just another summer escape

Coconut Beach Series

erin branscom

[signature]

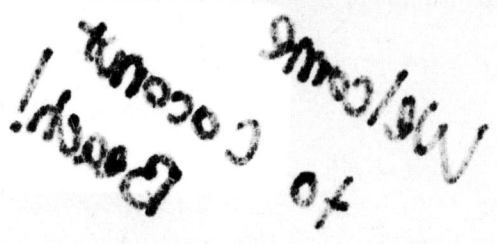

Copyright © 2026 Erin Branscom
www.erinbranscom.com

Just Another Summer Escape
Coconut Beach Series

Editor: Nicole McCurdy from Emerald Edits
www.emeraldedits.com
Copy Edits: All By Design

Cover Design
Illustration #1: Goldenmushroom
Illustration #2: Cover Design by Jillian Liota, Blue Moon Creative Studio
Typography and formatting: All By Design
979-8-88662-033-7
979-8-88662-032-0
979-8-88662-034-4
979-8-88662-035-1

just
another
SUMMER
Escape

about this book

Cal Bennett was supposed to be a solution. I need to be married before my thirtieth birthday, or I lose my family's billion-dollar company. He needs nothing from me except honesty and maybe a little fun. So we make a deal. A fake marriage. Simple. Temporary. Safe. What could go wrong?

Except there is nothing fake about this chemistry between us.

Between family dinners and early-morning surf lessons, I'm falling for a man who feels nothing like the cold boardrooms waiting for me back in Manhattan. I fall for his family and his friends. The messy, beautiful island life I was never meant to keep.

Everything seems manageable until I step into my role as CEO and the headlines start circling. New York expects its heiress back. Coconut Beach wants me to stay. And my fake husband is starting to feel dangerously real.

Now I have to decide if this was just **Just Another Summer Escape**...

Or the one love I'm brave enough to fight for.

coconut beach series

Just Another Summer Crush by Lyra Parish

Just Another Summer Romance by J.S. Cooper

Just Another Summer Escape by Erin Branscom

Just Another Summer Enemy by Ariel Hendrix

My friends and I wrote a beautiful series for you and they can be read in any order. I just know you're going to fall in love with Coconut Beach as much as we did.

Want to listen to the Just Another Summer Escape playlist. Scan here:

For every woman who has found their happily ever after. You deserve your Cal.

content warning

This book includes "on-page" adult content and language unsuitable for minors. If spice isn't your thing, they're easy to skip over. :)

silvie

. . .

I DON'T WANT to be here. In fact, I want to run far, far away from this wedding venue right now.

Anywhere but here.

But isn't a runaway bride a cliché? And what would people say?

Ugh.

My stomach clenches painfully at that thought and sweat beads over my upper lip, no doubt threatening to ruin my makeup.

Another thing to worry about, as if I'm not already unraveling thread by thread.

You can do this, Silvie.

Can I, though?

I have to.

There are over six hundred people expecting me to walk down the aisle in less than an hour. Not to mention the paparazzi parked outside waiting for juicy gossip to report on. And I'm pretty sure my parents would lose their ever-loving minds if I ran out on my own wedding.

Be brave, Silvie.

Do other brides-to-be feel this gut-churning, headache-inducing anxiety that makes you want to run away before it's too late?

Just hang in there, girl.

But I don't *want* to hang in there. I don't even *want* to be here. I'd rather suffer maddening thirst in a desert, or battle mosquitoes in a swamp...any other form of torture elsewhere is preferable than this one.

Now you're just being ridiculous.

This is supposed to be the happiest day of my life but I'm a thousand miles from happy. I can't explain it, but this feels...wrong. I've never felt so much dread as I do right now.

Breathe. It has to be nervous jitters.

Or maybe it's my gut telling me something important...

My heart rate skitters at that thought—at the idea that I might be making a huge mistake. Maybe it's one of those survival instincts telling me if I stay, I'll die.

Not to be dramatic or anything, but I kind of feel like I may not make it to the other side of this wedding alive.

I fidget uncomfortably. My dress is heavier than I remember from the fitting. Not physically, but emotionally. It digs into my ribs like it's trying to suffocate me. Like it was designed by someone who doesn't believe in bread or carbs in general and wants to torture me.

That's because it pretty much was.

My mother sent a nutritionist and a chef to me six months ago. If I were to fit into my dress, I had to follow a strict diet. Utter bullshit.

Luckily, I was so busy with work and wedding planning that I had no time to dwell on the fact my almond mom had a less-than-healthy eating plan for me. I simply ate what was provided and kept busy on everything that needed doing.

Perhaps that should have been a red flag.

My stomach grumbles as if to agree.

God, I miss bread. I miss all carbs, actually. I literally

dreamed about my cake today. The cake. Not the marriage. That should have been a sign, too.

I'm dragged from my internal meltdown, drawn to the humming of the wedding day chaos all around me. Curling irons clack together and makeup artists work on the wedding party for last-minute touch-ups. The lethal level of hairspray in the air makes it smell like chemical warfare.

Maybe I'll inhale too many fumes and go out quickly.

Why is that morbid thought so relieving?

My mother's voice floats in from the hallway, brisk and controlled as always. "Where is Belladonna? She's supposed to be helping her sister get ready. It's almost time."

At the mention of Belladonna's name, I grit my teeth so hard, I'm sure I crack a molar. I haven't seen my sister, and I actually don't care to. She and I have never been close, and the fact that my mom thinks that she might actually show up and help me is comical.

Belladonna hasn't helped anyone but herself her entire life. Why start now?

Of course, she's late. Again. She's made it clear in the past few months that she wants nothing to do with my wedding day. As much as I want to deny that it doesn't sting, it'd be a lie. There's a tiny part of me who remembers when she was born. I had all these visions of what having a built-in-best friend would be like.

Turns out, we couldn't be more opposite, and those idealistic views I had quickly vanished as she got older.

One of the makeup artists says something, but I realize she isn't even talking to me. This whole wedding is for me, yet I feel like I'm invisible. It's happening all around me and I'm being sucked into a black hole of flowers and tulle and eager wedding guests against my will.

And what does Tyler think?

The very thought of my husband-to-be has my stomach

clenching again. Another red flag? Or maybe it's just starvation from the stupid diet.

My mother once again mentions my sister as if the entire event relies on her presence. Still absent. Shocker. I'm certainly not holding my breath.

Belladonna is just a year younger than me, and my only sibling, but we couldn't be any more different. I'm a career-driven woman, and she's a socialite. Even at twenty-eight, she still hasn't grown up, loves to party, and stirs up drama wherever she goes. The tabloids love to see her coming. Not my cup of tea.

I'm more comfortable in boardrooms than shopping. I can't remember the last time I let myself relax and do something for fun. I've been so focused on building up our family's company and taking over before I'm thirty. That was the plan. My grandmother's will stated that I will take over the family empire at thirty as long as I'm married. I'm following the plan to save the company. Married before turning thirty in three months. Hence, my wedding day. Likely, had I not had this crazy will guiding my life, I may not have chosen to get married so soon. We could have had a longer engagement, and I would have felt better about things. Might not have felt like running away on my wedding day.

One of the makeup artists bumps into my chair, laughs shrilly, and then manhandles me around until I'm facing the mirror. It was much easier to avoid the inevitable when I didn't literally have to face it.

I suck in a sharp breath through my nose and then wince when I'm restricted from filling my lungs with precious air.

Who is this magazine-cover beautiful bride? I certainly don't recognize the woman staring back at me. Her eyes are hollow and her frown seems permanent. She blinks her heavily painted lashes, and still, there's no recognition. The sharp collarbones don't belong to my bread-loving soul.

Am I disassociating from myself or is this the new me?

Hysteria claws its way up my throat. I'm practically sewn into the loveliest dress I've ever set eyes on, and I want nothing more than to pluck at the seams, freeing myself from its prison-like hold.

Is this what marriage to Tyler will feel like?

Captivity. Loss of freedom. Despair.

And why don't I feel guilty for these rampant, horrible thoughts?

I absently pluck at the custom imported lace, the urge to ruin it overwhelming. I'm wrapped in thousands of dollars of luxury fabric molded to fit a version of me that exists only in other people's heads.

My heart is racing so fast at this point, I'm starting to feel dizzy. More sweat beads on my body and I wonder if my mother will come at me with more spray deodorant to pollute the air with.

"There she is," someone says, pleasure in their voice. I'm pretty sure the voice belongs to my mother.

Belladonna sweeps into the room as if it's her day, not mine. Her cheeks are flushed, and her dark hair is perfectly blown out. Her lips are swollen and lipstick-free as if she's put them to use before stepping in here. If I were to guess, she was probably making out with one of the groomsmen. Scotty? He's single and has always had a thing for her.

I'm eager to look at anything other than my unfamiliar appearance in the mirror, which means watching Belladonna as she commands the room with her intense presence.

She's wearing a pale green bridesmaid dress that our mother chose. It's flattering and hugs her curves in all the right places. It's not the dress I liked or even the colors I'd wanted, but admittedly, it looks good on her. This wedding, for all intents and purposes, though, is really for my mother. I am just another prop.

"Sorry," Belladonna says, not sounding remorseful at all. "Traffic was insane."

I tear my gaze from my sister to glance at the clock. That excuse is laughable. She has a driver, and there likely was no traffic.

When our eyes meet, she freezes. It's such an odd reaction, I find myself fixated on it. There's usually such arrogance rippling from my sister.

But I see a flicker of something reflected back at me that looks an awful lot like guilt. Since when does Belladonna feel guilty about anything? Triumph, absolutely. Smugness, sure. But guilt? Never.

I blink rapidly, trying to make sense of this. My heart aches to believe it's because she's shown up late, but my gut throws a fit. Something's off with her.

She tears her eyes from mine as I absently dab at the sweat on my upper lip and her attention falls on the glittering diamond on my finger. Her eyebrows pinch slightly, but it's enough to put my senses on high alert.

Something's wrong.

What did she do? She's conniving, but Belladonna never cares about anyone but herself.

"You okay, Silvie?" she asks, voice too bright as she inspects me with a pitying look. "You seem...tired."

And there it is. There's always a double-edged sword. A question, as if she cares, blanketed by an insult. Typical.

"I'm fine," I say automatically before I realize that I'm actually not even close to being fine. In fact, I'm so far from fine, it's not even funny.

But that's just what I always say. Everything's fine. It's been like that for so long that I don't know how not to just be fine. And frankly, I'm sick of it.

Is that what this is all about?

Am I having a mental breakdown at the most inopportune time of my life?

I don't have time to dissect that thought because Belladonna steps closer, reaching for my veil that's been painstakingly pinned to my head. Her fingers attempt to straighten it, but it doesn't move. She sets her phone down on the vanity in front of me so she can properly adjust the veil.

I'm unable to look away from her in the mirror. She still avoids my eyes, and her shoulders are unusually stiff. For once, she doesn't seem unruffled and always put together. There's definitely something going on with her. Alarm bells blare in my head.

Moments ago, I wanted to flee. Now, I want to poke into my sister's brain to discover what she's hiding.

Her phone lights up on the vanity, stealing my attention. A name flashes across the screen, accompanied by a message. Tyler.

Wait.

My Tyler?

I frown as I register another message from him. And another. Why is my fiancé rapid-fire texting with my sister who's acting oddly suspicious?

You know.

Of course you do.

Anxiety swells up inside me like a tidal wave. My brain works overtime as pieces start clicking into place.

Oh my God. How could I not have seen this before now?

The way she laughs at all his stupid jokes. His annoying way of taking her side whenever I complain about her drama. And that one time I swear they came out of the bathroom together.

A text flashes across the screen that stops my heart altogether.

Tyler: I don't want to do this. I miss you already.

No.

She's selfish, but she's not evil. At the end of the day, she's my sister. Surely, she wouldn't do this to me.

Belladonna grabs her phone so fast she fumbles it and drops it. It skips across the countertop and stops inches from my hand.

Without hesitation, I snatch it up. Another message comes across the screen.

> Tyler: Just tell me you love me, and I won't go through with this.

It's not just her. It's the man I'm supposed to marry, too.

I feel a roar between my ears and a ringing sound. Everything in the room feels like it stops and fades away around me. For me, everything narrows down to that single line of text glowing on the phone that's now in my hand.

> Tyler: I won't go through with this.

Belladonna is hissing at me, but I twist in my chair to avoid her, a death grip on the phone in my hand. I click on the message, grateful there's no lock on her phone. I pull up their text history and skim through them as quickly as I can.

"Silvie...give that back," she pleads, but there's no bite to her words. I think she wants me to read these and seems relieved.

The messages unfold before me, intimate and unmistakable. Nausea washes over me. Inside jokes that Tyler had with me for years that he's now sharing with her. A nickname he swore was for me. A photo of her naked on top of him. More photos that I can't unsee. They sure do like their naked photos.

I don't recall Tyler ever wanting to take an intimate photo of us, not that I would have wanted him to. Because I know those could be leaked. Belladonna apparently doesn't care. Hell, she'd probably sell them to the paparazzi herself.

There are people all around us preparing for my wedding and they have no idea of the bomb that just detonated in my hand. I bore my eyes into Belladonna's, imploring her to say something.

She makes a bored, smug sound. Then, she examines her nails as if waiting for me to say something. I'm sure my drama-loving sister's anticipating a freak-out.

A terrifying calm settles over me and camps out in my bones. I wait for tears to form, but nothing happens. I feel nothing.

"How long?" I ask, no emotion in my voice.

She opens her mouth and lets out an exaggerated sigh.

"Belladonna, how long?" I repeat, my voice so calm it scares me.

"I didn't want you to find out this way," she says, watching me like she's still waiting for the impending meltdown. "Tyler and I are meant to be, Silvie. We're in love."

Love? I didn't know Belladonna could love anyone but herself.

And that's not what I asked. This is almost laughable. She wanted me to find out. That's the only explanation. And minutes before we're supposed to get married.

What I thought was guilt was nothing more than another cruel trick in my sister's arsenal.

"How long?" I grit out.

"Five months." She smirks as if she's the victor in a battle I had no idea we were in.

Five months.

I nod slowly, blinking and taking in every piece of new information. For *five* months, my fiancé has been fucking my sister. The whole time I was planning this asinine wedding and running my company. Building a future for us. And while I was working eighty to ninety-hour weeks, this is what he was doing. *Her.*

I let out a cold laugh. It surprises both of us. She flinches, and confusion flashes across her face.

"We're in love." That's funny.

"Get him in here," I demand icily.

The room is still chaotic with voices and activity. They have no idea the destruction my sister and Tyler have caused.

"What?" she asks, her eyes wide.

"Get. Him," I repeat. "Now."

9

Belladonna shakes her head and glares at me like *I'm* the problem.

I stare at her, anger burning up my spine. I hope it's hot enough to set fire to this stupid dress.

She hesitates, then snatches her phone out of my hand to type out a text.

I stare at my reflection again. At least my eyes aren't empty anymore. Glimmers of my former self blaze back at me. I hate who I've become. This is not me. And I'm done pretending.

Tyler arrives quickly, breathless, tie crooked, and a fake smile plastered on his face. Several women chide him for "seeing the bride" before the wedding, but he easily charms his way past them. He stops short when he sees my expression.

"What's wrong, baby?" he asks, searching my face for clues. "I'm not supposed to see you in your dress yet."

I flick my perfectly manicured fingers toward Belladonna's phone, which still has his text messages open. She holds it up like a badge of dishonor.

His face drains of color, and he quickly looks away. The man says nothing in defense.

Coward.

The room around us has grown silent, everyone sensing something bad has happened. I hear the wedding coordinator murmur, "Let's give them a minute." People leave the room until it's just the three of us.

The silence between all of us stretches on for what feels like forever. It's thick and suffocating. I watch both squirm and say nothing.

"Well?" I say casually. "I hear you're in love with each other."

Tyler swallows nervously and lets out a big sigh. "This isn't what it looks like, baby."

Just hearing him call me baby makes me want to gag. My sister bristles as if that's *her* pet name and I stole it from her. She can have it.

Belladonna scoffs and whines. "Tyler. She knows."

I tilt my head and say, "Yes. I know. You've been sleeping with my sister for five months. *She's* your 'baby.'"

Tyler winces. "Silvie, don't be absurd. At least let me explain."

And the gaslighting begins. I shake my head and laugh at being called absurd. As if I'm the one who did this.

Belladonna lets out an exasperated sigh. "Just admit it, Tyler."

"Please do. Tell me," I say as I drag my gaze over him, trying to understand what I ever saw in this man.

He runs a hand through his perfectly styled hair, messing it up. "It wasn't our fault. It just...happened."

Accidents happen. Like spilling milk or backing into another car. Their affair was premeditated, sneaky, and well thought out. Anger burns hot in my veins, chasing away the panicky feeling from earlier.

My gut tried to tell me...

"It just happened," I mutter, mimicking his words. "And *whose* fault was it?"

I want to scream at the both of them. I'm so freaking mad.

"You've been working so much," he explains, looking at Belladonna for help. "And, with the wedding planning, you were so distant. I got lonely."

Distant. Wow. I was working and planning our wedding. Doing all of it by myself, I might add. He played golf, worked meager hours, and obviously was busy screwing my sister. I see where his priorities were.

I glance down at my expensive dress that now feels completely ridiculous. There were thousands of tiny buttons that required a special hook to button them, and it took over an hour to get them on. I can't even imagine how long it's going to take to get off.

"So, you repeatedly slept with my sister, and it's *my* fault? Is that what I'm hearing?"

Clarity matters.

11

Belladonna huffs. "Whatever, Silvie. It's not like that."

I look at her. "It isn't?"

"He loves *me*," she bites out. "Not you. Me."

Her words, shot out at me like arrows, don't penetrate. Belladonna makes everything about her, so this response is expected.

Tyler's mouth opens and closes. He sighs and then looks down. He shakes his head, but he doesn't deny it.

Something in me finally cracks. Like a snap, as if a taut wire is being cut. I'm vibrating with fury and it takes everything in me to remain seated, seeing this betrayal to the end.

"You were going to marry me today," I say quietly.

He nods. "Yes."

Unbelievable.

"And after today?" I ask, trying to understand. "Were you planning to stop sleeping with my sister?"

He hesitates. I knew it. I just wanted confirmation for closure.

I smooth my veil and straighten my shoulders.

I'm done.

And then my father appears in the doorway. "Everything okay in here?" He glances between the three of us and his eyes land back on me, searching for a clue as to why the tension is so thick in this room right now.

"I'm not getting married," I say resolutely.

My father frowns, confusion marring his classically hand-some face. "I don't understand."

"You do." I lift my chin. "I'm not getting married."

"Silvie, there are hundreds of people out there," he hisses, shock mixed with panic transforming his features. He glances at the hallway and back at us. "We don't have time for this nonsense."

That's exactly what this is.

Nonsense.

Our mother joins us. Her dress is almost as fancy as mine. In fact, as if coming out of a fog, I realize it's awfully close to white in color. *Well, it's her day after all, I laugh to myself.*

I can't believe I let it all get this far.

There was something inside me screaming to make it stop and I let it go on.

No more.

She shakes her head disapprovingly. "It is almost time. What are you all doing in here? Why are they saying that you're all arguing? We need to get ready."

I meet her gaze and say calmly, "Tyler's been sleeping with Belladonna."

The room explodes at my words. Voices rise. My dad looks livid. My mother's face tightens with calculation rather than concern. I watch her closely, and it dawns on me that she possibly might've have already known, judging by her reaction.

She's not outraged. She's doing damage control.

The betrayal cuts deeper.

Belladonna collapses into a chair, making a shrill, dramatic sound, reminding me of when she was a toddler. Tyler reaches for me, and I jerk my hand back.

"Don't touch me," I hiss and shudder, repulsed by him.

"Silvie," my mother says sharply. "We can handle this later. The guests are all seated. We're about to begin."

I stare at her and can't believe she has nothing else to say or to worry about besides the guests. That is her reaction to my sister and my fiancé having an affair. And the fact that she thinks we can 'handle' this later *after* we're married is insane. Literally insane.

This is the moment. The one I'll think about for years to come. The one where I decide whether I stay exactly where I am and who I am, or change. And I'm choosing me this time. I won't live like this, with these people. I realize everything I was working toward is no longer happening. The fog has lifted and I can finally see it for what it is.

"No." I shake my head.

Silence fills the room as if they can't believe I'm making this an issue. As if on cue, the music starts playing outside, soft and romantic. The opening notes of the procession drift through the building's open windows.

"Don't embarrass us," my mother hisses. "Just get ready to go out there. We're about to begin."

"Me?" I laugh. "*I'm* the one embarrassing us? Are you for real right now, Mom?"

She swats at my father. "Get them out there. They're inflaming the situation. I'll deal with her."

Good luck with that.

"Silvie, be the bigger person here," my mom urges, holding up her hands as if she's asking me to surrender. "Please."

The laugh that escapes me is bordering on hysterical. "I literally never want to be the bigger person ever again. In fact, we can all go to hell. I'll drive the bus."

Her jaw practically unhinges. It takes her a full twenty seconds to gather herself. Then, she scoffs angrily at me. "Stop it. You *will* marry Tyler. You know what you need to do for the family."

There's a twinge of guilt that threatens to yank me back into submission. I know my responsibility to my family and what's at stake here. But I refuse to be so utterly disrespected.

I smile, and not the practiced, forced one. The real one. At least it feels real. "I'm leaving."

Her nostrils flare and she stares at me with hatred.

It takes some effort getting me and my over-the-top dress out of the chair, but I eventually manage without help. My legs are a bit shaky, but my heart is racing wildly. My escape is so close I can taste it. I swipe an open bottle of chilled champagne from the bucket on a nearby table, take a swig, and wipe my mouth with the back of my hand.

Mom quietly barks out orders, but I'm done.

I pick up my purse and overnight bag and sling them over my shoulder. Then, I turn and walk out of the room, past the open doors and stunned wedding coordinator, chugging from the bottle as I go.

"Don't embarrass us."

Too late, Mom.

I don't look back as I make my way down to the pathway to the road. Cabs line the streets, and I lift the bottle to signal I need a ride.

A cab pulls up almost instantly. I open the door, throw in my bag, hike up my dress, and slide in as best I can. I don't know where I'm going. I just know I'm finally choosing myself. And for the first time in my life, that feels like freedom.

silvie

. . .

THE CAB SMELLS like stale coffee, and the driver has "Jolene" by Dolly Parton playing. I start laughing uncontrollably at the irony.

"You can't drink in here," the cab driver calls out as he eyes my champagne bottle in the rearview mirror.

Our eyes meet and I take another swig from the bottle, defiance gushing through me kind of like the tears that have unhelpfully began falling.

I don't want to cry over what happened, but now that I'm free of *them*—of that life—I can't help it. They're tears of relief. I almost made a horrible mistake marrying Tyler.

The cab driver frowns as he skims his gaze over my cheeks that are no doubt streaked in mascara. Considering the lipstick stain on the back of my hand, I imagine I have that smeared across my face as well. And, when I sat down in the cab *on my veil*, I felt several bobby pins rip the hair straight from my scalp.

Do I look like I've crawled my way out of a battle? Sure feels like it. The champagne bottle is my prize.

"Okay, okay," the man mutters, shaking his head. "You can drink in here. Looks like you need it."

My muscles lose some of their tension and I relax before

taking another hearty swig from the bottle. I lean back against the seat with relief to be free.

The driver twists around in his seat to study me curiously. He's older with a gray mustache and kind eyes. "Where to, miss?"

"I don't know. Just drive." I reach up, grab the edge of my veil, and rip at it. The rest of the pins tug painfully at my scalp, and I yank until the whole thing comes loose. I then fling it out the window, which ultimately inspires him to take off, because people are honking behind us and someone is taking pictures. Let them. I have no more shits to give today. None.

My blonde hair spills down around me in loose waves, finally free. I feel lighter. My life just got insanely complicated, and for once in my life, I have no plans, and I don't care.

He glances at the paparazzi and says, "Are we running from the groom or them?"

I blink. "Both."

What I don't tell him is that I'm racing to get away from the hurt that keeps clawing its way up inside me. Belladonna causes chaos. I know this. And, yet it still somehow took me by surprise.

Tyler, though?

That one cuts deeper. He was supposed to love me. Sure pretended to anyway. The entire betrayal is humiliating. They paraded around, practically in my face, and I was too distracted and overworked to notice. It's only fair Tyler has to deal with the embarrassment of telling everyone he got left at the altar for sleeping with the bride's sister.

"Definitely both," I say firmly.

The cabbie nods like this is just another normal day. "Got it."

I bark out a laugh, and it comes out as if I've officially lost my mind. "Okay, hypothetically speaking," I say. "If you were a runaway bride, where would you go?"

He chuckles as if this question takes him off guard, but entertains him, nonetheless.

"Depends," he says, tapping his fingers against the steering wheel, as he merges into traffic.

I lean forward, grinning, despite the way my mind races in a thousand different directions. "You act like this isn't your first runaway bride situation."

The city blurs past the window, and I watch my wedding venue disappear behind us. Good riddance.

"Honey, I've been driving a cab for thirty years," he says. "I've picked up three runaway brides. One groom. That was a weird one."

It's oddly relieving to know I'm not the only one out there eager to leave their bad decisions behind them, even at the very last minute.

"Where'd they go?" I ask.

"Two went back to their wedding," he says. "One went to Vegas and married a bartender. That one still sends me a Christmas card every year."

I sigh and take another swig from the bottle. For the girl who has every inch of her life planned out, it feels so freeing to have no plans. None. It's better than marrying that cheating asshole. And this is big. Because I'm type A. I have everything planned. But right now, all I feel is free.

He glances at me in the mirror. "You don't look like you're going back."

I shake my head. "I'm definitely not going back."

"Good," he says. "So, do you want chaos or peace?"

My stomach tightens painfully when I think about Belladonna's smug, stupid face and Tyler's lame excuses—a glimpse of what was going to become my future. My mother's voice telling me not to embarrass the family. I try to remember what my dad's face looked like, but I can't recall. I was too busy running away. He's probably so mad, too.

I try to suck in a breath of air, so I don't hyperventilate. This is overwhelming to say the least.

"Peace," I immediately respond. Always peace. I've had enough chaos.

He merges onto the freeway, and I lean my now-throbbing head against the seat, suddenly feeling exhausted. The adrenaline has drained out of me, and I am so tired.

He hums. "Mountains or tropical?"

I close my eyes and picture the beach with endless waves, cocktails, and peace.

"Tropical," I answer, dreamily. Then I sit up straighter. I know where I'm going.

Birdie.

I pull out my phone and groan when I see seventeen missed calls from practically everyone. And so many text messages. I ignore them all, pull up Birdie's contact, and hit dial.

She answers on the third ring cheerfully. "Hey, there, sugar. How's the wedding?"

Just hearing her comforting voice sends another wave of emotions rippling through me. My chin wobbles and more tears form.

"Birdie, I can't do it," I choke out. "I'm coming to Coconut Beach."

Birdie is my safe space. The place where I can be me. Or at least find the real me. I don't know who I am anymore.

Did Birdie know? Not the betrayal, because I'm sure she didn't, but about how this wedding would turn out? It hurt my feelings when she declined to attend the wedding, but there was the whole "Mom thing," so I got it. Now I wonder if there was more to it.

I hear her exhale, and she sounds relieved, further indicating her feelings about the marriage. "Sugar, I'm here. Just get here safe."

She doesn't ask what happened. She doesn't need to. She knows I'll tell her everything.

"Okay, I'll text you when I get there," I promise. My phone

beeps with an incoming call. A quick glance tells me it's my dad. "Gotta go, Birdie. See you soon."

After ending my call with Birdie, I sigh, knowing that it's inevitable that I'll need to speak to my father. I hit the answer button and wait for him to light into me.

"Dad," I say, voice raw and quivering.

He's quiet for a beat. I close my eyes, but then pictures of Belladonna and Tyler in various stages of undress flood my mind, so I snap them back open.

Instead of yelling, he says in a calm tone, "JFK. The jet is waiting."

Emotion tightens my throat, and at first, I can't speak. I blink back tears, trying desperately to find words.

I whisper, "Thanks, Dad."

He grunts and lets out a tired, staggering breath. "I'm sorry. About all of it."

I nod though he can't see me.

"And Belladonna..." He curses under his breath. "It was wrong, Silvie."

Sniffling, I nod again, grateful to have at least someone in my family on my side.

"I never liked Tyler anyway," he grumbles.

Despite the tears silently falling, I let out a small, choked laugh.

"Please don't tell anyone where I'm going," I say quietly.

He chuckles. "Honey, I don't even know where you're going. Just be safe, okay? And call me when you get where you're going."

"I will. I'm sorry I let you down. I promise I'll figure out a way to make it right. I just need some time.

"You have nothing to apologize for," he assures me. "Take care of yourself. Love you, honey."

"Love you, Dad," I say and disconnect. Then, to the driver, I say, "JFK, please."

As I put distance between me and my almost-wedding, I

can't help but momentarily feel like a failure. Is Dad disappointed in me? He was counting on me to save our company's family.

And now I'm destroying it all by running.

I chose me, not them. Despite the hardship that it put on my family and how scary that is, it's freeing. I won't be a pawn in their game anymore. I'm better than that. I deserve a real life. I deserve respect.

I down the rest of the champagne bottle and then curl up against my seat, already feeling the buzz of the alcohol. It's the first good thing I've felt all day.

I'm coming, Birdie.

"Miss Montclair, we're beginning our descent into Coconut Beach," a flight attendant says as she lightly touches my shoulder.

I open my eyes and sit up, realizing this was, in fact, not just a bad dream. It's real life, and it really sucks.

"Oh, thanks," I croak out, voice hoarse from sleep.

Heat floods my cheeks as I, once again, take in my current state. I'm still wearing my wedding dress, mainly because I knew I wouldn't be able to get it off by myself, and my face is a mess.

Thank God this is Dad's jet. His staff is paid well to be discreet. It's not lost on me that having the Montclair name comes with certain privileges. Getting to sit on a plane, half-drunk and looking like a racoon who stole a wedding dress and not get openly judged for it is one of those privileges.

Holy shit. It's beginning to truly sink in. I really left my own wedding, downed a bottle of champagne on the way to the airport, and slept all the way to Florida. I sit up and look out the window as the plane changes angles, just enough that the world outside opens up.

I press my forehead to the cool glass, soothing my throbbing head.

The bright blue ocean stretches out far as the eye can see. Every shade of blue possible. Navy blue farther out. Teal and aquamarine are closer to shore. Pale, sandy beaches where sunlight makes the sand sparkle like glitter. Palm trees lining the small beachy town, making it feel like paradise.

Paradise, also known as Coconut Beach, is home to my Birdie.

Birdie was our family nanny since I was born. She moved here and retired to Coconut Beach when I went off to college. And we've stayed close ever since. So close, it always made Mom jealous, though she'd never admit that. Birdie didn't come to my wedding because my mother wouldn't allow it.

I should have fought for that. Gone against my mother's control. Argued for something *I* wanted for once. But I didn't. Story of my life.

Until now...

I know Birdie would have hated the wedding anyway. She doesn't like my mother or Belladonna either. Today, she was missing out on what was supposed to be one of the most important days of my life, but now I'm here with her. And somehow that makes sense.

Coconut Beach looks smaller than I remember. Birdie brought me here on spring break in college. There were also a few Christmas breaks that weren't celebrated because my mom was off at a spa, so I'd spend them here as well. It was always a special place to me. If I close my eyes and picture home, Birdie's cottage comes to mind.

I spot the marina with the boats bobbing in neat rows, their wakes drawing faint white lines behind them like scribbles.

I swallow, and tears prick the edges of my eyes. I've missed Birdie, and I need her. It isn't lost on me that I'm not crying over losing Tyler. Sure, there have been times where I've been crying over what he and Belladonna did to me, but not because he broke my heart. I'm emotional at the thought of seeing Birdie. It feels like coming home. And I haven't had that feeling for such a long time. I spent my whole life in places with people who expect things from me. A special version of myself who meets their expectations. Work hard, go to college, and be next in line to take over the family company.

I'm done being pulled by their strings. I'm no one's puppet.

Birdie genuinely wants to spend time with me, and she loves me. And I need this. I need her.

The wheels touch down on the runway with a solid thud. I sit up and stretch, still agitated that I'm in this suffocating dress. As soon as I find a big enough bathroom, I'm going to make changing my next priority.

By the time I make it to the rideshare pickup, my feet hurt in the ridiculous wedding heels, my head hurts from downing champagne and not having enough water, and my phone will not shut up with constant notifications. The worst part is that some of them are reporters reaching out for comments. Thank God they don't know where I went. Hopefully, it stays that way, and I can fly under the radar for a while.

I shove the phone into my purse. Future Silvie can deal with the fallout. Present Silvie is wearing a wedding dress in the Florida heat, and that feels like enough ridiculousness for one day.

The rideshare smells like coconut air freshener and salty beach air through the open windows of the retro Bronco with no top. I give the driver Birdie's address, then sink back against the seat, watching Coconut Beach slide by through the window.

"Is that Birdie's address?" the driver asks with a smile. He looks to be in his fifties, wearing a palm tree-print shirt and looking laid-back.

I look up at him. "Do you know her?"

He grins. "Everyone here knows Birdie. She's one of the Bees."

I wrinkle my brow, not remembering Birdie mentioning anything about that. "What's a Bee?"

He chuckles. "It's a group of older ladies in Coconut Beach that basically, unofficially, run the town. In fact, tonight is their monthly bingo night. It's a big deal. Goes on until midnight, and she'll be there. She never misses bingo with her fellow Bees. Should I take you there, instead?"

I inwardly groan. I can't go to bingo, face the town and embarrass Birdie. Plus, I don't want her to think she has to stop what she's doing with her friends just for me. I didn't come here to be a burden. I guess I could just wait for her at her cottage.

"Just take me to her place," I say absently, marveling over the beauty of the palm trees silhouetted against a violet sky as the sun begins to set.

Then I see the weathered sign swinging slightly in the breeze. Cocktails & Chaos. A tiki bar. Maybe a good place to wind down before I face Birdie and unravel the last two years of trauma and drama. Because I know that when I'm with her, I'm going to finally fall apart. Birdie is the only person I can do that with.

"Wait," I blurt. "Wait, wait, wait."

The driver taps the brakes. "Everything okay?"

"Stop here," I rush out. "Please." I hand him a wad of cash and climb out before I can overthink it. I have no idea why, but something is telling me to stop here.

Just like your gut told you to run from your wedding?

Your gut was right.

As soon as the warm, salty air hits my skin, I'm flooded with relief. I grab my bag, sling my purse over my shoulder, and march up to Cocktails & Chaos like a woman on a mission.

It's a cute little establishment, open on three sides with a long bar running along the length of it. Smooth barstools are scattered from one end to the other. String lights stretch across the back bar, lighting up the bottles along the wall in a whimsical way. It's charming and I like it.

I trip over the threshold of the bar when my feet get tangled in my dress and I grab a nearby stool to steady myself. My bag slides off my shoulder, so I let it drop to the sandy wood floor at my feet. It's then I realize what shape my dress is in. I've somehow torn the bottom of it, and it's completely filthy. Well, there's that.

I hear someone mutter nearby, "Is she..."

In a wedding dress?

Yep.

Nothing to see here, folks.

The tiki bar is thankfully cool, with fans, and loud, with good music playing from the speakers. Glasses clink, and the air smells of fried food and something sweet. A breeze picks up and blows my hair behind me as I slide onto the stool. It feels like every head turns and stares at me.

Probably because I'm still very much wearing my wedding dress. If I could get the damn thing off, I would. It's like a strait-jacket straight from hell. I ignore the stares and plop my purse down on the bar top, dramatically exhaling when my phone buzzes again. I pull it out and shudder at all of the unread messages. So *many* unread messages.

I close my eyes and shake my head. "Nope."

Still not dealing with any of that. I need five minutes. Or five drinks. Or a lobotomy. It all sounds promising.

The bartender stops in front of me, and I stare at him, frowning. He's unexpectedly handsome, and I can't help but notice. Sun-kissed skin, dark hair that curls, and a smile that's as warm as the air breezing in off the ocean.

I'm not sure I'm mentally equipped to deal with a good-looking man when I've just left a mediocre one at the altar.

The man looks about my age and is completely at ease, like he knows exactly who he is and isn't trying to prove anything to anyone. There's something about him I can't put my finger on. I've spent all day running, unraveling, pretending I'm fine, and standing here under his quiet, easy gaze, I feel myself slow down. Like maybe, for the first time today, I don't have to be anywhere else.

He's calming. I bet it earns him all kinds of good tips. The nice grin doesn't hurt either. Selfishly, I'm glad to have something to distract me from my rampant thoughts.

He takes in my dress, slumped posture, and my exhausted expression. "Long day?"

"You have no idea," I murmur.

I'm curious as to how someone lands a job like this. Honestly, it seems kind of nice. I wonder what his story is.

"What can I get you?" he asks, smiling warmly. Not flirty, just safe and solid. I silently thank God because that's what I need right now. Just someone to be kind to me. Plus, he's easy on the eyes and I deserve a pretty view after my day from hell.

"Something that makes my current life choices feel justified." I snort.

He arches a brow. "Dealer's choice?"

"Surprise me."

He grins, turns, and starts mixing. I watch him work, grateful for the distraction. He throws a glass, catches it, dances a little, and hums to the music. He's in his element here, and I don't miss the fact that a lot of eyes are on him, watching him. Apparently, everyone is enjoying the view.

He slides a bright yellow and orange drink in front of me with a blue paper umbrella perched on the rim.

"Sex on the Beach," he says as if he's trying to get me to laugh. "A popular tourist favorite."

I laugh. "Of course."

I twirl the umbrella between my fingers after I take a sip and mumble to myself, "This will be the only sex I'll be having for a very long time."

He raises his eyebrows and wipes down the bar, not saying anything to that, but I know he probably heard. Great, he thinks I'm a lunatic who talks to herself.

"Need something to eat?" he asks, sliding a menu across the bar.

I suddenly realize how hungry I am. "I probably should eat something. I haven't eaten all day."

"Want me to surprise you with that, too?" he asks, dark hazel eyes glittering with flecks of gold and a splash of mischief.

I chuckle and nod. "Yeah, surprise me. I'm starving."

He winks at me before sauntering off. I catch a couple of women staring dreamily at his butt. I stifle an inappropriate giggle.

I needed this. Beach, drinks, food, and a cute, friendly bartender to remind me there's more to life than a shitty, cheating ex-fiancé and a monstrous sister who classifies as an enemy rather than blood.

Much to my delight, the patrons at the bar slowly forget about me. Or maybe they decide this is Coconut Beach and weird things just happen here. Either way, I suck down my sweet drink and wait for whatever food the bartender's going to bring me.

My new life starts now.

cal

. . .

THE FIRST RULE of bartending in a small beach town is that if a woman walks into your bar alone, wearing a wedding dress and mascara down her cheeks, you don't ask questions. Something's already gone sideways. You pour her a drink and keep an eye on her. She needs a minute.

The whole bar seems to clock her at once. Some make it more obvious than others. Conversations are cut off mid-sentence. A few people straighten in their chairs so they can get a better look. Every pair of eyes is on her. Marina, the other bartender, glances at me from the other end of the bar, brows lifted in silent question. I give her a small shrug. I have no idea who this mystery woman is.

And yet, something in me stirs anyway. I'm drawn to her. Not in a flirt-with-the-customers kind of way. More of a protective way.

That's new, Cal.

The woman looks tired, like she's reached the end of whatever road brought her here and decided this is the place she needs for now, and I get that. This bar has a way of drawing in nearly everyone who comes to Coconut Beach. Hell, it caught me in its net and dragged me in when I was lost.

Everyone knows everyone here, and if you're a tourist, we know it. We look out for everyone and consider this a safe space. I'm not sure what her name or story are, but I'm going to make sure she's taken care of here. Marina, clearly reading my mind, nods to me as if she'll do the same. It's just what we do.

"Tough day?" I ask.

The woman opens one eye. "You have no idea."

Her phone lights up on the bar. She flips it face down as if she's frustrated, without looking at it.

I slide a glass of water her way while I wait for her food order. She notices, and her shoulders ease just a little.

"Thank you," she says quietly.

We make small talk, and I push a plate in front of her loaded down with a savory burger and greasy fries. Nothing fancy. But it's the kind of food that will fill you up if you've been drinking. We like to feed people here when they drink. Music, food, and alcohol are what we're known for here at Cocktails & Chaos.

It's that simple, pure purpose that makes working here so fulfilling. I love running this bar, taking pride in every detail from taking care of the patrons all day and night to wiping off every sticky table at close. There's pride in what I do, and I can't say that's been the case for other jobs I've had.

I'm grateful for my friend, Jonah Black, who I manage the place for. He doesn't like people much and runs a local fishing charter. We have an agreement. I run Cocktails & Chaos, and he pays me a nice salary. It gets me out of the house, and I get to meet people.

What he doesn't know is I'd do it for free. Unlike Jonah, I genuinely love seeing new faces from all over, catching up with the regulars, and sharing inside jokes. It's the energy I thrive on. The music, the vibes, the food.

She's finished her drink and half of her water. I'm about to ask her if she wants another one when her eyes meet mine. They're haunted and sad. A moment ago, she was laughing at my attempts to lighten the mood, but she's not laughing anymore. The mask is gone, revealing a heartbroken woman. It makes my chest tighten. Helping people is in my blood. I want to make her smile again. To shake off whatever shitshow she just came from and enjoy this little slice of heaven.

"You were right," she says absently as she tears her gaze from mine to inspect the burger and fries in front of her. "This looks amazing."

"My tips are very important to me," I tease. "I'll grab you more to drink. Let me know if you want extra ketchup or something."

I casually check her out. Not in a creepy, pervy way. I'm just curious about her situation. The wedding dress she's wearing is wrinkled and a little ruined, like it's already lived a life before it got here. The hem is smudged. The buttons are holding on by pure will. And damn, there are a lot of buttons. This dress looks like a torture device, and I wonder what made her choose it in the first place.

Her hair is beautiful. It's long and blonde, falling in loose waves down her back, and her curls frame her face in that effortless way that looks soft and dangerous at the same time.

Not the time or place, man.

I glance up at her face, settling on her eyes once more. They're bright blue and look like they've been through enough today. She certainly doesn't need the bartender admiring her soft hair. Her mouth is set in an expression as if she's trying to be brave, but the occasional chin wobble gives her away. Despite being fragile and tired after whatever the hell happened at her apparent wedding, I can tell there's a strong woman underneath all that tulle and mascara.

Jewelry glints at her throat and ears, delicate and understated, like she doesn't need help being noticed. This woman is ritzy as fuck and confident in her jewelry selection. It tells me she's not from some small town around these parts. She comes from money. You can tell a lot about a person and their accessories.

Bartending sure sharpens a man's observational skills. Mine are certainly on point.

People stare at her because they can't help it. I stare because something in my chest tightens every time she shifts her weight, exhales, or looks like she's about to bolt.

Care to unpack that thought, Cal?

Maybe another time.

She looks like someone who ran hard and didn't quite know where she was supposed to land. I'm glad she landed here.

"Eat," I tell her. "You'll feel better when you have some food in you."

Finally, she does. Immediately, just inhales the food like it's her last meal and moans in delight, and damn if that sound doesn't shoot straight to my dick. I shake my head. This is someone's almost-wife. She's off limits. Every woman who comes into this bar is off-limits to me. I don't mingle business with pleasure. These days, I don't even seek out pleasure. I'm focused on what I have going on.

But something about this woman is different.

I place another fresh water in front of her, and she looks at it, then me.

"Hydration," I say with a wink. "We take it very seriously around here."

A CeeLo Green song comes on, and she laughs. "I love this song."

The laugh of hers is back and it warms me more than I'd like to admit.

She picks up the glass and drains half of it, needing it more than the food. Good sign.

I leave her to go check on a few regulars and even playfully thump one guy on the head for staring too long at the runaway bride. I know he means well, but there's a sliver of protectiveness in me I can't name right now.

A few minutes later, she leans across the bar to get my attention. "Hey."

I saunter over, snapping a towel over my shoulder, and raise my eyebrows. "Yes?"

She hops off her stool. "Can you watch my drink and bag while I go to the restroom?"

"Yeah," I say easily. "Of course."

She shoves it across surface toward me, and I set it behind the bar. I also reach for her drink, too, tucking it safe behind me.

I watch her hobble in her heels, and for reasons I can't explain, all I can think is that I'm glad whatever brought her here didn't get to win. I hope somewhere there's a groom regretting his life today. I know I would be if I lost a woman like her.

When she comes back, I hand her back her drink.

She eyes me like she's reassessing me. "Are you always this nice to your patrons?"

I smile and say, "Life's too short to be a dick."

It comes out smooth, automatic. Then I realize I'm not flirting the way I usually would. This is different. *She's* different. And I can't explain it, but it feels like dangerous territory.

She slides back onto her stool, then glances behind her where a bachelorette party has begun staring and whispering in confusion. They are wearing matching shirts and wide eyes.

"I can't imagine..."

"Do you think..."

She hears their not-so-quiet whispering and raises her glass to them. "I'm better off. Trust me."

And I don't doubt that. I glance down, and she's still wearing a huge engagement ring. The kind that could buy whole islands if she were to sell it for cash. At least she's not hurting for money.

She catches me staring, looks at her ring, then back at me. "I paid for that."

I chuckle and continue to wipe down the bar. She's blunt, outspoken, and it's honestly refreshing. She's kind of funny, too.

One of the bachelorette ladies gapes at her. "Did you get married today? Where's your husband?"

She shakes her head. "No. And he's probably off celebrating."

Who the hell would celebrate losing a woman like her? Some men are idiots. I know because I am one.

Just then, DJ Jeff starts playing "Where Is My Husband" by RAYE. I shake my head at Jeff, and he laughs and shrugs. He loves to pick weird songs to play at the strangest times.

That seems to break the tension and I'm grateful for it. The group of women laugh, and she laughs with them. She seems funny, like she's making the most of this day, but the defeat is still glimmering in her blue eyes.

The women in the bachelorette party beckon her to join them and make room for her. Introductions fly. Names I'll never remember. Except one. Silvie. It's a classic, beautiful name and suits her.

They compliment her dress, despite it looking like it's seen better days, and one woman says it must be custom-made. Silvie shrugs. "You can have it if you want. I'm never getting married. Everything is over."

Silvie turns back to me. "Okay, I need something less sweet for me, Mr. Bartender. I've had enough sex on the beach."

I chuckle. "Got it."

The group has more questions that she dodges with practiced ease.

I make her another glass of water and bring it along with a less sugary cocktail. She takes a sip of the new drink and nods approvingly. "Thank you, Mr. Bartender."

"His name is Cal," one of them calls out, snickering. "And he's the hottest guy in Coconut Beach. He's single I heard."

I resist rolling my eyes. Flirting is part of the job here, and I'm used to most nonsense.

And yeah, I am single. By choice. I have enough on my plate, and I'm too busy for a relationship. If they knew me on a deeper level, they'd know I don't want to be with someone who considers me a hot bartender. Nothing surface level. I want a real relationship, and I can't seem to find that here in Coconut Beach. We have tourists who come and go. Catching feelings for someone who isn't permanent is just plain stupid. And yeah, I've had my fair share of stupidity in that department, hence why I turn on the charm for tips, but don't ever let it expand past that. Even for pretty, sad runaway brides. Eventually, she'll go back to her castle in the city. And I know I'll never leave here.

I just wink and say, "Let me know if you need anything else."

Marina brings a tray of shots to the ladies, and they all say, "To finding the right one!"

I watch Silvie, and her eyes are sad when she takes her drink. She just lost who she thought was the right one. It's written all over her filthy wedding dress and tearstained cheeks. Unfortunately, love isn't for everyone. I, too, learned that lesson the hard way. Things changed for me about five years ago when I moved back to Coconut Beach. I've come to terms with the fact that this is my life now. Simple, easy, pain-free.

I can't help but listen to their conversation, but my ears perk up when I hear Silvie say that she's in town to see Birdie. I pick up her empty glasses and tilt my head in question. "You know Birdie?"

"Yeah, you know her, too?"

I smile at the question. "Everyone knows Birdie."

"That's what the rideshare driver told me, too," she says, wrinkling her brow in confusion.

I glance at the clock. "They're still doing bingo, though."

She smiles. "I know. That's why I came here to wait. I didn't want to interrupt her."

Interesting. I wonder if this is the woman Birdie used to nanny for. I can't remember her saying what her name was, but there was a woman she looked after for years, and she is like family to her. In the past, this woman has come to visit, but I've never met her.

Until now.

The bachelorette party pulls Silvie up a few minutes later for dancing. Which she does, because she's had at least three drinks in her at this point. She's barefoot, having lost her shoes since she got here, that ridiculous dress swishing, and she's laughing. Something tells me that she wouldn't have had this much fun at her wedding.

At least she doesn't look like she's about to cry at any second.

I don't look away as she sways to the music. When she spins a little too hard and stumbles, I'm already moving closer, just in case. She steadies herself and throws me a thumbs'-up as if she knows I'm watching.

I chuckle because she's certainly keeping me entertained. I move behind the bar, pull out my phone, and step away to make a call.

Birdie answers on the third ring, and I can hear bingo going on in the background. "Cal?"

"It's me, Birdie. I just wanted you to know that Silvie's here and I'll get her home...when she's done."

There's a pause, and a sigh of relief. "Thank you. I was worried when she didn't call."

I look back at the dance floor at the way she's dancing and laughing with strangers. "Yeah, she's okay."

Hours pass. Silvie drinks slower than when she first arrived. Laughs at the right moments, though I still sense underlying pain. She never flirts or dances with any guys which is to be expected. Just listens and participates in conversation with the bridal party.

It's last call, and the bachelorette party is long gone. Silvie is alone at the bar, opening and closing her umbrella that was in her drink as if she's pondering all of her life's choices.

"Cal."

I set down the glasses and look over. "Yes, Silvie?"

Her lips twitch when I say her name, like she enjoys hearing it from me. Honestly, I like saying it.

"I don't know how to get home," she admits, overwhelm

chasing away her buzz as reality sinks in. Her eyebrows are pinched with worry.

"I already called Birdie," I assure her. "She knows I'll bring you home."

She sighs with relief. "Thank you. I needed this."

"Needed what?"

She gives me a sad, half-smile. "Someone to be nice to me."

A flash of irritation burns through me. Not at her. No, I'm lowkey pissed at the guy who did this to her. I'm not looking to swoop in and be her knight in shining armor, but it's hard not to want to save this damsel in distress. Even I'm not immune and that's saying something.

We finish up closing, and I walk Marina to her car. She glances back at the bar where Silvie is waiting for me. "Are you sure you know what you're doing with that one?"

I shake my head. "She's Birdie's. Just getting her home safe."

She snorts. "Birdie would kill you if anything happened to her. The Bees would all help her bury your body somewhere."

"No doubt," I say as I wave.

I make my way back to Silvie, who's barely keeping herself upright on her barstool. "Are you ready?"

She looks at me with an absolutely gut-wrenching face. Fat tears well in her eyes and her features begin to crumple. She's had too much to drink. No matter how many waters I supplied her with or how many plates of fries, nachos, and snacks I brought her, she still took shots with the bachelorette party, and she's about to either lose her shit or her cookies. Neither will be pretty.

Her breaths come out sharp and uneven as her eyes frantically dart all around her. A whine of pure desperation claws its way out of her. I'm momentarily paralyzed because she's unravelling quickly and I don't know what to do.

"I need to get out of this dress," she says, breath hitching. One of the tears race down her cheek. "Before I lose my mind."

She rubs at the center of her chest as if that'll help her inhale more air. Her skin is paler than it was just a while ago when she was dancing. As she slides off the stool onto her feet, her entire body shudders. I recognize an impeding panic attack and it's coming on fast.

"You want me to help you to the bathroom?" I ask, voice low and gentle, hoping to calm her.

She swallows and shakes her head. "I don't think I can get it off alone."

"It'll be okay."

We make it outside of the bar, and as if being possessed by a demon, she starts clawing at the buttons down her back.

"I'm stuck," she cries out, panic threading her voice. "I'm actually stuck. I need it off of me. I don't want it touching me anymore."

"Hey," I say gently. "I've got you. It's okay."

She murmurs, her lip trembling. "Please help me."

I take in the dress, the lace, the way her whole body is braced like she's on the verge of a full-on panic attack.

"Do you care about this dress?" I ask.

She looks at me dead seriously. "I hope I never see this dress ever again."

"Got it."

I yank it off in one swoop. Buttons pop loose and scatter like confetti. The dress loosens and slides down, pooling at her feet.

She exhales like she's been underwater and finally came up for air. Her skin bears marks from the dress's tight fit. Jesus. This was, in fact, an honest-to-God torture device.

I hand her a beach towel and turn away while she wraps it around herself. As much as the glimpse of lingerie entices the lonely male parts of me, I don't act on it. Silvie doesn't even know me and is giving me her trust. Trust isn't something I take lightly.

"Thank you," she says, voice full of relief.

"You really are going to be okay," I assure her.

She smiles at that. Soft. Real. Then her knees buckle, and I'm already moving, lifting her without asking. She doesn't protest. She just relaxes in my arms as if she trusts I won't drop her. I won't. Especially since we left thirty pounds of dead wedding dress weight behind us.

I carry her to my truck and set her down on the seat. I don't wait for her to struggle with the seatbelt while trying to hold her towel on and just go ahead and buckle her in. I go back for her purse and bag and toss them into the back seat.

I pull my phone out and call Birdie.

She answers on the first ring. "Cal?"

"I've got your girl," I say. "We're on our way."

There's a pause. "Is she okay?"

"She will be," I tell her.

"I should have cancelled bingo," Birdie murmurs, guilt in her tone. "She needed me and—"

"She needed *tonight*," I interrupt. "I looked after her and now you can take over from here."

Birdie's voice softens. "Thank you."

I look down at the woman who's now asleep in the seat next to me, hair spilling down her shoulders, face relaxed and finally at peace.

"No problem."

cal
...

I'VE CARRIED a lot of random things and people in my life. A drunk fisherman. A raccoon taking up residence in the bar that absolutely didn't want to be relocated. A Christmas tree for a tourist that was wider than the doorway, and the tourist insisted it would fit. It did not fit, but I made it fit anyway, much to their dismay.

But, carrying a beautiful yet broken woman who had the worst day of her life is definitely the most enjoyable. Not the pain she went through. That shit sucks. There's something sacred, though, about her letting down her guard enough to trust me with such a task. I'm just grateful she landed in my bar and not at someplace shady. Not everyone would have handled her situation with respect.

Life hasn't been kind to her today. And that infuriates me.

Drool soaks into my shirt and I stifle a grin. Again, not the first time I've been drooled on, but certainly the best. Up close like this, I can smell her expensive perfume, but can't name what it is. When I stopped the truck, she protested for about ten seconds outside the vehicle, insisting she was mostly fine and could walk, before gravity won, and she melted into me like her body finally gave up.

Your shitty day is almost over, Silvie.

Birdie's porch light is on when I reach her cottage. That woman is one of the older women of Coconut Beach who meddle and look out for everyone. I turn the knob and nudge the door with my hip, letting myself in. Birdie looks up from the couch, a TV glowing in front of her, and she takes in the scene without missing a beat. I am carrying a beautiful woman, who's wearing nothing but her underwear, and wrapped in a towel. It doesn't look great.

She stands and asks me calmly, a frown marring her features, "Where are my baby's clothes?"

I clear my throat. "She was in her wedding dress."

An insanely expensive wedding dress. One that probably cost more than my truck. I think the way she looked at me when she said she needed that dress off will haunt me for a while. It was as if the dress was hurting her physically and emotionally when she begged me to help her get it off.

Birdie squints. "What happened to the dress?"

"She had a panic attack," I say carefully, "Wanted it off. I think it was sewn on her. That dress is now no longer operational."

Birdie exhales long and slow, as if this confirms something she already suspected.

"Lordy, Lou," she mutters and heads down the hall to her guest room. "This girl has been through it."

I nod and carry Silvie down the hall after Birdie, her blonde hair spilling over my chest, her breath slow and even. She murmurs something, and her fingers curl in my shirt. My chest tightens in a way I didn't plan for.

Birdie opens the door to her guest room and flicks on the lamp. The space fills with warm light. Worn and faded quilts are neatly folded at the bottom of the bed. Everything looks ready, as if Birdie had lovingly prepared this room for her. Silvie clearly means something to Birdie and is so special to her.

I gently lay Silvie on the bed and pull a quilt up around her. She murmurs a little and curls onto her side. "Thanks, Cal."

I give her a little pat and then follow Birdie to the living room.

Her face softens. "Thank you for bringing her home."

"Of course. So, this is your Silvie?" I ask quietly.

Birdie nods proudly. "This is my Silvie."

Silvie is beautiful in a way I can't put my finger on. She seems fierce but soft around the edges. And you don't fall asleep in a stranger's arms unless you're exhausted all the way through. You don't beg them to rip you out of your dress. It makes me care a little more than I should, which honestly, makes me a little uneasy.

I don't get attached to tourists.

But she's not a tourist, is she? She's Birdie's Silvie.

Birdie crosses her arms and tilts her head at me. "Did she tell you what happened?"

"She didn't say much," I admit. "She ate and hung out with a group at the bar to wait for you to be done with bingo."

There was a lot more than that, but I'm not going to spill all that to Birdie. It's her story to tell. Not mine. I still can't seem to shake from my mind how raw pain morphed Silvie's expression whenever no one was looking. No one but me. I'm a bartender, so we notice these things.

Keep telling yourself that, pal.

"I would have left bingo when she called me," she huffs.

"She said she didn't want you to do that." I gesture toward the back of the house. "I don't know what happened with her groom. Seems like he let a good thing go."

"You have no idea," Birdie murmurs. "Oh, honey. We should be celebrating that she didn't marry the tool bag."

That's something we can both agree on. I barely know Silvie, but I know enough that the man who let her go is a douchebag.

"How come you didn't go to the wedding?" I ask with a slight frown.

I shouldn't care. Normally, I don't. At least not past a surface level. It's unnerving to worry about someone I barely know. Birdie is clearly someone very important to her. Not having her at the wedding must've been hard.

Birdie frowns and she shakes her head. "Her mother doesn't care for me and wouldn't have me at the wedding. I told her I would celebrate with her later. I didn't want to go and make a fuss."

There's clearly history there.

"Her ex sounds like a piece of work," I blurt out, even though it's truly not my business. Still, I'm curious. I don't want to be, but I am.

You're going to get yourself in trouble with this one if you're not careful.

"Oh, he is," she says, scowling. "Anyone who fumbles Silvie is an idiot."

It was more than a fumble. The woman ran from her wedding. She was barely holding it together.

"She seems sad," I say softly.

Birdie studies me for a long beat. I'm not sure I'm comfortable with the inspection, but she eventually gives me a reprieve and looks away. "I don't know all the details, Cal, but she ran out of the wedding and came here. So, it can't be good." She pauses, then adds with a conspiratorial wink, "Or it *is*. Now she can find someone who deserves her."

I give her a pointed look. Birdie is a meddler and loves to play matchmaker in this small beach town of ours. My curiosity and eagerness to help Silvie doesn't play well in my favor. It makes me appear interested. Which I'm not.

Liar.

"It doesn't seem like she wants to be fixed up," I say to Birdie. "She seems like she wants to be left alone."

She scoffs and waves off my words as if they're silly.

"Well, if either of you need anything," I say, clearing my

throat and hoping to redirect this awkward conversation, "you know where to find me."

"I'll hold you to it," she says with a grateful smile. "We're gonna get my girl right."

I'm not sure about this whole "we" thing, but I do believe if anyone can help Silvie, it'll be Birdie.

I nod slowly. That feels right. Like, wherever she came from pushed her exactly where she needed to land.

Birdie studies me, eyes sharp and knowing. "You did good, Cal."

"I just helped her get home," I say with a chuckle.

"You looked after her. You're a good man. Love you, son."

"Love you, Birdie," I say kissing her cheek and giving her a hug. "Sleep well."

She smiles and reaches for the door. "Get on out of here. I'll take it from here."

As I step into the starlit night, something sticks with me. I can't explain the feeling. A premonition maybe. Whatever it is, though, I can't seem to shake it. It's imbedded in my bones, buzzing with warning.

I walk home slower than usual on the beach, taking in the moon in the sky. The air is warm, carrying a salty breeze, and the quiet of Coconut Beach fills me with a sense of calm.

What a weird night.

For the first time in years, something stirs in me. Curiosity, interest, maybe more. I have a rule. Never take anything seriously. Never have more than fun here in Coconut Beach. Serious relationships aren't for me. I've got too much on my plate.

But tonight felt different, and that's freaking me out. I want to know Silvie. I want to know where she came from, what she ran from, and how she ended up here. What made this kind of woman run in lace and heels and land in small town Coconut Beach?

Birdie's words echo in my head. My girl. She's talked about Silvie so much that I practically felt like I knew her. Silvie, the woman who never forgot Birdie's birthday. The one who sent her flowers just because. Birdie's always bragged about her like a proud mama. I didn't know her name, but I knew she existed.

That always made me happy for Birdie because she deserves that. Birdie has been a huge part of our town since she moved here over ten years ago. She fit into this town like a local, and everyone thinks of her as a local now. She loves with all of her heart.

I reach my place and let myself inside, the quiet evening enveloping me. I strip off my clothes and step into the shower spray, letting the water wash away the salt, sweat, and lingering scent of Silvie's perfume. Regret fills me at that last part.

Get it together, man.

My mind takes a while to settle when I lie in bed with the fan humming softly overhead. I close my eyes and see that honey blonde hair spilling over my arm. The way she trusted me without even knowing me. The peaceful way she looked while she slept, like she was finally able to rest here in Coconut Beach, her safe haven.

Whatever or whoever she's running from, I'm glad she's away from them. I have a feeling she's landed exactly where she's meant to be.

silvie

. . .

I WAKE up to the sound of a hush of waves through the window, blowing a breeze across my face. It's soft at first, like it's a dream. There's music in the distance playing softly. Something low and familiar, and comforting. And then it hits me. The unmistakable aroma of coffee and bacon. And something sweet I can't put my finger on, but if I had to, I'd say they were Birdie's honey biscuits she used to make for me when I was a kid. Anytime I had a bad day, those mouthwatering biscuits saw me through it. It got to the point where, no matter how bad a day I was having, if I told her I needed her biscuits, they were in the oven before I knew it. There's not much in life that Birdie's honey biscuits can't fix.

Even a rotten sister and a cheating groom.

God, I am so glad I got away when I did.

As quickly as the thought of yesterday's fiasco enters my head, I push it away. I'm here now, and out of that godforsaken dress, which means I can focus on healing myself. Things *will* get better.

I smile before I open my eyes. The breeze flows over me, and I let myself truly feel it. Love from Birdie. This has to be a dream. I have to be dreaming. Because yesterday felt like a nightmare.

I burrow deeper into the bed and pull the covers over my head, curling onto my side, the sheets soft against my skin. The smell of Birdie's home fills my senses like a hug. For a second, I let myself believe I've woken up in a new life. A better one than the rat race I've been living in.

Then my head pulses hard, reminding me of all the choices I made last night that led me to this wicked hangover. I groan and finally sit up. Sunlight spills across the room, painting everything in gold. I turn my head and spot a glass of water and a bottle of ibuprofen on the nightstand beside me. The room tilts a little, and I pop two pills in my mouth, draining half of the glass in one go.

Last night's events at the bar come back to me in embarrassing fragments. The shots. The dress choking the life out of me. The pleading for Cal to get it off me.

Cal.

Warmth pools in my stomach at the memory of his dark, honeyed eyes, so kind and honest.

He had plenty of opportunity to take advantage of the situation, but he didn't. Instead, he calmly assisted me through the worst night of my life.

And he was really, really cute. Not that I was looking. I'm so over men it's not even funny. But I do have eyes. A lot of the patrons flirted with him. He was friendly and fun. There was something about him that made him feel like a safe space. Plus, if Birdie approves, then he has to be okay.

She never liked Tyler and look how right she turned out to be with that assessment.

I'm still reeling over the fact I fled before the wedding. It was so out of character for me. Then, I allowed myself to get publicly drunk and relied on a bartender to take care of me. I'm not one to be reckless or impulsive. I'm the woman with spreadsheets, backup plans, and color-coded systems. I don't wake up with gaps in my memory due to a night of drinking. What if something happened to me last night?

Except nothing happened. And now I have to figure out my life. How to fix everything. To be honest, though, I don't even know where to begin. Or how to begin. How do I rebuild my life? How do I fix the mess I've made of my life, my company, and my family?

For the first time in my life, I feel like I have absolutely no control over anything. The thought sends a spike of fear through me, and it's scary. I press a palm to my chest and breathe through it.

I'm safe with Birdie. I'm here. There's no more Tyler, no more Belladonna, no more betrayal and drama. What a relief that is.

I push myself out of bed to find a folded T-shirt and leggings on the chair next to the bed. It smells like laundry soap and sunshine. I recognize the outfit as one I'd left behind on accident. I've never been more grateful for cozy clothes. I pull them on and head to the bathroom. I look in the mirror and cringe. Wedding makeup and wild, crazy hair. Lovely.

After brushing my teeth and hair and washing my face, I exit the bathroom and pause to admire the bedroom. Warm, muted colors decorate the space, and it fills me with happiness. Each silly knickknack or piece of art was painstakingly chosen with the purpose of making the guest feel comfortable. I could spend hours marveling over each figurine or carefully placed book.

I make my way out of the room and into the living room. The whole cottage is eclectic and so Birdie. Because of her, my childhood has color and playfulness despite the cold, perfectly decorated home I was raised in. There's a frame sitting on an end table and I can't help but pick it up. It's of me and Birdie. I must've been in elementary school. We're both grinning at each other, happy as can be.

I needed this escape.

I set the frame back down and step into the kitchen, smiling when I see Birdie. She's at the stove, humming along to the music, drizzling honey on her biscuits while swaying to the music. The kitchen is warm and bright, like coming home.

I can breathe again. It's safe to be...*me*.

She turns and beams at me. "Morning, sunshine."

She wipes her hands, and we meet in the middle of the kitchen for the biggest hug.

I swallow back emotion and say, "Morning, Birdie."

"There's my beautiful girl," she says as she pulls back. "Too skinny. But beautiful all the same."

I lost so much weight to fit into my wedding dress that my mother insisted could not be resized. I know she did that on purpose, and it's another reason to add to the long list of why my mom sucks. There was nothing wrong with my body size. She just insisted I be smaller.

I will never do that again. *Shrink to fit someone's needs.*

Birdie slides biscuits onto a plate and sets it at the table. "Are you hungry?"

I smile and nod. She ushers me to her little breakfast table with mismatched chairs. It's already set for two. She waited for me and set up a beautiful breakfast for us. It's the little things that I cherish about Birdie. The way she makes you feel seen and so loved.

She pours me a coffee without asking. But, of course, she does. She always knows.

We sit at the kitchen table together, eggs, bacon, and honey biscuits. Tea for her and coffee for me. It's a comfortable silence between us for a while, enjoying the open windows and breeze from the beach.

But I know it won't be for long. I can see it etched on Birdie's concerned face.

"You ready to talk?" she asks softly.

I know she's worried about me and how everything went down, and I know I would be too if the roles were reversed. It doesn't make talking about it any easier, though.

I focus on my food. "It was pretty bad."

Understatement of the year.

My eyes begin to water, and I hate that I'm about to cry for the millionth time. I'm usually so good at locking down my emotions.

She sips her mug and waits patiently. Birdie's always had a way of bringing out whatever I need to talk about.

"Belladonna," I say, voice hoarse and lip trembling. "Sorry." I sniffle and bat at a rogue tear. "I'm a mess."

Birdie reaches over and pats my arm, encouraging me to continue. "You're not a mess, Silvie. You're in pain."

I swallow hard and nod. "I wish I weren't. They're not worth it."

She nods as if she agrees.

"She'd been sleeping with Tyler for the past five months, Birdie," I choke out. "They admitted it right before the wedding. Who does that to their own sister?"

"Oh, honey," she says, frowning. "I'm so sorry. I can't believe that girl. What was she even thinking?"

"I know. I can't believe I didn't see the signs. I was so busy planning the wedding," I mutter. "What a joke."

She takes a bite of her food and chews as if she's thinking. My mom never liked Birdie, and Belladonna was awful. Birdie was always my kindred spirit. Dad knew that and never allowed Mom to let her go. No matter how many lies my sister made up or what she put Birdie through. Birdie tolerated a lot for me. I always hated that they treated her that way. In some ways, I think my mom was jealous of Birdie and me. And Belladonna was just plain mean.

"You're not the one in the wrong here," Birdie assures me. "You were planning a life while your sister was stealing it behind your back."

"Mom actually wanted me to go through with the wedding," I say through more tears. "Even after she learned what happened."

"That's plain insanity if you ask me," she huffs. "What a terrible thing to want for your child."

My mom and Belladonna are cut from the same cloth

whereas Dad and I are similar. That's probably why my dad and I are so close. We work together, and we share the same drive in business. I don't have anything in common with my mother other than our shared DNA. Sometimes I still can't believe my sister and I came from the same gene pool.

I stare down at my plate. "I think I lost myself, Birdie."

She doesn't say anything, just waits for me to continue. She reaches out and clasps her hand to mine.

"I don't know what happened," I continue. "But somewhere along the way, I stopped being me and started being...what everyone expected me to be. I don't even know who I am anymore. I don't like who I see when I look in the mirror."

Birdie's eyes soften. "Sounds like you needed a break, sugar."

Tears sting, and I laugh weakly. "That's one way to put it."

She squeezes my hand again. "You don't have to figure it all out today. You just need rest, baby."

"Okay," I say feeling exhausted.

"Eat your food. That's the first thing we'll do. Get you nourished," she says as she pulls my head to her and kisses it.

"Thanks, Birdie."

"Of course. I'm so glad you're here. And I'm also glad you didn't marry Tyler the turd. That boy never made sense for you. I know why you were going to do it. But it wasn't right." She shakes her head.

"I'm running out of time, Birdie," I say softly.

My stomach twists just thinking about my predicament. None of my friends or peers or anyone I know has to deal anything like this.

"There has to be another way," she says as she shakes her head. "I will never understand why your grandmother had that stupid stipulation in her will. You'd think it was the 1950s. Better get barefoot and pregnant in the kitchen while you're at it."

Bile creeps up my throat at the thought of chaining myself for life to Tyler. What a miserable existence that would have been. It was almost my sentence, and I escaped just in time.

"I only have a few months to get married, or the company defaults to a trust. Then, my family loses it," I say, feeling anxious just saying it. "We could lose everything. I can't do that to Dad."

"Tyler was not the answer," she says dryly, "and your father would understand."

But he wouldn't. Our entire lives revolve around the business. It would mean ripping everything away from too many people I care about.

"My grandmother had her reasons." She was one of the good ones in my family. While her stipulation doesn't make a lot of sense on the surface, I understand her reasons.

She was fighting the patriarchy. Well, sort of. In her own, slightly warped way, she was protecting her legacy and her eldest granddaughter by forcing her to choose love and marriage, first and foremost, which would then secure her future.

Unfortunately, in her efforts to do a good thing, she tied my hands. This idea of hers likely made sense for a woman of her time, but not a modern woman. I was going to college and learning the ropes of the business. Finding a husband was low on the priority list.

And then, time just sort of slipped by rather quickly.

Now we're down to the wire.

"I thought we were in love," I say as I think about my almost-husband and how close I was to completing this requirement. "Now I know it was all bullshit."

The anger feels good burning through my veins. Hurt over the cheating and the feeling of failure at keeping our company compete for space in my head, but it's fading a bit. There has to be another way through this will stipulation. If anyone can find it, it'll be me.

As far as the pain Tyler and Belladonna caused me, I vow to drag my way through it and to the other side.

Birdie leans back in her chair. "I have an idea."

I take a bite of eggs. "Okay..."

"What if you stay here for the summer and I help you figure out what you want to do?"

"Like, the *whole* summer?"

"The whole summer," she says as if it's already decided. "You were supposed to take six weeks off to travel with Tyler the turd anyway. I highly doubt your father would mind if you worked remotely from here in Coconut Beach. It'll do you good."

I snort at her calling him that now. Because it's true. He is a turd. "Yeah. I was going to travel."

"With the turd," she adds.

"With the turd." I laugh, shaking my head.

"The trash takes itself out."

I giggle, the sound surprising and real. "Did you just quote Taylor Swift?"

She shrugs. "Girl is wise."

I can't remember the last time I laughed over a casual breakfast. Lately, breakfast for me has been a protein shake on the way home from the gym. My nervous system thanks me for this moment. It needed a vacation too.

"You can stay here," she continues. "Work on getting back on your feet. No pressure, just breathe."

Relief fills me, and the fear eases up a little.

I wrap my hands around my ceramic coffee mug and let the warmth seep into me like a hug.

Maybe this is exactly what I need. Where else can I go? Back to the penthouse that I shared with Tyler? Back to the job that I've already taken six weeks off from for my extended honeymoon? The paparazzi are probably chomping at the bit to figure out what happened and where I disappeared to. If I went back home, it would be a nightmare. I would have no privacy. Here, at least nobody but Birdie seems to know me. She's my safe spot.

I think it's settled.

We finished breakfast, and I feel better. Nothing can fix a bad day better than a Birdie honey biscuit, and that's proved true once again.

Birdie hums as we clear the table. I wash up our dishes and set them in the dishwasher. I'm still wrapped in that fragile feeling that everything is unstable.

"Oh, I forgot to tell you. We're going to yoga," Birdie says brightly.

"We?" I blink. "I have never done yoga in my life."

Of course, this woman isn't going to take no for an answer.

"Shoes on," she calls as she disappears down the hall, returning with two rolled mats strapped neatly together with matching water bottles, like she's had this planned.

"Matching," she says proudly. "Because I'm thrilled to have a new yoga partner."

I stare at the pink and teal mats that are entirely too cheerful for this early morning, when I'm fighting a hangover.

"I don't know how I feel about yoga," I admit as I go to my room to throw on a sports bra. "I'm more of a cardio person, Birdie."

"I know. You and your running, I swear. You wouldn't catch me running. And if you did, you should find out what's chasing me," she says as I hear her filling up our water bottles.

I slide on flip-flops by the door where Birdie always has extras.

Birdie pats my arm. "You're going to love yoga."

"Have you ever done yoga?" I ask as I eye the brand-new mats.

"No, but we have a new class that Summer teaches, and I have been dying to try it out," she says excitedly.

The beach is already bustling with people when we arrive. We make our way past them to a quieter area where waves roll in steadily off in the distance. The sand is warm as I slide my flip-flops off and feel it between my toes. God, I missed this. When was the last time I felt the sun on me and the sand under my feet? When was the last time I let myself feel *anything*?

Someone who looks like she could be a sister to me stands on her mat at the front of the class. She has long blonde hair like mine and green eyes, and she smiles as we walk up. "Hi, Birdie. Glad you two could make it."

Birdie waves. "Hello. This is my Silvie."

My Silvie. I smile at how she introduces me. She's always done that for as long as I can remember.

The woman greets me with a wave. "I'm Summer. Welcome."

I nod. "Good morning. Thank you, although, I'm not sure what I'm doing."

She laughs. "You'll do great. This is a beginner class."

We roll out our mats and settle in. I lower myself onto mine carefully, head still a little fuzzy, body not quite sure what it thinks about stretching right now.

The class starts slowly. Breathing. Gentle movement. Summer's voice is calm but playful, guiding without demanding.

At first, my mind fights it. Wants to wander. Wants to sprint. Wants to control something.

Then I look up.

The ocean stretches endlessly in front of me, sunlight dancing across the water. Waves rise and fall without asking permission. Without rushing. Without apologizing.

My breath starts to match their rhythm.

I wobble and laugh. I nearly tip over once, and Birdie squeezes my hand like we're sharing a secret. No one is perfect, but everyone is relaxed and having fun.

By the end, my muscles hum, and my head feels clearer. Not fixed, but steadier and clearer. Wow. That was pretty amazing.

As we lie back on our mats, staring up at the sky, a quiet

thought slips in. Maybe I *can* do this. Maybe I *can* rebuild myself one day at a time, right here, with sand between my toes and nothing expected of me except showing up.

For the first time since I ran, that feels like it's possible. Showing up feels easy.

cal

. . .

"YOU HEADING over to see your mom today?" Jonah asks as he sits at the helm, like the ocean personally appointed him guardian of the Atlantic Ocean.

I glance at him. "Yeah, this afternoon."

Jonah grunts in response, which is typical because he's a man of few words.

The boat rocks beneath me, gentle and familiar. There's something soothing about being out at sea, the wind and sun on us. Now I know why Jonah prefers it to land. At sixty years old, permanently grumpy, he's somehow still revered by all of the people in Coconut Beach. In a way, he's like my mom, Carly, who keeps to herself. They love their solitude.

We fish in silence for a while. Jonah pretends he doesn't like my company, but I know he looks forward to our weekly time out on the boat. We catch up on bar stuff and spend most of the time just sitting together, watching our lines. I think he prefers the company of silence.

I cast again and wait. The sun warms my shoulders. It's not as hot today, and the breeze is perfect. I reach for my water bottle, open it, and take a swig. I stare out at the water that's calm and endless. Coconut Beach is paradise.

Jonah clears his throat. "You bring her books this week?"

"Every Tuesday," I say with a nod.

The mobile bookstore is parked by the marina this week. She likes anything romance right now. And anything with a strong heroine who kicks ass. It's getting harder to pick out books for her. I never know what she'll like.

Jonah grunts. "You're a good kid."

I don't say anything because compliments from Jonah are rare, but they mean something.

He squints at the horizon. "You just going to stay here forever? Be a bartender and take care of your mom?"

I scoff. "I manage that bar, too. Did you forget that, old man?"

He rubs his beard like he's deciding whether to argue with me or not. "Didn't forget. I just think you're built for more, kid. Once upon a time, you were going places."

I bristle at his words. "I'm thirty, Jonah. I'm not a kid."

"You're still a kid," he says with a stare that tells me not to argue. "And you spent all those years in school. Not using any of that tending bar."

That one sticks. I don't say anything because it's pointless to try and defend my actions. It is what it is. I made my choices, and I don't regret them.

I have a life here, and it's a good one. I fish with Jonah, check in on my mom, and run the bar. And I surf. I stay busy. *And lonely.* But we won't talk about that last part. I stay busy enough to beat that part.

After we dock, I swing by the bookstore before heading home. Mia, one of the owners of Salty Pages, waves, a million bangle bracelets clanging together, as I walk up, a big smile on her face.

She's an attractive woman—blonde hair, big brown eyes, dimples—but not my type. She wears a lot of jewelry, and I do mean *a lot*. Necklaces, bangles, rings. It must take her a good half hour to get it all put on each day.

"Hey, Mia," I call as I climb up and peruse some of the books.

"Hey, Cal, how are you doing?" she says as she tucks a few books onto a shelf. Her boho dress swishes as she moves.

"I'm good. Just getting books for my mom."

I scan the rows of books, quickly getting overwhelmed by the endless titles. There are tons with cartoon covers that seem interesting, but there are so many, they blur together. She'll be disappointed if I accidentally buy something she already has.

"I heard your aunt had a new release today," she says with a grin. "We nearly sold out of all the copies."

I nod. "She did. She already sent my mom a copy. And Donna is coming to visit at the end of the summer."

My aunt Donna has been writing romance novels for over thirty years. She lives in Wisteria Cove, Massachusetts, and has a beach bungalow here in Coconut Beach that her family and their friends use. My cousin Finn and his new wife, Rowan, came to stay here recently, and we had a lot of fun. I keep their house in order while they're away.

"It would be awesome if she could swing by and sign the books that we carry of hers," Mia not-so-subtly suggests.

I skim my gaze over a book that has a dude with eight-pack abs on the front cover. Yeah, not buying her that. I pick up a gold and black book that alludes that it might be about dragons. Now *that* I could buy for her.

"I'm sure she will," I say as I blow out a breath. "Mia, I have no idea what to pick for my mom. Is this one good?"

"Well," she says as she eyes the book in my hand, a patient smile on her face. "She already has that one. You bought it a few weeks ago." She hooks her thumb over her shoulder making all her bangles clatter loudly. "I already put back two paperbacks and one hardcover that I think she'd like. She doesn't already own those."

I sigh with relief. "Thanks. I never remember what she has or know what she'll like."

"It's no problem. These are good ones, I promise."

I'm grateful for Mia's help.

"Thanks, I trust you. You know your books. I just wish she could come pick them out herself," I say with a wistful smile.

She taps a pen to her lip, brown eyes glittering eagerly, and says, "What if we brought the truck to her sometime?"

The image of the book store rolling up to Mom makes my chest ache. I think she would enjoy that.

I soften. "You would do that?"

"For my top reader of Coconut Beach? Sure I would," Mia says as she flips the screen for me to tap my card.

"That would be great. Let me talk to her about it first, though," I tell her. Sometimes she's not up for going out in the yard, and I don't want Mia to go to the trouble for nothing.

"Let me know. See you next week, Cal." She waves, her millions of bracelets clanging their goodbye to me as well.

I make the short walk to my truck and stop by the Oceanside Market on the way home. I go through the list, get everything for my mom, and load it up. As I pull out of the parking lot, I pass a car that has "just married" written in shoe polish on the back window. Cans tied to yarn clatter against the pavement as it drives by.

Naturally, marriage makes me think about Silvie, the mysterious runaway bride from last night. I can't help but wonder how she's doing today. Each time my mind tried to drift to her throughout the day, I'd busy myself with something else. I'm still curious about her story. I wonder if I'll ever know it.

Once at my mom's, I find her in her usual chair by the window. Same spot she's claimed for years. She looks up when I come in, eyes bright when she sees me.

"Hey." She beams at me.

"Hi, Mom." I return her smile as I set the bags down and lean in for a hug.

She squeezes me tightly and says, "It's good to see you, honey."

"I got everything you asked for."

She pulls back and smiles at me like I hung the moon. "Thank you. You did well, kid."

"What is up with you and Jonah calling me kid today?" I roll my eyes. "Like I told him, I'm thirty."

She laughs softly. "You'll always be *my* kid."

I pick the grocery bags back up and take them to the kitchen. Once on the counter, I line them up the way she likes. Everything in Mom's house is neat, orderly, and well taken care of. If a complete stranger were to come over, they'd never know the mental warfare she goes through.

Mom sits in her chair by the window, sunlight catching in her hair. It's gone more silver than brown these days, but she still twists it back with the same clip she's had for as long as I can remember.

"You got the good apples?" She asks, eyes twinkling with love and happiness.

"The good apples," I say. "The ones that bruise if you look at them wrong."

She nods, satisfied. "Those are the ones I like."

I pull the paper bag from the bookstore out last. She straightens the second she sees it.

"Books?" she asks, already smiling.

"Three," I say. "Two romances and a thriller. Mia says she thinks you'll like them."

Her eyes light up. That alone makes the whole trip worth it.

I hand them over, and she holds the bag like it's something fragile and important. She pulls the first one out, flips it over, and reads the back.

"Oh," she says softly. "I've been wanting this one."

I owe Mia big. She never lets me fail.

"Mia says she can bring the truck here for you to buy from if you want," I say gently. "What do you think? Could be fun."

We both know there's nothing "fun" about her agoraphobia.

Mom looks at me wistfully over the top of the book. "I don't

know. You know I don't like to leave the yard. It's just...hard."
She trails off and shudders.

I nod, not pushing her. I've learned that if I push her to do
something, it's almost always a no. But, if I lay something out
and let her think about it, sometimes she surprises me and
agrees. I'm hoping this will be one of those times. We've come a
long way since the beginning when this all first started. There
were times I'd get a little frustrated with her, but we've found
how to maneuver through it. That's what family does for each
other.

I finish putting things away and lean against the counter,
watching her as she inspects the book selection. She opens the
second book, nods her approval, but then pauses when she sees
the third.

"A woman who restores old houses," she reads. "With
secrets."

I smirk. "Probably has a hot contractor dude in that one."

She hums, pleased, and sets it on top of the stack like it's
been promoted to her next read.

"Did you eat?" she asks.

"Not yet."

She clicks her tongue. "Sit. I'll make you something."

"You don't have to."

"I want to."

I sit at the small table anyway. She moves slowly but steadily,
pulling out the soup she made earlier and heating it on the stove.
She always cooks like she has all the time in the world. Soup in
the middle of summer isn't my thing, but I love my time with
my mom. I'll eat whatever she makes me.

She sets the bowl in front of me and watches until I take a
bite.

"Good?" she asks.

"Always," I say. "Thank you."

She smiles, then studies me the way she does when she's
thinking about something she hasn't decided to say yet.

"I'll think about the book truck coming here," she says softly.

And I know she will. She didn't always stay home as she does now. She never talks about why she doesn't want to leave. But the few times that she's tried, she's had panic attacks.

"Okay." I nod. "I think it would be cool if you could look at all the books they have to offer and see what *you* like."

She searches my eyes. "You look tired. Got a lot going on?"

"It was a long week."

"It's Tuesday." She laughs.

"Yeah," I say with a chuckle.

She looks back down at her books. "You like being busy."

"I do."

She flips a page, then glances up again. "But you've been quieter."

I freeze for half a second. "Have I?"

She smiles gently. "I know you, Cal."

I blow on the soup. "Nothing bad. Just thinking."

She reaches across the table and pats my hand. "Thinking is allowed."

I laugh. "Good. I was worried."

She squeezes my fingers. "I'm proud of you."

"For what?"

"For showing up," she says. "For taking care of things. For being so good to your pain-in-the-butt mother."

My throat tightens. "You don't have to worry, Mom. I'll always help you."

"I know," she says. "I just want you to remember you get to want things for you, too."

I look down at the table. "I have things."

She tilts her head. "Do you?"

I think about the bar. About the boat. Surfing. What I try not to think about is the woman in a wedding dress who trusted me without knowing my name.

"Yeah," I say quietly. "I think I do."

She smiles like she already knew. "Good."

I finish eating and stand to wash the bowl. She looks tired so I straighten up the grocery bags and push in my chair.

"Gonna head out," I tell her.

"Hot date?" she teases.

"Nah. You know I'm not looking for anything serious."

She cocks her head to the side, eyes narrowing as if she can see through the cracks in my words to the truth behind them. "Just because you're not looking doesn't meant it won't come looking for you."

"I'll keep that in mind," I say with a chuckle. "See you later."

She looks up. "Cal?"

"Yeah?"

"Thank you for the books. And the groceries. And everything."

I smile. "I love you, Mom."

She smiles back. "I love you, too."

I step outside into the warm afternoon, feeling lighter than I did when I walked in.

Sometimes love looks like big gestures. Sometimes it looks like books and soup with your mom.

When I climb into my truck and turn the engine over, "White Wedding" by Billy Idol blasts over the speakers. And, of course, Silvie's face pops up in my head. Again. Maybe I need to swing by and check to make sure she's okay. Then, I can finally move on.

That's all it is.

Worry over a sad, runaway bride.

Nothing more.

———

I turned around three times before I actually made it here. Three times. My brain tries to be logical and remind me I don't do *this*. Yet here I am.

Sitting in my truck across the street from Birdie's house

because I just can't let it go. I need, for some crazy ass reason, to know Silvie is okay.

With a frustrated sigh, I exit the truck and then stride toward Birdie's place.

I'm halfway up the front walk when I hear Silvie's voice. I glance over, and she's not on the phone. No, she's talking to something on the ground.

I slow to a halt and frown. She's sitting cross-legged on the front porch, in the shade, barefoot, with her hair in a messy knot on top of her head. She's in one of Birdie's oversized hot pink shirts and talking seriously to a very large iguana.

The iguana is staring back at her like he's considering her life choices. And I sort of am too.

"So, here's the thing," she says gently. "I didn't plan on coming here. But here I am. I feel like you understand me. Don't you?"

The iguana blinks. I stand, watching this unfold, my arms crossed. I'm wondering if this woman is sane or just adorably cute and a bit lonely for wanting to talk to an iguana.

She nods at him as if he's just responded. "Exactly. You get it."

I clear my throat.

She darts her head my way, startled, but I notice she seems nervous, and she fidgets, pulling her oversized T-shirt down. "Oh. Hey."

I gesture between her and the lizard. "Are you okay?"

"Yeah." She shrugs, then tilts her head at me. "Why?"

I squint. "I thought for a minute you were talking to an iguana."

She looks down at him and back at me as if I'm the odd one here. "Well, I was."

The iguana lifts his chin at me like he's challenging me.

I press my lips together, trying not to laugh. "Okay."

She smiles, all sunshine and zero shame. "His name is Iggy."

Her mood is considerably better than when I saw her last.

Being sober probably helps. There's a casual easiness to her that didn't exist before. I feel like it's good for her.

I move to stand in the shade next to her, and Iggy hisses at me. Great. An asshole lizard.

I take a step back. "Iggy doesn't like me."

"He doesn't trust men at first," she says solemnly. "We both have that in common."

I glance at her. "Is that so?"

She nods. "I think he could be an emotional support iguana."

Iggy takes another aggressive swish of his tail.

"You seemed to trust me last night. I'm a man." I inwardly groan because what the hell am I even saying. Are you flirting with her?

My brain hisses at me, much like the testy iguana, reminding me it already told me coming to see her was a bad idea.

"I don't think you count," Silvie says with a small smile. "You're a rare specimen."

Iggy takes another aggressive swish.

Great, now she's flirting back. This was not how this was supposed to go. She's heartbroken and piecing her life together. I'm over here trying to keep life simple and untethered. But, with a few teasing words, I can feel us entangling.

I should leave. My mouth opens to tell her goodbye, but no words come out. Idiot.

She stares at me for a beat, her face free of makeup and genuinely beautiful. She looks too young to be having the life problems she's clearly been up against. I wish I knew her story. I hate that I want to know because, *dammit, Cal, that's not keeping it casual*. That's called getting invested and I don't do that.

Not even for gorgeous runaway brides...

She pats the concrete beside her, and the iguana settles in next to her. "He lives under the hibiscus," she explains as if I've been waiting to hear the iguana's story my entire life. "Birdie says he's been here longer than most people on the island. Did you know they live a very long time?"

"That tracks," I say with a grumble. "He looks old and judgmental."

Iggy hisses again, louder this time.

She gasps. "Iggy. Be nice."

I laugh, full and surprised. "I'm glad you're doing okay, Silvie."

Now, walk away, man. You came, you saw, and now you must leave or you're going to get in too deep. This is dangerous territory.

She looks up at me then, *really looks at me*, and something soft settles in her expression.

"Yeah," she says. "I think I am. Even if I *am* talking to iguanas."

I shrug. "Especially if you're talking to iguanas."

Iggy scoots closer to her foot like he's chosen a side.

She smirks. "See? He likes me."

"You're not hard to like," I blurt out and then inwardly groan.

What is my deal around this woman?

She peeks at me from beneath her lashes as if my words embarrass her. "You'd be surprised. There are people who *really* don't like me."

Now that, I don't believe for a second.

"Then they're morons," I say simply.

I lean against the railing, arms crossed, watching her talk to the iguana like this is the most normal Tuesday activity on Earth.

She smiles and looks down at her hands in her lap.

Iggy hisses again, and she glares at him. "Stop threatening my friend."

Friend.

It feels safe. My brain agrees. But that word does something strange in my chest. There's an internal battle over how my brain and heart feel about it.

She stands, dusting off her legs, then looks at me like she's bracing for judgment.

"You think I'm weird," she says.

I meet her eyes. "I think you're talking to an iguana."

She waits.

"And," I add, "I kind of love that."

My heart thumps at those words as my brain misfires. Idiot. *What part about "don't flirt" do you not get, man?*

Her smile is slow and she looks pleased. "Good. Because this iguana is the only thing helping me hold it together right now."

Iggy lunges at my feet.

I jump. "Okay. I *don't* love that."

She laughs so hard she has to grab the railing. When she grows serious again, she says, "Thanks for last night. For getting me home safe."

I grin, unable to help it, because apparently my rules have flown out the window. "Any time."

She freezes for half a second, then looks at me, eyes bright. "Well, I guess I'll see you around, Cal."

"I guess you will, Silvie."

And, stupidly, I can't wait.

silvie

. . .

TWO WEEKS AGO, if you'd have told me I'd be excited about rolling out of bed to do yoga on the beach every day at sunrise, I would've laughed and ordered another latte. I'm a runner, not a yoga person. Also, a city girl, not a beach person. But now I'm surprised by how much I'm loving island life.

Now I'm at the door, itching to leave, before Birdie even finishes her tea. "Don't rush me, Sugar Bean," Birdie says, squinting at the clock. "My bones need a moment to wake up."

I have to laugh a little, because yoga was her idea at first. I dragged my heels to it, but now I'm the one excited about it every day. It gives me a purpose and something to look forward to every day. Yoga has been good for me.

"Come on, we don't want to miss the sunrise," I tell her, bouncing a little.

She eyes me. "Who are you and what have you done with the woman who questioned yoga on day one?"

"That was the hangover," I say. "And trauma."

Birdie snorts and grabs her hat, "You're going alone tomorrow. I'm sleeping in and meeting my Bees for coffee."

"Okay," I say cheerfully. "But I bet you'll regret not doing it. It's the best start of the day."

Even though yoga makes me ridiculously happy, these past two weeks haven't been worry-free. I had to hide my phone in a drawer so I wouldn't be tempted to look at it. While work isn't missing me, I know my friends and family are confused, and likely upset or angry. Plus, there's the tabloids and all their speculating. It's a lot to obsess over.

And yet, I'm finding ways not to. I've been exploring the cute shops in town, taking long, reflective walks on the beach, cooking what I want versus what someone else wants for me, and prioritizing my wants and needs over anything else.

It's strange, but nice.

"I've created a yoga monster," Birdie says with a huff.

I sigh, feeling happy. "I'm finally sleeping and eating actual food. I might just be a human now."

The sleep has been orgasmic. And not just because a certain handsome bartender keeps appearing in my dreams. I've finally been able to relax for the first time in forever.

Birdie studies me as if she's trying to take it all in. She's been doing that ever since I got here. Watching me closely as if I might break. "You're glowing."

That part is true. I am glowing. I don't remember the last time I felt this rested. I feel like someone swapped my batteries.

She eyes my T-shirt and leggings, the same ones I have been washing and re-wearing. "You know I love you, sugar. But you've got to go over to Coral Moon and get yourself some clothes. You have been wearing the same thing on repeat."

It's so comfortable, though.

"Hmmm, not a bad idea," I muse. "There were a couple of shops with cute things inside. Maybe I'll check them out tomorrow."

In New York, I admittedly had a stylist. She got me tailored suits and all my clothes. I never had to worry about what to wear. They just appeared in my closet. But now that I've been hiding out in Coconut Beach with an overnight bag that didn't hold much, I do need to grab a few things. It might be fun to go shopping for clothes that I actually like and pick out for once. Maybe I'll even get something daring that would have my mother clutching her pearls.

The thought makes me giddy.

———————

Sunrise yoga on the beach feels less like exercise and more like permission to breathe again. And not to have to think about anything whatsoever for an hour. Just listening to Summer's relaxing soothing voice and stretching and bending in ways my body isn't used to. And the best part is that I'm starting to physically feel better. *Stronger.*

And Summer is the actual best part. She's pure sunshine in human form, always barefoot, laughing, and comfortable wherever she is. I feel like I'm making a friend, and I love that. I'm going to ask her if she wants to grab a coffee and go shopping later. I can't remember the last time I did something like that.

I'm embarrassed to admit that my only friend back in New York is Wilby, my assistant. And he was so mad that I left without telling him. He's over it now, but when I got back to him after those first few days here, he gave me hell.

We've been texting whenever I fish my phone out and turn it on. Wilby is relieved I didn't marry Tyler. I always knew that Wilby wasn't a huge fan of Tyler's, but he never said much.

Until now.

Now, every text insults my ex, and frankly, it's therapeutic.

After class, Birdie wanders off to chat with someone, and I linger, watching the waves. That's when I see him.

Cal.

And I try not to look. I do. The last thing I need is to crush on the cute, local bartender. He literally saw me at my worst. But he makes it really, really hard not to notice him.

He's on a surfboard and *wow*...his body is beautiful. He's in board shorts, shirtless, and effortlessly riding a wave. Afterward,

Erin Branscom

he shakes out his hair and paddles out again. I watch him do it over and over, entranced by how gorgeous this man is.

Which is exactly why I need to stop looking. My pride is still tender and bruised from the beating it took a couple of weeks ago. Drooling over Cal complicates an already brittle situation.

I've seen him around, but I haven't talked to him since he walked up on me talking to Iggy. I've caught glimpses of him everywhere. At the marina. At the market. Once at dawn, jogging along the beach in the opposite direction. We never cross paths long enough to talk. Which is for the best. I'm not sure what I'd say.

I certainly don't trust myself. At least not yet.

With a sigh, I turn away from the stupidly gorgeous, distracting man to roll up my mat.

Summer flops down next to me like we're already the best of friends. "Hey girl, how are you doing?"

I'm grateful to have something other than Cal *and all his muscles* to focus on.

"I was actually wondering if you were busy later?" I say, trying to act casual, as if this hasn't been brewing all morning.

"Well, that depends. What are we doing?" she says with a grin.

"I didn't bring clothes," I say. "Like...any. Birdie is tired of me looking ragged and wants me to go shopping, and I need a partner in crime."

She looks excited, "Oh, that sounds like a lot of fun."

Relief floods me. "Really?"

"Absolutely," she says. "First rule of Coconut Beach is you get fresh clothes."

"Second rule?" I ask.

"We get coffee first."

Relief hits me. I made a friend, and I'm finally going to dress decently. Win, win.

———

74

We meet an hour later at a little walk-up spot near the beach where there's a coffee truck. Summer orders us iced matchas and tells me I'm going to love it. It's green, so we'll see. I don't have high hopes.

"Trust me," she says, handing one to me. "This will change your life."

I take a sip and groan. "Oh no. This is dangerous. It's actually good."

She laughs. "It's my favorite drink ever."

Shopping with Summer is effortless. She hands me dresses, linen shorts, and flowy tops, as if she already knows what will work. I try things on. Twirl. Say yes to colors I'd never pick back home. Because most people here on Coconut Beach wear bright and happy colors, and I love it.

"This one," she says, pointing at a sundress. "You look like you're a local."

I check out my reflection in the mirror and barely recognize myself *in a good way.*

"You've got a story," Summer says lightly. "And, if you're willing to tell it, I can be a listening ear."

A part of me wants to blurt out every awful, sordid detail, but I refrain. I like Summer, but I'm not sure if I'm ready to explain what a mess I am. I'm just barely making sense of it myself. I don't want to trauma dump on her and run her off after our first friend date.

"I'd like that," I say and mean it before changing the subject. "Should I try on swimsuits next?"

"Heck yeah."

By the time we're done, my arms are full, and my cheeks hurt from smiling.

I didn't just buy clothes. I bought a version of myself that feels like she might actually feel like me. Not a tailored black suit in sight. I realize I don't even think I liked those suits. I wonder if I can get my stylist to help me pick out different outfits when I go back to New York. Clothes that feel more like me. With color.

I've tried so hard to fit into the corporate world that I dressed like the men I work with. I'm realizing it's okay to be me in that world. I can be bright. I can embrace being feminine.

"Earth to Silvie." Summer grins.

"Sorry, I just got lost in my thoughts." I chuckle and look at my watch. "I'm starving. Want to hit up a food truck I saw back there?"

She nods, eyes glimmering. "Hell yeah. I could legit order everything on the menu right now. I'm that hungry."

We don't end up ordering everything on the menu, but we do order street tacos and sit at a picnic table. The tacos are savory with just the right amount of spice and fresh veggies loaded on top. I'm glad I ordered three.

"So, what do you like to do back in New York City?" Summer asks around a mouthful of food. "See a Broadway show? Visit the Statue of Liberty? Stand in the middle of Times Square?"

I like that she's a messy eater. It makes me feel less awkward about my own eating in front of my new friend.

"Hardly. I'm not a tourist." I say with a snort and then sip my soda. "I basically just work."

She arches a brow. "Sounds boring."

"I mean, I don't think it is," I say honestly. "I'm a VP at my family's company. It's a private investment and asset management firm. We help people manage their portfolios. In simple terms, we help people stay rich."

She leans in and whispers, "Are you rich?"

I laugh. "Sorta. I have money in investments. But not like a ton of money in the bank. I guess I do okay, though."

I don't know how to explain my strange world to people sometimes. I grew up with my mom's side of the family who was very wealthy. But my dad was not wealthy when he met my mom. Which is sometimes something I think about. They are pushing me to save the company, but at what cost? Money isn't everything. I've made enough to honestly retire somewhere and live a very simple life. But I love the company. I love helping people. And I love watching it grow and thrive. I don't want to stop. And if we lose it because of me...I don't know how I'll ever forgive myself.

Thankfully, we switch topics and she tells me funny stories about her yoga students. By the time we finish our food, I'm relaxed and truly glad I worked up the nerve to ask her to hang out with me.

"We totally need to do this again," Summer says when we wrap up our day. "I had a lot of fun."

"Me too," I agree and then give her the world's most awkward hug. "I'm looking forward to it."

"Give me your number and I'll text you." She holds up her phone ready for my digits. I blurt out my number and then she grins. "There. I texted you."

After I get back to Birdie's, I'll need to turn my phone back on to check it. Not just for Summer's texts. I've been ignoring everyone, except Wilby, of course, and my dad's texts and emails. I'm technically on vacation, but when you're the VP, vacation is just a different work location with worse Wi-Fi. One thing I've always done to try to prove myself is work non-stop like my dad. And I hate it. I wish I had more of a life than just working.

Like shopping dates with a friend.

Even while being on vacation, something is buzzing inside of me. I have so much energy and am restless. I take a deep breath. Which is wild because for the first time in a long time, I don't feel suffocated. I'm just...here. And I'm starting to think that here isn't such a bad place. I *like* it here.

———

I jab at the soil with my trowel. "I don't know why this plant isn't doing so well, Birdie. I've been trying to get it healthy like you showed me."

Birdie squints at the plant and sways a little, since she's on her third glass of sangria that she and the Bees have been drinking. "Sugar, it's not your fault. That plant should've tried harder."

The Bees lose it and laugh.

"Lordy, you're a hoot, Birdie," January calls from her chair, her own glass of sangria almost gone.

Birdie ignores their laughter and hands me another plant that I'm repotting as if I'm performing a sacred duty. "Here. These need encouragement. And probably gossip."

The Bees have a more active social life than anyone I know. They're partying with Birdie's homemade sangria and listening to music, gossiping, and making each other cackle with laughter. When I'm old and retired, I want this life, I've decided.

They are clustered around the wicker patio table, the massive pitcher of sangria almost gone. I've declined their offerings because someone has to stay sober around here. Birdie stops and tops off everyone's glasses.

January, Glenda, Bitsy, and Lucille are a hoot. And they encourage Birdie in the best possible way. Sometimes in questionable ways. They're hilarious.

Glenda looks at me and says, "So, tell us about your ex-fiancé. What should we do to terrorize him, ladies?"

A chorus of groans arise at the mention of him. Birdie must've spilled all the dirty details about her dislike for him.

I roll my eyes and grin. "You don't need to do anything. Tyler's hellbent on destroying his life himself, I can promise you that."

"Tyler," Lucille bites out as if it's a sour taste in her mouth. "He sounds like a turd."

"He is," Birdie chirps.

Bitsy leans forward. "Can I see a picture of the offender?"

Birdie's already got her phone out and is scrolling. I grab another plant and shake my head with a snort. I wouldn't want to get on their bad side.

Birdie thrusts the phone out and shows them. All their heads crowd in to look at the picture on her phone.

Then, Lucille sighs deeply. "In my opinion, I'm extremely disappointed that this is the person you were crying about. He is *not* worth crying over."

January looks at me, dead serious. "You can do much better."

Someone feigns a cough and mutters, "Cal."

A memory of water sluicing off his muscular chest while he rides the wave hits me out of nowhere and sends a flash of heat rippling over me. *Ugh.*

I look at all of them. "Don't be playing matchmaker. I'm not here for that. This is my vacation this summer. No men. I'm swearing off all men. I have to figure out how to save my family's company."

"Women, then?" January asks as she sips her wine.

"No," I sputter. "I'm getting my life together. One plant at a time."

"It doesn't look like it's going well," Glenda muses over her glass at the plant in question.

"No fun." January shakes her head in disappointment.

"Well, what should we do tonight, ladies?" Glenda asks, examining her nails.

Birdie leans in and whispers loudly, "We could go moon Jonah Black when he brings his boat in."

They hoot and holler at that idea.

"He's so grumpy," one of them mutters. "He can't get any grumpier."

Lucille smiles wickedly and says, "Giddy up, sparklefarts. We've got fuckery to spread!"

I laugh so hard as all of them set their glasses down and wander off to do whatever nonsense they're going to do. I feel sorry for Jonah Black and whatever he deserved to get mooned by a bunch of old ladies.

For the first time in a long time, I feel at peace and calm with life.

Even though I can't get a certain hot bartender out of my mind. Or the fact that I'm still running from my life. At some point, I'm going to have to go back to New York and face everything. I can only ignore Tyler, my mom, and my sister for so long.

I get cleaned up and go for a run to clear my head. I end up down by the beach and strip down to my new swimsuit and sit in the waves. The warm water feels good, and the waves lapping up on my legs give me something to focus on.

I know one thing for sure. I'm going to figure out what to do about the company. I'm Silverlyn Montclair, and I won't go down without a fight.

I have no idea what was going through my grandmother's mind when she left in her will that I could inherit the company if I was married by thirty. She had all sorts of ridiculous stipulations in there as well like I had to be *happily* married. And I had to prove to the trust that it was a legitimate marriage and that I wasn't faking it.

Where can I find a husband in two months? And convince him to marry me?

If I don't, I'm out. And then my parents and the board will move on to the contingency plan—the one where my sister can take my place and marry within two months after my thirtieth birthday. Same rules: happily married, no faking, legitimate. They'll want Belladonna to rescue the company.

Hell no.

cal

. . .

I GET TO COCKTAILS & Chaos early because the paperwork won't do itself. And if I don't get to it before the bar opens, it'll never get done, and I'll get even more behind.

Lately, we've been slammed, and I've barely had time to think. I don't mind it. Work is easier than downtime, because downtime leaves room for Silvie.

Ever since she got to Coconut Beach, she's been stuck in my head. I keep telling myself it's just proximity, small town, same routines, but that's not it. She's just... there. Talking to iguanas like they understand her. Falling in with the Bees. Showing up to yoga with Summer every morning like she's been here all along.

And I've noticed.

The sundresses are new. So is the way she carries herself, like she's more relaxed, more sure.

It's like something about this place unlocked her, and now she's everywhere I look.

I don't need that kind of distraction.

I stop short when I realize she's sitting in an Adirondack chair in front of the bar when I get there, legs crossed, hair pulled up in a messy knot on top of her head, wearing another

81

one of those sundresses. This one is a pale blue and shows off the tan that she's acquired since coming to Coconut Beach. I certainly don't notice the way the material creeps up her smooth thighs. Nope. Not happening.

What I do allow myself to notice is she's holding two coffees like she's guarding them with her life. She has a bag next to her chair.

She looks up when she hears my keys and smiles. "Oh, good," she says, brightening. "You're here."

I try to play it cool and not like the weirdo who was just thinking about her. "Silvie. What are you doing here?"

She hops up and holds one of the coffees out to me like an offering. "Please let me work here. I promise I'll sit in the corner and you won't even know I'm here."

I take the coffee because she's pushing it toward me. And I desperately need that coffee right now. I've been sleeping like crap and working so many hours it's not even funny.

"What do you mean?" I say, trying to understand. "You want to work at the bar?"

"I have work to do on my laptop," she says, picking up her tote bag and putting it over her shoulder. "I promise I won't disturb you. In fact, you won't even know I'm here. I'll be quiet as a mouse. Promise."

Yeah, right. I don't say it out loud, but the thought lands fully formed in my head. I couldn't *not* notice her here. Even when she's not around, she takes up my thoughts. That realization makes me clear my throat and focus very hard on unlocking the door.

"I thought you were on vacation," I call as I turn and unlock the door. "Why are you working?"

She sighs. "I'm on vacation. But when you're one of the bosses, do you ever really get a vacation?"

I realize I don't actually know what Silvie does. And, somehow, I'm interested. More than I should be, probably, but not enough to admit it aloud.

"Okay," I say, opening the door and holding it for her. She follows me like this is already settled, which I guess it is.

"Thank you so much. Birdie and the Bees are insistent I make a friend my own age. I think Birdie might be getting tired of me."

I doubt that. Birdie is just meddling like she usually is, but I don't tell her that.

"How's your pet iguana?" I ask as I flip on the power behind the bar.

Her grin is instant. "Great. We're having a birthday party for him next week."

I freeze, turn slowly, and look at her. "What?"

She points at me and giggles, "A joke, Cal."

I laugh before I can stop myself. "You're funny."

She beams. "I try. Anyway, are you up for being my friend? That way, I can get the Bees off my back and tell them that I have three friends now. You, Summer, and Iggy."

I snort at her joke.

She heads for a table with a great view of the ocean and sets up camp with practiced efficiency. Laptop in front of her chair, her coffee within reach, and phone flipped face down as if it might distract her.

Am I up for being her friend?

Right now, I can't trust my mind when it comes to her. And I don't like it. Being actual friends means more time spent together. That could be catastrophic for my whole "keep it casual" schtick. Friends means letting your guard down.

Can I even do that?

But it's not like I'm going to deny her. She's...happy. I don't want to be the one to steal her smile.

"I can be your friend, Silvie," I find myself saying against my better judgement.

It's fine. I can keep my cool around her. Maybe this is better. I'll get used to talking to her. Eventually I'll even be immune to her pretty smile.

She sips her coffee and smiles at me triumphantly. "Thanks for being my friend, Cal. Questionable life choice, but I appreciate it."

I grab my clipboard and settle in at the other end of the bar, pretending I'm not aware of her presence like gravity. "Don't you have friends back in New York?"

She looks down and pretends to pick an imaginary piece of lint off her dress. "Yes, my best friend is a guy. He's also...my assistant. Which might sound weird, but we've been best friends for over four years. It probably seems lame, but I work a lot and don't have time for a social life. That's why being here has been nice."

I feel bad for her, but I get it. I, too, was once a city boy with big ambitions. It's all too easy to get caught up with work and abandoning your personal life.

"Well, then, I'm honored to be your friend. You can come up here anytime I'm here if you need a quiet place to work."

"Don't worry." She smiles, leaning back slightly, as if daring me to doubt her. "You won't even know I'm here."

I snort, glancing down at my clipboard, then back at her. "I don't think anyone can go without noticing you."

Her eyes flick up to mine, sharp and playful. "You won't notice me. I promise."

"I always notice." I shift on my stool, trying to keep my posture casual, but my fingers tap the clipboard faster than necessary.

The words hang in the air a beat longer than either of us should let them. I shake my head, clearing my throat, and jab lightly at the paperwork. "I've got... paperwork anyway."

"Oh yeah?" She leans forward just a fraction, tilting her head, the corner of her mouth twitching. "Paperwork?"

"Yeah," I say, adjusting the clipboard like it gives me some kind of armor. "I manage the bar, too. Not just a bartender."

I glance away because my heart is thumping louder than it

should. Why does she do this to me? Why does one woman make me feel like I'm about to stumble over every word?

"Well, look at you, boss man," she says, giving the chair across from her a sharp kick. It scrapes loudly against the floor in the quiet morning. She leans back, eyes on me, and I can't help but read it as an invitation. Or a dare. "Let's get our work done together, friend."

I tell myself not to, that I shouldn't. Still, against my better judgment, I pick up my coffee, head over, and slide the chair out, settling across from her. Somehow, despite every warning my brain throws at me, I'm drawn into the space she's carved out.

"What do you do for work?" I ask, curious since she's the boss.

She's already started typing, her fingers flying, expression focused but calm. She's wearing glasses now, the kind that make her look capable, serious… not just a girl in a sundress, but someone who could run a Fortune 500 company and make grown men cry. And I can't deny it, she's even more compelling this way.

She looks up. "I'm Vice President of Montclair Holdings."

I pause, letting the words sink in. Montclair Holdings. Holy shit. I've heard of them. Big players, and serious money. She's not just another visitor here, she moves in a different world entirely.

She continues when I don't respond. "It's a private investment company. Real estate, tech, hospitality. The boring answer of what we do is manage portfolios and partnerships."

There's a tone to her words that I can't quite pinpoint the meaning. Almost robotic. Detached. As if she's reading from the company manual. From what I know of her so far, it doesn't quite connect with her personality.

"Anyway," she quickly says. "The honest answer is we clean up messes and make sure generational wealth stays generationally wealthy." She grimaces slightly as if that last part frustrates her. I can understand that.

I nod and utter out something stupid, like, "Cool," but she's too focused to pay attention to my lacking conversational skills. Her fingers are flying over her keyboard a mile a minute. Every once in a while, she mutters something under her breath that makes no sense to me. Deadlines. A call she doesn't want to take. She wasn't kidding when she said she had work to do.

Once I realize we really are going to work, I get to doing what's on my list. I file invoices and check inventory. I lose my place twice, though, because I keep glancing up at her.

Silence settles in, but it's peaceful and relaxed. Sunlight spills through the open windows. The ocean hums somewhere in the distance. I make us both a breakfast burrito and brew some coffee in the back since ours are long gone.

I carry out the burritos and the fresh pot of coffee, setting them on the table.

She looks up and says, "Oh, you didn't have to do that." But she must be eager to eat because she eagerly snaps her laptop shut to make space for the food.

"Just made extra. It's my routine. It's nice to have a friend to share it with," I say with a smirk at the friend part.

After a bite of her burrito, she closes her eyes and groans. "This is so good. I didn't realize how hungry I was."

I'm amused as I watch her eat. Every bite is better than the first based on the sounds she makes. And, for someone as ritzy as a VP from the city, she eats messily without a care in the world.

Sauce dribbles down her chin and I absently hold a napkin up, eyes locked on hers. Her cheeks turn slightly pink as she takes the napkin to clean up the mess.

Dammit, I knew I wouldn't be good at this friend stuff. Friends don't like staring at their friend's pouty lips.

"Anyway," she says, tearing her gaze from mine, changing the subject. "I just love the Bees. Did you hear they all got on the cliff and mooned someone named Jonah Black when he was parking his boat?"

I laugh. "No, I didn't know that. But I will be sure to give Jonah crap about that."

"They're hilarious," she says.

"They're something."

"They *really* are," she murmurs, a wistful tone lacing her words. "And this is *really* good. You keep spoiling me like this, I'll be here every morning with coffee."

I wouldn't hate that.

Marina showed up later and looked at me with a smirk when she saw Silvie working in the corner. She's still got her laptop open, one leg tucked under her, and she's been working non-stop.

I ignore Marina's smirk and pretend to organize receipts, even though I've already done it twice.

"Since when do customers bring laptops here to work like we're a coffee shop?" she whispers as she walks behind me and puts on her apron.

"Ha, ha." I roll my eyes playfully. "She needed a place to work, and it was quiet here."

"Mmmm, hmmm," she says as she clocks in on the cash register. "I've seen you chase off tourists for that."

"She's Birdie's. She's not really a tourist," I say as I restock the shelves.

The bar is still quiet, and early beachgoers have trickled in for food and drinks. Marina stops to chat with Silvie, who smiles at her and laughs at something she says. I love the way her whole face lights up when she talks to people. Like you're the only person in the room. She gives her whole attention. It's mesmerizing to watch.

Another hour goes by, and I slide back into the chair across from her. She looks up as if she forgot where she was. "Oh my gosh. I've been here for a while. I should get out of your hair."

I hold up a hand. "Just came over to check on you and see if you wanted lunch."

She bites that sexy, plump lip that *I've* thought about biting.

"I wouldn't mind a bite to eat," she says as she reaches for a menu on the table. "Can I buy you lunch?"

I laugh. "No, you don't have to do that. But I can place your order if you'd like."

"Can I please get the chicken cobb salad with extra croutons?"

I smirk. "Sure. I'll get that going."

I put it in and made up a bunch of orders for the beach crowd. Music changes up, and when I look her way again, she's dancing a little in her chair, and it's adorable.

"You always look like that when you work?" I ask as I set down her salad and a water that she didn't ask for, but I brought anyway.

She glances up. "Like what?"

"I don't know. Happy?"

She snorts and closes the laptop. "That couldn't be a farther assessment from the truth."

I lean back against the counter. "You ever take a real break? Like a real vacation?"

She looks like she's considering what I'm saying. "I'm trying to. That's kind of the point of this summer."

"Yeah?"

She nods. "I'm trying to find myself. Or at least figure out who I am when I'm not working ninety hours a week. I'm supposed to take over the company, but I don't want the life my dad had. No time for a life and everything revolved around work."

"That sounds exhausting," I admit. But then I call myself out on it because I work a heavy load as well. But not near that much.

She smiles sadly. "It is. But I do love most of it."

Her phone buzzes on the bar. She looks at the screen, and the light in her face dims just a notch. Her jaw goes tight, and she gives a small sigh. She flips the phone face down without answering it. But I did notice "Tyler the Turd" flashing on the screen.

"Who is Tyler the Turd?"

"My ex." She fidgets in her seat, a frown marring her features.

"Ahh. Turd worthy."

"Yep, not worth discussing," she says as she takes a sip of her water. "And thank you for this."

Since we're "friends" now, I wonder if she'll ever confide in me. She says it's not worth discussing, but it can't be good bottling it in.

"So, what did you mean when you said you were going to find yourself this summer?" I ask instead of probing about her douchebag ex like I want to. "Are you lost?"

"You could say that," she says thoughtfully. "I've spent the past five years working hard to take over my family's company. And I haven't taken breaks. I work non-stop. And last month...everything just fell apart."

I wait for her to continue. She doesn't.

"What about you?" she asks instead as she takes another bite. "What's your story?"

I lean back in the chair. "Nothing much. I'm from Coconut Beach. My mom had me young and raised me here. I'm close with Jonah Black, who owns Cocktails & Chaos. I manage the place for him and bartend."

"Oh, yes. The guy the Bees mooned," she says as she grins.

I like her bright smile that's brought on by the mention of the Bees so much that I want to see more of it. She's clearly entertained and happy. It inspires me to lean into this new "friend" role just to see if I can make her smile some more.

"What do you like to do?" I ask after a beat.

She blinks. "What do you mean?"

"For fun. What makes you feel good?"

Her eyebrows pinch together as if the question confuses the intelligent workaholic city girl. "Um, well, back home, I have a pretty solid routine. I get up early and run. Then I work until late and get up and do it again the next day." She frowns. "And every day after that looks much the same." She shakes her head. "When I say it out loud, it sounds pretty lame."

I'm glad she found her way to Coconut Beach. This place has a way of making you focus on the things that matter. People can shake off the mundane of their everyday life and do a little soul searching.

"It's not lame," I assure her. "I work a lot too. I fish with Jonah on his boat once a week, and I manage the bar and work shifts here. I get it. I work a lot, too."

Fishing with Jonah though is one of my times of peace where I can just be me. I can turn my brain off and just live in the moment.

"I do like being outside," she says thoughtfully. "Moving my body until my brain shuts up. Yoga has been surprisingly fun."

I don't like thinking about her "moving" her body. Okay, so I *do* like thinking about that, but I don't *want* to.

"I'm a runner too," I blurt out to shake away the image of her stretching and bending on her yoga mat.

Her eyes flick to mine and she smirks. "Well, well, well. Maybe we do have a few things in common. We both run and work a lot."

She giggles and my stomach tightens in response. I really like that sound. Being around her is easy. Too easy. My brain is screaming warnings at me: *We don't do this, man.*

She's just a friend, my heart argues back.

"Running keeps me sane," I admit softly. There's a pause as she eats her salad, and I say casually, "Maybe we could run together sometime. You know...as friends."

The word "friends" sits between us, comfortable yet charged.

But "friends" is supposed to be safe, dammit. Why doesn't it feel safe at all?

She smiles and looks down. "I'd love a running partner. You sure you can keep up? I'm pretty competitive, Cal."

"Oh, really? Like super-fast or what?" I tease.

"The fastest," she says, a taunting glint in her eyes. "I'm just kidding. I run like a normal person. Running for me has been a way to think. To get my anxiety and frustrations out. Now...I've been doing yoga, and that's been a change of pace."

Again, with the yoga and imagining her contorting her lithe body into a million different positions.

I look out at the water, and it clears the filthy images from my mind. "What about surfing?"

"What *about* it?"

"Ever been?"

She laughs. "No, but I've seen *you* surfing, hot surfer."

Oh, fuck me. What happened to friends? She's playing a dangerous game, and my brain isn't strong enough to resist, no matter how much of an inner pep talk I give myself.

I face her fully, unable to keep from playing with her. "Have you now? Well, I may or may not have happened to notice you doing yoga." I shrug and shoot her a wink.

This isn't keeping your distance, Cal. This is you stupidly trying to charm her pants off.

"Oh, really? Are you flirting with me, Cal?" she says.

My lips curve before I can stop them, "Nah, friends don't flirt. Would you like to go surfing with me sometime?"

She laughs. "Sure. I have no idea how to surf, but I'd be down to try."

"Can you swim?"

She nods. "I swam competitively in college. I told you. I like to win."

Relief hits me because I don't love that my brain jumps to worst case scenarios. I just want her to be safe in the water.

"There's no need to be competitive in surfing," I say as I glance out at the ocean, sun catching on the surface, making it glitter. "Just ride the wave. Let yourself have fun. Relax."

Her gaze remains fixated on the ocean as if she's visualizing herself out there right now.

"How about tomorrow?" I ask, suddenly feeling nervous. It's dumb to get the jitters because I love surfing. It calms me. Never makes me anxious.

Maybe it's just her. A change in the routine.

I don't go surfing with anyone aside from a few friends I've had since high school. I have fun at the bar when I work, but I don't date, and I don't flirt with tourists.

But she's been here over a month now. Hell, she's starting to feel like a local.

She drums her fingertips on her thigh as if she's taking this in and considering it.

"Okay," she finally says.

Relief settles into my chest. "Great. Meet me at sunrise. I'll have the boards."

She stands and slings her bag over her shoulder, laying down a few bills even though I never brought her a ticket. "I should go before I talk myself out of this bad idea I just committed myself to and take up more of your day. Thank you, Cal."

"Surfing is never a bad idea." I chuckle. "You'll do fine. See you tomorrow."

She hesitates and then smiles. "Thanks for being my friend."

There's a tender thread of vulnerability in that statement and it lands harder than it should. Because no one thanks you for that unless they really needed it. She's a mega-successful board-room boss babe and yet she's grateful for a new friendship with the surfer bartender bro. It makes me want to haul her to me and hold her in my arms.

As friends, of course.

"Any time, Silvie."

She leaves, humming, almost bouncing, and smiling easily at everyone. She's different from the woman who blew in here a month ago in a wedding dress. Silvie fits in here. And when she's gone, the bar feels lonelier without her in here. Like the energy in the air has shifted.

Tomorrow we're surfing. For the first time in a while, I have something to look forward to.

Standing behind the bar, with the ocean humming outside, I realize I'm looking forward to it way more than I probably should.

silvie

. . .

"THIS IS UNACCEPTABLE, ISN'T IT?" I say, holding up one of the only two swimsuits I have here in Coconut Beach.

I'm sitting cross-legged on my bed at Birdie's, surrounded by the clothes I have, trying desperately to find something appropriate to surf in. I don't know how I didn't think to buy more swimsuits when I went shopping with Summer the other day. The one I grabbed with her was basic. I also have the granny one I left here at one point when I visited Birdie about eight years ago. That one is definitely not going to work.

Wilby's face fills my phone screen, his dark brows already pulled together like he's not sure what I was thinking wearing that swimsuit then, either. He's sitting at his desk in New York, immaculate as always, white button down, coffee cup clutched like a lifeline. And given that he has impeccable choices in fashion, I know he'll always tell me the truth.

"Silverlyn," he says patiently. "Those are not swimsuits, they're punishments. I can go to your penthouse tonight and pack up some of your things and ship them to you."

He's not wrong. One's generic and the other is a granny suit. I can't wear them surfing with Cal. He'll think I'm one of the Bees. He probably already does. And maybe that's how he should think of me. But that's definitely not how I want him to think of me.

Why is that anyway?

After the hell Tyler put me through, you'd think I'd be turned off of men. Initially, I would have sworn that I was. But, over the past few weeks, I've done a lot of soul searching. What I had with Tyler wasn't real love. It was convenience more or less. Of course, it doesn't excuse his infidelity, with my sister no less, but it makes it less painful.

The lowkey flirting I've been doing with Cal has a fire burning in my belly. Maybe having a little fun with him will be nice. I certainly feel safe around him, especially when he's always taking care of me and bringing me food.

Does he have the same buzzing attraction that I do?

Considering I've caught him a time or two staring a little longer than appropriate, I'm going to assume so.

"Seriously, no," Wilby says, interrupting my thoughts. "Stop waving that ugly thing at me. Birdie called, she wants her old lady swimsuit back."

"Ugh." I glance down at the navy one-piece in my hands. "This one's functional at least. Great for surfing, right?"

"It's giving grandmother," he corrects. "Add a little moomoo, and you're all set, Bertha. Grandmas don't surf."

"Stop." I laugh, tossing it onto the bed. "I've been wearing both of these for days."

"That's a crime," he shudders as he sips his coffee.

I miss Wilby. He made work fun, and he's my right arm man. I know everything about him, and he knows everything about me. I have never had a closer best friend than him.

I snort and start digging through another bag. "I just haven't had time to think about fashion choices."

"You have had nothing but time," he says. "You simply chose yoga and beach walks and emotional healing instead of appropriate swimwear."

"You're not wrong," I murmur.

"You need me to fly down there and get you straight? I can go get you clothes and make a weekend of it," he offers.

The thought of having my bestie here makes my chest tighten. We would have such a blast trying new restaurants, sunbathing, and, of course, sipping cocktails served up by the cutest bartender in Coconut Bay.

"It's not a bad idea, Wilby. I've put on a little weight, so I'm not sure what I have in my closet will still fit me. I could use some new stuff. I've gone up a size...or two."

Bitterness creeps up inside me. I was a ghost, drifting through the motions, allowing my mother to control my food intake. Now that I have some weight on me and a sunkissed glow, I can admit I look a million times better than I did the day of my wedding which was supposed to be the most beautiful version of me.

"As you needed to," he says, frowning. "I told you that the wedding diet was bullshit. You're stunning, and you need to be healthy."

Wilby always sets me straight. I knew talking to him would make me happy.

"I'll come," he says. "Send me your measurements, and I'll bring you some things. What's your vibe right now? Looks like you're leaning towards beachy boho?"

I just proudly showed him all of the clothes that Summer and I picked out. He hummed in approval, so there's that.

"Yeah."

He nods his head. "I gotchu."

I love Wilby.

"I'm so excited you're coming!" I say with a grin. "Birdie will be so happy to see you, too. How soon can you get here?"

I see the reflection of the computer screen in his glasses. "I'm looking at flights now."

I pull out a bright green bikini top and freeze. "Oh. I forgot I'd put these in my bag for my honeymoon."

Wilby's eyes narrow. "Why are you making that face? Let me see it."

"Because this feels like a version of me I was with Tyler."

He leans closer to the camera. "That is literally the point of a summer reinvention. You are finding out who you are without Tyler the Turd."

I told him what Birdie called him, and it's kind of stuck with everyone now.

I hold it up. "Is this too much for surfing?"

"For Coconut Beach," he says, "it's perfect. Wear it until I can bring you some more swimsuits that will make your hot bartender swoon."

I laugh and toss it onto the bed. "I don't think I'm ready to be more than his friend," I lie. "I have got to figure out how to save this company. And that is what I need you to come and strategize with me, Wilby."

"We totally have this. Now, for flights," Wilby says, tapping on his keyboard. "I can be there tomorrow. Tonight, I have to go shopping." He playfully rolls his eyes.

"You know there are stores here, too," I say with a chuckle.

"Yeah, but I'll need to bring some reinforcements just in case. Plus, you're rich. You can let me shop for you. You know I live for this stuff."

"I appreciate you. Buy yourself some beach attire with my card, too," I tell him. I know he won't go crazy, but he works hard for me, and I want him to have a fun little trip away. He's been bored in the office without me.

"Oh, I'll get myself some linen shirts and trunks. Gotta check out the pretty ladies in Coconut Beach and have to look hot myself." He smirks. "Oh, and I booked my flight first class. You owe me for having to deal with Tyler the day of your wedding."

I'm not sure what all that entails, but I'm sure he's going to tell me all about it.

I grimace. "Yeah, sorry about that."

"He looked like a lost puppy. A stupid lost puppy. Then he left with your harlot of a sister."

I won't lie and say I haven't thought about Belladonna. Is she happy that she won "the prize"? I have a hard time believing they're truly in love. With my sister, there's a motive to everything she does. Tyler is no different.

"No more turd talk." I shake my head. "You will love it here. You deserve a break putting up with everything at the office without me. First class all the way, bestie. Just hurry up! I miss you."

He smiles and then it falls as he grows serious. Since he's a mostly playful person, I prepare myself for whatever he's going to say next.

"One more thing I wanted to tell you. You're not going to like it," he says as he takes a deep sigh and clicks something on his keyboard.

"Okay, what?" I brace myself.

"I checked your mail like you asked."

My stomach tightens. "And?"

"Tyler still hasn't moved out."

My jaw clenches, and I roll my eyes. "Of course he hasn't."

"And," he adds, clearly enjoying this part less, "I saw evidence that your sister has been staying there."

The audacity of that woman. First, she takes my fiancé and tries to steal my home too?

"What? How do you know?" I demand as I shoot to my feet and begin to pace. "I don't want her there."

"She is very much there," Wilby says, grimacing. "I saw her in her underwear."

"Eww."

He shudders. "I can't unsee it, Silverlyn. I'm traumatized."

Rage floods my chest, hot and fast. "The penthouse is mine, and I want Tyler evicted. Immediately."

He doesn't blink. "Do you want me to start the process?"

"Yes," I say. "Today. Get our team on it. I don't care what you have to do. He needs to be gone, immediately."

He smiles, making a note on a pad of paper next to him. "Sure. Evict the turd. It will be my pleasure."

Because Wilby hates Belladonna and Tyler almost as much as I do. I can't believe the nerve of these two.

I sink back onto the bed, heart pounding, phone still in my hand, clothes scattered everywhere.

"Thank you," I say quietly.

He softens just a fraction. "I'm here for you, Silverlyn. I'll get the ball rolling."

"I can't wait to see you. You're the best, Wilby."

He scoffs. "I know. Have fun surfing with the hot bartender!"

Then, with a pointed look, he says, "Wear the green swimsuit, Silverlyn. You are not healing nothing in that navy crime against fashion."

I laugh, glance at the mirror, and for the first time since I left New York, I feel empowered.

I feel like I'm finally starting to find myself.

———————

"Are you ready?" Cal asks as he reaches for my hand, his board tucked under his arm.

Last night I was uneasy. Now, I'm straight up nervous about surfing with Cal. He's a great teacher and spent the better part of the morning showing me, while safely in the sand, how to lie on the board, paddle, and pop up safely. Each time his hand shot out to assist me, my skin would burn at his touch. If he's that protective on dry land, I know he'll keep me safe while on the water. Still, I'm nervous.

"Ready as I'll ever be," I say, trying for casual and pretending that my heart isn't beating a mile a minute as I slide my hand into his, feeling goosebumps dancing up my arm. *Just a casual surfing experience with a friend*, I try to tell myself.

He clutches my hand, and we run out into the waves, laughing. We paddle out together, waves rolling easily today. Cal said it's a good morning to surf, the kind of morning that the locals don't waste and tourists haven't figured out.

The ocean feels different when you're with someone who is making your pulse do stupid things.

He keeps glancing back at me like he's checking I'm still there. Like he's responsible for me. It's ridiculous and sweet and makes my chest feel tight in a way I don't want to examine too closely.

I didn't have that with Tyler. Tyler was the kind of guy who always walked four feet in front of me and was constantly on his phone. He couldn't care less. And now I'm seeing what I dodged.

It wasn't all his fault, though.

As much as I hate to admit it, I didn't exactly foster a great relationship between us. My ninety-hour work weeks didn't leave much room left for romance. Maybe I was subconsciously avoiding what wasn't true love. Unfortunately, I wasn't aware enough to realize that until recently.

Tyler is a total cheating scumbag. That won't change. However, I have to take some accountability for what went down.

The next relationship I have, I want to do better. I want to have lazy weekends with my partner and to build a family I can be present for. It's strange how my escape to Coconut Beach has opened my eyes about what I want my future to look like.

I'm tired of being passive in my own life.

I want to take control and be happy in it.

Cal looks over at me and winks, making my heart flop inside my chest. It's easy to imagine this future with someone like him. Not just because he's the hot bartender who makes me feel alive. He's kind and genuine and caring.

"You're doing great," Cal says, grinning at me.

"Hardly." I'm out of breath and my muscles are already screaming, but I'm having fun.

Cal's shown me a few times how to do it, and I'm trying to pick it up, but the truth is I'm so uncoordinated compared to him, and I'm terrible at surfing. I fall off every time, and we both laugh when he catches me. His hands on my waist send zings to my lady bits, and it's more than obvious that I am wildly attracted to Cal.

We take a break, and I'm standing barefoot in the sand, the board on the ground. Cal sits next to me on the sand, his legs stretched out, watching the sun rise. It's already rising, and it's beautiful. I make a mental note to get up earlier and watch more of these sunrises. I never paid attention back in New York. I always felt like it was a rat race. I was running from one thing to another. Here, life just feels slower and steadier, somehow.

I'm trying my best not to stare at him. And when I look at him, he seems to be doing the same. The sun hits his shoulders, his dark hair wet with water. I'm failing. I am absolutely staring at him. I love his tattoos. I want to trace them all with my fingertips and ask him what they mean.

He turns and catches me looking, a little color rising in his cheeks, which shouldn't be possible for a grown man who is probably used to being eyed like candy.

"Cal, I think I might be the worst surfer of all time," I admit, tearing my eyes from his abs.

He shakes his head and chuckles. "It's your first time. You're allowed to figure it out, Miss Competitive."

It's strange not to be the best at something. I think it's pretty much engrained in me to be top tier at everything I do. Surfing humbles me in the best possible way. I'm also learning I can have fun doing something I totally suck at.

"I'm taking that back with surfing," I say to him with a sigh. "I'm terrible at it."

He scoffs. "You just need practice."

He lies badly.

I laugh and feel lighter than I have in months.

"You're a good teacher," I murmur, gaze locking with his.

And he is. He's given me tips on when to paddle and when to stand. He's hovered and helped, but he is good at teaching.

He's a good friend, I remind myself. A very hot friend. But a friend.

We sit side by side, sun warm on us, while he tells me about the bar and the history of Coconut Beach. I'm interested in each fact he tells me, gobbling them up as fast as he can divulge them.

"What was it like to grow up here?" I ask, curiously.

His lips curl up on one side as he thinks about it. "It was good. We got up, surfed before school, did school, and mostly knew everyone. It's a small town. It was paradise."

He's not wrong. This place is definitely paradise.

"Jonah is like a dad to me," he continues. "I never knew my dad. He was a tourist, and my mom was working a summer job here when she was eighteen. She met a guy and had a summer-long fling, and at the end of summer, he went back to New York City to work. He ghosted her. She tried to tell him about me, but he and his family wanted nothing to do with my mom or me." He frowns and looks away.

I can't imagine how that felt for him as a young boy. It breaks my heart for him.

"I'm sorry, Cal."

He shrugs as if it's nothing, but I know it bothers him. His shoulders are tense and the frown lingers. "I had an aunt and uncle I'm close with. My uncle passed away a few years ago, but my aunt still lives in Wisteria Cove, Massachusetts. I'm close with my cousins, too."

I have the urge to hug him, but I keep my hands to myself.

"Do they come to visit?" I ask.

He nods. "Yeah, all the time. My aunt Donna has a cottage here close to mine."

"Does your mom still live here in Coconut Beach?"

A flash of something passes across his face that I can't read. "Yes, she's still here in Coconut Beach."

Interesting. I wonder what's going on there. Maybe he's not close to her. I'm not close to mine. And after the wedding, I don't know that we ever will be.

He laughs, that low and easy sound that makes me smile. "But one cool flex is that my aunt is Donna Bennett. Have you ever heard of her?"

My jaw drops. "Donna Bennett, the author?"

He nods.

"Donna Bennett, the *New York Times* bestselling author?"

He laughs. "Yeah, that's the one."

"You've been hanging onto that little gem and just now felt like sharing with the class?" I ask, in awe.

He shrugs. "To me, she's just my aunt. And she's pretty great."

"Um, yeah. She's an icon. I've been reading her stuff since high school. Way cool, Cal."

"Maybe you'll meet her when she comes to visit."

I gasp in shock. "Here? I can't wait."

"Sometimes she comes here to write when she has a tight deadline," he says. "Around here, she's just Donna. She's pretty chill."

Wow. Incredible.

Not just his flex about being related to one of my favorite authors, but this time together. Getting to know little kernels of information about him and his life. Our conversation is unhurried and comfortable. I could stay here all day chatting with him and never get bored.

"What about you? What do you have going on this week?" he asks, as he leans back on his hands, his arms flexing and looking amazing.

"Well, my friend is coming to visit. He gets in tonight."

"Oh, another friend, I see. Cheating on me already?" he teases. Then his face changes, and he looks embarrassed. "Actually, that was super dumb. I'm sorry. Your wedding...ugh, too soon."

Truth is, it didn't sting like it might should have. Cal has a calming effect on me. It's easy to forget about my problems when I'm in his orbit.

"It's fine," I assure him, giving him a warm smile. "Wilby's the one I was telling you about anyway. I think you'll like him."

"Yeah? Where's he staying?"

"The hotel was full. Some kind of festival or something. But he got the Seaside Bed and Breakfast booked."

Cal chuckles. "Wendy, the owner is really nice. He'll have fun."

We head back up the beach, and Cal says, "I'll grab us some water."

I nod and use my towel to wipe my face. Who knew surfing could be such a workout? I'm going to need a nap later.

My phone rings, and I glance at it. It's a work number calling from Montclair Holding. I answer it, guessing it's probably someone from my team or Wilby. Although Wilby usually calls me from his cell.

"This is Silvie."

"What the fuck, Silvie?" Tyler bites out. "Evicting me?"

I'm startled at first hearing his voice. I never noticed how whiney it is. How was I ever attracted to this man? I close my eyes. Fucking Tyler. I have been avoiding his calls since the wedding and haven't spoken to him. Figures he'd use a work phone to get through.

"Get the hint, Tyler," I say calmly. "I don't want to talk to you, and you need to move out of my house."

He lets out a frustrated huff. "Are you serious right now?"

I steady my breathing and say, "We're done, Tyler. Get the hell out of my apartment and take my skank sister with you."

That felt really, really good to say to him. I kind of wish I could see his facial reaction.

"We have nowhere to go, and you know that," he says, voice

rising a few octaves. "We're family, Silvie. You're just going to kick us out?"

Is he for real right now? He thinks *he's* my family? And the way Belladonna treated me sure as hell isn't how family treats family. Both of them can go kick rocks.

"You're not my family, Tyler. And yes, I can," I say firmly.

"You can't just do that," he sputters. "That's your sister."

I pinch the bridge of my nose, a headache forming from the stupidity that I'm hearing right now. "Tyler, you need to get your things and leave. If I hear that Belladonna has been there again, I will have her officially trespassed. I am done with you both. You can go fuck yourselves."

He gasps as though I've punched him in the gut. I bite back a laugh.

"You're being dramatic again," he hisses. "It doesn't have to be this way."

I laugh, but it's short and humorless. "I don't really care what you think. Just get out of my house, my life, and don't ever call me again."

"Listen," Tyler pleads, grasping at straws. He's lost control, and he knows it. "I just didn't know if I was ready to be married to you, okay? I thought I was and then...I needed time. I wasn't sure if you were the one for me. But...Maybe we could try again? Why don't you come back to New York? We can talk."

Is he for real right now? I've never met anyone so delusional. He wants two different realities—one with my sister and one with me. She can have him because I am so beyond done.

"Silvie," he says again, voice even needier than before. "Please—"

I end the call before he can finish his sentence. I don't argue with losers. And Tyler is a loser.

When I look up, Cal's standing there with two waters, his jaw tight. Oh my God, how much did he hear? How embarrassing.

"That didn't sound great," he says carefully as he settles in next to me on the sand, handing me a water.

"It wasn't."

"You don't have to tell me," he says. "But you can. I'm a good listener."

My chest warms at his words. Like I said, Cal is caring. It's nice to be cared for, even if only in a "friend" capacity.

I take a drink of the water and stare out at the ocean. "He's a loser. And he won't get out of my life."

His jaw tightens. "What do you mean?"

"He just told me that he didn't know if I was the one for him or not. And I guess that was his excuse for hooking up with my sister."

Cal's jaw drops and then he closes his mouth. Then he shakes his head in disbelief. "What an asshole."

"Yeah. And now he's mad that I'm finally choosing myself, and he can't be a leech anymore."

"Can you just ignore him?"

I snort. "I wish. He works for our company, and apparently, still lives in my apartment. But my team is evicting him right now, and he doesn't like that because that's where he's been shacking up with my grifter sister."

Cal's eyebrows shoot up as if he can hardly believe my words. It's pretty outlandish for sure, but alas, it is my life. Ugh.

"We can go to New York tonight," Cal half-jokes, scowling. "I can throw that fucking loser out for you."

I laugh and try to picture Cal in my world in New York City. And...I kind of *can* picture him. Whoa. Where did that thought come from?

Friends, girl. He's your friend.

"I mean it. You think I can take him?" he jokes, bumping my shoulder with his, trying to make the conversation lighter. I have noticed that he's good at that.

"I think you could definitely take him. He's about, maybe five-eight. He plays golf and drinks beer as a hobby." I joke as I glance over at Cal. He's well over six feet tall. More like six-four if I had to guess. He's built and has what looks like muscles on top of muscles. And his tattoos...*damn, I really need to stop looking at him.*

He smirks but then looks intently at me. "I'm going to tell you something, Silvie. Listen. Most guys? We know within the first ten seconds if we like someone. And we know in the first month if they're wife material. That guy knew he couldn't measure up to you. It was his problem, not yours."

I blink and look at him, my breath hitching. "You're very insightful for a hot surfer."

His mouth quirks. "You can stop calling me that anytime now."

"I absolutely cannot."

He smiles and says, while looking out at the ocean, "Silvie, you're wife material. And that asshole? He wasn't worthy."

My skin prickles with awareness. The waves roll in and the sun keeps shining, but something in what he just said shifted things between us. A thousand thoughts flip through my mind, sending a thrill shooting down my spine.

For the first time in a while, the shitshow I've been dealing with back home doesn't feel like it's drowning me anymore.

cal

. . .

THE BAR ISN'T SO busy at the moment. It's that sweet spot between dinner and chaos where the glasses clink, and I can catch up. I'm behind the counter at Cocktails & Chaos, wiping down the counter that's already clean. It's a habit and something I do to stay busy and listen to what's going on around me. My hands know this place by heart. But my head is somewhere else. I'm thinking about Silvie.

Surfing with her started out innocent enough, but as our morning together waned on, I felt myself hanging on her every word. Revealing parts of me while learning parts of her was intimate. Her ex is a grade-A douchebag, and I meant every word about her being wife material.

I just wish I was thinking about her as wife material, generally speaking, and not as wife material for me. My heart thuds a little too hard in my chest and I rub absently at it.

Jonah sits at the bar with fish tacos, a plate of fries with aioli sauce, and his usual Coke. Jonah's not one to drink, even though he ironically owns the most popular bar on the island. He's never said why, and most people know little about Jonah. The man's a quiet guy who doesn't let many people in. He comes in for dinner a few times a week. I think it's more about having the limited social interaction he craves but won't admit to as the unofficial town grump.

"You seem distracted," Jonah says, not looking at me as he takes a bite of his food.

He has no idea. I'm distracted by one thing. She plagues my mind and haunts my dreams. It's getting ridiculous.

"I'm working," I say, evading the truth. "I'm focused."

He snorts. "You've been polishing the same spot. You're going to wear a hole in the counter."

I move the rag a few inches. "Happy?"

He takes a sip of his Coke. "I saw you surfing with the pretty blonde. Looked like you two were having fun."

I pause just long enough to give myself away. "You stalking me now, old man?"

"Hard to miss," he says with a smirk. "Whole town probably has a wager on you and the pretty blonde."

I huff. "She has a name."

"I bet she does." Jonah grins, provoking me. "Hot bartender."

He says this, then throws his head back and laughs.

I roll my eyes playfully.

This is how we interact. We give each other shit constantly, and it's fun.

"I heard that you got mooned by the Bees the other day."

Jonah rolls his eyes. "Weirdos."

I laugh at that and turn around when I see a group of people walk in and take a seat. Marina nods and hurries over to take their order.

Summer and Silvie roll in together, laughing and chattering happily. Oh, man. Jonah's going to love this. More ammo. They're wearing bright summer dresses. Silvie's in a fitted pink dress that should be illegal. Her shapely, tanned legs are in strappy sandals. Those legs go on forever. Toned and strong.

For a second, my mind betrays me, and I picture her legs wrapped around my waist. I swallow and close my eyes, shaking my head as if I can physically knock these thoughts away.

Get it together, man.

Summer and Silvie have bright pink hibiscus flowers tucked behind their ears, their sun kissed skin bright and glowing. Silvie spots me and waves, clearly happy to see me. Summer whispers something to her and Silvie gives her a smirk.

"Hi, Cal!" Silvie calls as she makes her way over, Summer beside her.

"Hi, ladies." I smile. I can't help it. I'm happy to see Silvie.

"Hi, Cal," Summer says as she slides onto a stool. Silvie sits on the one next to Jonah. He glances sideways, eyebrow lifting like he's watching a movie play out.

I grab the menus, hand them over, and set out drink napkins. My hands need something to do because she's here and I feel like I've just gotten caught thinking about her.

"Mmmm, I'm starving," Summer croons. "I taught two classes today. I need food."

"Glad I could catch your afternoon class," Silvie murmurs appreciatively. "It was a good one."

My brain short circuits when I imagine her doing her yoga poses in the dress she's wearing now. I'm losing my mind.

"Jonah," I say, clearing my throat and nodding between them. "This is Silvie. Silvie, this is Jonah. He owns the bar."

I don't know why I put that last part in. I've talked about Jonah enough that I think she would put two and two together. Hell, I'm nervous. And Jonah knows this, which he is no doubt finding amusing right now.

"Oh," she says, eyes widening. She turns and reaches out and gives him a side hug, like it's the most natural thing in the world.

Jonah freezes. Because no one hugs Jonah. He looks like a statue, and his eyes flick to me like he's wondering what is happening right now.

Silvie pulls back and talks to him as if they've known each other forever. I'm entranced and can't stop watching them.

"I just love your bar," Silvie says, bright and sincere. "And Cal speaks so highly of you. It's so nice to finally meet you. I heard you have a boat?"

Jonah clears his throat and sits up straighter. "I do."

Summer watches all of this with fascination. She studies the menu, looks at me, and grins knowingly.

I watch this exchange with absolute fascination as well. Wow. Did she just charm our town grump?

I watch her lay her hand on his arm and laugh at something he says, and I see Jonah smirk under his big bushy beard.

Holy shit. She did.

Of course she did. She's sunshine personified.

This pleases me for some reason. Like she just passed a test I didn't know I'd given her. More proof in the "wife material" department? I inwardly cringe because I don't do this. I don't get smitten.

But neither does Jonah, and he's just as charmed by her.

I get Jonah's dumbstruck look. I know exactly why he's frozen. I've been caught like this before, and it's impossible to resist her.

Dangerous. This woman is dangerous to my heart.

I notice Jonah relaxes by a fraction. "Are you visiting long?"

Watching Jonah's cheeks blush whilst making small talk has got to be one of the highlights of my evening.

"For the summer," Silvie says. "I love it here. I never want to leave."

Jonah nods as if this is a satisfactory answer, but my stomach sinks, and the moment crashes back to earth. A reminder that she won't be around forever. My pulse slows, and suddenly the worry that's been lurking under the surface rises.

Summer taps the menu and says to Silvie, "Do you know what you want?"

Silvie nods. "I'll have what Jonah's having. That looks so good."

"I'll have the same," Summer says.

Jonah smiles at me. Wow. She's good.

"What time does your friend get in?" I ask as I place their orders.

"Wilby got delayed. He's coming tomorrow instead. So, Summer and I decided to go out to eat and go dancing."

Summer nods enthusiastically. "We earned it."

"Cal, can we both have a sex on the beach?" Silvie asks.

Jonah practically chokes on his Coke.

"Sure." I grin and turn to make them.

I know Jonah's going to give me crap later. It'll be worth it.

I busy myself getting drinks for them and helping Marina fill her orders. When I glance over on occasion, Silvie's eyes trail after me, like she's tracking me in the bar. I don't miss it. The connection between us is undeniable. I just don't know what to think of it. Friends? Potentially more?

No. I shake it off. I can't be that guy. The one who meets a nice woman and falls for her, but then she goes back to New York at the end of the summer. I can't do it.

My world is here in Coconut Beach. Hers is in New York. Period.

If only it were that easy. Nothing is ever that easy.

Silvie meets my eyes again when she sips her straw. I inwardly groan at her mouth wrapped around that straw. There's a look in her eyes that makes my chest feel tight. My body feels warm. And damn, I wouldn't mind tasting that mouth of hers. Silvie's dangerous.

Summer and Silvie eat with Jonah, who I notice lingers longer than he usually does and seems to listen to their conversation, even grunting in response when Silvie includes him. I even hear him tell her about his boat, something I've never heard him do. Usually, he eats and leaves.

Later, they say goodbye, and when Silvie hugs Jonah again,

he pats her back. Summer and Silvie then head to the dance floor, and music swells through the bar. Laughter follows them like a trail, and eyes in the bar lock on them as well. I hate that. I don't want anyone looking at Silvie.

I turn back to Jonah, who's watching me watch them. He grins, slowly and knowing.

"Stop it," I murmur.

"This one's different," he says.

"No, she's not," I say dryly.

But she totally is. I can't deny it. I have no idea what's happening here. I'm rejecting all of these feelings, but they're still coming at me head-on like a freight train.

I wipe the bar and pretend everything is fine.

Jonah stands to leave, laying down bills even though it's his own bar. "You gonna keep pretending or are you going to let yourself live a little?"

"I live plenty," I argue.

He arches a brow. "You surf at dawn, work the bar, take care of your momma. You do that rinse and repeat. That's not living, son."

I don't answer because I don't know what to say. The music shifts, and Silvie's intoxicating laugh fills the air. She tips her head back, dancing, that flower behind her ear, bouncing with her movement. They spin, and both laugh as they sing along to a popular beach song.

"Don't be stupid," Jonah says as he takes off.

Too late.

I keep working, thankful for the distraction. Orders come in and go out. I send glasses to be washed and polished. The night air thickens. But my attention is never far from Silvie. And judging by how she's looking at me, hers is never far as well. Silvie closes her eyes and dances to the music like she belongs. Confident, and she knows exactly who she is. She says she's trying to find herself this summer. I bet she doesn't need to find herself. She's been there all along, just waiting to discover herself.

She meets up with Mia and her Salty Pages co-owner, Juniper, and they all order waters and keep dancing.

Yeah, she's different. Jonah's right.

———————

The bar finally empties just after one. We've got all the chairs up and the lights low. The waves crash outside, and I'm still running on high energy even though my body is tired in that good way from work. And, naturally, I can't stop thinking about Silvie.

I set the last clean glass behind the bar and step out to lock up. Silvie is outside, sitting in one of the chairs, sandals on the ground beside her, her toes brushing a pattern in the sand. Her dress is wrinkled from dancing, and her hair's wild, the flower gone.

She looks up when she sees me and smiles like she's been here a while. "You're finally done."

"Been waiting?" I ask, surprised.

"Summer ditched me," she says cheerfully. "She has an early yoga class in the morning and needs her sleep."

I grin and lock the door, tucking the keys into my pocket. "That tracks. What about you? Don't you need your sleep, too?"

"Yeah, except I'm used to not getting that much sleep."

She yawns, despite her words, as she absently reaches for her sandals beside her and misses. Without skipping a beat, I kneel in front of her to assist. I pick up one of the sandals and our eyes meet. Her eyebrows are drawn together as if she doesn't know what to think about me wanting to help her with her shoes.

That makes two of us.

Yet, I grip her delicate ankle in my grip and slide her shoe on. Once I set her foot back down, I pick up the other sandal. She offers me her other bare foot. I grab onto it, rubbing my thumb over the top of it, liking the softness of her smooth skin.

The air is charged between us, neither of us speaking, as I slip her other shoe on.

Once they're both on, she shyly smiles as I rise to my feet. I offer her a hand, which she takes, and pull her to her feet.

"You good getting home?"

"I just thought we could walk together," she says. "If that's okay."

It's more than okay.

I tried to reason with myself most of the night to draw that invisible line in the sand between Silvie and me. But then she was out here waiting, and there's something about the way she's vulnerable with it, like this is new for her as well, that hits me right in the chest.

"I'd be happy to walk you home," I say, voice rough.

"Okay," she says. "Lead the way, hot bartender."

I groan at her hot bartender reference and she giggles.

We fall in step together, easy, as if this isn't new. The streets are quiet now, the sounds of the waves fading the further we get from the bar.

She walks close to me, not touching, but just enough for me to feel her arm swinging near mine. Every nerve in my body lights up at the hint of her presence.

"So, Cal," she says. "Can I ask you something?"

"Depends," I tease.

"Why did you say that I was wife material? And what did you mean by that?"

I stumble slightly but recover.

She waits and watches me as we walk for my answer.

I look at her and wonder why she can't see it. "Silvie, you're the whole package."

Her pace slows and she listens.

I glance over and continue, "Your ex was an idiot. He never deserved you."

She stares and blinks at me when I say that.

I stop walking, and she does too, turning to face me. The streetlight and the stars light up her face. Her eyes catch mine and linger.

That's what hits me, so I continue.

"You listen better than anyone I've ever seen. You notice people. And you make them feel validated. You're like a light in the dark. A rainbow at the end of a storm. You make everyone you come in contact with smile. Even Jonah Black, who is the town grump, by the way. You charmed the man who couldn't be charmed. I don't know how you did it, but you did."

Her breath catches.

"That's a hell of a compliment," she says quietly.

"I mean it. I've never met anyone like you. And that turd fumbled you bad. I hope you know that. You are wife material. And I hate that they hurt you the way that they did. But I'm glad you didn't marry him. Because he could never be good enough for you."

The air between us goes thick, and the energy feels charged. She steps closer. She's close enough that I can smell the coconut from her shampoo or body wash.

My hands lift, and I put them around her, pulling her into me. My heart beats faster against my ribs. Her lips part in surprise. I could kiss her right now.

Then she exhales, shakes her head once, and gives me a small, sad smile. She wraps her arms around me and pulls me in for a hug. Her arms are tight around me, and mine pull her in just as tight. It practically knocks the air out of my lungs.

She presses her cheek to my chest, and I close my eyes, holding her just long enough to imagine holding her like this as if she were mine.

But she's not.

"Thank you," she murmurs.

"For what?" I ask softly.

"For seeing me," she says. "And just being my friend. Being kind to me."

I close my eyes, and she pulls back first. Her smile is soft and careful, and it's as if she has no idea what she just did to me.

"Good night, Cal. See you tomorrow."

I wave. "Night, Silvie."

She walks inside Birdie's, and I turn when I hear the lock click into place.

I don't move and stand there longer than I should, my hands now shoved in my pockets. I know one thing for sure.

If kissing Silvie felt as amazing as it did to hold her, I'm in trouble.

I don't think I can fight these feelings like I thought I could.

silvie
. . .

I CHECK my phone for the tenth time in the past few minutes. I've been standing here waiting for Wilby at the single terminal in Coconut Beach. Eight fifty-seven. His flight landed at eight forty-three, which means he's due at the baggage claim any moment now.

The Coconut Beach airport has exactly one baggage carousel and absolutely no sense of urgency. Here in Coconut Beach, that's just the way. You're on island time, and it's pretty chill here. Everything and everyone is, including their airport.

There are three people in the baggage claim area. One of them is asleep, and another one is eating a hot dog, staring out the window. The third is me, nervous and anxious to finally see my friend.

The music flips to *Free Fallin'*, and the glass doors slide open. Wilby DeSoto steps into baggage claim, and the air shifts with his larger-than-life energy. He's tall, fit in that quietly lethal way, all long lines and easy confidence. His haircut is perfect, sharp at the edges, styled like he woke up handsome and stayed that way. His skin is olive and golden, his jaw strong, his mouth unfairly nice, the kind of face that belongs on billboards or magazine covers, not waiting for luggage with the rest of us. Linen pants, immaculate leather shoes that have never known struggle, sunglasses worn indoors because he can get away with it. He pulls a dark, sleek, wheeled bag behind him, posture relaxed but purposeful, like he always knows where he's headed and assumes the world will clear a path. I don't even pretend not to stare. Some men walk into a room. Wilby arrives like a headline. And I love that about him. He's confident, sure of himself and the best friend a girl could ask for.

He looks so far out of place here on the casual island that I almost laugh. But I'm too relieved to see him.

He stops dead and looks around, sliding off his sunglasses. "Oh."

I wave enthusiastically, and he raises an eyebrow at me, full of shock and concern.

"Welcome to paradise," I call out.

He looks up at the ceiling and sighs. "Why didn't you tell me that this place was tiny and smells like sunscreen and beach?"

I jog over and throw my arms around my human equivalent of a black cat personality. He stiffens for half a second and then hugs me back tight. We play this game where we irritate each other, but the truth is we're besties. Whether he likes it or not, I've claimed him and he's claimed me. We have our work hats...and then we have our friend hats. And right now, we're wearing our friend hats.

"You look tan and relaxed," he says into my hair. "That's alarming. Who are you and what have you done to my suit wearing workaholic best friend?"

"And you look overdressed. What happened to island casual?" I tease.

He scoffs. "This is casual."

Back in New York, I dressed the same. But here? Something's changed. I love the casual, and I'm fully embracing it. Most days, I spend in yoga shorts and a sports bra, and then in sundresses. Casual is my new favorite look.

"You're smiling more. I'm suspiciously hopeful." He pulls back and looks at me, eyes narrowing. "Should I be worried?"

I shake my head, grinning at him. "For once, you don't have to worry. I'm enjoying the relaxed, summer life." Then, I pat my stomach. "And I'm eating at all the good restaurants and food trucks, not even thinking about my dress size. My mother would be horrified at my calorie carelessness."

"The woman turned you into a skeleton this past year. Her opinion doesn't matter." He motions for me to turn around so he can admire my new curves. When he whistles and gives my butt a little smack, I crack up laughing. "My girl has cake now!" Then, as if scandalized, he gasps. "What are you wearing on your feet? You went and ruined the whole look with those."

"Flip flops?" I grin. "They're comfortable and you don't have to worry about sand in your shoes. All you have to do is give them a little flip and a flop and *voila*! Sand is gone."

He looks pained. "I knew it. You're becoming a local."

I shrug. "I do live here. For now."

Despite his razzing, there's visible relief in his gaze. It melts my heart how much he cares for me. I know I worried him, but hopefully he'll see how much I've healed since coming here.

"I knew it," he mutters, looking around as we exit the airport. "This place is like a postcard."

We walk out onto the street to where I parked. I brought Birdie's golf cart here to pick him up. A woman walks by, pushing a stroller with her dog in it, and smiles at us. Wilby nods politely, then leans in. "Why did that woman seem to know you?"

"She does." I smirk.

He blinks. "Silverlyn. Who are you? Who have you become?"

Happy. Myself. Free.

I grab his arm and pull him to the golf cart. "Come on. You need breakfast and a tour."

Outside, the sun is already hot, beating down on us with a tropical feel. Wilby squints at the palm trees lining the parking lot. "This place is gorgeous. I'm beginning to see why you haven't come home."

Home.

I shudder at the thought of New York City being home. It feels like another planet right now.

"This place looks like a time capsule. Like it's still living in analog mode."

"It definitely fits the vibe," I tell him.

"That's...interesting," he adds, still looking around and taking everything in as I stuff his suitcase behind us on the golf cart. "This is your mode of transportation?"

"Yep! Buckle up!" I call as I get in the driver's seat.

He sighs as he slides in next to me and says, "If anyone asks, I rode in a respectable Uber."

We ride through town, music spilling out of shops and restaurants, even though it's barely morning. A man in board shorts waves at me from the coffee stand. Wilby takes everything in like he's watching a nature documentary.

"Why is everyone waving at you?" Wilby asks, confused. "You haven't even been here that long."

"Everyone waves at everyone here. It's not like New York," I add.

"Yeah, if everyone smiled and waved in New York, we'd think they were psychopaths." He cringes as if the thought is traumatizing.

I laugh. "It's different here. It's good for the soul. I wish everyone could come visit Coconut Beach at some point and relax. You'll love it, Wilby. Trust the process."

"Okay, but I'm not wearing flip flops," he says, shaking his head with disgust.

"Trust me, by the end of the weekend, your dogs will come out to play," I tease, knowing that sentence alone will make him crash out.

"Never, and I repeat never, say that to me ever again," he says, giving me a look of disgust.

"No promises," I singsong.

"So, there's a bar called Cocktails & Chaos? That gives me *Cocktail* movie vibes. You know, the one with Tom Cruise, before he got all weird?" he says excitedly.

"That movie is a classic," I agree. "B&B to check in first or Birdie's?"

"As if you have to ask. The B&B can wait. I want to see all the things, including Birdie. Plus, I can't check in yet anyway."

I head in the opposite direction of his B&B. We pull up in Birdie's little driveway that fits her golf cart. I turn to Wilby, and he's watching me, grinning slowly. "You look happy here."

I smile despite myself. "I *am* happy here."

He doesn't say anything for a moment, then finally smiles. "It looks good on you."

"Thanks," I say as I step out and lead him up to Birdie's cottage. I look at it as if I'm taking it in through what he's seeing. It's a light blue cottage with white trim. It's framed by flowering bushes, making it cozy. There's a small screened-in porch on the front full of plants. I have always loved Birdie's cottage. And I'm curious to see what Wilby thinks.

He looks around, taking it all in. I grab my purse, and Wilby screams. He jumps back onto the golf cart, holding onto it for dear life.

"Oh my God," he says, clutching his chest. "Why is there a dinosaur?"

I glance over at the hibiscus bush where Iggy is peeking out. "Oh. That's Iggy."

"The prehistoric creature," Wilby whispers, "is walking toward us."

Iggy blinks, completely unbothered by Wilby's emotional collapse.

I lean down and pet his head. "Hi, handsome. Did you have a good night? Did you have good dreams, buddy?"

Wilby turns to me, his eyes wild. "You named it, and you *talk* to it?"

"Yeah. That's Iggy. He's my friend."

"No." He shakes his head.

"Yes."

"That's it," he says. "I'm having you committed. I flew down here to make sure you're okay, and you're talking to reptiles."

Iggy flicks his tail, and Wilby yelps and pulls his legs up onto the seat. "How does it know I'm talking about it?"

"He's friendly." I shrug.

"His face says otherwise. Like he's going to go get his gang of other iguanas and they're going to beat me with their tails until I scream for mercy."

Birdie opens the door right then, smiling. "Iggy, move, sweetheart."

Iggy waddles aside, obediently.

Wilby stares in shock. "It listens?"

"Better than most humans." Birdie beams and then gestures for Wilby to move his butt. "Come here, sugar. It's been what...two years?"

"Yeah, you haven't been up to New York since," he accuses as he relaxes and gives Birdie a hug.

Birdie came to visit a few years ago and stayed with me. It's then she met Wilby. Those two hit it off, and he always asked about her ever since. It's impossible not to love them. There's a reason why both are my favorite people on the planet.

"Who knew that you lived in paradise and commanded iguanas?" he says as he pats her back.

"I'm very happy here," she says with a grin. "And happy that you both are finally here."

He exhales. "I might never leave. New York doesn't seem to compare anymore."

"Wait until you're on the beach with a cocktail, watching the dolphins," she says, smirking.

Wilby looks over at me. "This explains why you've been hiding out down here. I'd never want to leave either and deal with the crap back in New York."

"I'm not hiding," I say.

"You are absolutely hiding, and I can't blame you," he says as he stretches and takes in the view. "This place is stunning."

"It's about time you came to visit," Birdie says as she straightens the kitchen towel over her shoulder.

"You smell like cookies." Wilby raises an eyebrow. Sweets are the way to Wilby's heart, and Birdie knows it.

"I made lemon blueberry scones," she says. "Come in and have one. They're fresh out of the oven."

Wilby looks at me, eyes wide. "I love her. Do you think she could adopt me?"

I nod. "See? This is why I came here. Your soul is about to get a big ol' hug, too."

"I get it now," he confirms as he follows her inside.

We sit at Birdie's kitchen table with scones on our plates and coffee. Wilby eats as if he's never been fed before, and he's so happy.

Birdie puts another scone on his plate. "Where are you staying, sugar?"

"At the Seaside Bed and Breakfast," he says. "Although, I can't check in until later."

"Oh, good! Silvie can show you around," Birdie says.

"This," he says between bites, "is the best thing that's ever happened to me."

Birdie pats his cheek. "You know you can come visit me anytime you want, Wilby."

He nods and jokes, "I live here now. Wherever the boss goes, I go."

And thank God. Because I've missed my best friend.

———

Wilby and I have a lot to catch up on workwise, so we pack a beach bag and head over to the beach. We might as well catch up by having cocktails and lounging at the beach.

We set up our chairs and towels not far from Cocktails & Chaos, and I glance over, wondering if Cal is working.

When I don't see him, I deflate, shoulders slumping. I chew on my bottom lip, wondering where he could be.

I tie my sarong a little tighter around my waist. I'm wearing my green bikini since it's still the best option I own. Wilby sets up our chairs facing the water and smiles with that smug confidence he has in all his city-boy audacity.

He looks unfairly good shirtless. Annoyingly fit.

"My goodness, Wilby. You're like a chiseled Greek god."

He has ripped arms, a six-pack, and a tan that should not exist on a man who lives under office lighting. Sunglasses perch on his nose, and I grin when I see he has sandals on his feet. Not flip flops, but still, sandals.

He grins, "Hey, I blame you. You dragged me on all of those runs and workouts for your wedding body prep."

My chest tightens and my stomach sinks. I say nothing, shifting uncomfortably and glancing down at my honey-toned thighs, not missing those grueling workouts.

He sighs and says, "Sorry, Silverlyn. I shouldn't have brought up the wedding."

"It's fine. I'm over it. I mean...pretty much over it. I haven't gone back and faced it all, yet. But I have no feelings for Tyler anymore. In fact, I don't even think about him. I will never let another man know my soul like that. Because it crushed me in ways I didn't think were possible."

"I've missed you," he says as he glances over at me. "You look really great. Strong."

"It's the daily yoga," I admit.

He grins. "*You* are doing yoga? This I would like to see."

"Good. Because I'll be dragging you there with me. Birdie got me hooked on it and then she abandoned me. So, I go by myself in the mornings most sunrises."

He shrugs. "I'm down for yoga on the beach at sunrise. Sounds amazing."

Our chairs are close enough to Chaos that I can hear music drifting down from the bar and smell fried food and fruity drinks in the air. Wilby leans back in his chair and immediately shifts into shop talk.

"Okay," he says. "Do you want it straight or filtered?"

I love that Wilby always gets me.

I glance over at him through my sunglasses. "Hit me straight."

Despite my wishes for the directness, my stomach twists with nerves. I've been so detached, there's no telling what he's about to say, and that gives me anxiety.

"First off, I am relieved you never married Tyler. Good call," he says as he leans in.

I brace myself, afraid that whatever comes will make me mad.

He ticks off on his fingers. "Tyler's still a douche canoe."

"Obviously."

"Your sister has been at the office every day visiting said douche canoe and asking for money and attention from anywhere she can get it. Mainly your parents because Tyler doesn't have any, and he's hanging onto his job by a thread. Your father has had it with him. And word is that the board has as well. He is lazy and got away with it because he was marrying you. Now that he's not? Nobody cares about his loser ass anymore."

Well, no surprise there on Belladonna. Word has it she's burned through her inheritance. I invested mine and kept working. But that's what a normal person would do. Not a grifter like Belladonna. How someone can blow through that much money in just a few years is beyond me.

"She's exhausting." I sigh.

"And your father," he lowers his voice, "is angry."

That makes my stomach twist with guilt. "What's he most angry about?"

"Everything," Wilby says. "About Tyler, optics, and losing

control."

I pick at my fingernail as I stare out at the water. "Great."

"And," he adds carefully, "your mother's been coming around constantly."

I groan and snap my head to him. "What?"

"She's actually attended board meetings," he says.

I'm stunned by this fact. It's...*unusual*.

"I have never seen her attend a single meeting," I say, and can't help but wonder what her angle is here. I don't like it.

"No," he agrees. "It's not good. They're circling. Something is going on. They're planning something, Silverlyn."

I blow out my breath. "What are you thinking?"

Wilby looks around slowly, as if he's scanning the beach, the bar, and the easy rhythm of this place, and about to drop a bomb.

"I'm saying," he says, casual but sharp. "Maybe you could find a temporary fake husband."

My heart stutters to a halt. He can't be for real right now.

I bark out a laugh. "Come on, Wilby. Be serious."

"I *am* serious. You just need to think outside the box here," he says. "Can you think of anyone?"

"You know it's not that simple. My grandmother had rules set in place. I can't just choose some rando and make it work."

He frowns and lets out a frustrated huff. "I feel like we need to make it happen one way or another. Your time is slipping away. I'm afraid if you wait too long, the vultures are going to swoop in."

My head throbs as I try to work out who the vultures might be. In my gut, I know, but I've been playing blissfully ignorant in paradise.

"I could marry you," I say, wondering if that's too far outside the box.

He recoils. "Ew. No offense, darling, but you are absolutely not my type."

"Rude," I joke back.

"I love you," he says, "but you have to convince the board

that this is a real marriage. And the optics of marrying your assistant is not going to fly. In fact, I'm terrified of what your father would do to me. He scares me on a normal day at work. As a son-in-law? Never, ever going to happen."

Anxiety makes my chest tighten. I circle over and over to my problem that needs solving. Unfortunately, all the answers are vague and out of reach.

"Ohhh." Wilby's head jerks and he looks behind us. "Ohh-hhh my."

I swivel in my chair and follow his gaze. Cal is walking toward us from the bar, barefoot, shorts slung low on his hips, a button-down shirt flapping in the wind, unintentionally showing off his chiseled abs. He's smiling and waves at me.

Wilby's jaw drops.

"Him," Wilby says faintly, looking stunned by Cal.

Cal comes around and stands in front of us, eyes flicking between us with curiosity.

"Hey," he says, wearing a friendly grin. "This must be your friend."

Wilby stares and doesn't blink. He's entranced. Then he slowly turns to me. "You know this exquisite man, Silverlyn?"

Cal's mouth turns up when he hears my full name. "Silverlyn," he repeats. "Beautiful name."

I never told him my full name. Not that I don't trust him, it just never came up. And hearing it on his lips is nice.

I smile. "Cal, this is Wilby. Wilby, this is Cal."

Wilby stands and offers his hand like a gentleman who has lost control of his motor functions. "Hi," he says. "Hello. Wow."

Cal shakes his hand, looking at me, amused. "Nice to meet you, Wilby."

"Is Cal short for something?" Wilby asks, something I've been wondering myself.

"Callahan," he says. "Callahan Bennett."

I laugh. "That's sexy too, hot bartender."

Cal groans playfully. "Not this again."

"She keeps calling me hot bartender," he tells Wilby.

Wilby looks at me, his eyes widening, and mutters. "Well, if the shoe fits."

Cal snorts, shaking his head. "Can I bring you two some food or some cocktails?"

Wilby sinks back into his chair with a sigh, staring up at the sky. "I've died," he mutters. "And gone straight to heaven."

cal

. . .

"MORNING!" I call as Wilby and Silvie cross the sandy beach to me.

When I asked them yesterday if they wanted to surf this morning, Wilby lit up like I'd offered him free drinks for life at Chaos. I didn't sleep much last night. I was excited to see Silvie again. And Wilby seems cool. The waves are clean, the air feels great, and there's no way I'm missing another morning with Silvie.

Silvie smiles at me, looking hesitant. The other day she fell more than she surfed but I have to hand it to her, she stuck with it. "You already got the boards?"

"All set." I nod toward the lineup. "You guys ready?"

Silvie smiles at me, and yeah, that makes the lack of sleep worth it.

Wilby cracks his neck. "I was born ready. I think so, anyway. To be honest, I've never actually been surfing before. But it looks really cool. I've always wanted to learn."

"It'll be fun. Silvie's pretty much a pro now," I tease.

"He's lying. I'm terrible. Trust me, no one is worse than me," Silvie says as she picks up her board.

"Hey, now! A for effort!" I call as we head down to the water, boards tucked under our arms.

The sun is already starting to rise, and the beach is still quiet, the perfect time of day to come down and find peace before the chaos of the day.

Silvie paddles out as I showed her last time, confident and smooth. I'm proud of her for trying again, even though I'm not sure how much she enjoyed it last time.

God, she looks stunning in that bathing suit.

Wilby follows, just as determined as Silvie. Those two are competitive I've discovered. He does a few rounds with me and gets the hang of it and stays upright.

At the end, he pops up, laughing and sputtering. "I love it here. I'm never leaving!"

Silvie attempts again and wipes out spectacularly. I laugh and swim to her, and she pops up laughing. "I'm trying!"

"You're doing great!" I call cheerfully.

We surf for a while, and Wilby and I catch a few good ones. He's a good sport, and we cheer each other on. Silvie whoops and finally lands one that she rides all the way in, her grin wide.

"Did you see me?" she calls, excitedly.

"I did!"

Wilby walks through the shallows and lets out a scream that makes Silvie and me both turn instantly.

"Oh, my God," he says, his voice high with panic. "No, no, no, no."

"What?" Silvie says, panicked. "What happened?"

"Something bit me!" Wilby gasps. "I stepped on it!"

He hops on one foot, slapping at his foot.

I scan the water. "Oh, shit. Jellyfish."

Wilby squeals. "I'm sorry, what?"

Silvie's eyes go wide. "Oh, no. That's bad. That's really bad."

Wilby limps toward me, starting to panic. "What do I do? Somebody help me!"

Silvie grabs his arm. "I know what to do!"

"Do it!" Wilby moans.

I open my mouth to offer advice, and Silvie beats me to it.

"I can pee on him," she blurts. "I read that you're supposed to pee on it."

There are a few seconds of intense silence amongst us.

Wilby stares at her in horror as if she's lost her mind.

"You're not peeing on me!" he says, his voice cracking.

"I'm serious," she insists, looking at me for confirmation. "I think that's what you do."

I lose it and bend over laughing, trying and failing to breathe. She's completely serious when she offers to pee on her friend. She's ready to help. And damn, if that's not a good friend, I don't know what is. But she's absolutely not peeing on him. Contrary to what people believe, that doesn't actually work.

"Oh, my God," Wilby says. "You were serious!"

"I just want to help you," she says and adds lamely. "I'm a helper."

Wilby yelps and dives behind me, clutching his foot. "Don't let her pee on me, Cal. I'm begging you. I draw the line. You don't pee on your best friend and assistant!"

I'm laughing so hard my stomach hurts, and my whole body is practically shaking so hard I can barely get the words out. "I won't let her pee on you, Wilby."

"Thank you," he says breathless, looking relieved.

"She's not peeing on you," I finally manage. "You'll be fine. It's a mild sting, but we can stop by the first aid station. This happens often at the beach. Just part of beachside living."

Wilby sniffs. "I can't believe you tried to pee on me."

"I didn't try. I just offered," Silvie huffs. "I was just trying to save you. That's what friends do."

"I appreciate the effort, just keep your pee away," Wilby cries in disgust.

I help him rinse his foot and promise he won't get peed on or lose a limb. Eventually, his panic fades. "Well, look at it this way. It was a memorable first surfing experience."

"It definitely was a memory, I'll be telling this lore forever," he says.

We get Wilby cleaned up, and the first-aid helper laughs at the pee and says it's from a *Friends* episode and not accurate at all. Wilby is still horrified, and Silvie looks relieved she didn't have to do it.

She teases him by saying, "You're ungrateful for my love and devotion for you."

I wipe my face with a towel, still grinning. "You guys want to get breakfast?"

Wilby nods emphatically. "Yes, I'll even buy. I'm not touching the water ever again. I'm a land type of fella."

Silvie chuckles, and I smile at her. Yeah, I like Silvie. And Wilby.

———

By the time we get semi-cleaned up and head to Iggy's Grill, I'm starving.

"I'm so hungry," Wilby says as he walks like a man who has been victimized by a jellyfish and the ocean now personally offends him.

"I was trying to save you." Silvie grins.

"You were trying to traumatize me," Wilby says. "There's a difference."

"Can I give you a hug?" Silvie offers.

"No."

"Please?"

Wilby looks as if he's considering it, then gives her a hug and holds her tight.

I'm slightly jealous of their connection. I want to hug Silvie again.

"Why are you hugging me like that?" Silvie mutters.

"I'm trying to measure you, so I know how big of a hole to dig if I have to bury you if you ever try to pee on me again,"

Wilby says.

I choke on a laugh. "Dude, you are funny."

"I try." Wilby grins and playfully squeezes Silvie's shoulder. "This crazy lady keeps me on my toes."

By the time we get down the street to Iggy's Grill, the place is already buzzing with the breakfast crowd. It looks like a mix of tourists and locals. The smell of bacon and coffee hits us as we get closer.

Wilby squints up at the sign. "Are you kidding me? Is this place named after the iguana?"

Silvie snorts and looks at me for confirmation. "Maybe? I'm not entirely sure."

"Iggy's has been here for decades," I tell them. "I don't think Birdie's iguana has been around that long. But that would be funny if it were."

"I can guarantee you that by the end of your trip, you're going to love Iggy." Silvie smirks knowingly.

"Doubtful," Wilby calls.

We grab a booth by the window, and Silvie slides in beside me, her blonde hair still damp, hanging in two braids, looking relaxed in a way that makes my chest tighten. She's got a smattering of freckles across her face that feel new. Everything about her is adorable. Wilby slides in across from us, sunglasses still on like he's protecting his pride from the jellyfish incident.

The server drops our menus and a thermos of coffee with cups and says, "Morning."

We all greet her in return.

"I'll give you a minute," she says cheerfully and saunters off.

"What's your favorite thing to get here?" Wilby asks.

Silvie laughs. "Wilby is a foodie. He loves trying new places."

"You do, too. We have been simultaneously eating our way through all of the restaurants in New York since we've worked together," Wilby says, examining the menu.

"You have spreadsheets," Silvie adds.

"I do." He shrugs.

I wish I could take Silvie to more places to eat. Damn. Am I really getting jealous of her assistant, who seems completely platonic? I couldn't dislike the guy if I tried. He's hilarious and devoted to Silvie. I'm glad to see she has a guy like him in her corner. Hell, I want him to be my best friend, too.

And do I even have a right to be jealous of Silvie? She's a friend, nothing more, I remind myself.

I clear my throat and answer the question. "Breakfast burritos."

"Oh, yes, I need that," Wilby says immediately, reaching to pour a cup of coffee.

"Pancakes," Silvie says.

"I'm so glad you're eating carbs again," Wilby says with relief.

She nods. "Same."

"Yooohooo," we hear, and we turn to see Birdie, January, and Lucille waving from another booth.

"The Bees have arrived." I smile and nod.

Wilby asks over his mug, "Who are the Bees?"

Silvie grins. "Birdie's friends. You'll love them."

They hoot and wave and laugh about something.

"Where have you guys been off to this morning?" January calls.

Lucille eyes me. "Cal. Honey, you look good. Damp."

This makes the others laugh. Jonah was right. They're weirdos.

I clear my throat. "We went surfing."

Birdie gasps dramatically. "Without inviting us?"

"You were asleep," Silvie says, looking smug. "Just like every other morning that you skip yoga."

"That's fair," Birdie says, then leans closer. "We're about to go stir up some trouble."

Wilby's eyes light up, and he whispers to Silvie, "You're right. I adore them."

Lucille calls out to him, "You're new."

"I flew in yesterday," Wilby says proudly.

"Welcome," January calls. "We're headed off to cause chaos."

"Where?" Silvie asks, throwing concerned frown at Birdie.

"We've got errands," Birdie waves, looking like they're definitely not off to run errands.

They clatter out as loudly as they came in, leaving the place buzzing and laughing.

Wilby exhales. "I'd go cause chaos with them. They look fun."

Silvie smiles, reaching for her coffee. "Told you this town was special."

I watch her for a few seconds longer than I should. Sun-kissed and happy. Silvie is special.

Wilby's phone rings while we're still laughing about the Bees, and the shift in him is instant. He glances at the screen and stands. "I need to take this."

Like he switches from friend hat to assistant hat and makes his way out front of the restaurant.

"I hope everything is okay," I say, pouring myself some coffee.

"Me, too," Silvie says as she frowns.

We watch him through the window. He paces and stops and then runs a hand through his hair. He says something and motions with his hands as he says it, clearly worked up on whatever conversation is taking place right now.

Whatever is happening, it doesn't look good.

Silvie watches, her shoulders tense like she senses this, too.

Wilby ends the call and kicks a pebble, clearly pissed. He takes a deep breath, then comes back inside.

"It must be bad," Silvie mutters.

Wilby slides back into the booth. Silvie and I watch him, concerned.

Silvie leans across the booth. "What happened?"

Wilby shakes his head. "We can talk later. It's not good."

Silvie looks at me, then back at him. "Just tell me."

Wilby leans in and whispers, "Your sister and Tyler are getting married this week."

Silvie blinks and practically hisses. "What?"

"They filed the paperwork this morning," Wilby says. "Quietly and strategically. They're trying to secure the company before you do."

Silvie is still staring at Wilby. The air feels heavier all of a sudden. Is her sister marrying her ex? Low. What a piece of shit.

Wilby continues, his voice dropping even lower, "Silverlyn, you need to get married. Fast."

Silvie looks out the window and shakes her head, "There has to be another way. What does the lawyer say?"

"That *was* the lawyer. And we're out of options. You're going to lose this if you don't."

Silvie closes her eyes. "Crap."

"Yeah," Wilby bites out. "Crap."

Wilby looks at me and looks back at her. I feel it, then, what he's pushing her to do. She needs a fake marriage.

Silvie barks out a nervous laugh, which doesn't sound like humor. "No. I'm not getting married just to save the company."

"Silv," Wilby says, urgently now. "They're moving on this. And your father knows. Your mother is backing this. This is not a drill."

She pushes her cup back and whispers, "I'm not marrying someone just to win a power play. That's...so wrong."

Her eyes flick to me for half a second, and she looks embarrassed and apologetic.

I don't say anything. I just watch it all play out. It's seriously the craziest thing I've heard in a long time.

Wilby exhales slowly. "Then they take everything. They win. You lose. Everything you've worked for. Gone."

Silvie swallows. "No."

Wilby looks at me and then out the window. Our server drops off our food, and no one says anything except a murmured "Thanks."

Our food sits before us, neither of us touching it. Both of them seem to be having a conversation with their eyes.

She says it again, quieter but firmer. "No."

I casually pick up my burrito and take a bite, watching this play out. I don't say anything. I want to. A curious person probably would. But my brain is still stuck on the words "get married fast," replaying them over and over.

Fake marriage. That's what this is, I realize as I watch them strategize and argue about it. I see both sides. I never saw myself getting married, ever. I've got too much going on.

None of this should have anything to do with me. And yet I catch myself wanting to offer to help, anyway.

I picture it without meaning to. Her being my fake wife. Standing next to me while someone takes photos of us. Pretending something while everyone else thinks it's real.

I could do it. That thought hits too quickly. Then I feel sad when I realize it'd be fake. If I did want to be married, it would be because someone chose me. Not because I'd be a solution to a problem.

The idea of a fake marriage doesn't scare me. Losing someone like her would undo me.

I glance at her and see a steely expression on her face, like she's thinking and daring the world to push her. Because I have no doubt that she'll push back harder.

She doesn't need saving. She needs backup.

I could be backup, I reason.

Because if she's going to choose someone to help her do this, I want to be the one standing beside her, backing her up.

I look at her and say, "I'll do it."

silvie

. . .

I'LL DO IT.

Wait. He's serious.

"You don't have to do that," I say quickly, voice firm.

My mind is reeling with what Wilby told me. Tyler and Belladonna getting married? That means my family and the board are moving on to the contingency plan. My sister.

I really need to call Dad. Wilby said he was angry about everything. Was this why? I'll be out of the running, and she'll swoop in to "save" the day.

What a disaster.

That's why it needs to be me. There's still time. It was always supposed to go to me. And, because of a stupid time limit and some ridiculous rules, it's all about to slip through my fingers.

I have to figure this marriage thing out and put on one hell of a show. All I have to do is convince my grandmother's attorneys. They don't know me. This should be easy.

"You don't have to do that," I say again, the certainty leaving my voice.

Because what if he did?

That would save me, the company, a family legacy.

It would be for show and for a short time. Cal did say I was "wifey material."

"You already said that," he says softly. "And, I know."

Cal just sits there eating his breakfast burrito, adding more hot sauce to it like he didn't just flip my entire life upside down with one sentence. He doesn't even seem phased.

I'll do it.

Who does that? He said it like he'd take me to lunch or go surfing. Not signing a legally binding contract agreeing to marriage. Also, it's so much more than that. Marrying a Montclair is a legal nightmare. Not to mention a paparazzi nightmare. I close my eyes and wince at the idea of paparazzi swarming this place that has become a sanctuary to me. I can't bring that shit show here.

It's too risky. I shake my head before my brain can catch up. "No, I can't ask you to do that."

But that being said, it's truly my best shot. Plus, I know I could convince the attorneys I "love" Cal Bennett. I mean, I'm quite smitten with him, so it's not a stretch. I could always say I ran to Coconut Beach after the betrayal and accidentally fell in love. It happens in movies literally all the time.

"It's only temporary," Wilby says quickly. "It wouldn't last forever. Just until the ink dries and the company is hers."

Cal's eyebrows slightly furl at the mention of how it wouldn't last forever. He's not the type of guy who randomly gets hitched to a woman he barely knows. This would be messy in his life and he doesn't deserve that.

"You're not asking," Cal says, sitting up straight and boring his gaze into mine as if he's convinced himself this is the only answer to one of life's biggest questions. "I'm offering."

This makes my stomach knot in a way I don't appreciate. And if I am being honest, it's because having him do this would be a lot harder than having a stranger whom I have no feelings for.

God, I do have feelings for Cal. BIG feelings for Cal.

Wilby clears his throat. "Okay, back it up. I just need to confirm something. You are willing to be fake married to my best friend and boss to help save her family's company?"

Cal looks at him. "Yes."

"And what do you gain from this?" Wilby asks, eyes sharp and assessing.

I hold my breath because, honestly, it's a valid question and also a scary one. And considerably rude since Cal just offered to save my ass. There are layers to this one.

Cal turns to me, gentle but kind. "I'm not trying to talk you into anything. But if you need my help, I'll help."

"Why, though?" Wilby counters. "For money? I'm sure there'll be a stipend for your 'trouble,' however, this doesn't grant you keys to the kingdom. There will be an ironclad prenup with whoever she marries."

"Wilby." I shoot him a warning glare.

"I'm just covering all of our bases here. It's my job," Wilby emphasizes the last part.

"I don't need or want your money." Cal sets down his fork. "Listen, I'm not married. Never been married. I'm single. If I could help you, why wouldn't I?"

"Well, for one," I say. "My family is crazy."

Wilby nods, and his eyes widen. "Can confirm."

Cal smirks. "Okay..."

"You would have to sign an NDA *and* a prenup?" Wilby challenges, as if he's trying to scare him away.

I kick Wilby under the table and glare at him. He ignores me and continues in his professional voice he uses when he can talk anyone into doing just about anything.

"Of course." Cal shrugs and takes another bite. "Wouldn't want you taking all of my money."

If Cal's uneasy about the idea, his poker face is on point. I stare at him for a little longer than necessary, wondering if he's hiding his true feelings about it.

Wilby laughs. "I love you, Cal."

"Thanks?" Cal smirks and takes another bite.

"I'm sorry. This is really weird. Like a really weird conversation. How did we go from surfing to discussing a potential marriage?" I ask, pinching the bridge of my nose as a stress headache forms.

"Eat," Wilby orders. "You get a headache if you don't eat."

I sigh, pull my plate closer, and drizzle syrup on the pancakes, which look perfect. Fluffy and buttery. I close my eyes. A weird day this has turned out to be. But at least there're pancakes and sausage.

Wilby looks at Cal. "I didn't mean to imply you didn't have money. But I'm just covering bases. Because if this goes any further and makes it to the lawyers, that's what they will be asking."

"Good," Cal says. "I wasn't worried about it."

Wilby taps his chin. "This could work."

I cross my arms over my chest. "You have no idea what you're volunteering yourself for. Some of my family is terrible. Horrible. Like *stealing your sister's husband* horrible."

Cal's gaze stays on mine. "I'm not worried about your family. But I do think it's ridiculous to lose everything to two people hell-bent on trying to destroy you. That concerns me. And it concerns me that your family is okay with them doing that."

My heart rate quickens in my chest. Cal is my friend, but when he says things like that—so protective and from the heart, it blurs the lines between friendship and something more.

And a fake marriage won't?

"Oh, her dad is *not* okay with that. Trust me." Wilby shakes his head. "He is livid. But he's also getting desperate. He stands to lose it all."

Guilt consumes me as I think about how much I've left on my dad's shoulders. I ran with my tail on fire from the wedding and he's been cleaning up fires without me since.

We've always been a team.

I definitely need to call him.

"This is such an inconvenience for you, Cal," I say with a frown.

He doesn't answer right away. His eyebrows furl together as if he's thinking long and hard about something. He looks at the table and adds more coffee to my cup, then Wilby's, and tops his own. Then, his shoulders relax as if he's made peace with his worries. "You're my friend, Silvie. And I don't like seeing good people get taken advantage of. It makes me mad."

And there it is. The crack to my armor that I've so carefully constructed for most of my life.

I swallow down the emotions clawing at my throat. "You need to know what you'd be signing up for. Your entire life would change."

"I'm sure it wouldn't change as much as you think."

Wilby sighs. "It absolutely would. Have you ever Googled Montclair Holdings?"

Cal pauses. "I know who they are, Wilby."

"The paparazzi would dig into your life," I murmur, already hating what that would look like for him. "They'd look for dirt. And pressure you. They'd try to pay you off."

Cal shrugs. "I'm not for sale."

"I know. We'd be in the spotlight, though," I say, voice slightly rising. "There would be constant press, gossip, and assumptions."

The marriage would be the easy part. It's everything that comes with the Montclair name that makes life so utterly difficult.

"I can handle that," he says confidently.

"And when it ends," I say quietly. "That's when it'll be the hardest. Awkward even."

Wilby rolls his eyes. "This isn't a romcom."

"No one said it was," I say dryly.

Wilby straightens. "Okay," he says. "If we're entertaining this further, I have some more questions."

I glare at him. "We are *not* entertaining this."

But it's a lie. I've already begun moving chess pieces in my head. Cal wears a determined glint in his eyes.

"Humor me," Wilby says, already turning to Cal. "Do you have debt?"

"Nope."

"A criminal record?"

"Nope."

"A temper? Because I would kill you if you acted sideways to Silverlyn. And I can promise you her father would do a million times worse than anything you could ever imagine."

I bite back a smile. I hope he's making Tyler's life a living hell.

Cal smiles faintly. "No temper."

Wilby nods like that tracks. "Children?"

Cal hesitates. "Maybe someday. With the right person."

My heart stutters.

Wilby laughs. "No. I mean, do you currently have any?"

Cal shakes his head.

Wilby exhales slowly and grins. "This makes sense."

"It doesn't," I insist, though there's not much fight in my tone.

Wilby sits up straighter. "It does on paper. Which, unfortunately, is where your future is being decided right now."

I shake my head. "I feel like I'm trapping someone into this."

Cal leans in and says softly, "You wouldn't be trapping me. I offered."

That's worse. When it ultimately ends or falls apart spectacularly, I'll feel guilty for that, too.

I look away, blink hard. "I didn't come here to get married."

"I know."

"I came here to breathe and have peace," I say, gesturing between us. "And this will take away both of our peace. I don't think you fully understand."

Cal smiles softly. "Bring it."

Wilby watches us, quiet now, like he's calculating. "This is going to save your company."

I squeeze my eyes shut. "Okay."

———

We finish eating and chat about the logistics. Wilby emails the company to say he'll be working remotely for the next week, but doesn't offer any details on where or why. So far, I've been able to keep my location private, and I want to keep it that way. He researches and steps outside to make a few calls.

Cal leans back and looks at me. "You okay?"

I shake my head. "No, I'm not okay. This is proving to be the weirdest day ever."

Cal snorts and nods.

"I'm sorry. It's not that I'm not grateful. But I think statistically this is going to be a shitshow, and I'm worried about that for you."

"You don't have to worry about me. But I do have one request," Cal says sheepishly. His cheeks redden and he can't meet my eyes.

I give him a curious look, my nerves making my pancakes sour in my gut. "What?"

Cal sighs and looks out at Wilby on the phone, who's no doubt setting up an impromptu wedding. "I need you to come meet my mom."

Oh.

Oh my.

I soften. "Your mom?"

Cal nods. "Her name is Carly. It would break her heart if she heard about you from anyone else. And I don't keep things from her."

My heart melts a little. Cal is such a good guy.

"Yes, I'd love to meet her. Just say when," I agree. "But she's probably going to think this is the weirdest thing ever."

Or the most horrible. If she's a normal mom, unlike my crazy, controlling one, she won't like the idea of her son marrying out of convenience to help some tourist who blew into town wearing a wedding dress and carrying a suitcase full of issues.

While I like the idea of meeting her, I wish it were under any other circumstances. I'm suddenly nervous but also excited at the same time. What if she's really cool? I've never had a cool mom. Just my sorry excuse for one.

"Well...she probably won't think this is that weird," Cal assures me. "But to be on the safe side, we'll pay her a visit so she's not blindsided."

"Does she want to go out to dinner? We could..."

Cal shakes his head. "The thing is...she doesn't leave the house."

"Oh. Like ever?" I ask, suddenly feeling worried.

"No."

"Where does she live?" I ask, curious.

"Over by Birdie. It's Tuesday. I usually go visit her and bring her groceries and her books. If you want to come with me...you can."

This feels big. Like more than a way to rescue my company through marriage. More than just being friends with the hot bartender. This feels like a next step. Something deeper. Something more.

Life is getting complicated, but I can't stop it now.

"Yes. I'd love to go with you," I say with a smile. "What do you mean by books?"

His cheeks turn pink and his grin is entirely too cute as he says, "She's a big romance reader. She's always been a romantic at heart. I stop by the mobile bookstore and get her a few books to read for the week. It's just something she looks forward to. It means a lot to her."

And apparently it means a lot to him too.

If Cal can "fake" marry me, I can visit his mother with him

and bring her books. Knowing I can do something for him for a change warms my heart.

"Oh. I've been wanting to go to Salty Pages Books," I tell him with a cheesy grin. "Can I help you pick out some books?" I'm excited by this.

Cal leans back in relief. "You have no idea how much that would help me. I am terrible at picking out her books. Mia and Juniper have been awesome at helping, but I might need reinforcements."

"Well, let's go," I say, bumping his shoulder gently. "Wilby has the wedding stuff."

I grab my black nylon crossbody purse and Cal's hand lays on mine gently. A zing of pleasure shoots up my arm at his touch. Whoa.

Cal lays down bills and nods to our server. "I got it."

"Wait," I say. "I can't go meet your mom looking like this. I look like a drowned rat. She will think I'm so weird."

Cal laughs. "She would never think that."

"Can I take a shower and get presentable?"

"Of course. Why don't I drop you off and take Wilby to his B&B. Then I'll get ready and come get you?"

I grin. "Sounds perfect."

And this is how I met my future husband's mother.

————

"Okay," Cal says carefully. "I usually only bring her three books."

I look down at the towering stack in my arms. Paperbacks, hardcovers, and a cookbook I'm sure Carly would love. *I* love it.

"Shhh," I tell him.

The Salty Pages mobile bookstore smells like paper, sunshine, and happiness, which feels on point. I absolutely adore it. And this has become my new favorite place in Coconut Beach. I can't believe I haven't been here before. It's been what feels like forever since I've been able to read a book for fun. I'm going to see if Carly wants to lend me some of these. Maybe we can be friends.

Juniper and Mia are behind the counter, glowing with the kind of joy that comes from watching someone buy a ton of books from their store and get excited about them. I put them all on the counter and start making another one in my arms. I can't help it. There're just too many good ones to choose from. I have to get them all for her.

Cal clears his throat behind me, and I glance over at him. "What?"

He gives me an exasperated look.

I slide another novel onto my second pile. "You said she likes books."

Juniper grins, and Mia gives me a thumbs up as if they're both confirming.

"Yes," Cal agrees. "But this looks like you're stocking a bunker full of books for like the end of time."

I step a little closer to him, lowering my voice. "Cal... I love books. Your mom does too. This means a lot, so please don't take it from me."

He watches me for a moment, eyes flicking to mine, and then, just slightly, to my lips. A small jolt of awareness runs through me, and I shake it off, focusing on the books in my hands, aware we have an audience. "I hope she'll really like this too," I add softly, pointing at another book.

He smiles, shaking his head. "She's going to think it's Christmas morning."

"Exactly," I say, letting myself relax a little as I slide the book onto the stack. Juniper beams at me, grabbing one pile of books, and Mia hands me another. "Thank you," I say quietly, smiling at them both. "Of course. I'll be back. I need books, too."

"You're doing the Lord's work," Mia says with a wide grin. "We'll be restocking for you!"

"I aim to serve," I reply, with a mock salute.

The drive to Carly's house is quiet. I worry she might not like me. What if she thinks I'm a weirdo trying to bag her son for some weirdo reason? Well. That last part is true. Kinda.

When we pull up, my nerves spike. The house is modest and neat, curtains drawn, porch swept. It looks loved and cozy. It's a little pink bungalow with a eucalyptus wreath on the door. I love it.

As we approach the house, my stomach tightens and my heart races. I didn't realize how much this visit would unnerve me. I'm used to commanding board rooms, but this feels so outside my wheelhouse. I don't want to disappoint Cal.

Carly answers the door before Cal can knock. She's younger than I expected. Softer. Her smile is wide, nervous, and warm all at once.

"Hi," she says, looking timidly at me.

"Mom, this is Silvie. We have some news," Cal says.

I barely get out a hello before she pulls me into a hug. A real one. And I realize I've never been hugged like this by my own mother. Birdie, yes. But not my own mother. My nervousness about meeting Cal's mother fades instantly, and I like her.

"So nice to meet one of Cal's friends. I'm a hugger. And it's just so nice to meet you. Let me help," she says as she picks up a bag, and her eyes grow wide when she sees all the books. "What is all this?"

Cal brings in a few bags of groceries he'd had tucked in a cooler in his back seat. I helped Carly unpack all the books on her dining room table.

"Just a few books we thought you'd like," I say with a smile. "I'm a big reader, too. I mean, I was. I want to get back into it, though. Maybe we could read some together and talk about them. Like a book club?" I say sheepishly.

We spread them all out and looked through them. I noticed Cal watching us from the kitchen, pretending to stay busy as he put away groceries. He's meticulous and careful about his task. My heart squeezes because I'm moved with how much love he puts into something as simple as putting the groceries into cabinets.

Carly's hands hover over the books and then over her mouth like she can't believe it.

"For me?" she keeps saying. "All of these are for me?"

Cal watches her like she's his favorite person in the whole world, and that's when I truly know he's a good man through and through. He loves his mom. He brings her books. He takes care of her.

And you get to marry him...

A thrill shoots through me and I quickly squash it. As much as I want to romanticize what we've agreed to, it's nothing more than just that. An agreement. A contract. A marriage on paper.

"Come sit, kids," Carly says, gesturing to the living room. "I have cookies."

Who says no to cookies? Not this girl.

After we sit, cookies in hand, Cal and I explain our crazy plan. To Carly's credit, she doesn't freak out or tell me to get out. If anything, she seems amused and entertained by the whole thing.

She just laughs when we finish. "It's like a romcom."

I smirk and look over at Cal. That's what Wilby said. He grins and shakes his head, too.

"Fake or not," Carly says gently, "welcome to the family."

There's nothing real about this marriage, aside from what the law will see, but my heart still trips over itself to be included in their family. Carly is the sweetest. And Cal...

He's just about perfect.

Later, when we step back outside, I can't stop smiling.

"She's younger than I thought," I say quietly.

He nods. "She's forty-eight. She had me young."

"She's really great."

I want to ask about what happened to her but can't find the nerve to voice it. He must sense my question, though because he answers it.

"About six years ago," he says, eyes on the ground, "she stopped leaving the house. Anxiety. It got bad. I came back home to take care of her."

Something in my chest cracks open.

The way he said it so plainly. Like love doesn't need explaining. He would do anything for the mother he loves.

"She obviously adores you," I say and mean it. It's something to be cherished and grateful for. Not everyone has that.

He smiles. "She's probably going to ask you a million questions next time. She seemed kind of in shock by everything."

"I like her a lot," I admit.

"She said she'll support us," he says. "Whatever we need."

I glance back at the house, light glowing warm through the window.

I don't know how this all ends.

But I know one thing.

Anyone raised with that kind of love is someone I could temporarily trust with my heart.

cal

. . .

THE WATER IS calm and steady this morning, and Jonah's next to me, quiet like always, as we get our lines ready to fish. I cast mine out and watch it disappear into the blue and let my mind wander over the past couple of days.

Jonah clears his throat and says quietly, "I've been seeing you with the pretty blonde a lot."

Pretty is an understatement. She's mesmerizing. I feel like she puts me under a spell anytime she's nearby. Hell, even when she's not, my mind is on her as if lured into magically thinking about her.

Is that why you offered to marry her?

I shake away those thoughts and mutter, "You know her name."

He grunts, which is as close to agreement as I'm going to get with Jonah.

"I introduced her to my mom."

That gets me a glance my way, and he says, "Bet Carly loved her."

I smirk. "She did. Those two hit it off."

I'm worried, though, about Mom getting too attached to her. Even though she knows the marriage is temporary, Mom isn't

155

one to just stop caring about someone. Unfortunately, the apple doesn't fall far from the tree.

Jonah glances over again. "Knew it."

"She practically bought out the entire mobile bookstore," I add. "Two huge bags. I tried to stop her, but she's hard-headed."

"Good luck with that." Jonah chuckles. "Sounds like the perfect woman for you. Someone to keep your stubborn ass on your toes."

I reel in and cast again. My voice comes out nervous, and I just tell him. "We're getting married."

It's strange admitting that to him. These are words I never thought I'd say out loud. I've been perfectly happy with the bachelor life. And now just look at me.

You're not marrying for love, idiot. You're helping a friend.

Jonah stops moving, and he turns slowly to me and grumbles in shock. "Well, that escalated quickly."

The boat drifts, and his line goes slack. Jonah is just staring at me like I've lost my mind.

"I'm helping her," I say with a sigh. "She's got some will thing going on with her family. She has to be married by her thirtieth birthday, or her family's company gets turned over to a trust, and she loses everything. And now, she's contending with their contingency plan. Her awful sister who already stole her fiancé." I scrub a palm down my face. "Silvie's a good person. She doesn't deserve that. This is something I can do to help her solve this problem."

Jonah squints. "Wait. You're serious?"

"Dead serious," I utter. "You can't tell anyone, either."

He huffs out a laugh. "Who am I gonna tell?"

"One of your many girlfriends. The Bees. The ones who like to moon you."

"I'm going to throw you overboard," he decides.

I laugh, reach for my water, and take a swig. And I think about how this all sounds when I actually say it out loud. It does sound insane. But maybe something Jonah said about Silvie was right. She is different. I can't explain it. Maybe I never will be able to. But this feels right, helping her.

He's quiet for a while, then says, "I told you this one is different."

That hits me in the chest harder than I thought it would. But I know, deep down, somehow, this is true. She is different. I have no idea how or what, but something is different.

I've never had feelings like this for someone that run as deep as they do for Silvie. We're friends, but I think there's hella potential for more. Watching her with my mom. Seeing how she looks after Birdie. She's a powerhouse VP of her company. And that's sexy as hell. I like her a lot. I love hearing her laugh and being playful with Wilby. She's someone I could see myself with beyond a marriage of convenience, and that also scares the hell out of me. I've never met anyone like her.

The voice of reason inside my head tries to calculate what the end games looks like for all this. Do we stay here or do we need to spend the allotted time in New York? Is there a time period where we stay married and then divorce? My gut clenches, not necessarily loving that thought. But I barely know her, so it's not like we could stay married if it worked out, right?

I haven't even kissed her. *Yet.*

"I like her," Jonah finally says.

I look at him, and that's when it hits me how insane that statement is. Jonah never admits to liking anyone. If he likes you, he'll show it by showing up for you. But he's a man of few words. He came to every one of my high school sporting events. Just showed up. Sat alone. Watched me. Then got up and left at the end.

He's always shown up for me. Even when I went to prom. He showed up and snapped a few pictures on his old digital camera, grumbled something, and left. Only later did I see that same photo and several others he had of me at important life stages, taped to the side of his fridge. Quietly, in the background, he's always been there. Always supported me. And that's

157

another reason I don't want to leave Coconut Beach. He and my mom. They mean everything to me. I'd do anything for them. And I don't want to miss these years with them. They don't get it, but I'm not sacrificing my time for them. I'm sacrificing other dreams to have them. I want them in my life. That's what family means to me.

But when this is all over with Silvie, will it leave a crater-sized hole in me? I have a strong feeling it will. The hurt might just be worth it, though. I know I should steel myself. This is temporary, and I'm just doing a good thing for someone who needs my help. That's it.

But that's not true. I like her, too. So much. I knew being attracted to her and letting myself get attached would bite my ass in the end.

The marriage part doesn't scare me. No, it's the way I know this all ends. She returns to New York, to her real life. I'll still be here. Bartending and managing Cocktails & Chaos. Fishing with Jonah. Taking care of my mom. Same beach, same boat, same thing every day.

But maybe it won't hurt as badly as I think. Maybe I'll push through. Either way, I'm doing it.

———

I'm headed home from fishing to shower and get ready for the day when I pass my mom's house. Sometimes she waves from her front window, but this time she's not there. I make my way around the side and pause when I hear it. Laughter. And more than one person is laughing.

What the...?

The sound of laughter spills out the open back door and drifts across the yard, light and easy, as if this were an everyday, normal thing, which it's not. My mom doesn't let any visitors come besides me. And she doesn't leave her door open. Ever. Or unlocked. I slow down, and my chest tightens as I make my way closer to take a look.

I recognize my mom's laughter and her voice. She's happy and talking, but I can't make out what she's saying. I get closer, and sunlight pours in the wide-open door. That's when I see them.

Silvie and Mom are sitting at her kitchen table with plates of scones between them. They have mugs of coffee in front of them, and my mom's leaning back in her chair, laughing so hard, she's wiping at her eyes. I haven't seen her like this in years.

My heart thuds painfully in my chest. I watch silently from the doorway for a while, neither of them aware of me being here. Silvie's holding up a book and saying something to my mom, and that makes her laugh even harder.

"And it was so funny because in this one part..." Silvie trails off when she realizes I'm standing here. Her eyes widen and skim down my chest. It's then I remember I'm not wearing a shirt. I cross my arms over my chest and lean against the doorway.

"Hi." She gasps. "Cal."

"You guys good?" I ask, trying to keep it casual as I look from her to my mom and back at her.

I can't remember the last time I saw my mom this happy. My chest is tight, and the overwhelming feeling of many emotions fills me. Happiness. Gratitude. Regret. All a strange combo.

My mom looks at me and beams. "Hi, honey. I was just having scones and coffee with Silvie."

She says it as if it's absolutely normal to do on a random day. It's not. I mean, I've always wanted her to do this. In fact, for years, people have tried to come visit. She just wouldn't take any visitors without me being there. Ever. They give up and just leave her random goodies and notes on her porch now. Which she loves...but I've never seen anyone here.

Silvie nods, confirming. "Yeah. We're good. We're talking about books. Your mom has read so many good ones. So, many.

Cal, she's got the lowdown on the best series. Like ever. I have to write these down."

"Did you tell her what her job is?" I prompt, looking at my mom.

"Yes," Silvie says, shaking her head in disbelief. "Coolest job ever, by the way. Your mom is just way cool."

Mom looks down, not sure what to do with the compliment. "Thanks," she says softly, but I know she's so happy right now.

"I can't believe you're an editor for a major publishing house. You get paid to read books. Not fair," Silvie says, tucking her pretty hair behind her ear. "You're living the life, Carly."

It's the perfect job for my mom, who refuses to leave the house.

"Silvie and I are going to have our own little book club," Mom says cheerfully. "And set up regular coffee dates."

Interesting. Like this is normal. Like, Silvie didn't just slide herself into the center of my life and make my two favorite people fall in love with her. Jonah and my mom. This is like freaking sorcery. Like the universe is sending me the biggest joke ever. A fake wife who my family is into almost as much as I am. Because, let's face it. I'm *really* into her.

"Come join us, honey," my mom calls as she stands to grab another plate out of the cabinet.

She knows I'll never turn down time with her. Even though I need to get home and get ready. I can't ever tell her no.

I grab the shirt thrown over my shoulder, put it on, and make my way to the sink to wash my hands. "Fair warning, I smell. I've been out fishing with Jonah."

"Oh, how is Jonah? He's supposed to bring me a fish today to fry," she says as she slides a mug onto the table and pushes the plate toward me. "We have a thing where he leaves one already in the cooler by the back door."

I actually did not know that. Another interesting fact that I'm learning about my mother today.

I watch Silvie reach for another scone in the center of the

table. She eyes me curiously. I didn't miss the way her eyes trace my tattoos on my chest and arms. That was one hobby I've had the past few years, collecting tattoos. And it seems like she likes them.

"He's good. I told him we were getting fake married. He knows not to tell anyone, so don't worry," I say as I take a bite of a scone.

Silvie nods. "Of course, I trust Jonah."

"Me, too." Carly nods. "He's a good man."

We make small talk, and I don't miss how Silvie's eyes drift between my mom and me like she's trying to figure out a puzzle.

This is when it hits me. I'm so screwed. I'm in deep. I like her. And all of the walls that I've carefully built around me here in Coconut Beach to keep myself safe are crumbling one by one, and I feel like I'm watching it happen in real time. Like I'm sitting here, and there's nothing I could do to stop it if I even tried.

The divorce after the fake marriage is going to hit me hard.

And there's nothing I can do about it.

silvie

. . .

COCKTAILS & Chaos has become our early-morning office for all things wedding planning and strategy over the past few days. Wilby commandeered an entire table with his laptop open, sunglasses up on his head, and he looks comical here rather than back in our New York Office. In fact, he fits right in.

Wilby and I just finished sunrise yoga with Summer while Cal surfed. And honestly, I'm still a little embarrassed, so I'm glad Wilby is here as a buffer now. Wilby told us both, under no uncertain terms, that he would never surf again. In fact, I'm not sure he's ever going into the ocean after the jellyfish incident that seems to have scarred him for life. He's never going to let me live that one down.

And this is what I love about Coconut Beach. Back home, I have to be the corporate Silvie, with her life together. Here, I can be Silvie, who tries new things, makes funny memories, and finds myself turning out to be more fun than I thought.

Wilby's locked in wedding-planning mode. Meanwhile, I'm leaning against the table, drinking a coffee, trying not to stare at Cal. Which is funny, because I'm pretty sure he's trying not to stare at me. He's opening up the place and moving with confidence. He has his hat on backwards, and I'll admit, it's doing things to me. He looks *so* hot. He's wearing a T-shirt and shorts, and he moves like he does this every day. Which he probably does. But he's definitely nice to look at.

Then he cooks us up breakfast, and I think, yeah, this man is marriage material. Real marriage material.

What happens when you have to get divorced?

Wilby must sense I'm deep in thought as I watch Cal, and he pauses and looks over at me.

"You know...I like this guy for you," Wilby says cautiously. "I never thought we'd be sitting here over a thousand miles from home and you'd be marrying a bartender, but hey, life is weird. I guess we should just embrace it."

I laugh. "My father's gonna lose it. You know that, right?"

"Your father scares the holy ever-loving shit out of me, Silvie. He is going to go ballistic. But he's not who we have to worry about. Your psycho mom and sister scheming is why you're literally racing to the altar."

I can't wait, I think sarcastically.

Part of me feels bad for my dad. He just wants the company to be solid. Nobody likes this stupid clause my grandmother left in her will. But it's something we're all dealing with. I just want a real life. Not a fake one. But if this is what I get right now, I guess I'll take it. It's better than the life I was living with Tyler.

I shudder at even the thought of his name.

Wilby watches Cal walk toward us with a tray of breakfast, and he leans closer to me. "If you don't lock this one down, I swear I will. He cooks, Silverlyn."

I laugh and stare at Cal dreamily. "Yes, he does."

Cal sets down plates in front of us like it's nothing. Eggs, toast, fruit, and bacon.

"Thank you, Cal," I say as I push out the chair next to me so he can sit by me.

Wilby stares at all the food and back at me. "Okay, but what is seriously wrong with him?"

Cal grabs a pitcher of coffee and returns, sliding into the chair next to me. "What?"

"How are you so perfect?" Wilby shakes his head in disbelief.

Cal chuckles and grabs a fork. "I'm not perfect."

Wilby turns to me. "Silverlyn. I can't find anything wrong with him. Neither could our investigator."

Cal pauses and looks up at him, his fork mid-air. "You had me investigated?"

Wilby looks at him and nods. "Standard practice for marrying a billionaire and my best friend."

Cal chokes on his food and covers his mouth with his napkin. He looks at me strangely and takes a sip of his water.

Wilby, not reading the room, continues. "We've looked. Trust me. Never seen a more honorable member of society."

I take a bite of eggs and close my eyes for a second. "These are good, Cal."

"Thanks," he says as he slides the jelly over to me.

None of us are addressing the elephant in the room Wilby just casually mentioned I'm a billionaire. Which, I'm actually not. Not technically, anyway. My family's company is worth billions. I have millions, but all in investments and stocks.

It's not lost on me that Cal hasn't had any questions about my company or marrying me. We're both just been going about our lives as if this is perfectly normal. There's nothing normal about all of this. It's totally weird.

We eat while Wilby also works on his laptop between bites.

"Okay, I have the wedding all planned out. I think you're going to like it," Wilby says. "We keep this quiet and fast. No announcements or social media."

"Okay," Cal agrees.

"Agreed," I say.

"Birdie can know," he continues. "Jonah, and your mom. That's it."

"And Cal," I tease.

"Well, obviously," Wilby says. "The groom should be informed."

Cal laughs softly. "Appreciated."

Wilby looks over at him. "You still good with all this? Feel like running?"

My chest tightens all of a sudden at the thought of Cal not being around. I hold my breath as I wait for his reaction.

"I'm fine," Cal says, glancing over at me. As if he can sense I'm nervous, he lays his hand on my thigh.

He doesn't do it in a sexual way, but a calming, *I've got you*, way. As if he's saying, *I'm here. Everything is fine.* And I have no idea how Cal can do that, but he does seem to calm me when I'm anxious.

It's a small gesture, but my body still reacts. Heat blooms where his palm rests, and my panties, embarrassingly, are soaked.

No one ever touches me like this. Tyler never did. He had no interest in soothing or caring for me.

I glance at him, expecting him to pull back and realize what he's doing, but he doesn't. His eyes stray to mine, and they're calm and steady, too. He isn't afraid or intimidated by any of this.

My body relaxes and my shoulders loosen. I relax under his hand and let myself feel it. Safety. And I swallow, picturing for a second what it would be like to always have this. To feel safe. To have someone in my life who wants me to feel safe. I have always wanted a relationship deep down. I know I was never going to get that with Tyler. He wasn't half the man Cal is.

And that's when it hits me. This might just not be pretend anymore for my heart.

That complicates things.

Wilby brings me back to reality as he continues his checklist. "I'm surprised that the paparazzi haven't found you yet. This is really good. But I'm just surprised."

"I know," I say.

"And honestly, even more shocked that Tyler didn't leak your location to mess with you," Wilby adds.

I stare down at my coffee. "I'm not sure he knows."

Cal stiffens and jerks his head up. His eyes narrow and jaw clenches. He sweeps his gaze around us as if searching for the paparazzi threat that isn't here. His voice is sharp as he says, "That's unsettling that he would do that and risk your safety."

It's the first time I've ever seen Cal remotely anything other than chill surfer dude. Right now, he's alert, tense, and protective. My heart patters wildly in my chest. I've never had someone care that much, to the point of anger, so naturally, it does dangerous things to my attention-starved heart.

"Everything about Tyler is unsettling," I say quietly.

Cal looks over at me, moving his hand, as the brief anger melts away to concern flickering across his face. He doesn't pry but pours me another water from the pitcher that's sweating at the center of the table. He's always making sure we have food and something to drink, specifically me. I love that about him.

Wilby watches this too and seems to file it away. "Oh, hey, good news. That turd is officially moving out of your penthouse. I'm going to have the locks changed and have it deep cleaned. I also ordered a new bed. It'll be here next week."

"You think of everything." I smile appreciatively, feeling relieved.

"It's my job," Wilby says as he continues to type.

"You're getting a raise."

Wilby grins and keeps typing. "Excellent."

"This guy is a miracle worker," Cal states, smirking.

"You have no idea," I say. "Right-hand man."

Wilby closes his laptop with a decisive snap. "Okay. Everything is locked and loaded. You are winning, Silverlyn. Period. Tyler the turd and your skank sister will not be getting your company. Our plan is foolproof."

"Thank you," I say.

"It's going to be fine. We're sticking to the plan. I gotta run and figure out my B&B situation. Since I extended my trip, they are saying there's no room. I'm hoping to get in at the Palms. Thanks for breakfast, Cal."

"No, problem," Cal says.

"Thank you!" I call. "Let me know about your room situation."

And somehow, I feel so much relief when he says it's going to all be fine.

Because right now everything feels more than fine. It feels pretty great.

———

I need to work off some of my nervous energy. Birdie's off with her Bees doing God knows what. I clean her cottage and get it sparkling. It smells like clean laundry and lemon cleaner, which feels wildly productive for someone like me whose life is currently a massive shit show.

I've got her bedding switched out and mine in the washer. I'm folding towels when Birdie comes in from the porch with her purse over her shoulder. "Well. If this isn't a treat to come home to. What are you doing, sugar?"

"I'm anxious," I say. And I clean and organize when I'm feeling anxious.

"I know. You have a lot going on," she says as she hangs up her purse. She saunters over, takes out the jar of iced tea, and pours two glasses. "Come sit down."

I reluctantly fold the last towel and set them all in the basket.

"Well," she says gently. "I bet you didn't see your trip playing out this way."

"Nope." I laugh as I take a sip of my tea. "But here we are."

She sets her tea down and says, "I like Cal for you, sugar. Are you sure this is a fake relationship? Looks like it could be pretty great if you ask me."

Perhaps that's the underlying reason for my anxiety. I know

she's right. What happens when it all ends? The whole thing is *designed* to end. Cal is helping me achieve a goal, and when I achieve said goal… That's the part that stresses me out.

"Everyone likes Cal, apparently," I say, trying to keep my tone light despite the rampant thoughts in my head. "Wilby's trying to find something wrong with him."

She shakes her head. "You'll probably never find anything."

That makes me feel better, even though I already knew, deep down, this was the case.

She continues, tracing the sweat ring of her tea on the table-cloth. "I do want you to be careful."

"Why is that?" I ask, curious.

"You're both soft souls," she says, her voice kind. "Underneath that badass CEO exterior of yours, you're still my sweet sugar."

My throat tightens, and she continues.

"And Cal," she adds, smiling, "is a good man. He loves his momma. He works hard, and he shows up. He's good to everyone in this town. Good people, that man." She looks at me, her eyes sharper, but still warm. "I want you both to be happy."

"If I couldn't even keep Tyler, I'm not sure I can keep a good one like Cal," I say admitting my thoughts aloud. "I'm not doing well in the relationship department." When it's all over, Cal may be more than eager to move on from me.

She scoffs. "*You* were never the problem. Tyler was the *whole* problem."

"He rejected me. For Belladonna," I remind her. "It's embarrassing."

She cups my cheek. "Sugar, he didn't reject you. He rejected the man he would have to become in order to be with someone as incredible as you."

"Thanks," I say softly, my heart melting.

"Don't make yourself small to fit into a small man's world. You let that turd choke on your greatness."

I laugh and nod. "I want to be a career woman. But sometimes I look at life and wonder if I want a family instead."

She tilts her head. "Why can't you have both?"

"I watched my dad not be able to have both. And my mom chose neither," I remind her.

"That was their choice. And you aren't either of them. You might share DNA, but you're your own person. And thank God for that."

I snort at her candor.

Birdie grows serious. "Any chance this doesn't have to be fake?"

I shake my head. "We just met. He's helping me. That's it. Like you said...he's a good guy."

She hums, unconvinced. "That's not what it looks like."

"This is temporary. And strategic. We have a solid plan."

Birdie grins. "I've seen a lot of things, sugar. I can tell when two people are pretending and when they're real."

I don't answer. Because the fact is, everything is blurred now. I'm questioning everything. And it's got me so anxious.

She pats my arm, gentle and reassuring. "Just be careful with each other. Soft hearts bruise easily."

I nod, even though I have a feeling that broken hearts are inevitable in this case.

———

Later on, I'm at the Seashell Diner with Summer. She's venting about her stepbrother, Dayton. We order coffee, and I get a sugar-free banana-nut blondie with a caramel drizzle. Her matcha was good the other day, but I'm more of a coffee lover.

"Okay, girl. What's up with the sugar-free? Why is everyone ordering sugar-free these days?" she demands, looking offended.

I chuckle and shrug. "I don't know, actually. I just started getting this back in New York, and I like it."

Summer's on a tangent right now. Dayton has her in a mood.

He's been keeping her from making the updates to her parents' house she wants to make. I know it's not necessarily about sugar-free coffee. But I let her rant.

"Why does everyone hate sugar?" she complains.

"I don't hate sugar. I'm a big fan," I tell her.

"Who stood by everyone when they were sad? Not lettuce, that's for sure. It was sugar. Sugar!"

I pat her shoulder. "I know."

"I just want my mural. And my painted tiles. Why is Dayton ruining that for me?"

"I don't know," I tell her. "I think it's going to be beautiful."

"And why does *he* hate sugar?" she bites out.

And there it is.

"He's a psychopath," I tell her.

"Exactly," she agrees.

"Want to go do some yoga? Will that make you feel better?" I ask her.

"Yeah," she says softly, sipping her matcha.

My phone buzzes, and I look down and see a text from Wilby

> Wilby: Heads up. Your dad grilled me today about what's going on with you. He's on the warpath. He is livid.

Great. I see I have several missed calls from my father. No more hiding from the inevitable, especially since Wilby is having to intervene on my behalf. Time to be the big girl I am and deal with him.

"Summer, I have to make a call. Meet you down at our spot?" I ask.

"Sure, I have to go get changed and get my mat. See you there." She waves.

I take a steadying breath and dial my dad. He answers immediately.

"Silvie," he growls, frustration dripping from my name. "I have been trying to call you."

"I'm aware. What's going on?" I ask, fighting back, rolling my eyes.

"Things are escalating here," he says hesitantly, his anger dimming. "Your sister...is going to marry Tyler."

"I know. I heard."

"You know?" he barks out, once again pissed off. "And you're doing nothing? What the hell, Silverlyn! You have to fix this. Come back to New York, right now. Fix this! You are supposed to run this company. You know this. If your sister gets control, she's going to put Tyler in there. It's bad enough he works here at all. I won't have him in a position of power."

That sounds like a nightmare and a half. I shudder at the thought of Tyler sitting at my desk in my office.

"Dad, you have to trust me. I'm fixing this. I need you to just wait it out," I tell him calmly. "When have I ever let you down?"

That's the truth. I've poured my heart and soul into our company. There's no way I'll let it crash and burn in the final hour. He knows this.

He breathes heavily, obviously worked up. And I can't blame him.

"Okay," he finally says. "But hurry."

I'm doing my best.

cal

. . .

WILBY'S PACING when he opens the door to his room at the B&B. He's got a phone in one hand and a coffee in the other, and he looks agitated. Relief washes over his face when he sees me. He motions for me to come in.

"Okay, I have an appointment, sir. Yes, I'll keep you updated," he says as he rolls his eyes.

He hangs up and sets his phone down on the table where his laptop is open. "That was Silvie's father. And no, I won't be keeping him updated. He's scary as hell, so I have to lie to him. But my allegiance will always be to Silverlyn."

This comforts me for some reason. I can see it written all over Wilby's face. He'll run through fire for her. I'm beginning to realize she has that effect on people.

"As it should." I snort and shove my hands in my pockets, noticing his suitcase is packed up. "Are you leaving?"

He shakes his head. "Not the island. But the B&B is all booked up. I have to find another place to stay."

"Tourist season." I nod. "This place gets pretty booked up."

"This brings me to something we need to discuss," he says. "Hear me out."

"Okay," I say hesitantly. I'm not sure where he's going with this.

"I need a place to stay. And Birdie has her guest room," he says, stacking a few things on the table he's working at.

I wait for him to continue.

"I need to stay at Birdie's. Which means Silvie needs to move in with you," he says, waiting for me to react.

A flutter of panic takes flight in my stomach. Suddenly, this whole thing is all-too real. And fast. I agreed to it, and have every intention of helping her, but it's now creeping into my personal life. Literally. But I'll be marrying her and this is an inevitable step.

"I don't have a guest room," I tell him, with wide eyes.

My brain quickly catalogues what it would look like to have the gorgeous woman in my home. Sitting on my sofa, bare feet near me. Half-dressed in my kitchen making coffee. Dripping and dressed only in a towel as she exits the bathroom.

This is going to be difficult.

How do I refrain from pinning her to every surface, kissing her until she's whimpering my name?

"It doesn't matter," Wilby says quickly, stealing me from my wicked thoughts, as he motions for me to sit at the table with him. "Paparazzi could show up at any time. And if the attorneys handling the trust believe this is not a legitimate marriage, Silvie will not get her company. It will all be for nothing. You have to make it look legit, my friend."

Before I can respond, there's a knock at the door. He opens it, and a woman steps into the room. She has a measuring tape and a clipboard. Wilby's already moving onto the next task. This guy is efficient as hell.

"Cal," Wilby says, "this is Denise. She's here to measure you."

Denise smiles warmly. "You ready?"

"I think so," I say, though that feels optimistic.

This is happening at warped speed. All I can do is strap in and go along for the wild ride.

Silvie's worth it.

That settles my brain a bit because it's the truth.

Denise circles me, tape ready. "I was going to have linen pants and a button-down shirt. Maybe a light jacket. But," she adds, glancing at Wilby for approval, "I'll need his full measurements for future events we'll need to dress him for."

Future events? I freeze and glance at Wilby, but he's already crossing things off what looks like a massive to-do list on his computer.

"Future events?" I repeat, voice hoarse.

Wilby nods like this is obvious. "Galas. Dinners. Board things. Charity stuff."

It's all temporary, remember? Wilby implores me with that silent message. I nod, understanding the unspoken words.

Denise keeps measuring, unfazed. "We like to have everything on file."

My chest tightens. I didn't realize we'd be doing events. And where?

"Yes, you will look powerful in a suit," she says. "Sleeve length."

She measures my arm while my brain spirals.

This is more than paperwork. This is showing up. Standing beside her. Being seen as her husband. Silverlyn Montclair's husband.

I take a slow, calming breath so I don't hyperventilate. I wish Silvie were here with us. She has a calming effect on my soul.

Wilby winces at something on his list and comes back to our conversation. "Eventually, Cal, you're going to have go to New York."

My stomach drops. I can't go to New York. Panic claws its way up my esophagus. This woman flitting around me like an annoying fly is only adding to the anxiety.

"To meet her parents," Wilby adds and winces. "I'm so sorry about that by the way. Her mom is actually a terrible person."

This jolts me from my mini panic attack as the urge to protect Silvie grounds me.

"That bad?" I ask, frowning.

"She's the type of person who takes pleasure in being mean to Silvie," he says. "Her dad, though, isn't a bad guy."

Mean to Silvie? What? I don't like that. At all. If her mom is making trouble, that's not going to go over well with me.

"He's just," Wilby continues, searching for the word, "hella intimidating."

Denise finishes measuring and steps back. "All set."

I nod, barely hearing her.

New York. Her parents. Events. Galas. A life that isn't mine. Away from Coconut Beach, my safe space. The place I came back to and thought I'd never leave. I didn't think this through.

I thought I was agreeing to be her husband on paper.

I didn't realize I was agreeing to step into her world.

Wilby claps me on the shoulder. "You'll be great."

I force a smile.

Because backing out was never really an option.

Somehow, terrifying as it is, the idea of standing beside her through all of it doesn't feel wrong. It feels necessary. For her sake. To protect her.

Wilby glances at his list on his computer. "We need to get temporary rings. We can't have anyone seeing either of you buying them."

"I already have the rings covered," I tell him.

Wilby's eyebrow hikes up in surprise. "Really?"

I nod. "They're coming today. Nothing to get excited about. Just temporary fake ones I ordered."

"Okay," he says, letting loose a long breath of air. "Did not have that on my bingo card. You are on it, Cal."

I shrug. "I just figured that was my job."

As husband. I'm going to be her husband. My mind is beginning to latch onto everything that entails. It's a lot. I suppose that's one of the downsides of marrying a billionaire.

"Another thing," Wilby says, cutting his eyes my way. "I saw in our report that your father is from New York and was here in Coconut Beach on business when he met your mom."

My stomach twists uncomfortably. "Yeah, so?"

"Do you know who he is?" he asks.

"I don't think that's relevant. It's not a big deal," I say firmly.

He stares at me for a second, then nods. "Okay, sorry."

I stare for a moment. "Do you know?"

He shakes his head. "I could probably find out, though."

I shake my head. "That's okay. I'm good."

He's watching me now, curious instead of investigative. "Okay."

The room goes quiet. Too quiet.

There's a knock at the door, and Wilby opens it to Silvie standing there in a yellow sundress, looking like pure sunshine. The relief I feel at seeing her nearly has me sagging. I inhale her sweet scent, the smell of her a soothing balm to my soul.

"Hi," she says, taking in both of us and our serious tones.

Wilby glances at me, smirks, and blurts out, "Did you know that Cal has money?"

I scoff and give Wilby a dirty look. This dude is a menace. He's changing the subject and giving me shit.

She smiles then, slow and warm. "There's a lot I don't know about you, hot fiancé."

I groan. "Don't call me that."

"I'm going to find out anyway," she says to me in a teasing voice, eyes twinkling. "You can tell me all of your dark secrets."

I shoot Wilby a nervous look, and he shakes his head slightly as if to tell me he didn't tell her what we were talking about earlier.

She reaches for my hand like it's natural. Like this marriage is already ours.

"Let's go on a date tonight," she says. "A pretend date. You can tell me all of your secrets."

My chest tightens at the thought of taking her out. "Okay."

Wilby darts his gaze between us and then blurts, "I have to go to a meeting. I'll be back."

This has my heart skipping a few beats, eager to be alone with her. Maybe all the chaos overtaking my brain will leave with Wilby.

"Bye," Silvie calls out to him.

He grabs his bag and heads for the door, muttering something about needing air and therapy.

She bites her lip and admits. "I'm nervous for the wedding."

"That makes two of us."

"Do we kiss?" she asks quietly. "I've never kissed you. What if it's weird?"

The question lands between us, fragile and honest, and something in my chest gives way.

Nothing about "kissing" and "Silvie" could ever be weird. That much I know for a fact. She's sweet and a damn knockout. It'd be my honor to prove just how "not weird" kissing her can be.

I step closer before I can talk myself out of it. Close enough that I can feel her warmth, see the way her breath stutters just a little. I don't rush. I lift one hand to her waist, steady and sure, like I've done it a hundred times in another life. With my other hand, I tilt her chin up so she's looking at me.

Her eyes search mine. Trusting. Nervous. Wanting.

Then I dip my lips to hers and kiss her.

It starts slow. A brush of lips, barely there, like I'm asking permission with my mouth. She inhales softly, and when she leans into me, that's all I need. The kiss deepens, unhurried but certain, heat building in a way that makes my pulse kick hard.

She tastes like coffee and sugar and something that's entirely her. Her hand slides to my shirt, fingers curling around the material like she's anchoring herself. I tighten my grip at her waist without even thinking about it.

It doesn't feel strange or foreign, like I'm kissing a stranger I just met. No, it feels a little like coming home, like every moment we've had up until this point has brought us to this kiss. And it's one I won't ever forget. Nothing about Silvie is forgettable. She makes every moment feel special and fun.

I pull back just enough to rest my forehead against hers, our breaths tangled, my thumb brushing slowly along her jaw.

"Now you know," I say, my voice lower than I expect.

Her eyes are bright, lips flushed, breath unsteady in the best way.

"Yeah," she whispers. "I do."

And I know, right then, that pretending this is fake is going to be the hardest thing I've ever done. Nothing feels fake about this at all. And I'm ready to risk it all for her.

———

I knock on Birdie's door the evening of our date. Which is a fake date, because this is a fake relationship, even though I'm nervous as hell after that kiss. Damn. That kiss was everything. There wasn't anything fake about that kiss.

Silvie opens the door and pauses, a grin telling me she's been informed of the plan.

"So," she says. "Apparently, I'm moving in with you."

I laugh, slightly caught off guard. "Yeah, Wilby has a way of making things happen when he wants to."

"I've never moved in with someone on the first date," she adds. "Feels bold."

"I've never lived with a woman other than my mother, so there's that," I say with a small chuckle. "It'll be a first for me."

Her humor morphs into concern. "Are you sure you're okay with this, Cal?" she says, searching my face.

There's a lot I'm not okay with about this—galas and her mom and New York—but what I am okay with is her. If that stuff comes along with it, so be it. As long as she benefits in the end, it'll be worth all the headache.

Silvie deserves good things and I want to help deliver them to her.

"Yeah," I say with a smile. "Of course, happy to help. Plus, we're not that far away. Still close to Birdie and now Wilby. Makes sense."

She studies my face for a second and says, "Okay, let me get my things."

After we grab all her things, which isn't much, we head to my place. She steps in slowly, taking it all in. It's not much different from Birdie's house, just not as cozy. Silvie sweeps her gaze over the worn but comfy couch. The way everything has a place. She runs her fingers along the back of a chair and glances out the window at the darkening sky. A storm's coming in.

"This place feels like you," she says.

"Is that good or bad?" I ask.

I'm shocked at how much her approval means to me.

"It's comfortable," she says. "Like you know who you are, and it fits your vibe. Solid, steady, sturdy, and home."

Interesting.

"I only have one bed. I'll be taking the couch," I inform her.

She frowns and looks at me like she doesn't like that plan.

I show her the guest room with wall-to-wall bookshelves and my desk in the center. She examines all of my books, running her fingertips over the spines, reading the titles.

She stops short when she sees the framed photos on the wall of me in high school and during college. Surf shots. When I was a lot younger, leaner and had longer hair. A few newspaper clippings are tucked into the frame corners, headlines faded but still readable.

She turns slowly and grins. "Well, it turns out you do have a few secrets."

I lean against the door frame, arms crossed. "Not really. I surfed and did some competitions to pay for school."

She points at one photo. "You look... intense."

"I was," I say. "I needed that prize money. I surfed pretty hard for several years."

"I didn't realize you competed," she says, stepping closer. "Like seriously competed."

I shrug a shoulder. "It was a long time ago."

"Cal," she says, reading one of the clippings. "Regional finals, sponsorship offers." Her eyes flick back to me. "You were a big deal."

I hesitate. "Didn't know it mattered."

She studies my face, hers softer now. "Of course it's a big deal. I want to know everything about you."

Her words soften parts of me I didn't even know were hard. I like that she wants to know things about me. The feeling is mutual.

"It feels like another life," I say softly. "It was a means to something that I thought I wanted. Then it wasn't."

She nods as if she understands.

"Yeah," I murmur. "I live a different life now."

She's quiet for a second. Then she smiles, gentle and real. "That's kind of a big secret, Cal."

I laugh under my breath. "Wait until you hear the rest of them."

She arches a brow. "Oh yeah?"

"Come on," I say. "I'm cooking you dinner. Then we're going to sit and watch the storm roll in and tell each other all our secrets."

Only there's some I won't be telling her.

She grins. "I can't wait. Apparently, you've got layers."

She has no idea.

───────

So much laughter.

My jaw hurts. Not from the savory steaks I grilled. No, from all the laughs I've had with Silvie. She's fun. While I cooked, she insisted on helping, and she was sort of clumsy, unsure of where anything was located. It made for a humorous affair.

Thunder rattles all the windows in the bungalow. There's an eagerness in Silvie's eyes that has me abandoning kitchen cleanup after dinner to take her onto the porch. We sit side by side on my porch swing, close enough our thighs touch.

"I'll learn my way around your house soon," she says, turning slightly to smile at me. "I love the smell of a storm."

I inhale the ozone scent, but her sweetness quickly overtakes it. When she shivers, I slide my arm over the back of the porch swing and pull her to my side. We sit quietly as the wind whistles and the thunder rumbles. Each time I push the swing forward, she kicks her bare feet out toward the edge of the porch, letting the raindrops speckle the tops of them.

What was supposed to be a "secrets confessional" turns into a charged, intimate moment between us while we enjoy the sounds of the storm. Silvie, having had enough of getting her feet wet, turns more toward me, and hooks her legs over my thigh.

Nothing about this feels fake.

My heart stammers in my chest as I toy with a silky strand of her hair.

"Cal," she whispers, barely carrying over the sound of the storm.

"Hmm."

"I have a secret."

I turn to smell her hair. God, she smells good. "Yeah? Tell me."

"I really like this. You."

"Silvie?"

"Yes?"

"I have a secret too," I murmur.

She giggles, already reading my mind. "Oh, do you now? What is it?"

"I like this. And I really like you, too."

The most difficult thing about this entire fake marriage with Silvie is that I'm going to have to not fall in love with her.

She's not making it easy.

silvie

. . .

"I CAN TAKE THE COUCH," *I say, heat flooding my cheeks. I feel like a jerk stealing his bed from him. "It's fine, Cal."*

He grunts and shakes his head. "No. Get your rest. I'll be fine."

Everything about him is attractive—his smile, his body, his smell—but it's his heart that's the most handsome part about him. I feel cherished and taken care of in his presence. Before I can stop myself, I stand on my toes and kiss him. Again.

This time, it's more familiar. I drag my nails through the hair at his nape, loving how he shivers at my touch. Our kiss goes from sweet to not-so-sweet in three seconds' flat. But, before he can scoop me up and take me to bed, he pulls away, slightly shaking his head.

"Sleep," he murmurs, leaning his forehead against mine. "If you don't, I'm going to do something we'll both regret."

I highly doubt that.

His rejection stings, but I respect his boundaries.

"Goodnight, hot fiancé."

"Night, future wifey."

I wake up before my alarm, the memories of last night clinging to me like a second skin. I ached to have him join me in the bed, but this morning, I'm sort of glad he didn't. This whole fake wedding thing is confusing. It's easy to get swept up in the lie of it. If I'm not careful, I'll fall for the man which will hurt way worse than the betrayal of what Tyler did to me.

Losing Cal feels catastrophic.

And I don't like feeling so vulnerable.

The waves crashing out the window and the early morning ocean breeze brush across my skin. For a moment, I just lie here, staring at the ceiling fan as it turns slowly and lazily above me. The air is cool, drifting in through the window, the beachy scent making me feel at home. And it dawns on me, aside from the oddness of the situation I'm in with Cal, I feel at peace.

He's safe.

Steady.

And I'm grateful that it's him on this marriage journey with me because I can actually trust him.

Today's my wedding day. My second wedding day. A shiver of anticipation ripples through me, but there's no panic and nausea. No urge to run off to a desert or swamp to hide. Just a quiet peace.

Huh. Strange. I thought maybe all wedding days felt like the previous one. Today feels pretty great.

It's a fake wedding, and that could be why. But I don't think that's it. I feel like anything with Cal feels peaceful. I've never felt chaos with him. He isn't Tyler, and he never will be.

I sit up and swing my feet to the floor. The wood is cool under my feet. Somewhere down the hall, I feel his presence. Cal. He took the couch and refused to let me take it, even though it made sense that I sleep there. I'm smaller.

I open the door and see Cal moving around shirtless, in shorts, and his feet bare. He has a mug and presses it to his lips as he leans against the counter. His large frame is comical in such a small space. His tattoos span over his chest and arms, something I've traced in my head several times. My fingers twitch at the thought of actually touching them.

"Good morning," I murmur, feeling slightly shy in his half-naked presence.

He watches me walk toward him, a smile on his handsome face, as if he's been waiting for me. "You sleep okay?"

"Yeah," I say. "You?"

He shrugs. "Enough. I've been up since four."

"I feel bad taking your bed," I admit. "I'm taking the couch tonight. I insist."

He slides a mug across the counter toward me. Coffee and cream. Exactly how I like it. I reach for it and wrap my hands around it, letting the warmth sink in. I inhale its aroma and sigh. "Thank you."

"No way you're taking the couch, Silvie."

I pin him with a narrowed stare. "We'll see, hot fiancé."

Heated tension crackles between us. Every day, it multiplies. Like he's gravity, I feel myself being pulled into his orbit.

"So, today we're graduating to hot husband?" He playfully rolls his eyes.

"That's the plan. Are you still on board?" I ask, nervous that he might be having second thoughts.

Yesterday, after our first kiss, we picked up our marriage license. We were able to waive the out-of-state three-day waiting period thanks to Wilby's maneuvering. I still have no idea how he managed that, but he made it happen.

"Oh, I'm on board. Just making sure you're not going to be a runaway bride again," Cal teases.

Even though he's joking, I sense a thread of unease in his words. Cal's the kind of guy women run to, not away from. He's magnetic and incredibly good looking. And soon, he'll be mine.

Fake mine, but still mine.

"No, not this time," I assure him. "Thanks again for doing this." My eyes wander up his arms, and I mentally trace the muscles he has on top of muscles. A chiseled body from a life of working and surfing. Not one that sees the gym, but one that lives an active life.

"Come here," he says as he sets his mug down and pulls me to his side. He presses his head into my head. He's warm, steady, and solid. I sigh and lean into him, breathing him in.

Our second kiss was even better than the first. How will the third, fourth, and fifth one feel?

"Are you nervous?" I ask.

He chuckles. "No. Are you?"

I shrug. "Not really."

He holds me there in his kitchen, and somehow, being in his arms gives me peace, comfort, and a feeling I haven't had with anyone... *ever*.

A knock on the door breaks us apart, and he goes over and opens it. Birdie says, "Yoohoo, good morning, love birds."

She's a mess but I'm glad to see her.

"Good morning," I say as I give her a hug, ignoring the love birds comment.

"Big day," she says, not dramatic, not teasing. Just factual.

I nod. "Yeah, I'm glad you're here for this one."

She studies my face, her eyes softening. "How do you feel, sugar?"

I consider her question honestly. Before, I would offer the typical answer, "I'm fine." That was my answer to everything because I felt like I couldn't be anything other than fine. But being here in Coconut Beach with people who don't have an agenda for me, I can be real. I can be me. And right now, I feel good.

"Calm," I say, surprised that it's true. "Strangely, calm."

Cal winks at me and warmth pools in my gut.

Birdie's smile deepens. "That's usually when you know you're doing the right thing."

Before I can ask where he is, Wilby shows up, carrying two garment bags. He's already dressed and put together, as if this is another morning for him. Wilby loves events and getting dressed up. He lives for weddings and planning events.

"Good morning. I brought the dress and suit," he says as he holds them up proudly. "They made it in the nick of time."

"I haven't even seen the dress yet," I muse. "But I know which one you picked."

"Optics are everything, Silverlyn. We need the photos to be perfect. We have to sell this as a real wedding," he says as he lays it over the couch.

The calmness falters as I mentally prepare myself for the realness of what's coming.

"You still good?" he asks Cal.

Cal nods. "Yes."

I long for that hug Cal and I were having when we were interrupted. I wish I could go back into his arms and just stay there right now. There's something grounding and relaxing about Cal.

Wilby heads over to the coffee pot and pours himself a cup. "I need this. Also, your dinosaur chased me over here. What is wrong with that thing?"

I frown. "Iggy?"

"Yeah, the monster that lives in the bushes in front of Birdie's. That's the one." He shudders. "Unless it has a whole monster family I don't know about."

"I don't think Iggy likes men," I muse.

He lifts an eyebrow. "He's a very rude iguana. Sexist."

"He's just misunderstood," I say. "You just need to bring him a treat or something."

"You have truly lost your mind," Wilby says. "I'm not bringing him a treat."

I shrug. "I'm just saying. That's the way to your heart. Maybe it's the way to his, too."

Birdie laughs and goes back to fussing with the little bouquet she brought me. It's beautiful with purple flowers and white daisies.

Wilby sips his coffee and glances to where Cal has gone back to his room to get ready. Then he says, "Girl."

189

I brace instinctively. "Yes?"

"Your husband is the only family member you get to choose."

The words hit harder than I expected. They drop straight into my chest and sit there, heavy and undeniable.

Wilby continues, still casual, still scrolling his phone like he didn't just crack something open inside me. "This time, you're not picking a loser."

I huff out a breath. "Pretend husband. And yes, Cal is great for doing this."

Cal is so far from a loser, it's not funny. He's amazing. Funny, kind, strong, protective, and so freaking hot. I could go on and on, but that's just the tip of the iceberg.

Wilby looks up again, eyes sharp now. "We'll see about the pretend part."

There's a smirk on his face that says he knows exactly what he's doing. I open my mouth to argue, then close it. Because part of me doesn't want to.

"I'm still your boss, you know."

He scoffs. "We know who gets the work done. And you know I'm still your bestie."

I grin. I finish my coffee and set my cup in the sink. "All right, let's get ready."

I glance at Birdie, and she meets my eyes and smiles. I'm so glad she's here. It feels right to be here with her. I think about what Wilby said.

The only family member you get to choose is your husband.

But I am lucky that I've gotten to choose Birdie and Wilby. Really lucky. I wish my dad were here. I wish I could tell him about the marriage, but, I can't. I don't know where he stands on everything, and I have to focus on the company. This is for work. And also, if Dad were involved, he'd have my mother and Belladonna pulled in too, and I don't want either of them anywhere near Coconut Beach.

This feels like a safe space for me, and they don't belong.

Birdie and I decide to go to her house to get ready. We gather up everything. Wilby agrees to stay with Cal, work, and help make sure everything is ready to go.

Once back at her place, Birdie gingerly pins my hair back, smooths it, and helps me get it into beachy waves, which feel unnecessary since my hair has been defaulting to curls since coming to Coconut Beach and letting it go natural. It's wavy and has turned even blonder in the sun. My hair looks simple and beautiful when I finally look in the mirror. I feel...like me.

As she helps me with my makeup, Birdie smiles, happy, proud tears in her eyes. "I always dreamed of your wedding day. And I know you said this is just to save the company, but to me, sugar, it feels like a good day."

And she's right. It feels like a really good day.

When she's done, she steps back and nods once. "Perfect. You are stunning."

I look at myself, and I recognize myself this time. My makeup is light, my sun-kissed skin glows, I'm smiling. On my wedding day to Tyler, I felt and looked cold. Sterile. Professional. Unhappy. And today I look like me.

I step into my satin wedding dress, a mock replica of Carolyn Bessette Kennedy's wedding dress for JFK Jr. I've always loved this dress. It's shorter, satin, simple, and me. The ostentatious dress my mother picked, which required a designer's special hook to remove all the buttons, was never for me. In fact, who thought of something like that and thought that was a good idea? Who has an hour to remove a dress at the end of the night? Who wants to spend time doing that?

I wonder about what my mother would think of all of this. I know she'd never approve of Cal. She wouldn't like his job, his tattoos, and she definitely wouldn't like how he'd never let anyone treat me badly slide. He wouldn't tolerate any disrespect, period. And I love that about Cal. He just is who he is. She'd try to assume he's a bartender and that would be less than for this family. She'd never care that I saw on his diplomas he graduated Cum Laude at the top of his class at NYU. That wouldn't matter. She'd only care about how he'd fit into her society-focused world. And he wouldn't. Because Cal is a Coconut Beach guy. He is a man who cares for his mom and his friends. He's the best. And he would never fit in that cold and sterile world. I wouldn't want him to.

I grab my phone and text Wilby.

> Me: Change of plans. We're moving the wedding to Carly's house. We can go to the beach first and take pictures. I'm not having Cal's mom miss this.

> Wilby: Let me make some calls.

Outside, the sky is blushing pink and gold. The beach is quiet, waves lapping up on the shore. A light breeze blows my hair as I stand and wait for Cal. A thought pulses through me that maybe he's the runaway groom this time.

But he's already there. He's down by the water, in his white pants and white shirt. He looks so good. He turns when he hears us, and something in his expression shifts when he sees me. His shoulders relax, and his mouth curves into a smile.

"We're not getting married here," I tell him, breathless.

"Uh...what?" he asks, confused.

I shake my head. "We're just taking photos. Then we're moving it to your mom's house. I can't let her miss this. Don't worry, I've already texted her. She's nervous about this many people, but she is excited. She's getting ready."

His eyes soften. "I love that. Thank you."

"Of course. Thank you, Cal. For doing this."

His hand brushes mine, tentative, like he's asking permission to hold my hand even though we're already here. I lace my fingers through his, grounding myself in him. Something that isn't hard to do. Cal is steady and calm.

Birdie clears her throat and steps into place with Wilby as the photographer snaps photos.

We pretend to do a ceremony, and at the end, Cal gazes into my eyes and cups my chin, pulling me in for a soft and deep kiss.

The sun crests the horizon as we kiss, warm light spilling over us like a blessing. The kiss itself is slow, intentional. Not rushed. Not performative. Real.

His lips command mine, taking his time, cupping my jaw. I lean into him, my arms around his waist.

As we pull back, Birdie wipes at her eyes.

Wilby watches us closely with amusement. "That," he murmurs to Birdie, "doesn't look fake."

I grin at Cal, his eyes on mine. He tips his forehead to mine. I close my eyes and breathe him in. Photos snap.

I am no longer performing for a photographer. I'm lost in him. Until they clear their throat. We get more pictures and then load up and ride to Carly's.

Jonah got the message from Cal and Wilby, and he's sitting on Carly's back porch steps when we arrive. He's wearing a button-down shirt tucked into his pants. His beard is trimmed, and it looks like he got a haircut.

I make my way to him and he stands, his kind eyes on mine. "Jonah Black. You clean up well and are the most handsome man here."

He chuckles and Wilby clears his throat and nudges Cal. "Looks like you have competition."

Cal snorts and claps Jonah on the back. "Hey, Jonah."

I love seeing Cal and Jonah together. They may not be related by blood, but they are so sweet together the way they show up for each other.

I make my way inside and find Carly in the hall bathroom, fighting with a curling iron. She sees me and looks relieved. "Hi, Silvie."

"Can I?" I ask, motioning to the curling iron.

She hands it to me and relaxes. "Thank you."

"It's always easier when someone else does it," I say softly as I curl her hair into long waves that match mine.

"Beautiful," I murmur, meeting her eyes in the mirror.

"Thank you for everything. I've felt more like myself with you around. You're so good for my son."

You're so good for my son.

But am I? Because this isn't real. And then it makes me feel guilty that when this is over, Carly will be hurt, too. I shake the thought out of my head and focus on today. Today. Today with me and Cal. And including Carly.

"Are you ready?" I ask.

She nods, eyes twinkling with excitement. "Are *you* ready?"

I laugh. "I am. We took photos at the beach. But now it's time for the ceremony."

We head out to the living room, where Birdie is officiating, and Jonah, Cal, and Wilby are waiting.

Cal's mouth turns up when he sees us. I walk to him, and he takes my hands. The ceremony is simple. Nothing exaggerated. And it's fast.

When Cal says his vows, his voice is steady, and his eyes never leave mine.

When I say mine, I look at his eyes, and my heart feels like it's going to beat out of my chest.

Birdie smiles and pronounces us man and wife.

Jonah claps Cal on the back. Carly wipes her eyes, smiling bigger than I've ever seen her smile.

Man and wife. So strange, yet so right. How can this be? For the first time in a long time, I'm not paralyzed with anxiety and worry. It feels like hope.

"You may kiss your bride," Birdie says.

Cal's eyes never leave mine as he leans in, lips brushing mine, and a surge bursts through me. His kiss is warm and grounding, confident in a way that makes my panties wet and my knees go soft. One hand settles at my waist, pulling me closer like this is exactly where we belong.

I moan softly into his mouth, and he deepens the kiss just enough to make my heart flutter. It isn't rushed or showy. It's tender, as if he knows this moment matters to us. And it also feels like he's memorizing me, the way he lingers, soft and firm all at once, and I kiss him back, just as passionately.

Because I do love kissing Cal. And standing here right now, being married to him feels impossibly right. Like it's the beginning of something.

cal

. . .

I CAN'T REMEMBER the last time I saw my mom this happy and excited. She's not had people at her house in years. And never this many people at one time. Granted, most of these people are like family to her, except for Wilby and Silvie. But she's becoming Silvie's biggest fan. Next to me. I'm definitely Silvie's biggest fan. Whether she knows it or not. I know she's doing this for me, and that makes me even more grateful. And it also feels like progress.

Laughter spills out of the living room as I follow Mom and Silvie to the kitchen. She holds up a cake that she's made for us.

"Oh, Carly! It's beautiful!" Silvie exclaims, looking surprised and emotional. "You didn't have to do that."

"Oh, I wanted to," Mom says sheepishly.

"Mom, that is so nice," I add, looking at the simple triple-layer cake that she decorated to perfection. My mom has always been a great baker, and she has made cakes for every birthday or any other special occasion she can think of. It makes sense that she made us a wedding cake. I bet this made her so happy.

"I knew you'd want your favorite cake. And when I spoke with Wilby, he said Silvie loves a classic wedding cake, too. So, I hope you both love it."

"We do," I say as I take the cake from her and set it on the table.

"It looks so good," Silvie says, sighing. "I love cake."

"I can't believe you changed your wedding to my house," she says. "I woke up and checked my phone and was so happy. I thought you'd both come by, but this...this was so nice."

Silvie smiles, "Of course. I'm glad we were able to do it this way."

We cut the cake, set it on plates, and carry it to the living room, where everyone enjoys it for breakfast. Fitting for this day that makes no sense and every bit of sense, somehow at the same time.

"Carly, this is delicious," Birdie says as she takes another bite.

We drag chairs into a loose circle in Mom's small living room, except there aren't enough. Birdie takes one and Carly perches on the couch next to Jonah and Wilby.

Without thinking, I gently pull Silvie into me, and she sits on my lap in the chair.

She pauses for half a second, then settles onto my lap like it's the most normal thing in the world. She fits perfectly there, and my hand comes around to hold her, without thinking.

I'm strangely content. I know this is all fake, but it feels real. The crazy thing is I'm not panicking. Up until now, the idea of marriage has seemed a foreign concept to me. And, yet here I am. Married to the most beautiful woman I know.

She grins at me and takes a bite of her cake, as if this is perfectly natural. I can't believe she surprised me and moved the wedding here to my mom's. That meant everything to her and to me as well. Mom has already made a lot of strides since Silvie arrived. That one small thing meant everything.

Jonah's brows lift at me as he takes a bite of his cake.

My mom shrugs and smiles as if this is the greatest match-making endeavor ever. "No more chairs."

Birdie agrees. "Perfect fake marriage already."

Everyone talks at once, overlapping stories and teasing. My

mom and Birdie talk about the books overflowing on Mom's shelves. Birdie tells her she's missed her, and I notice my mom's eyes get misty.

Silvie keeps everyone laughing, and her body is relaxed against mine. She's glowing and happy. And ridiculously sexy in that wedding dress. I almost have to shove my hands into my pockets to keep myself from tracing the thin spaghetti straps on the back of the dress.

Nothing is staged or fake about how she's acting right now. She's so relaxed around my mom, Jonah, Birdie, and Wilby.

Wilby pulls out his phone and snaps a few pictures of us. He's subtle about it, but I see every shot, clocking it immediately. He seems happy for us. But I know that this is all part of the plan. Make it look real. Save the company. And I get it. I'd want someone to help me, too.

Silvie's too busy laughing at something Mom says, her hand braced on my shoulder, her body loose and happy. Wilby catches my eye and lifts his phone and takes more photos. He looks part proud friend, part working assistant.

After our cake and coffee, Wilby straightens and says, "I have to head out."

Silvie blinks as if she's back to reality. "Already?"

"Yeah," he says. "I'm going to file the certificate. Make it official before Tyler and your sister beat us to it."

"Oh, right," she agrees.

She steps forward and wraps Wilby in a hug. He stiffens at first, then relaxes into it, and pats her back gently. She whispers something to him.

He nods. "Anytime."

He shakes my hand and says, "Congratulations, Cal."

"Thanks," I say.

When he leaves, Birdie claps her hands together. "All right. What now?"

I glance at Silvie. "What do you want to do? Technically, this is our honeymoon time."

She considers it, then smiles slowly and mischievously. "I want to go to Chaos and drink."

Jonah gives us a look and a nod and quietly ducks out the back door. And that's Jonah. Never misses an important occasion but is a man of few words.

We head down to Cocktails & Chao. It might be just her and me having drinks.

I hold her hand as we drive to Chaos and park the truck behind it like I usually do. I come around and help her out. When she steps out of the truck, I pull her to me and kiss her forehead. "You look so beautiful," I murmur.

"You look pretty amazing yourself, hot husband."

And hearing the word "husband" on her lips doesn't sound so bad. I'll even allow the ridiculous hot part.

The second we round the corner and step into the bar, the place explodes with cheering and "Congratulations!"

Cheering, clapping, music, and someone whistles. There's a white-and-silver banner strung above the bar that reads "Just Married."

Flowers are on the table everywhere. Marina and Jonah stand behind the bar. Marina looks like she's been planning this all day and is excited for us to finally show up. Locals I recognize fill the room, grinning and raising glasses.

Silvie freezes beside me, fingers tightening in mine. Wilby comes in behind us.

"Is this okay?" she whispers.

"They all wanted to celebrate you both," Wilby says. "Figured it was alright. It'll probably get leaked but at this point, it's okay. I wanted the wedding to be official so that you get married before they do. Now, it doesn't really matter who knows."

Silvie presses herself into me, and I wrap an arm around her and rest my hand on her lower back. It seems to steady her.

"You okay?" I murmur.

She nods. "I just didn't expect this. It's so nice."

I nod in agreement. "It is. Where it all started."

Drinks appear in front of us, and food follows. Summer hands Silvie a flower and tucks it into her hair. Music shifts into something warm and familiar. It's an Asher Walker song and it's one of my favorites.

We eat and drink. So many laughs and stories told. I never leave her side. My hand stays on her, on her lower back. Holding her hand. At her waist. Making sure she's okay and I pass her water in between drinks. We both eat and have snacks laid out.

When a song comes on that I like, I ask her to dance. She pulls me with her to the floor and wraps her arms around my neck, pulling me close. And God, I like it. She feels so good. So right. If fake is all I ever get with her, it'll hurt. But it's better than having nothing.

Every time our eyes meet as we dance, she smiles and leans in closer. "Thanks for today, Cal. It's been a good one so far."

"Yeah, it has."

She dances with Mia, Summer, and Wendy, another local and friend. People toast us and someone buys us all a round. Someone insists on taking photos. Wilby takes more pictures, and they're mostly candid shots.

Silvie looks so damn happy. From the outside, it would be hard to tell this is fake. People in Coconut Beach have to be so confused. They're all just going with it, though.

Before we know it, we've danced the day away, and the sun is starting to set. We've both drunk a lot, she more than I. I mostly can't keep my eyes off her and make sure she's staying hydrated.

It's time to head out, and Silvie leans into me as we walk.

"I'm tipsy," she announces.

"I know." I smile.

"But I'm happy, though," she adds. "I have a hot, hot husband. Like I never thought I'd seen a guy as beautiful as you when I first saw you. And here you are as my husband now. How did I get a guy like you?"

Is she for real right now? She thinks she got me? No, I got her.

"I think I'm the one who got lucky here," I remind her.

We get dropped off at my house, kick our shoes off, and collapse on the bed without even turning off the lamps. It's early, but we've partied all day. Silvie curls into my side and rests her head on my chest.

"I wish you were really my husband," she whispers as she drifts off to sleep.

I close my eyes to hear that. Me too.

I lie there for a while, listening to her breathe, feeling the weight of what we've done settle into the new reality we are living in.

She's here in my arms. And for now, that's enough.

———

I sleep better than I have in years. Even after a day of drinking, that was a ton of fun. Our wedding day. It's crazy to think we're married.

Silvie is curled into my side, one arm draped over my chest, her leg thrown over mine, warm and grounding. My cock is rock hard and painful as it's been every day since I met her. And I need to probably go shower and do something about that.

I don't want to move and risk waking her, so I just lie here, listening to her breathe.

She sighs softly and tucks her face into my chest, and my palm spreads, holding her, feeling protective of her without even giving it a thought.

Yeah. This is dangerous.

Eventually, the light shifts, and I know the sun is about ready to come up. She stirs and blinks awake.

"Morning," I murmur.

She hums instead of answering, closing her eyes, her mouth

curving into a lazy smile. Then she blinks her eyes open again and freezes.

"Oh," she says.

"Good oh or bad oh?" I ask curiously.

She lifts her head just enough to look at me, her hair wild, face soft. "Good oh. I thought I was just dreaming. It turns out you're real."

Relief floods me. I want to bring up what she said last night. I want to ask her if she wants to be real with me. I want to so badly. But something in me says not to push it.

She smiles again. "I slept really, really good."

"Me, too."

"No, you don't understand. Something about you is just so calming to me," she explains.

I understand this completely.

We don't rush to get up, and we linger, me tracing her shoulder, her holding me, not addressing the elephant in the room, which is my hard, throbbing cock that I'm desperately trying not to think about.

Eventually, she groans. "If we don't get up now, we'll miss the sunrise." She sits up and then says, "Want to help me out of my dress? This time, you don't have to rip it."

I laugh and help her unzip her dress.

She turns and grabs clothes. "I'll be ready in ten! We have to hurry!"

And right then, I realize I don't ever want to miss a sunrise or sunset with Silvie. I want them all with her.

I'm getting too permanently invested in something that's supposed to be temporary. If I feel like this the first day in, how will I feel in another month or two?

We're at the beach twenty minutes later with coffee mugs in our hands, and our other fingers linked together.

The sun starts to rise, seagulls squawking and the waves crashing in front of us.

"This is my favorite part of my day," she says softly.

Erin Branscom

I glance at her and think she's never looked more beautiful. Her hair is piled on top of her head in a messy bun and her face is makeup-free. The smile she wears is content as she sips her coffee.

"This is magical," she murmurs. "The best."

We listen to the waves crashing, side by side, and watch the horizon, her leaning into me. I'm sneaking glances her way. She's happy, her eyes bright. She traces a heart in the sand and picks up a shell, tucking it into her pocket.

I realize that I can't stop watching her. She's magical to me. Not the damn sunrise.

On the way back to the house, she's quiet. We walk leisurely, waving to people, her hand in mine as if it's already a habit. I squeeze hers, and she squeezes back. Silvie is just as affectionate as I am.

We rinse our feet in the outdoor shower in the back and towel off. We move around the kitchen together, bumping into each other as she pours us juice and I crack eggs into a cast-iron pan. Music hums low from the old radio under the counter, there for decades.

I grin at her and lift her easily onto the counter so I can get a bowl behind her, leaning in between her legs. She squeals and laughs.

"Manhandling me already?" she teases.

"I think touching you is my love language," I say.

She watches me, amused. "I appreciate your love language."

"You're so fucking sexy," I counter.

Her eyes drop to my mouth, and I take it as permission and lean in to kiss her. There's no one watching. No one to put on a show for. And yet, this is natural and feels really, really good.

The phone rings, interrupting us. I silently curse whoever is calling right now.

She reaches over and glances at the screen. Her shoulders tense and her smile disappears. "It's my dad." She hesitates, then presses accept. "Hello."

I can hear him from next to her. He's loud and sounds furious.

"This is not funny, Silverlyn," he shouts. "Do you have any idea what you've done?"

Silvie stiffens. "And just what have I done, Dad?"

"You married a goddamn bartender! You know what you did! Why would you do that?" he shouts.

She glances at me, embarrassment flashing across her face.

"I've got lawyers calling me," he snaps. "Board members asking questions. They're investigating this. You think you can just run off and get married without consequence?"

"Actually, yeah. I do," she says, voice tight but controlled.

"This is not a joke!" he roars.

"I didn't say it was," she argues. "And I didn't run off. I've been here for weeks, Dad."

He sounds even angrier, which I'm not sure how is possible. "You always make things harder. You could have done things differently!"

I step closer, without thinking, resting my hand on her back.

"You know what, I gotta go, Dad. I'll call you later when you've calmed down." She ends the call, and lowers the phone.

"So," she says with a nervous laugh. "That's my dad."

I exhale slowly. "He sounds intense."

"Yep. I'll give him this one pass. But the next time I talk to him, he'd better have it together, or I'm putting him in his place."

Holy shit.

I try to be positive. "He'll come around."

"You don't know my dad."

I shrug. "People do eventually."

She studies my face like she's trying to figure me out. "Are you always so positive?"

I smile. "Sometimes."

She shakes her head, half laughing. "Weirdo."

"You married me," I pointed out.

She laughs more softly this time. "Yeah. I did."

We finish breakfast quietly, and somehow, we always find excuses to touch. My hand rests on her knee. Her fingers brush the tattoos on my forearms, which I've noticed she's been obsessed with tracing. We stand close when we wash the dishes. God, I can't get enough of her.

She wanders off to shower, and I start a load of laundry. I see her journal laid out on the coffee table next to her bag, a pen resting on top. I don't mean to pry, but I see my name and can't help it.

At the top, it reads:

> *New Things for Me to Note*
> *1. Never trust a man with a trust fund*
> *2. Don't let Birdie and the Bee's drink too much sangria and wander off again.*
> *3. Cal's arms = illegal. Investigate those sexy tattoos further.*

I laugh and set the pen back down.

Then I look further down and see my name underlined twice. And the words safe and happy next to it.

My heart warms at the thought that she feels safe with me. That's all I want for her.

silvie

. . .

CAL and I are surprisingly both early birds. I learned that he doesn't always close the bar. He's more of an opener. And the night he met me at the bar, he was there by chance. Something he said he's grateful for. We both got up and went about our usual morning routines. I did yoga with Summer on the beach, and he went and surfed until I was done. He picked me up on the way home.

And now he's off having his weekly fishing date with Jonah, and I'm setting up shop in his kitchen to work. Morning light spills across his wooden table in warm stripes, the ocean humming outside, waves splashing steadily in the distance. Cal's kitchen is cozy and quiet in the best way possible. I open my laptop and pull out my notebook and pen, my water bottle full and ready beside me. It's time to get to work. Face the music.

I'm halfway through my emails when there's a knock at the front door. I open it to find Wilby standing there with two coffees and his laptop bag slung over his shoulder like he's ready to work.

"Hey," he says. "You working?"

I step aside and hold the door. "I am."

He hands me one of the cups. "I found the good coffee."

I grin. "Best friend ever. Get in here."

Wilby scans the room, takes in my setup, and joins me at the table. He pulls out a chair, and his movements are efficient. I'm reminded of why he's my right-hand man.

"I'm surprised you aren't working from the bar with him," he says casually. "You two are awfully inseparable these days."

I shrug and take a sip of coffee. "He's fishing with Jonah this morning."

Wilby's eyebrows lift slightly. "You two are so domestic. It's adorable."

"Yeah. He has his routine, and I have mine," I say. "Plus, we have work to do."

Wilby's mouth curves into a knowing smile. "I have already been on calls this morning with our team back home."

My stomach tightens a bit. "I'm guessing there's a lot being said."

Wilby nods. "Oh, they all know. And we definitely beat Tyler and Belladonna to the altar. You got this fair and square."

I blink and scan through more emails. "Oh. Fun."

Wilby leans forward in his chair. "My intel from back at the office tells me that people are secretly celebrating that you'll be taking over. And others...not so much."

I snort. "Shocking. Well, I'd love to know who is not celebrating."

"Oh, it's an entire shitshow back there," he continues. "They're scrambling for breadcrumbs of information."

My lips curve into a smile. "Which you have."

He grins. "Which I have carefully curated to release per your permission."

I sit up straighter. "Let's see it."

Wilby turns his laptop for me and clicks a few keys. A folder opens, and thumbnails fill Cal and my screens. They are carefully curated photos, it seems, meant to prove that we are, in fact, a real couple. There's just one problem. They don't look fake at all. In fact, in each photo Wilby captured, we experience real emotions and real-life moments. There's nothing fake about it.

My breath catches. Because they're beautiful. We're beautiful. We're a real-life looking couple. The way I gaze into Cal's eyes and the way he holds me? It's real. At least it feels real to me. And these are intimate and real-life photos.

Now they suddenly feel very, very personal.

"I don't want to share these," I say quietly.

Wilby's grin fades. "What? Why?"

I swallow, and my throat feels tight. "I don't want to share Cal. Or anyone here."

The words feel so vulnerable as they leave my mouth, but I mean every word.

Wilby studies me for a long moment, something softer replacing his usual sharper edge.

"Silverlyn," he says gently. "This was the plan."

I look down at my lap. At my fake wedding ring, catching the light. At the normalcy of sitting and working at Cal's table, waiting for him to come home from fishing so I can make us lunch.

I think about how he joked I could fry up his catch, and I told him that I wasn't cutting up dead fish, and he laughed.

Our life here on Coconut Beach doesn't feel fake. It's starting to feel very real, and that's scaring me.

"I know," I say.

For the first time since this began, the cost of it all hits me full force. The cost to Cal and the people I'm growing to love very much here. The people who have shown up for me in ways that some of my real family never would.

I don't want to share this. But I know I have to. Otherwise, I'll lose it all. But is it really worth saving? Because right now if I just lived in Coconut Beach, would that be enough? Surely, I could find a job somewhere? Something remote even? I don't even care about the money at this point.

The next morning, Cal and I wake up tangled together. Literally. My leg is thrown over him, my arm draped across his chest, and I'm pretty sure I drooled on him. Gross.

The sheets are twisted around us, the room washed in early morning bluish light, and my brain finally catches up.

I had the most vivid sex dream about Cal. It's unfair that the intense level of hotness that happened in this dream. A dream where Cal's hands were everywhere on me. His mouth was slow and devastating as he devoured me. And in the dream, no one was pretending anything. It felt so very real.

I shift and realize Cal is already awake.

"We need to talk."

"I'm so sorry," I say as I mentally cringe. He must think I'm such a weirdo.

He puts his arm around me. "I think if I keep sleeping with you like this, I'm going to explode. You're making me crazy, Silvie."

My body reacts before my brain can fully intervene. Well, that escalated quickly. I want Cal so bad. And I wasn't sure if he wanted me. Or was just being a nice guy.

His hand tightens at my waist, fingers holding me like he's grounding himself. I lift my head to look at him. His hair is a mess, his eyes are dark, and his jaw is tight. There's absolutely no mistaking what is happening between us right now. His body is solid and hot and very aware of mine. He wants me, I want him.

We stare at each other for a moment too long.

"I'm an idiot." I scramble to try to get off of him, limbs suddenly everywhere, mortification flooding me. "I will take your couch from now on. I can sleep on the couch forever. You know what? I'll sleep on a hammock outside with Iggy. I'll build a pillow fort. I'll exile myself."

"Silvie."

I keep going. "I don't know what's wrong with me."

"Silvie."

"I will never touch you ever again," I promise.

He sits up suddenly. "You're not sleeping on the couch, in a pillow fort, or outside. Or anywhere else."

I sigh. "I can't be trusted. What do we do?"

"We bang each other senseless," he says in a teasing voice that doesn't feel like teasing.

My jaw drops. Then I close it. "You think that's the solution?"

"It absolutely is."

"No."

"Fine, if that's what you want." He smirks.

"I don't want to make this weird." I shake my head. "It's already so weird, isn't it?"

His gaze softens. "Whatever this is? I like it. I like *you*."

I open my mouth to argue again, and that's when he stands up. One second, we're at eye level, and the next, his hands are on my hips, and he lifts me clean off the floor and onto him like I weigh nothing.

I gasp, instinctively wrapping my legs around him.

"Cal," I breathe.

His jaw tightens. "I want you so bad, Silvie. And I think you want me too. Why are you running from this?"

"I'm not running," I lie.

"Yeah, you are."

I grab his shoulders. "Put me down."

"No."

He carries me a few steps and then presses me up against the wall. I feel his hard cock against me, and I practically pant. His hands are firm on the backs of my thighs, grounding, not rough, but greedy.

"It's okay to want this."

My breath hitches. "I didn't say I wanted this."

His eyes drop to my mouth. "Yeah, you did."

My pulse races. "This is not a good idea."

"Why not?"

"Because..." I drift off. Why *isn't* this a good idea? Why *can't* I have sex with my husband? Greedy, hard, nice, hot sex with my hot husband?

His mouth drops to my neck, and he kisses it, slowly, sensually making his way down to my collarbone.

I shake my head, trying to think of a reason. "Cal."

He looks up and kisses me, taking his time, holding me firmly, showing me what I could have if I knocked down these stupid walls that already feel like they're crumbling around me.

I kiss him back before I can stop myself. I put my hands in his hair, pull him down to me, and moan into his mouth.

"I will make you feel so fucking good, Silvie," he whispers into my mouth.

Holy shit. This is not a dream. This is happening.

His forehead rests against mine, his breath still uneven. "You want me?"

I nod, dazed. "Yeah."

"Tell me right now if you don't," he demands.

"I do."

He brushes his thumb along my jaw, gentler now.

"You always take care of me," I moan. "You feed me, hold me... Why are you so good to me?"

"Baby." He stops for a second, his eyes darkening. "If a man doesn't check to see if you've eaten or need to be eaten? He's not taking care of you."

And just like that, my panties are soaked. Holy shit. I am so fucked. Literally. *Hopefully.*

"You're making this very hard." I moan.

He huffs a laugh. "Trust me, you're the one making this very hard."

His phone starts going off and he reaches to silence it. When he sees the text messages, though, he pauses. "Shit. There's a problem at the bar. I gotta go down there. I will be right back," he promises.

I sigh, thinking of how close we just came to having sex. And that's my luck. He quickly changes and grabs his keys. "Be right back," he says as he kisses me softly, then pulls the door closed behind him.

I quickly shower and get ready, putting on a sundress and thinking about what I need to get done today. I'm sure Wilby will have a list for me.

And suddenly there's a loud knock on the front door. A banging knock. Not like a friendly Wilby knock or a Birdie "yoo-hoo."

I freeze and frown.

And then another knock, even louder this time. Geez.

I look out and holy shit. It's my father.

Deep breath. This isn't going to be pretty.

I open the door, and Dad stands there in his aviator sunglasses in a button-down shirt, jaw tight, nostrils flared. He looks past me and scans the inside of the house.

"Where is he?" he demands.

I stare him down. "Excuse me?"

"Your husband," he bites out, looking murderous. "Where is he?"

I step out onto the small front porch. "No," I say calmly. "You're not talking to me like this."

His mouth tightens, and he opens it to speak.

"Stop," I say, sharper now as I hold up my hand. "You don't get to barge into my life and interrogate me like I'm some little child."

We have a silent standoff where he glowers at me and I glower right back. When Dad gets stressed, he acts like a prick. We've had our fair share of battles at work. This one is a little more complicated, but one we can navigate through, none-theless.

"You're behaving like a little child," he says, gritting his teeth. "You think your little stunt doesn't affect anyone but you?"

I laugh once, and it's short and humorless. "You're out of line."

That catches him off guard.

"You're embarrassing the family. Marrying a bartender. Some random stranger," he growls.

"Careful," I say cautiously. "You're starting to sound like Mom. Like a royal bitch."

"Guess you think you're running things now, do you?" he challenges.

"I know one thing I'm running, and it's my own life. You or anyone else do not get a say about my life and what I do," I say evenly.

His face darkens. For a flicker of a second, I see a flash of uncertainty. Guilt. There's hope for him yet.

"Go back to your hotel," I say, pointing in the general direction of town. "Get your shit together. And call me when you're calm."

He glares. "You don't get to tell me what to do."

"I absolutely do," I say, "because I won't be spoken to like that."

The silence stretches between us, and he turns sharply and walks toward his car. He yanks open the door, slams it shut, and peels away from the curb.

I stare until he's gone.

Then I look over and see Wilby staring at me from the front yard. He must have come over from Birdie's when he heard the commotion.

"That was," he says slowly, "so scary."

Maybe for Wilby. Not for me. My father can be a hothead, but he's still my dad. We've come to blows over many things in the past and always came through to the other side together.

"He's going to stay at his hotel until he can speak nicely," I tell him.

I exhale, the adrenaline, finally letting down.

"Damn," Wilby adds. "I almost peed myself. I can't believe he came here."

"There's going to be a board meeting," I say to Wilby. "Set it up."

Wilby sighs. "I'm on it."

"It'll be a quick trip. We'll take the jet with Dad."

He winces. "I'd rather sit on a commercial flight. In the back, like a peasant next to the bathroom. And a woman holding a crying baby."

Sometimes he's so dramatic and silly.

I tilt my head. "I think it's time to get down to business. And let my dad and others know who is in charge here."

He taps away on his phone and then smirks at me. "Board meeting is scheduled. They're all going to lose it."

Yeah. New York is going to be interesting.

cal

• • •

I WALK THROUGH THE LOBBY, and it doesn't take long to spot him. I knew he'd be staying at the Five-Star Grand Palm of Coconut Beach. It's where the rich come to play and stay. And it's exactly what you'd expect. High-end and beautiful, and nothing ever looks out of place.

I don't mind The Grand Palm. In fact, I worked here in high school on their maintenance crew, and I'm still good friends with a lot of the staff. This is where my mother worked when she met my father. And growing up, knowing she worked here, and he was a guest who treated her poorly, never landed well for me. It's not that I don't like people who have money. It's that I don't like people who treat others badly just because they have money.

When Wilby said he could find out who my father was, part of me was curious. But part of me doesn't want to know. What would it change? I've had good people in my life like Jonah, and I don't need someone who doesn't care about my mother or me. Knowing who that man is changes nothing. He did what he did. He left.

So, people who have money don't bother me. Never have. I know who I am and how I show up for the people that I love.

Charles Montclair sits alone at the bar, jacket draped over the stool behind him. He has one elbow planted on the immaculate bar and another wrapped around a glass of bourbon. His jaw is tight, and he looks pissed as hell.

I know a little bit about Charles. I Googled him before I came over here because, unlike him, I show up for meetings with knowledge of who I'm dealing with.

The bar sits just off to the right, dark wood and soft lighting, leather stools, and a long mirrored back wall that makes the whole place feel bigger than it already is. A muted golf tournament plays on the TVs, sound low, applause polite.

I take the stool next to him and sit.

The bartender looks at me curiously, and I order a bourbon too. Neat.

Charles doesn't look over, not at first. He's locked in on staring at his bourbon and probably contemplating how he's lost control of everything in his life.

The bartender slides my drink across. I take a slow sip and let the silence stretch between us. I have no idea whether Charles knows who I am, but judging by his silence, probably not.

"Terrible swing," I say casually, nodding to the TV.

Charles scoffs under his breath. "That's because he isn't adjusting his grip."

I glance over at him and sip my bourbon. "Exactly."

That earns me a look, and he assesses me. Then sips his bourbon again.

We drink in silence for another minute, and I wait.

"Are you a golfer?" he finally asks.

I chuckle and shake my head. "No. I hate golf."

He sighs with relief. "I do, too. Stupid sport."

"You know enough about it, though," I joke.

He shrugs. "Doesn't mean I like it. Sometimes you have to play the game, you know? Play golf with other people and show up."

We drink in silence for a few more minutes. He has no idea how accurate what he just said is.

Just Another Summer Escape

"Vacation?" I ask finally. "Or business?"

He exhales sharply. "Business."

I smile slightly and sip my drink. "Not a bad place for business."

He chuckles, and it's humorless. "I have no idea. It's my first time here."

We order another round. Then food. I order the steak sliders and truffle fries. He orders the same. I forgot how good the food was here, and I made a mental note to bring Silvie here for a date.

Conversation comes easily after that between us, as I figured it would. I have experience talking to people at a bar and getting them to open up. We talk about the stock market and finances that run at the bottom of the screen. He even laughs and jokes with me.

Charles eats his food and checks his phone every so often. Probably hoping Silvie will text him. And maybe she will.

"You with a firm back in New York City?" he asks as he looks over at me. I realize I finally earned his respect. He still has no idea who I am. And this couldn't be going more to plan.

"Nah. I'm a local. Born and raised in Coconut Beach," I say as I take a sip of my bourbon. I ask the bartender for a glass of water and keep eating.

"Really?" he glances over in surprise. "I would've pegged you for a trader or an analyst back in New York."

I don't answer. Just take a few bites and drink my water.

He takes a slow sip of his bourbon, jaw tight. "My wife hates it here. But my daughter has visited here often. She has a ...friend here."

I nod and take a sip of my bourbon. Still waiting for Charles to catch up. But I wanted him to meet me first before he judged me. And it worked. He still hasn't the faintest idea who he's sitting next to.

We finish eating and set our plates aside. I order two more bourbons neat for us.

Charles looks over and nods with thanks.

Then he clears his throat and says, "I've come here to meet with my daughter."

I nod and take a sip of my bourbon. "I know."

He frowns and turns to face me. "You know?"

He looks confused, as if he's trying to figure out who I am. His eyes narrow, and he's processing this.

I set my glass down and meet his eyes. "Yeah."

The silence is loud between us, and Charles goes still as he studies my face like he's reconciling this. The bartender clears our dishes, and the TV crowd cheers at something on the screen.

"I'm her husband," I say calmly.

Charles glares at me with narrowed eyes and says, "You."

"Me." I nod.

He leans back in his stool, lips pressed together, gaze sharp. "I want to hate you for marrying her like this."

I nod in agreement. "I don't think I'd be pleased either if I were a father and my daughter did that."

His eyes narrow in suspicion. "Then why did you do it? What's in it for you?"

I let out a deep sigh. "That is for you and Silvie to discuss. I'm here for other matters."

He huffs. "Figures."

"Figures what?" I challenge.

"You have an angle here. Nobody gets married to a billion-aire heiress they just met. And a bartender, at that."

I don't flinch. "You seem to think you've got me all figured out, don't you? You sat here with me for over an hour and had no idea that I was a bartender."

"But," I continue, my voice steady, still composed. "Just know that if you ever come to my house and speak to my wife the way you did this morning, we're going to have problems, Charles."

That gets his attention.

"So, I don't care what you think of me, what preconceived

notions you seem to have. Have them. I don't care. But what I do care about is Silvie. And I will never tolerate someone speaking to her the way you did this morning."

My words land heavy and deliberate. I'm still calm and steady.

And Charles, even though he's been upset, seems to be thinking about this. He knows I'm right.

He stares at me for a long moment as if he's gauging me. Then he purses his lips and takes a sip of his drink.

A few minutes later, he says quietly, "Fine."

He stands, reaches for his wallet, and lays down a big bill on the counter. He slips on his jacket and looks over at me one last time. He shakes his head, turns, and walks away into the hotel lobby as if nothing happened.

I finish my drink and let the warmth settle in. Yeah, he's not a bad man. But he's been warned. I'm a good man until I'm not.

I protect what's mine.

And that's my wife.

———

I didn't head home right away. I sat there thinking about what he said. He questioned why I was marrying his billionaire heiress daughter. And hearing that reminds me just how different the worlds we live in are. And the family we come from. I don't know how Silvie and I could make this work if this were really real. And it's feeling pretty damn real for both of us. We have to figure this out before it goes further. What this would look like and how we keep it together. Because family is important to me. My mom is everything to me. And I want Silvie to have that, too. She deserves that.

I don't give a shit about her money. Money doesn't motivate me.

When I walk home, the lights are on low, and the house feels like a home. For once, I'm not coming home to a dark and quiet house. I get to come home to Silvie.

Silvie is propped up in bed, laptop open, glasses on. The hot ones that make her look like a badass CEO. She's got on those tiny shorts and a tank top that looks like it might actually be mine. She's tucked one leg under herself, focused and biting her lip like she's pondering something important.

Fuck me. She's so beautiful. And she's mine. Well, almost mine.

I pause in the doorway and watch her. I just spent time putting her father on notice, and now I'm supposed to lie down next to her and sleep like my heart isn't hers. Earlier, we were so close to having sex. She felt so good. We have to talk before we have sex, though. We have to be on the same page before we take it further.

"Hey," I say.

She looks up and smiles. "Hey. Where have you been?"

I cross the room, then lean down and kiss her. She melts into it, soft, familiar, and then pulls back and grins. "You taste like bourbon."

"Guilty."

She closes her laptop and sets it aside. "I was just getting some work done."

"When are you going back to New York?" I ask.

She shifts, making space for me, and says, "I wanted to talk to you about that."

"Yeah?"

She clears her throat. "I have a favor."

"Sure," I say. "What?"

She hesitates. "I know it's last minute, but I was wondering if you'd like to go with me."

I mentally go through what I'd need to do to get things done here to go with her, and she's watching me, waiting for my reaction.

"I can make that happen."

"Wait. Really?" She studies me. "You want to go?"

"Yeah," I say easily. "Whatever you need."

Truth be told, I'm not keen on the idea of being apart from her. Things are smoldering between us, and I want to keep burning with her.

Her shoulders relax, like she didn't think I'd say yes. "Okay."

"Okay," I say as I trace her wrists with my fingers.

"We can go after my book club tomorrow. Does that work for you?"

I grin. Her book club is with my mom. But I know they both look forward to it. I love that she's making my mom a priority. I lean in and kiss her neck. "Sure, we can go after book club."

She adds casually, "We're flying back with my dad. But don't worry...I'll talk to him before we go. He won't be giving you any trouble."

I shrug. "Okay."

She narrows her eyes suspiciously. "Why are you so chill about all of this?"

I sit up on the edge of the bed and say, "Your dad's not that bad."

She looks at me as if I just said something wild. "What do you mean, not that bad?"

I glance at her, take her hand, bring it to my mouth, and kiss it. "I talked to him today. That's where I was."

She pulls her hand back and sits up straighter. "What?"

"I went to his hotel," I say. "We had lunch."

She stares at me as if I just told her I wrestled sharks for fun.

Her mouth opens. Closes. "And?"

"We came to an understanding," I tell her.

"You went to my father's hotel," she repeats slowly. "Sat next to him at the bar and had lunch."

"Yes," I confirm.

Her eyes drag over me, assessing, and something that looks like heat flickers there. "That is...unexpectedly so freaking hot."

I laugh softly. "That wasn't the goal, but I guess that's a good perk."

"Was he nice to you?" she asks.

My eyes soften. "Silvie, it doesn't matter if he's nice to me. It matters that he's nice to you."

Her expression softens. "Cal..."

I tuck a lock of hair behind her ear. "He's complicated. But he loves you. I get that now. This whole thing is just messy and stressful to everyone. I'm not here to add to that. I'm here for you."

She sighs. "Complicated is one way of putting it."

I meet her gaze. "He knows to never speak to you like that again."

"He said that?" she asks quietly.

I nod. "He agreed."

She looks at me and says, "I'm glad you're coming with me. I can fight my own battles. But it sure is better fighting them with you."

I smile. And that means more to me than she'll ever know. I don't want to be needed. I want to be wanted.

Silvie says, "Oh, and Wilby says he wants you to come to New York, too. He said you can be his emotional support animal with my dad. Apparently, he likes fighting battles with you, too."

I grin, and silence settles between us. "I'd be honored."

She yawns, and I suddenly feel tired, the heaviness of the last few days hitting us. Feelings are still tangled, and there's still so much unsaid between us. But this has been enough for tonight.

silvie

. . .

I LIE awake with Cal's arm heavy around my waist, his breathing slow and even against my back. I love sleeping with Cal. He feels safe and solid. I can't get over the fact that he went to see my dad.

The thought still doesn't feel real to me. I can't imagine any other man that I've dated having the balls to go confront Charles Montclair. And then have drinks and lunch with him? This is wild. And I have no idea what was said at that lunch, but whatever it was, Cal is not intimidated by my dad, and he said he'd go back to New York with me.

I didn't know I was allowed to have that. A man who would just be by my side and have my back like that. I've had my own back for so long. He just stepped in and set boundaries as if that were the most natural thing in the world. I've always assumed that I couldn't have someone like Cal. I'd have to have someone my parents picked or someone who was good for the company. But I never thought I could have someone *for me*.

Cal saved my company and me. And asked for nothing in return except for meeting his mom, whom I adore. He's stood beside me. And that changes everything.

We can work out logistics. Cities, schedules, boardrooms, and beaches. All of that is solvable. I've been busting my butt for years. I know how to make things work out. But what I didn't expect was to fall in love with someone like Cal. Who is steady, grounding, protective, and confident. He knows who he is and isn't afraid to be himself. And that to me is sexy as hell in a partner. If I were allowed to dream up a perfect partner, it would be him.

This is terrifying because I feel like I have everything now. And I have something else I could potentially lose.

———

The next morning, I wake up to find Cal gone. His side of the bed feels cold, which likely means he's been gone a while. I slept in and realized I'd forgotten to set my alarm.

I pad out to the kitchen to start coffee, and it's already made, with a note next to my mug that he left out. I notice Cal's neat, slanted handwriting.

Silvie,

I went fishing with Jonah. I'll be back, packed, and ready by 2 pm.
Love, Cal

Love, Cal. My heart warms when I read it again. I sip the coffee and smile like a dork. He wrote "love." I tuck the note into my journal on the counter. I take in the empty kitchen, tidy as usual. It doesn't have much clutter, but it's cozy and functional.

I make my way to the bathroom, stare at my reflection, and imagine the board members seeing me. My hair has gone curly with its natural glory. It's lighter and could definitely use a deep-conditioning treatment, a trim, and a blowout. I'm a simple girl, but I like my blowouts. Something I haven't had in months now. My nails are a mess. If I don't look put together, the board won't take me seriously. I'm the new CEO of Montclair Holdings, and I want to look the part. They're going to try to swallow me up if I show up like this.

I need a massive maintenance day. I sigh.

I grab my phone and call Carly.

She answers on the second ring. "Hi, Silvie."

"Hey," I say. "I have something to run by you."

She hums. "Sounds interesting."

"If I bring someone with me, can we do hair and makeup at your house today while we are doing book club?" I ask. "It's totally okay if you say no. But I was thinking we could do it together, like a spa day. We could both be pampered while we eat snacks and talk about books."

She pauses for a bit.

I wince. "Again, totally fine if you say no."

Carly clears her throat, sounding nervous. "Do I have to go outside?"

I smile. "Nope."

Another beat of silence.

"Okay," she says, excitedly. "Yes, definitely yes. I haven't had my hair done in years."

Relief floods me. I never want to upset her or overstep. I just want to include her. "Okay. I'll bring snacks and coffee."

"I'll make us sandwiches," she says cheerfully.

"Okay, let me get it all set up. See you soon!" I say as I disconnect.

I fire off a text to Wilby, letting him know our new plans. He'd already arranged a team to help me get ready.

He had texted me very nicely, in the best way he could, that I needed to be "cleaned up" before we go back to New York.

I laughed because he's not wrong. But I like how I feel and how I look here on Coconut Beach. When I'm here, I can just be me.

I pack an overnight bag and take a quick shower. I go to

Birdie's, peek under the bush, and find Iggy. "Hey, buddy," I call to him.

Birdie's gone and not home. Wilby's at her kitchen table, headphones on, when I knock and open the door. He looks up and waves. "Almost done," he mouths.

I nod and sit across from him.

He finishes up his call and slides his headphones off. "The stylist and makeup team will be at Carly's in an hour."

"Thanks. Are you coming?" I ask.

He looks at me as if I'm crazy. "No. I have things to do before we go."

Then I realize he looks sad.

"Do you like it here, Wilby?" I ask, tilting my head.

He shrugs and looks down. "Yeah. I'm going to miss it."

"Do you want to come back with me?" I ask.

He brightens. "Kinda. Is that crazy?"

I snort and shake my head. "No. This place grows on you, doesn't it?"

"If you tell anyone, I'll deny it," he says, deadpan.

"I'd never tell," I say as I stand. "I'm going to get coffee, snacks, and head to Carly's."

"I got you a new power suit. You're going to love it," he calls.

"Can't wait!"

———

Carly's house turns into a glorious disaster within twenty minutes. Make-up brushes and make-up are on the counter. I had no idea Carly loved makeup, hair products, and styles as much as she does. She was nervous at first when they arrived, and I saw her glance at the door and back at me a few times. I made sure the door was shut and sat by her.

Curling irons are heating up, and makeup is being applied to both of us. Someone has a playlist going that belts out nostalgic throwbacks. Carly and I laugh and sing along.

We end up ordering more coffee and snacks for everyone, and we burn through it all quickly. Carly tries to make food, and I wave her off, instead ordering takeout from Chaos & Cocktails. The delivery driver leaves it at the back door. We all eat and talk about music, make-up, and anything else that comes up.

I'm getting a manicure at the kitchen counter while my hair is in gigantic rollers.

"We're like that scene from Steel Magnolias." Carly sighs. "I love that movie."

"A classic," I agree. "My colors are blush and bashful."

She snickers. "And no one is allowed to die at the end."

"Absolutely not. That movie wrecked me," I admit.

By the time we get to discussing the book, the hair stylist has already sent her assistant to the mobile bookstore to see if they have any extra copies so they can read them as well.

"It's a great series. I love the first one, *Forever To Me*. Walker is so hot," Carly says, fanning herself. I love a musician romance."

"Definitely a good series. I can't wait to read Cami's story next in *Wild As Her*."

Bryn, our stylist, sighs. "I'm going to have to just order the whole series. You ladies have me convinced. I love small-town romance books. And hot ranchers? Say less. I want to move to Bridger Falls."

"You look so beautiful, Silvie. From the inside out. It's no wonder my son is wildly in love with you," Carly says with a smile.

I pretend not to get emotional about that. I don't know if Cal loves me. Too soon for that. Or ever. But I'm pretty much head over heels for him, just not ready to admit that to his mom before I admit it to him.

"It's a good thing I'm equally as obsessed," I joke.

I feel lighter than I have in weeks and love that we can do this together.

Before long, our hair is done, makeup perfect, and we're

sitting in her front chairs by the window. Cal pulls up out front and hops out, pulling bags from the trunk.

I sit up. "I forgot to bring you books!"

Carly laughs and glances over at her still overflowing bookshelves. "Honey, I think I'm good for a while."

Cal steps inside, and his eyes land on us. "Wow. You two look beautiful."

"Hi, to you too." I laugh.

"You like our hair and makeup?" Carly says, flipping her freshly blown-out, styled hair similar to mine.

He crosses the room in three long strides, grabs my hand, and pulls me outside before I can process what's happening.

"Cal," I protest and glance back in Carly's direction. She's smirking.

The second we're on the porch, and he shuts the door, he cups my face and kisses me like he's been thinking about it all day.

I melt into him. His hands roam my face, and he breathes me in. "You look so gorgeous."

"Why are you acting like a caveman right now?" I laugh.

He smiles at me proudly and kisses my nose. "You're pretty great. You know that?"

Heat spreads through my chest. "You're pretty great yourself."

"You're good to my mom," he murmurs and kisses me again. "That means a lot to me."

"Yeah, well, she's not hard to love," I admit.

That gets me another smile. He laces his fingers through mine. "You ready for New York?"

I squeeze his hand. "Yeah. I did a little makeover. Wilby says he has a power suit for me."

We head inside and spend time with Carly. She knows we're going to New York, and is excited for us.

"I want to hear all about it and take pictures of your old stomping grounds!"

I wave, and I wonder what she means by that, but I'm side-tracked as Cal picks me up and throws me over his shoulder playfully and carries me to his truck, me laughing.

———————

I slide into my seat on the plane by the window, Cal settling in beside me with that easy calm that is always grounding to me. Wilby drops into the seat across from us and is rummaging through his bag.

Then, my dad appears. He nods at us and doesn't say anything. No scowl. He just says calmly, "Silvie, can I speak with you for a moment?"

I follow him to the back of the plane, into the back bedroom, and he closes the door.

"I wanted to apologize for how I spoke to you." His eyes are kind, and he means it.

I soften. "It's okay, Dad. You just have to trust me that I know what I'm doing."

He sighs. "I know. I'm trying to do that. It's not easy."

"I heard you had lunch with Cal," I tell him.

"I did. Quite a young man you have there. Very intriguing."

I laugh. "He is. I thought you'd like him when you got to know him more."

He tilts his head. "I think I will. Your mother will hate him on sight."

When he mentions my mother, I roll my eyes. "I don't want to talk about Mom."

He nods. "Let's just get to it. The board is very curious about what you're going to do with this meeting."

I lift my chin confidently. "Good. I hope they're ready."

He smiles. "There's my girl."

We exit the bedroom and head back to Wilby and Cal. Dad sits next to Wilby, which is hilarious because Wilby is scared of my dad. Wilby eyes me, then slaps a deck of cards on the table we're all sitting around. "Bullshit. Who's playing?"

Cal raises an eyebrow, but Wilby's already shuffling the deck. "We play bullshit. Passes the time."

Wilby hands the cards to me and says, "Shuffle, I'm going to check on dinner."

He stands to head to the front of the plane.

My dad nods toward Wilby. "I should fire my assistant and hire him. He's good."

I scoff. "You can't have Wilby. He's mine. Plus, he's terrified of you. You're mean."

"Silverlyn, I'm not mean," he says in mock horror.

"Dad." I tilt my chin to him. "You've been through more assistants in six months than I can count."

Wilby comes back and says, "I had pizza and drinks brought in. This is going to be a fun ride."

We taxi and lift off, Coconut Beach shrinking beneath us, all blues and greens and sunlight.

I feel sad, I realize.

"We're really playing bullshit?" Cal asks.

"It's a classic," Wilby says. "Have you played?"

My dad glances at him curiously. "That's the name of the game?"

Cal leans closer to me. "It is. I love this game. Growing up, I played cards with my mom often."

The pizza is served, and it's hot and delicious from Iggy's. "Wilby, good thinking," I tell him as I take a bite.

Wilby goes first. "Two queens," he announces confidently, sliding two cards forward.

Cal squints at him. "Bullshit."

Wilby flips the cards, not queens.

Those two go to war over this. It's hilarious to watch.

I laugh so hard I almost drop my cards. My dad watches this all quietly, chewing his pizza, eyes darting between us like he's studying a new species.

My turn. "Three sevens," I say sweetly.

Wilby narrows his eyes. "That smile tells me everything."

"Bullshit," Cal says immediately.

I flip my cards. Three actual sevens.

Wilby groans. "I don't like this version of you."

My dad clears his throat. "Can I play?"

Wilby freezes. "Are you familiar with the rules?"

"I am," my dad says. "I used to play in college."

I blink. "You did?"

"Yes," he says dryly.

Wilby slides him his cards. "Welcome to the table."

My dad plays conservatively at first. Quiet. Careful. Then Cal calls him on a move.

"Bullshit," Cal says calmly.

My dad looks offended. "You don't even know what I put down."

"That's why it's fun," Wilby says.

My dad flips his cards. He was lying.

Wilby whoops. "Sir. I respect you so much right now."

My dad actually laughs and acts surprised.

As the game goes on, the lines blur. We lose track of whose turn it is. Wilby accuses everyone of cheating. Cal keeps winning with infuriating ease. I get called out three times in a row and swear vengeance.

My dad watches Cal closely. Watches the way he leans in. The way his hand finds mine without thought. The way he lets me win one round on purpose and then smirks like I won't notice.

At one point, my dad says to Cal, "You're very good at this."

I'm not sure if he's talking about the game or marriage. Either way, it's the truth.

When the cabin lights dim, and the city lights appear beneath us, the laughter softens. My dad grows quieter again, gaze fixed on the window across the aisle. He looks as if he's thinking through everything.

After landing, we stand to deplane. Cal reaches up without effort, muscles in his arms flexing as he pulls our bags from the overhead bin. His broad shoulders fill the narrow space, and for a second, it feels like the plane was built too small for him.

He towers over everyone around us at the airport, solid and unmissable, all long lines and quiet strength. People step aside without thinking, like they can feel his presence before they see him. I clutch my bag and try not to stare, but it's hard when he looks like this, strong and steady and completely in control.

I swallow, suddenly very aware that he's with me. And that maybe I like the way he takes up space in my world just as much as he does in this airport.

"I hope you know what you're doing," my dad says quietly.

I don't hesitate. I nod my head once and smile. "I believe in myself, Dad. I've got that covered."

He looks at me for a long moment. "I need to catch up."

"Yeah. You do."

He exhales. "I'm trying. I just want you to focus. You have a lot on your plate right now. I don't think you realize how much this job is going to take out of you."

Even though Dad still seems a bit hesitant about the whole marriage thing with Cal, something has shifted in him.

For now, that feels like progress.

cal

...

LANDING IN NEW YORK and seeing the city lights and bridges stretch beneath us as we were making our descent hit me harder than I thought it would. I've always loved New York City, and its loud, restless energy. It's different than life in Coconut Beach. It's hard to explain that to Silvie because with her and me, things still aren't defined.

The limo that picked us up at the airport glides away from the airport, and outside the window, everything stacks upward, lighting up every square inch it feels like. We drive past steel-and-glass buildings, their office windows lit, casting shadows and silhouettes of people still at work. Because we're in the city that never sleeps.

Traffic crawls and horns blare, with people cutting in and out, not even glancing at others as they do. Everyone here seems to have a sense of urgency. I think about how time slows back in Coconut Beach. People stop to chat, lunches are slow and often include other locals catching up, and people stroll the beach with nowhere to be. Here, it's different.

The energy is charged.

Chaotic.

Anxious.

Silvie sits beside me, legs crossed, phone resting in her lap. She looks different... as if she's more dialed in. Her hair and make-up are stylish and fitting for the city. She looks polished yet effortless. She's wearing a tailored blazer, with slacks and heels. Her New York attire is completely different from her makeup and sundresses back in Coconut Beach. I prefer that version, but this one is stunning and sexy as hell. She looks very much like the CEO badass she just became.

Honestly, I love seeing her in her element, relaxed and confident. Pride fills me just watching her. She looks happy. Her hand slides into mine, and I squeeze it. I don't miss her dad's eyes on our hands and our faces as we smile at each other. It's not a façade. Not this part. I'm proud of Silvie and am her biggest supporter.

But I still can't help the warning bells that are threatening to go off in the back of my head. Because what if she never comes back to Coconut Beach? What if she needs me to move here and... I can't. I couldn't imagine leaving my mom and Jonah.

Wilby's across from us, scrolling through emails on his phone, and says, "Feels good to be home. But I already miss Coconut Beach."

Silvie sighs. "Me, too."

Wilby looks up. "When do you want to return to Coconut Beach? I need to set that up."

"We'll be heading back tomorrow after the meeting," she tells him.

Silvie's dad's eyebrows raise. "So soon?"

"I have everything I need to work in Coconut Beach," she says. "I already told you I was taking time off. That hasn't changed."

He says nothing, just nods and gazes out the window. Charles is an interesting man. Still not sure how I feel about him, but as long as he treats Silvie right, I have no problem with him.

Silvie turns to me and studies my face. "You're quiet."

"Just taking it in," I say.

The limo slows and slides up to the curb as a building comes into view. Our driver hops out, opens the door.

Wilby says, "This is me. I will see you all tomorrow. Good night."

Silvie smiles. "Good night, Wilby. Thanks for all your hard work."

He nods at all of us, and the door closes. Wilby disappears into his building, and we pull away again. It's just her father and us now.

Silvie rests her head on my shoulder, her voice soft but electric. "Tomorrow's going to be...big. I've worked hard for this for years. I can't believe it's finally here. Thanks to you."

I tighten my grip on her hand, grounding us both. "You did it. You built this with every late night, sacrifice, and hard choice that led you here. I'm proud of you and happy to help you." I lift her knuckles and kiss them. "You've got this. And you should be proud of yourself."

Her dad says nothing. He's reading something on his phone, but I can feel him listening. He looks up and tells the driver to drop us off, and then he's going back to the office for a while. Silvie says nothing, just looks out the window. I wonder how her and her dad are doing now that they talked on the plane. Wilby was a genius bringing pizza and cards. For a while, they seemed almost normal. Just a father and daughter playing cards and eating pizza. We all had a lot of laughs, even Charles. It gave me hope that they can work things out. I don't know them or how their relationship works, but I hope they can get to a good place.

She lays her head on my shoulder as if it's the most natural thing in the world. I wonder if she's made for this place and not Coconut Beach. And I can't help but wonder what that means for us.

The elevator doors open, and her penthouse almost makes my brain short circuit. She has the entire top floor of the building, and if I had to guess, it's probably well over five thousand square feet. This is far from my small and cozy cottage back in Coconut Beach.

Her penthouse has floor-to-ceiling windows, and city lights that pan out all around us as if they're part of the decor. I wonder what the views look like during the day. Despite the penthouse's grandeur, it still very much feels like Silvie. Warm and intentional. Warm lamps cast a glow throughout the penthouse, and throw pillows fill the couch with cozy throws. Everything smells fresh and clean. This is Silvie. She may have money, but this is her space, and I like it. It feels like her and what she would pick out. Whites and beiges and soft blush tones. Plush couches that somehow look elegant and nap-approved at the same time. It shouldn't feel cozy, but it does. Like someone thought about comfort instead of just appearance.

"Wow," I say before I can stop myself. "This is gorgeous. Great place."

She kicks off her heels, getting comfortable. "Thanks. I've actually been thinking about selling it."

"Really?" I ask, surprised, and glance around. "Well, with the view, it's probably going to sell quickly. It's nice."

She glances out at the view. "No, I mean the building."

I freeze. "Wait. You own the whole building?"

She shrugs. "Yeah. I used my inheritance for investment properties."

She says this so casually, as if she doesn't own hundreds of millions in investment property.

My laugh comes out, full of disbelief, and I shake my head. "We come from two different worlds, Silvie."

She grins and flops on the couch. "Nah. We're in the same world. This one is just...weird. I prefer your Coconut Beach world."

I relax hearing her reassurance.

She flips her hair, watching me. "Besides, it's probably yours now, too. I think it's community property."

"No, thanks. I'm all set," I say with a grin. "I also don't think that's how that works."

She shrugs. "It might."

Plus, I signed everything Wilby gave me to sign from the lawyers. I'm not interested in any of her assets. I'm not this level of rich, but I do okay. I'm actually really good with finances, too. I just don't own buildings.

I hope she doesn't really think I need that from her or would want any of her assets. "I don't need a building. Like I said. All set. Thanks."

I laugh again at the ridiculousness of it and suddenly realize that the two worlds are definitely different kinds of normal.

Fake marriage, I remind myself. This isn't real. I don't have to make sense of it. She just needs my help.

"It's only seven thirty," she says. "Let's put on comfy clothes and order pizza from my favorite pizza place."

I relax a little bit at that. "I like that plan."

I carry our bags into her massive bedroom that overlooks another view of the city. "Wow," I whisper, standing and taking it all in.

We change and meet back in the living room. Silvie has an additional bathroom and closet that's bigger than my whole cottage.

"I really like it," I tell her. "It suits you."

"Thanks," she says easily. "Wilby had the entire place deep cleaned, and I have a brand-new bed."

I shake my head at the reminder. "Gotta erase the evidence of the turd."

She grimaces. "And Belladonna, my sister." She eyes the couch. "I should probably burn this, too."

I laugh. "I think the couch is fine."

We settle in on her sofa, and she picks *How to Lose a Guy in Ten Days*. The opening credits roll just as the door buzzes. A doorman, whom she apparently knows well and enjoys chatting with, brings in the pizza and sets the boxes on her gleaming white kitchen countertops.

She thanks him and catches up with him like they're old friends. Before he leaves, she gives him a hug. I smile because that doesn't surprise me at all that she's friends with her doorman.

She grabs paper towels and two plates. "Moment of truth."

We open the boxes, and I inhale the aroma. The perfect pizza to fold and eat.

"I had to try Joe's first," she says. "I haven't had this in over a year since my mother had me on a ridiculous wedding diet."

I am not looking forward to her mother. I have a feeling we're not going to like each other. She treats Silvie like trash.

"Yep. This is as good as I remember." She chews and moans, and holy shit, that sound goes straight to my dick. I try to focus on the pizza. *Don't think of her like that*, I tell myself. *She's your fake wife*.

We swap and take a bite of each other's and nod like we're serious judges on a very important panel.

And then we stop and look at each other. "Mine's better," we both say at the same time.

Then we burst out laughing.

She grabs another slice, and I snag a couple of sodas from her fridge for us. We already operate and move like we've been doing this for years. With Silvie, things are just easy. We make our way back to the sofa, plates in hand, the city glowing around us.

I take another bite of pizza and watch her as she settles in next to me and crosses her legs. She picks up her plate from the coffee table and settles in.

"So, what happens tomorrow?" I ask.

She doesn't even look up, just chews and swallows, and says, "Tomorrow we measure our dicks and make sure they're the same size. If anyone has any problems, we clean house."

I cough and cover my mouth, then reach for my soda. "Jesus, Silvie."

She laughs, and her eyes are bright and unapologetic. "I'm serious. You're about to meet corporate Silverlyn. She's a barracuda."

"I can tell," I say, still laughing. And I can't wait.

She wipes her hands on a napkin and leans back. She's so casual, and at home here, it's cool to watch. "Some people don't want to see me succeed as CEO. They don't want to see a woman in charge. Especially one who isn't asking for permission. This is my company, and I worked hard for it."

She continues, and I chew as I listen to her.

"And I wouldn't have this without you, Cal. I'm so thankful for you. For being here with me by my side. You're a big part of this."

My smile fades a little, and she keeps going.

"They're either going to get on board," she says calmly, "or get off. I'll be doing what I have to do."

There's certainty and confidence in her voice. "We're not changing the company," she adds. "My dad was running it well. He and I will be a great team until he decides to retire. But the old men cronies who can't stand to see a woman in charge will be an issue."

I nod, impressed and a little in awe. "That sounds...messy."

She grins. "It might be painful to watch."

I take her in, sitting there with pizza and comfy clothes, the whole city at her back, and think about the boardroom and power plays. I love it that they are underestimating her. She's going to be so damn sexy to watch.

"It'll be interesting. Damn, I can't wait." I say, and I mean it.

I know one thing is for sure. I'd pay good money to watch her clean house of all the idiots who chose not to support her.

For a moment, this feels like a completely normal life. Like, maybe we could make this work between us.

silvie

. . .

MORNING LIGHT now fills the windows of my home office, all glass, and my laptop's open, reports stacked next to me in rows, numbers and projections lined up on my desk like little financial soldiers. I've been awake for quite a while. I probably slept for maybe three hours. Time goes by quickly when your brain won't turn off. I'm not nervous, I'm excited. I've worked so hard for this. Today is my day.

I look up and find Cal leaning in the doorway looking sexy as hell with his hair messed up, watching me. "You're up early," he says.

I laugh softly. "Bold of you to assume I slept."

He frowns, crossing the room. "You need your sleep, Silvie."

"I can sleep on our way home tonight," I say.

He stops in front of my desk, taking in my organized chaos. "How can I help?"

"Nothing to help with." I shrug, closing my laptop. "I just couldn't sleep. Had a lot of ideas churning."

He leans down and kisses me, slow, and says, part joking, "If you don't listen to me, I'll tell Birdie. She'll make sure you're not staying up all night."

I shudder. "You wouldn't."

His eyes are on mine. "I would."

I scoff. "You know she'll have my ass."

"She absolutely would," he says, serious. "And I happen to like your ass. So, let's keep it safe and rested."

I laugh, rubbing my tired eyes. "Fine."

He glances in the direction of the kitchen. "I saw you have breakfast food. Let me make us something while you get ready."

I nod and reach for my phone to check the time. "I have time for a quick soak in the tub."

I don't tell him this, but I need it for my nerves. I'm starting to get nervous.

"Good," he says. "You get ready, I'll cook. It's going to be a great day. You'll see."

The confidence in his voice settles me in ways I didn't know I could be grounded. He's done that since we met, and somehow it feels way less daunting to have him here by my side.

He kisses me again and saunters off. I watch him go and take in all of his tattoos and sigh. In the bathroom, I turn on the tub and pour in my favorite salts and oils, filling the water with bubbles, and lavender and eucalyptus fill the air.

I open the door, still standing in my pajamas, and Cal stands there, with messy hair and holding a mug of coffee and my water bottle, probably filled.

"Thank you," I say as I set them on the edge of the tub.

"No, problem," he says easily. "I'll bring you a plate when it's done if you want to eat in here."

I wrinkle my nose. "But I want to eat with you."

"Okay," he says, smiling, and disappears down the hall.

I slip out of my clothes and sink into the bubbles with a long sigh. Today's my first day as CEO. I fought so hard for this for years. I fought daily for respect and a seat at the table I now command. And now that I have it, I wonder if it needed to be such a battle. I wonder if it'll feel like I imagined. Earned.

I rest my eyes, and time passes. A knock at the door makes me open my eyes. After I tell him to come in, Cal saunters in, carrying two plates. He's so nonchalant about it. Like, I'm not naked in the water in front of him, covered in bubbles. He says nothing about it and is a gentleman. I wish he were not a gentleman. I wish he'd join me in this tub and fuck me senseless. But his food looks so good.

"You still want me to eat with you?" he asks, looking at me and back at the door. "I can eat in the kitchen."

I nod and motion. "Yes."

He sets my plate on the tray over the tub. I'm covered in bubbles from the neck down, but I still notice the way his pupils darken when he sees me, like he wants me just as bad as I want him.

And the realization that this man will bring me breakfast in the tub when he knows all I want to do is soak, and he does it to just be with me. I think I'm falling in love with him. I'm not sure when I started falling for Callahan Bennett. But I did. And I'm falling stupidly even harder. I can't even stop myself.

He sits on the floor, across from me, his plate resting in his lap while he eats. He made us eggs that are cheesy and fluffy, toast with my favorite jam, and bacon.

"Breakfast of CEO champions," he says, taking a bite.

"This is so good," I say, covering my mouth.

He grins. "I'm surprised you don't have a chef."

"I have you," I say with a smirk. "Nobody can make me breakfast and eat in the bathroom with me like you, Cal."

He winks at me.

"Besides," I continue, "I had a meal service before. Delivered prepared meals, but they were so bland. I missed good food. I'm not going back to that."

He doesn't laugh at that, because he knows I wasn't being healthy before my first wedding.

We chat about the bathroom, and he marvels over how massive it is.

"In the winter, I turn on the floor heaters," I tell him.

He grins. "I bet it feels great getting out of the shower when it's cold."

"It does," I agree. "But this tub is my favorite part of the whole penthouse."

When we're done, he stands and takes our plates. "Finish up. I'll get ready in the other bathroom."

I bite my lip, wishing he'd stay, wishing he'd get ready in here with me. But I don't push it.

Some things are worth letting unfold at their own pace.

———

I head out to the living room, still in my robe, but my hair and makeup are done. I got new makeup yesterday from the makeup artists to match my newly sun-kissed skin. I think I did a pretty good job if I don't say so myself. My hair is still good from its blowout yesterday.

Cal's in the living room, sitting on the couch with a mug of coffee, sleeves rolled up on his dress shirt, looking unfairly hot for someone who doesn't need as long as I do to get ready.

He smiles and says, "Feeling better?"

"I am," I admit. "Wilby should be here soon with my suit."

The elevator dings, and the doors slide open. Wilby strolls in confidently. He's dressed in an impeccable suit, and his tie is perfect. Calm confidence, and I remember that he's stepping into his new role today, too. Executive assistant to the CEO. I wouldn't be here without him, either. It's a big day for him as well.

"Good morning," he says cheerfully as he holds up two garment bags. "I brought yours and Cal's suits."

Cal's head snaps over, and he says, "What?"

Wilby grins. "That's right. I got one for you, too. And if we're being honest, I got one for me, as well."

I laugh and shake my head. Wilby is literally the main character, and I love him.

He unzips the first bag and reveals an all-black suit, sharp and tailored, with a light pink dress shirt tucked neatly inside. It's so pale, it's almost white.

Cal just stares. "Holy shit. That's nice."

Wilby takes a bow and then opens the second bag. My breath catches in my throat.

It's a power suit in the same shade as Cal's dress shirt. Strong lines, perfect cut. And it's unmistakably feminine, soft, but intentional. Wilby knows I've loved pink and dialed that back at the office the past few years. I always wanted people to take me seriously. And now? I can wear whatever the fuck I want. Hell, yeah.

I smile because this was my dream. Walking into a room full of people who underestimated me, wearing pink like a crown. Like a statement and a reminder that softness and strength are not opposites.

This suit feels like a giant, elegant fuck you to the old meanies who whispered and smirked. The ones who rooted against me and called me sweetie when I started out. The ones who assumed I wouldn't make it to this day. I read the reports and the forwarded emails. I know what was said. I've filed those thoughts away. I never forgot.

I made it. I'm here, and today is the first day of me running a family business that I earned.

I run my fingers over the fabric and look up at Wilby. "It's perfect."

He nods, excited. "I knew you'd love it!"

"Damn it, you're getting a raise." I shake my head, thinking about how I don't deserve Wilby.

He laughs. "You always say that. Just know I get myself presents, too, sometimes. Like this suit."

Cal says, "I look like I'm about to overthrow a corporation in this suit or testify in court."

Wilby claps him on the shoulder. "Both could happen. The day is young. All right. Your ride's here in twenty."

I laugh and take the tailored suit, which feels like karma. Today isn't just another day. It's my day, and I'm ready to collect.

———————

Wilby, Cal, and I are on our way to the office. A tray of coffees is waiting in the car, and I'm so thankful, I could practically cry. I need all the coffee today.

We pull up in front of the building. I feel like I should have Cal take my picture like it's my first day of school. I don't think I've ever paid attention to what our building looks like until today. I feel like I'm seeing it through Cal's eyes. It's massive, glass and steel stretching straight into the sky.

Cal leans toward me, his voice low and teasing. "Do you own this building, too?"

I laugh and whisper back, "No. But, the company does."

He squeezes my hand, and I'm starting to get so nervous.

We step out of the car. Reporters are waiting, taking pictures and shouting questions. I forgot to prepare Cal for this, but he handles it with ease. He gets out first, shielding me, holding his hand out and pulling me alongside him, protectively. I don't think I could even prepare him, because he already feels like he's two steps ahead of me in preparing *me*.

Heads turn as we walk toward the building, and conversations pause. My hand is steady in his, and I feel the second people start clocking us as a unit. I glance at our reflection in the front of the glass building. Hot damn, we look like a power couple.

Wilby trails behind at a careful distance. When we reach the elevators, he leans in to whisper, "You two look so good."

Cal leans over and whispers back, "We had help."

Wilby smirks. "I do have good taste in suits."

"Thanks," we say at the same time. "Yes, you do."

The elevator ride is quiet and fast. When the doors open, the vibes shift. The floor hums with power and testosterone, something I've always hated. I've always wanted to bring more women into finance with me and show them they can do it, too. I've encouraged more opportunities for women. Previously, all of my ideas were shot down. Now? I'm going to make damn sure that happens. When I'm done, maybe there'll be pink everywhere. I smile at that thought.

My mother is standing across the lobby with a small group of older men. She hasn't seen us yet, but I can see her shaking her head, lips tight, clearly displeased about something. One of the men glances over her shoulder and spots us heading their way. Then another man turns. Both of their eyes widen in surprise. My mother keeps talking, and I hear her mention getting the board to vote on it.

Her voice trails off as she turns, and her gaze sweeps over us, taking in every detail of our outfits, our confident posture, and our hands still linked. We look damn impeccable. And unstoppable.

I haven't seen or spoken to my mother since my wedding day to Tyler, and everything fell apart. She never reached out, and I didn't bother to, either. There wasn't much to say that wouldn't have ended in bloodshed. I'm done with her bullshit.

She doesn't say hello or hug me. Or ask to meet my husband. She doesn't even pretend for the people standing around us.

I try to imagine Carly acting this way, and I simply can't. The comparison alone makes my teeth clench.

"I see you're still going to be a problem, Silvie," my mother says, cooly glancing between Cal and me.

I stare at her for a long moment. Long enough for the men behind her to shift uncomfortably.

Then I slowly smile.

"Mom," I say evenly. "I'm about to be the *whole* problem if you keep running your mouth at my work. Why are you here?"

Her lips thin, and her hands go to her hips. "I'm a part of this company."

I don't laugh. I just feel so unbothered by her right now. "No, you're not. You're married to the VP. And you can be removed from the premises if you want to disrespect anyone in this building, including me, the CEO."

I don't add daughter. Because she hasn't been acting like a mother to me. She doesn't deserve that title.

I step closer, lowering my voice. "Don't make me do that. Because I will."

Her eyes flash, but she turns on her heels and storms toward the other end of the lobby, looking furious.

I move toward the hallway to my office, and Cal follows, Wilby behind us. We pass my dad's office, now labeled "VP" on the door.

My dad steps out when he sees us. "Good morning," he says evenly, eyeing Cal.

I let go of Cal and hug him tight. "Morning, Dad."

"I'm proud of you, Silverlyn. You've worked hard to get here," he says as he pats my back.

Then it's time for the meeting. We head toward the boardroom when Tyler appears in the hallway. He stops short, an enraged expression twisting his features when his eyes land on Cal.

"Oh, hell no," he practically spits. His eyes rake up and down Cal. Which is comical because Cal is massive compared to Tyler.

"You brought your bartender here, Silvie? That's so embarrassing," Tyler says, looking at me with disgust. "You have ruined everything. You won't get away with this."

I don't let go of Cal's hand. I just stare at Tyler as if he's a bug in the hallway we might need to step around.

Cal looks down at Tyler and says without missing a beat, "You're not tall enough to talk to me like that."

Wilby laughs and then coughs behind me, unable to stop himself.

We step around Tyler, who is gaping at us, not even sure what to say to Cal, checking him like that. Because it was hilarious and true.

I ignore Tyler, smile sweetly, and tell Wilby, "We're about to turn it up a notch. All gas, no brake."

"I can't wait," he mutters as we continue past a confused-looking Tyler the Turd, who is still glaring at us.

"Let's get to work," I tell them as we head into the board-room, and I saunter up to my place at the head of the table. Cal and Wilby take theirs at the other end.

It's a beautiful day to fuck around and find out.

cal

. . .

THE BOARDROOM IS all glass and polished wood and screams expensive and money. It's not a cozy room, but more of a room where dick-measuring contests happen. I remember those rooms when I worked in finance right out of college. I didn't like them then, and I don't like them now. A long table that seats a couple dozen with leather chairs. Everyone's in suits that probably cost more than my truck back home. I stand near the wall at first, hands loose at my sides, watching. Wilby is next to me, his eyes on Silvie, serious and watching to see if she needs something. One thing I've noticed is that he doesn't play when it comes to Silvie. He's dedicated to her and his job. I like Wilby a lot.

The rest of the men in the room, though? They look at Silvie like she's a novelty. Like it's bring-your-daughter-to-work day, and she's here to entertain them. Assholes. I fucking hate all of them.

Most of them are not openly disrespecting her. Nothing they could be called out on easily. It's the little things. The bored glances passed between two men at the end of the table. The way one of them checks his phone while she speaks. The low

253

comments muttered just under their breaths. Smirks that say they think they know how this is going to go.

I feel something ugly twist in my chest. I want to knock all of their heads together and chew them all out. But I don't, and I wouldn't. I'm here to support my wife. But I shoot a few of them glares that take them back a bit. Just like fucking Tyler in the hallway. The balls on that guy. He needs to be taken down a peg or two.

Charles notices the behavior of these assholes, too. I can tell by the way his jaw muscle tightens. He glares at anyone he catches being dismissive, and a few men straighten when they realize they've been seen. Still, not all of them bother.

Charles is confusing to me. I see him love his daughter, but I am still on the fence about whether I trust him. I didn't like the way he talked to her. And I don't like the way he condones his daughter and wife treating Silvie the way they do. And why is that tool, Tyler, still here? He should have been removed immediately. But it's not my company, so what do I know, though? I'm here for Silvie. I want to support her in any way she needs.

Silvie steps to the front of the room, calm and composed. Not nervous, even though I know she has to be. This is a huge day for her. She has nothing to prove. Yet to some of these assholes in this room, she'll never be respected. I know that, and she knows that. That's why she's doing what she has to do.

"Welcome," she says clearly and confidently. "It's my honor to be your new CEO."

A couple of heads lift. Not all. One guy is still on his phone as if whatever's happening there is more important than her.

"I'm excited to continue as we have been when Charles was running the company. He's done a great job, and I look forward to working side by side with him to continue operating the way it's supposed to be run."

Someone at the far end exhales like he's bored. Another man leans back in his chair, arms crossed, eyes already drifting. It's disrespectful. Plain and simple.

Silvie sees it. I know the moment she does. Her lips thin just a fraction.

"That being said," she continues, "the company will run the same. The big question in the room is who will remain to run it with us?"

That does it. She's got their attention now. I love seeing the faces of those who didn't think she had it in her. Chairs scrape softly. Backs straighten. Eyes narrow and lock on her like predators suddenly interested in the prey.

Silvie starts pacing slowly in front of the table, heels clicking against the floor. She doesn't rush. She doesn't raise her voice.

"Some of you are being downright rude and disrespectful to me right now," she says. "And I want you to know that won't be tolerated further."

The room goes still.

"But this is the last conversation we're going to have about this. This is the only time I will address it. From this moment forward, you will treat me with respect. If you don't, you will be gone."

A few men bristle. One scoffs quietly.

"I don't care if you've been here thirty years or five. I don't care. We treat everyone with respect here, regardless of gender, age, or experience."

She stops pacing and leans forward, both hands braced on the table. "I hope you're really taking this seriously, because I won't hesitate to fire any of you."

She turns her head slightly. "Starting with Tyler."

Every head whips toward the man halfway down the table. His face drains of color, and he sputters, "What?"

Silvie looks up and nods toward the door as two security guards step inside.

"Escort Tyler off the premises," she tells them. "He won't be returning. We'll send him his things."

A man I don't recognize steps forward and holds out a manila envelope to Tyler. "You've been served."

Tyler stands so fast his chair tips back, and he snaps up the folder.

"You stupid bitch!" he shouts at Silvie. "You're going to pay for this. I will sue you!"

Silvie waves at him and smiles like she's saying goodbye to a neighbor.

He's still yelling as they escort him down the hall. But I can't make out what he's yelling. He's embarrassing himself. Charles is watching all of this, sitting back, his hands crossed in front of him as if he approves.

"I'll fire any of you who treats anyone as less than," she says calmly. "This is not a threat. It's a promise." She straightens. "I've worked my ass off to get here. And I'll be damned if anyone even looks at me sideways. Do you understand?" She waits. "Nod your heads and respond verbally."

They do. Every single one. Wilby and I glance at each and every one of these men.

"You're all getting a contract to sign," she continues as Wilby opens a folder and passes out papers to them. "It's basically everything I just told you. If you can't treat everyone with respect here, you'll be removed. No severance. No pension. Be respectful. It's not hard."

There are murmurs. She cuts them off with a raised hand.

"I won't be taking questions or comments. This is basic kindergarten knowledge. If you've made it this far in life and still need that explained to you, then you don't deserve to go further."

She smiles again.

"Now, everyone have a great day. There are snacks and coffee in the lounge. It's a beautiful day. Enjoy it."

She nods toward me.

I don't hesitate. I cross the room and slide my hand into hers. Her fingers curl around mine instantly. We walk out together, Wilby following behind us. His face is neutral, but I know better. He's eating this up.

We head toward her office. Wilby shuts the door behind us.

"That was epic," he says, fist pumping. "I've been patiently waiting years for you to do that, Silverlyn. Well done."

Silvie exhales and sinks into her chair, crossing her legs.

I sit on the couch across from her. Wilby sits down beside me.

She meets my eyes, smirks, then looks away.

"Okay," she says. "That felt good."

"I bet," I say. "I'm proud of you."

She glances back at me. There's something softer there now.

"What was Tyler served with?" I ask.

"A restraining order," she says easily. "And a lawsuit for emotional distress, damages, and to recoup for the entire cost of the wedding since he was cheating. He's cooked."

Wilby lets out a low whistle. "This is perfect."

She shrugs. "He'll settle out of court. But we won't have any further trouble from him."

There's a knock at the door. Charles comes in and sits in a chair near us.

"Well," he says. "That was interesting. Did we have to have Tyler served?"

"I meant every word, Dad," Silvie says. "I'm setting the standard. Something that should have been done a long time ago."

"You're rocking the boat with the board, just so you know. But this is effective."

"And just how are you okay with that?" she asks, tilting her head.

"I never said I was," he says quietly.

"And yet, you allowed it, encouraged it, and let Mom talk shit and embarrass me at my own company."

"I'll handle your mother," he says.

"Please do. I don't want her here. Tell her she's not to come here, and I don't want her poisoning my workplace with her drama," she continues. "Things are going to be changing, Dad. Her and Belladonna aren't welcome in my life. And if you want a place in it, you'd better make sure you act accordingly."

"I said I'd handle it," he bites out.

I glare at him, and he doesn't notice, but Wilby does, and I can tell he's trying not to laugh.

"I'm going back to Coconut Beach tonight," she says. "I'm staying there for the time being. I'll be working remotely and taking meetings. Wilby has my schedule. I'll fly back if it's absolutely necessary."

Charles frowns. "How long are you going to be gone? We have a company to run, Silvie. You can't just take off like this, especially not now that you're CEO."

"I can run it just fine from anywhere in the world. And just because you ran it working twenty-four-seven doesn't mean that's how I'll do things. We're running this together. And I will have work-life balance."

Wilby grins, trying to hide it. I can tell he's so damn proud of her, just as I am.

"I'll also be hiring an assistant for Wilby," she continues. "Actually, two. They'll be here in NYC. And Wilby might be coming to Coconut Beach as well."

I don't say a word.

I just sit there, watching her, knowing one thing for sure.

Anyone who ever thought she wasn't cut out to be the CEO has no idea what hit them.

———

Leaving with Silvie feels different than when we arrived. She moves confidently and people nod and greet her by name. She stopped to shake hands, pat their arms, and remember their names. She laughed easily and was at ease. This is where she's comfortable. It's her world, and it's fascinating to watch.

I stayed half a step behind her the whole time because I wanted her to feel supported. Coming here brought up a lot of feelings for me. And, in some ways, it made me start healing in ways I didn't realize I needed to.

The doors open, and the doorman straightens when he sees her. "Ms. Montclair," he says warmly. "Good to have you back."

"Henry," she beams. "Good to see you."

I'm already thinking about getting air outside, stripping out of this suit, and going back to casual clothes, when his gaze shifts to me. He frowns slightly and studies my face. And the recognition hits me just as his eyes widen at the same time.

"Cal?" he says. "Cal Bennett?"

I turn to face him, and the city rushes back all at once. The version of me that was here six years ago.

"Henry," I say carefully. "Hey, good to see you."

He breaks into a grin. "I thought that was you. Wow, I haven't seen you around in years. You look good."

Silvie pauses beside me, and I can feel her confusion before I even look at her. She's still, and her head is turned watching us.

Henry continues, "You just disappeared."

His words hit harder than they should. But he's not wrong. I did just disappear.

Silvie's eyes continue to flick between us. She doesn't say anything, just watches. I feel my shoulders tense, and I paste on a smile that doesn't quite stick.

"Yeah," I say. "It's been a while."

He shakes his head like he's still catching up with me and not making things really messy. "Everyone talked about you back then. You were sharp and focused. We all thought you were headed somewhere big."

Silvie's breath hitches, and she says, "You two know each other?"

Her question changes everything between us.

"We worked at the same company together," I say quickly. "A long time ago."

As if the last part makes anything less confusing.

Henry laughs. "Long time? It's only been what...five years? Feels like yesterday. Don't disappear again, man."

I swallow and look at Silvie nervously. Her brows are together and she looks so confused.

"Anyway," Henry adds. "Good to see you, Cal."

"Yeah," I say. "You too."

Silvie thanks him politely and slips her hand into mine as we continue to the car waiting for us. The door closes behind us, cutting off the memories of a life I didn't get to finish. Memories that still cut deep when I let myself think of them.

She doesn't say anything, and that feels worse.

We get a few blocks away when she finally says, "What was that?"

I stare at the buildings, the familiar buzz of the city that makes my throat tight. "I didn't know how to bring it up. I don't talk about it."

She waits.

"I loved it here," I admit. "More than I meant to. And leaving felt like the greatest failure of my life. Just talking about it makes me have to face who I didn't become when I thought that was my dream."

Her hand slides into mine and squeezes, and it pushes me to continue.

"I went to school here. Then I worked in finance at Smith and Townes."

She exhales slowly, like something is clicking into place.

"Why didn't you say anything?" she asks, surprised.

"I don't know...it was like a past life. Not me anymore. You know?" I shrug. "I'm just a bartender from Coconut Beach now."

"Why did you go back to Coconut Beach?" she asks softly.

I look out the window for a few seconds, and then I say, "I went back for my mom."

For a while, the city hums around us as we make it back to her penthouse. Life continues even though I feel like I'm failing.

"I didn't mean to hide anything from you," I promise. "I just don't like talking about it. I miss it more than I thought I did. And coming back has shown me that."

And I realize that's the first time I've let myself fully admit it.

"You weren't hiding," she says. "It sounds like you've been grieving."

I nod, because she's right. And I haven't been able to fully process it until I met her.

"Why didn't you just tell me?" She laughs. "You let me play tour guide like it was your first time in the city. You lived here for years."

"I didn't want you to know someone who doesn't exist anymore. That's not me," I say quietly.

Silvie leans closer. "I like knowing you. All of you. The sweet man who takes care of his mom and Jonah. The hot bartender. The hot surfer. All of you."

I look at her and realize this isn't about secrets or not being who we think we can be. It's about us. And somehow, we've been orbiting each other in this lifetime, yet we still ended up together. Even in some strange capacity, like a fake marriage.

Fake marriage. Fake rules. Fake lines we promised not to cross. One look at her and I know the truth. Whatever this is, it's already real. And we're running out of time to stop it.

silvie

. . .

MY CHEST FEELS heavy in a way I didn't think it could. I'm shocked. I had no idea that when I took Cal to New York with me, he was practically coming home. He went to college there and studied finance at NYU. He built a whole life here that looks a whole lot like mine. His family didn't own the company, but he was climbing his way up, and it sounds like he was good at what he did. Henry was practically in awe of him. And now I'm shocked. Who the hell is Cal?

The plane hums beneath us, and I am still trying to figure out this version of Cal that I didn't know existed until today. And he was just so chill about it, like it wasn't a giant piece of his life that I had no idea about. I wouldn't have brought him here and rubbed his face into it if I had known.

Cal's next to me, his broad shoulders relaxed and his gaze fixed on the window like he's watching memories and not clouds. He looks the same and feels the same. Yet everything feels different. I feel somehow closer to him, now. Like he gets me and gets my world after all.

How many moments did he understand me in ways I didn't realize when I was working and taking calls at his kitchen table? It doesn't feel like he betrayed me. It feels like I'm discovering something about him that is incredibly attractive, and that part makes me wonder if our paths had crossed years ago. I went to NYU, too. I likely would have been a year behind him. But did we see each other and never know? Part of that makes me sad. What if he'd been the right guy, wrong time? What if we were meant to be, so the universe laughed and moved Birdie to Coconut Beach, so I'd somehow go there someday and meet Cal. The world works in weird ways.

And this changes things. Things that scare me and pull me closer to him. I have questions. So many questions. I have to unravel this man bit by bit.

He must feel my crazy thoughts churning because he looks at me and says, "What?"

"I'm still in shock that you're like an undercover hot finance guy."

He rolls his eyes playfully. "Not quite. You know, Wilby probably had all of that information in his reports. Did you not read them?"

I shake my head. "No."

He frowns and laughs. "Why not? You just married a stranger?"

"Why would I?" I say softly. "I trust you, and you'll tell me when you're ready."

His expression softens. "I'll tell you anything you want to know."

"Do you miss it?" I ask.

"I still do stuff for Jonah and me." He shrugs. "Nothing crazy, just playing around. I'm good with money."

That's what Wilby was saying when he was teasing that Cal had his own money.

I stare at him, and he continues.

"The bar's paid off," he continues. "Along with my cottage, Jonah's, and my mom's. I like finance stuff."

I stare at him because all of those places paid off are a huge chunk of real estate.

His gaze drops to mine, dark, warm, and familiar. "What are you thinking right now?"

I shake my head, as if I can't believe this. "I'm thinking, how did I end up with a secret hot finance guy for a husband?"

He exhales a quiet laugh and leans his head back as if he's tired of my shit again.

I continue because I live to tease him now. "I feel like I just went on an epic side quest with you. I kinda love it."

He closes his eyes and sighs, then looks over at me. "Now what?"

I lean closer, my mouth brushing his ear. "Now you take me to the back of this plane, and you make this right."

He swallows, and his breath hitches. "What?"

"I don't even care how," I add softly. "Kiss me. Touch me. Make me come. Fuck me senseless. I don't care. You started something the other day and got pulled away to the bar. Then we were tired and traveling, and then you had the nerve to look that fucking hot in a suit. So now I need it." I pull back, just enough to lock eyes with his. "I need you."

His eyes darken, and something low and mistakable is happening behind those eyes. And it feels dirty. He doesn't say a word, just reaches down and slowly unbuckles his seatbelt.

My panties are soaked.

I stand, and his hand immediately finds mine, and I tug him down the narrow aisle toward the back of the plane, my pulse racing with need. Every step feels like it's taking forever. I can't wait anymore.

We slip into the bedroom, and I shut and lock the door behind us.

"What if someone comes back here?" he asks, his voice low.

"They won't," I say, pushing him gently toward the bed.

He catches my waist instead, his strong hands pulling me close, spinning us, so I stumble back against him. God, he could manhandle me every day. His body is so solid, warm, and hard. I feel dizzy with the scent of his soap and cologne. He's so fucking intoxicating.

He leans down, mouth at my neck, and I can feel myself forgetting where we are. "You may be in charge in the board-room, Silverlyn. But in the bedroom, I'm in charge.," he says, tucking hair behind my ear. "Don't forget that."

I shudder and whimper, pressing my thighs together.

"And I didn't get my in-flight meal yet. I'm starving," he says as he pulls my suit pants down and throws them off to the side. He puts his fingers around my lace panties and slides those down, too, me stepping out of them.

He grins at me and pushes me back on the bed, using his hands to guide my thighs apart. He looks at me and says, "Per-fect for me."

I whimper, and he says, "Gotta be quiet. Otherwise, they'll hear you."

"I don't care," I murmur.

He kisses his way up my thighs, finding my center wet and ready for him. He swipes his tongue up my center and lands on my clit, sucking softly and moaning quietly. "For me."

He takes his time, and every time I build up, he slows down. I know he has to be doing that on purpose. "First time you come will be on my cock, baby."

"Then you'd better get ready to fuck me now, Cal, because I am ready and have been ready," I gasp out.

He stands and takes off his belt, and I swear I almost come just watching him. He unbuttons his shirt quickly, throws it aside, and slides his pants down, revealing black boxers. I watch as he releases his cock, and holy shit. Now I know what I've been missing, and I'm kicking myself for not doing this sooner. What were we waiting for?

He leans down, mouth at my neck, and I forget where we are. The only thing I care about right now is Cal being inside me. Immediately. Yesterday. Today. All day.

He pauses. "I have a condom in my wallet. Hold on."

I grip his shoulders. "I'm on birth control, and I got tested at the Coconut Beach clinic when I got there. I haven't had sex with anyone in over six months."

A look of confusion crosses his face, and he says, "Yeah, I'll ask you more about that later."

"Please don't," I murmur as I practically pulse for him to be inside of me. "Just fuck me, Cal."

"My wife," he bites out as he pushes inside me, filling me.

I whimper, and he says, "Want more?"

"It's not all the way in?" I ask, my eyes wide, moaning slowly.

He shakes his head and pushes further, and I could never describe this feeling. Of being full and of him. At this point, there's nothing I wouldn't do for this man. Have his babies someday? Keep him forever? Anything. I love him. I love his family and friends. And I love him so goddamn much. I'd worship him if that wouldn't be fucking weird.

"You good?" he whispers in my ear.

"I'm really good," I murmur.

"I've wanted to do this since the moment I saw you. I knew you were mine. I couldn't explain it. But I knew," he says as he thrusts and makes me forget my own name.

Weeks of tension snap between us, and when he thrusts and kisses me in between thrusts, it feels inevitable. I'm so fucking gone for this man. Like this was always going to happen. Like the world was going to do everything in its power to get us together. No matter what.

My orgasm builds hard and fast, and I feel him too. He says, "I won't ever come until you do. Ladies first, baby."

And then I do. I come harder than I've ever come in my life.

And he does too.

I pull his face to mine and kiss him, because there's nowhere else to be, and I am never going to stop kissing Cal. I melt into him, into the way he makes me feel safe, grounded, and free to be me.

Erin Branscom

Time blurs. He gets up, comes back with a washcloth, and helps me clean up. And I'm reminded that it's the little things like that. The small moments that build up to the big moments.

He settles me against him, and everything else feels far away. Because in his big strong arms, his chin resting on my hair, I feel the best I've ever felt.

A soft knock at the door lets us know that we're descending into Coconut Beach, and I gently wake him.

For the first time in days, I feel relaxed. And real. Something I thought we could pretend our way out of is never going to be fake again. There's no way. Not after this trip.

And I'm going to tell him that.

———

By the time we head out through the doors of the Coconut Beach airport and into the Florida warm, salty and familiar air, I feel like I've lived many lives in one week. Coconut Beach feels like a relief compared to the electric, bustling race of New York City. I don't know why my father can't understand why this is where I want to be right now. He was here. I know he felt it too.

Cal's hand finds the small on my back, and just that simple touch relaxes and charges me at the same time. It must feel similar to him, because his shoulders are relaxed and he seems happier. Content. Hot sex on the plane didn't hurt, either.

I wish he'd have told me about his past in New York, but I know he wasn't ready. There's still baggage to unpack with Cal. And he's working on it. Regardless, I don't care what his secrets are. I want him.

When I look at Cal, I want it all with him. I can't even begin to explain it, but I just can't imagine not being with him.

Birdie's house comes into view as we pull up in front of Cal's, and we park.

My hope is to take a shower and have a quiet night in with

Cal and some takeout. That hope is gone when the front door flies open to Birdie's house.

January steps out and calls back inside, "They're here!"

I barely have time to get out of the truck before Birdie squeals my name and barrels toward me. Her arms wrap around me, and she laughs. "You're back!"

I laugh. "Of course I'm back. I told you I would be."

Glenda catches up and says, "Her husband is here after all, of course she came back."

Husband. I love the sound of that. I glance at Cal, and we share a small, secretive smile.

The Bees surround me, and I smile. They are so happy to see us, wrapping us both in hugs.

"What are you all up to tonight?" I ask as I take in their chatter and chaos.

Glenda says, "We were tracking when you all landed. Birdie was worried you wouldn't come back. We consoled her with sangria and kept her busy by playing poker."

I laugh and pull Birdie into another hug. "Of course I'm back."

Cal sets our bags down, and one of the Bees claps him on the shoulder. "You make it out alive?"

He smiles. "It was good."

They laugh and joke with him as if they've known him forever, and then I remember they probably have. I watch as he leans into the chaos here, and he looks at home. This version of him feels slightly different than the man walking beside me in Manhattan. He's himself here, and there he feels like a ghost of himself. But still strong by my side.

Birdie stands back on the porch, smiling as if she's relieved. Hugging Birdie feels like coming home in a way that I need.

"You survived New York and your first day as CEO?" She beams at me proudly.

"I did," I say. "Barely."

She looks at me more closely and says, with her kind eyes that always seem to know. "You look different, sugar. Happy."

Before I can ask what she means, a cold glass is pressed into my hand by Lucille. "Drink. And cheers to being back where you belong."

I glance at Cal, and he shrugs. "Go have fun. I'll put our bags up and order food for everyone. I need to check in at the bar, anyway."

But I don't want him to go, and he must sense that because he comes over and kisses me softly and says, "I'll be right back."

"Okay," I say softly. "Bye."

Inside Birdie's house, it's loud and chaotic. Shoes piled up by the door, and half-empty plates stacked on the counter. Our coming home clearly interrupted their party. I lean against the island, feeling overwhelmed and happy in the best possible way.

We eat fondue over a big fondue pot that the Bees have set up. If there's one thing about the Bees, they sure do know how to have a good time. I listen to them talk about an upcoming wedding and a couple of other events.

Birdie catches my eye from across the room and tips her glass toward the porch. I slip outside, the night air wrapping around me, the waves crashing in the distance, steady and familiar to me now. That's the sound I fall asleep to and the sound I wake up to.

I check in on Iggy, and he's curled up on a rock under his hibiscus bush. "Hey, buddy," I whisper.

Cal joins me a few minutes later, sliding onto a chair next to me, wearing shorts and a T-shirt now. We don't say anything at first, he just slips his hand into mine.

"I forgot how quiet it is here," I say.

He glances over at me. "Not quiet with the Bees."

I laugh softly as someone inside laughs loudly, and another person breaks out into song to the music. "They missed us."

"And how does that make you feel?" he asks.

I look over at him and think about New York and how someone recognized him and missed him there. No one misses me in New York. And I think about how this life in Coconut Beach is a place I've come to find home. A real home. With real people I love.

I squeeze Cal's hand, and he strokes my knuckles.

We go inside, and I say goodbye to everyone, giving them hugs. A familiar flutter reminds me that this could be home. I can choose this. This place feels like it's choosing me.

Birdie kisses my cheek and tells me that Wilby's room is ready for when he comes back.

"I'll tell him," I promise.

Cal waits patiently beside me and when we head back to his house, I realize something.

New York showed me who I was trying to be. But Coconut Beach showed me who I truly am. And coming here was the best choice I've ever made.

cal
. . .

THE NEXT MORNING, the sun hasn't risen yet, and the soft sound of the ocean comes in the open windows. Silvie's curled up against my chest, her leg draped over mine, her hair fanned across my shoulder, and I breathe her in. I just made her come twice, and then we had the best sex I've ever had with anyone. The connection I have with Silvie is palpable.

I stroke my thumb in circles along her shoulder, back and forth. Her fingers move lazily over my chest, tracing lines I know by heart. I've had my tattoos for so long that sometimes I forget that they're there. She follows the ink down my arm, and my breath catches. Goosebumps ripple across my skin from her touch.

She smiles. "You sleep okay?"

"Yeah," I say as I shudder when her fingertips slide lower. "I always sleep well with you next to me."

Her mouth drops and kisses my ink, and she looks at me, curious. "Tell me about them."

"My tattoos?"

She nods. "You've got a lot. And they look like they tell stories."

I exhale slowly. "They weren't supposed to be a story at first. I just liked them."

Her fingers trace a familiar curve, slowly. "But now?"

"Now they are kind of personal," I admit. "I think I started mapping out life experiences without realizing it."

She studies my arm, following the lines. "This is New York."

I still for a second as she realizes.

"I see it now," she says quietly. "Skyline shapes."

"Yeah," I say. "That was a whole chapter."

She leans in and presses a soft kiss there, right over the ink.

"And this?" she asks, moving to the waves across my ribs.

"Home," I say. "The water, where it's quiet and peaceful."

At least I thought this was home. But now that I'm with Silvie, I think home is wherever she is. She makes me feel like I can have it all with her.

Her fingers keep moving, over patterns that don't have names, shapes that only make sense to me. "And these?"

"Those were survival," I admit. "Times I didn't know what I was going to do, but I kept going anyway."

She rests her head on my chest again. "I like that you have these."

I pull her closer, pressing a kiss to her temple. "I've never really explained them to anyone before."

"I like being the first," she murmurs.

So do I.

We stay like this until the sun begins to rise, the ceiling fan turning lazily overhead.

"I've got to get to yoga," she murmurs. "Are you surfing today?"

"No, I've got to catch up on bar stuff," I admit.

Eventually, we drag ourselves out of bed. She disappears into the bathroom, and I take a minute to steady myself. This feels dangerously like love and a real marriage. Like I could get used to this.

When she comes out, wearing a new yoga top and bottoms, I almost drag her back to bed. I pull her to me and kiss her softly. "I've got something to show you."

I lead her down the hall, and she says, "What is it?"

I open the door to my rarely used office. Her office now.

She goes quiet.

"I figured you'd need a space to work," I say. "Somewhere that's yours."

I'd had Marina's brothers clear it out and set it up with a new desk and chair. It's not much, but I wanted to make my space more her space, too.

She turns and takes it all in, her eyes shining. "You did this? For me?"

"Well, yeah. Of course. I know you need to work here," I say, leaning against the door.

"You didn't have to do this. I can work from anywhere, Cal."

"I wanted to," I say simply.

She steps closer and wraps her arms around me. "You're really good at making room for people."

I swallow. "Only the ones who matter. You matter to me, Silvie."

Her arms pull me tighter at that. "Thank you."

"What are you doing today?" I ask.

"I'm going to the crochet club with the Bees later," she says casually. "Then I'm stopping by your mom's with coffee."

Something pulls in my chest when she mentions my mom, as it always does.

"She'll love that," I say.

"We have so much to catch up on," she says, like it's obvious.

Before she leaves the room, I catch her hand and pull her back to me gently. She laughs and stumbles into me.

I take my time, kissing her, breathing in her vanilla-and-coconut scent. "Have fun at yoga."

"I will. I'll plan dinner tonight," she says.

"I like doing life with you," I say.

Her expression softens. "I like doing life with you, too."

She kisses me again and then pulls back, giving me that smile I feel all the way in my soul. I stand there watching as she heads out.

I don't know how this will work yet. I just know I don't want to go back to the version of my life that didn't include her.

Tonight, Silvie planned dinner at the Seashell Diner. Silvie, I have discovered, is not much of a cook. And when she says she's going to take care of dinner, she means either picking up or choosing the place we'll get takeout from. And I don't mind, because every day feels like an adventure with her.

Silvie, wearing cutoffs, sneakers, and a tank top, is as casual as ever.

We peruse our menus, and I glance over at her, still unable to believe that this is my life and my wife.

"How was work today?" I ask after we place our orders and our menus are collected.

She leans across, and her cleavage is on full display. I can barely focus. Jesus, she's stunning.

"It was good. I had meetings all day. Wilby is coming tomorrow. He's going to stay at Birdie's until I can find a place for him to rent," she says. "I'm glad he wants to come back. He says he loves it here. Who would have thought?"

"Good. I've missed him, too," I admit. "You think you can work here and back in the city and make it work?"

She nods. "Listen. It's a double standard. My father has traveled all over the world while running that company. It's no surprise that he did it to avoid my mother. He ran it by doing meetings over video and calls. And I picked up the slack back home. Now it's my turn. I can be wherever I want in the world, and he can pick up the slack back home."

I listen, and she continues. "It's insane that he is trying to get me to come back by telling me that I need to be there to run the company. That's simply not true. And also, I don't need to work eighteen to twenty-hour days as he did. I believe a good CEO has a work-life balance. Sure, we'll have calls later in the evenings and travel. But it doesn't have to be all-consuming. It's just not necessary."

Our burgers and fries arrive, and we dig in. I can't stop staring at her.

"What?" she asks when she notices.

"I just like seeing you so casual. Happy. Being you. Knowing what you want and going after it and not taking crap from anyone."

She smiles. "Thanks. I'm not sure I have everything quite figured out. But I do know what I don't want. And I don't want my dad's life. He doesn't seem to ever be happy."

"Have you heard anything about your mom and sister?" I ask.

She shakes her head. "Wilby said she hasn't come around, and my dad has been working even longer hours. Tyler and Belladonna have moved into my parents' house."

I shudder. "That's so wild that they are married. And rubbing it in everyone's faces. I don't like the way he talked to you, and I don't want him near you. He has no respect for you."

She grins. "Look at you being so protective. It's sexy, hot husband."

I shake my head at her and change the subject. "I have a surprise for you after this."

She pops a fry in her mouth. "I like your surprises."

I like her.

———

Hidden Cove is a local's best-kept secret. One that few tourists know about. Locals guard it and rarely share. It's about a mile to get to, but worth it. The views along the way are spectacular, and once you arrive, the waterfalls are the best. I know Silvie will love it.

She walks behind me, humming softly, stopping every so often to touch a leaf or comment on the light filtering through the branches. She looks relaxed and happy. Like the noise fell away the second we entered the trail. I've always found peace here, and now I'm happy to share it with her.

"You bring all your girls out here?"

I look at her like the answer's obvious. "Only the one I married."

She laughs, and she grows quiet when the waterfall finally opens up in front of us. She stops short. Mist hangs in the air, cool against our skin, sunlight catching in the spray like it's holding on to whatever daylight is left.

"Oh," she breathes. "I can't believe this place."

"This is my favorite place on the island."

She looks at me then and nods. "Your waterfall tattoo."

The water is cold when we step in, shocking at first, then exhilarating. She squeals and grabs onto me, shivering as her fingers dig into my arms, and laughs.

I pull her to me, her legs hooking around my hips as I move us under the waterfall. Water rushes over us as her hands slide into my hair. Mine are at her waist, pulling her against me, my dick hard and ready for her. There's nowhere for us to be. Just us at sunset in one of my favorite places. Where we're exactly supposed to be in this moment. Together.

I dip my head down to hers and kiss her softly, needing her, wanting her, and giving her what she needs. I slide her swimsuit bottoms down and kick my trunks off, pulling her up and slamming into her, both of us panting with need and desire. I feel her grip me and come around me, and my body shatters into hers, us becoming one.

Later, we stretch out on warm rocks, the sun drying our skin, the sound of the water steady and constant. Silvie's head rests on my chest, her fingers tracing lazy circles there like she's memorizing me.

"I want this to be real with you," I say quietly.

The words surprise me even as they leave my mouth. I don't take them back.

She lifts her head, eyes searching my face. "It is real."

"I love you," I say. It doesn't feel dramatic. It feels honest.

Her smile is soft and sure. "I love you too. It stopped being fake a long time ago for me."

Relief hits me so hard I have to close my eyes for a second. Like I've been holding my breath through this whole thing and didn't even realize it.

We stay there for a while, wrapped around each other, the world narrowed down to water and sun and skin. It's slow and unhurried and feels nothing like the frantic wanting I used to mistake for love.

Eventually, she shifts, propping herself up on one elbow. "Can I ask you something?"

"Anything."

"Do you want kids?"

The question lands softly but carries weight. I don't deflect. I don't joke.

"Yeah," I say. "I always have."

Her brows lift slightly. "Really?"

"Really," I say. "I didn't have a dad growing up. I think that stuck with me."

She listens, quiet and attentive.

"I want to be there," I continue. "Not just around. I want to show up. Make breakfasts. Go to games. Teach them how to surf and how to treat people right. Family means everything to me because I had to build mine from scratch."

Her eyes shine, and she swallows. "I want that too."

I pull her closer, pressing my forehead to hers. "Maybe this could work," I say.

She smiles. "Maybe it already is."

Erin Branscom

The waterfall keeps rushing behind us, steady and constant, and for the first time in a long time, the future doesn't feel like something I'm bracing for.

It feels like something I want.

silvie
· · ·

"I'M JUST SAYING," Birdie says calmly from the stool on the kitchen island as she sips her coffee, "that the instructions of three fifty are not a suggestion."

I just almost set Cal's kitchen on fire because I wanted to bake him a treat. This feels important to note because the smoke alarm is screaming, reminding me that I'm horrible in the kitchen and I should never be trusted in here ever again.

"I didn't think it was a suggestion. I just forgot to set the timer, then got on a work call." I cough as I use a tea towel to try to shoo the smoke out the window. It's useless and not helping.

This is how I know I'm madly in love with Cal. I'm a woman who runs a billion-dollar company and can negotiate deals seasoned financial professionals wouldn't fathom taking on. But put me in a kitchen and try to follow a simple recipe to bake brownies, and suddenly I'm close to arson.

Birdie's eyes slide to mine over her cup. "Mmhmm."

"What?" I ask

"It sounds like my baby is in love." She smirks.

Even though this budding love between Cal and I feels like our little secret, I know my cheesy, lovestruck grin gives me away.

281

Luckily, the smoke alarm finally shuts up, interrupting her teasing. Whatever is left of the charred brownies is a stark reminder of my nonexistent kitchen skills.

"I was just trying to bake something," I add.

"Sugar, I raised you. You have never baked anything in all of your life."

Wilby knocks and opens the front door, poking his head in, looking concerned. "What in the fresh hell is this?"

"I'm baking," I tell him.

He takes one look at the smoke, the oven, and me. "Who let you bake?" he asks slowly, looking confused.

"I can bake," I snap. "Why is this so hard for everyone to understand? Can't a wife bake something for her husband?"

He narrows his eyes. "Who are you and what have you done with my best friend?"

"Stop." I groan.

"No," he says. "This is freaking me out."

Birdie snorts, enjoying this.

Wilby steps closer, turning on the ceiling fan in Cal's living room. "Have you been kidnapped?"

"Wilby," I clip.

"Blink twice if you're okay."

I blink twice.

He gasps. "Oh my God. You should never be left alone in the kitchen. Everyone knows this."

"I can try new things," I insist.

Wilby puts his hand over his heart and slides onto the stool next to Birdie. "This is worse than I thought."

I roll my eyes. "When did you get in anyway? I thought I was picking you up at the airport."

Wilby shrugged. "Birdie got me. We had plans."

"Plans?" I huff. "What plans?"

"Relax, you've been busy falling in love, baking brownies, and you're practically on your honeymoon. I didn't want to bother you." Wilby shrugs.

Birdie stands and heads to the coffee pot, pouring herself more coffee and another cup. She sets the cups before Wilby and heads to the fridge for creamer. "Wilby is an unofficial Bee now. He's joined the hive."

I open my mouth to say something when Cal walks in, hair damp from surfing and smiling at me as he crosses the room and dips his head to kiss me softly.

"Still doesn't look fake," Wilby mutters.

"Oh, stop it. You know this stopped being fake a while ago. Cal and Silvie are in love." Birdie smiles with approval as Cal holds me.

"What's going on in here?" Cal asks, shaking his head at Birdie, not able to hide his grin.

"I tried to bake you a surprise," I say.

He looks at the oven and back at me, and his smile softens. "You didn't have to do that."

"More like shouldn't have done that," Wilby mutters.

"I know," I say. "But I wanted to."

He leans down and kisses my temple like his kitchen isn't a disaster, and I didn't almost burn his house down. He looks like he couldn't care less.

"It's perfect," he says.

"It's charcoal," I tell him.

"It's the thought," he says, pressing his forehead to mine. "And it's very nice."

Wilby groans behind us. "Why do they have to be so adorable and sickeningly sweet?"

Birdie smiles like she just won something. "They're perfect."

Cal wraps an arm around my waist and smiles down at me like I hang the moon instead of committing crimes against baked goods.

And I realize, standing in a smoky kitchen with a ruined pan and a man who looks at me like I'm magic, that I would absolutely set the world on fire for him.

Preferably just not his house.

I knock on Carly's door, holding two cups of coffee. Extra cream for Carly's with cinnamon sprinkled on top because I remember that's how she likes it.

"Come in!" I hear from inside.

"Carly?" I call as I let myself in.

No answer. I step fully inside, the door clicking behind me when I stop short.

Donna Bennet is stretched out on the couch, smiling at me. "Hello."

She says this like she's just a normal person, not a *New York Times* bestselling author I've been reading since I was twelve. She's my favorite author of all time and seeing her here just casually sitting in Carly's living room is like having my two different worlds collide.

She looks just like the photo on the back of all of her books and from the few interviews I've seen of her. She looks incredible.

She's wearing sunglasses pushed into her hair, and a giant, brightly colored tote bag rests at her feet. A laptop is propped open on the table next to her. She has a coffee mug in her hand.

She looks at me and smiles. "Oh, good," she says. "You're here. Come in."

I just stare, my jaw dropped. Because this is the very woman whose books I stole from my mom's bedside table in high school and from friends' mothers. The woman whose name people talk about in any romance book conversations, the mother of all romance. *The* Donna Bennett. In real life and on Carly's couch in Coconut Beach.

"I'm sorry," I say faintly. "I didn't expect to see you here."

She laughs. "That's the response I usually get." I walk forward slowly. "I'm sorry. Hi. I'm Silvie."

"Hi," she says warmly. "I figured that's who you were."

My heart does a little flip-flop. "I didn't know you knew who I was."

She waves a hand. "Of course I do. I had to come to Coconut Beach and see for myself the very woman who married my favorite nephew and brought my sister back to life."

I glance down at myself. "This is unexpected."

"So is hearing a billionaire heiress married my favorite nephew."

I choke.

Before I can recover, she gestures toward the hallway. "Carly's in the shower. She'll be down soon."

"Oh," I say, pretending to be chill. "Great. I brought coffee for her. I would have brought you one...you know, you can have mine."

"Not a chance," Donna says. "I'm all set."

I set the cups on the coffee table, nervous as Donna watches me with curiosity.

"She's doing better, thanks to you," she says. She studies me for a moment, and her eyes are kind.

I pause and glance over at her. "What do you mean?"

"You've helped," she says. "I appreciate that."

That hits me straight in the heart. Because when I fell in love with Cal, I didn't expect to fall in love with his mom as well. She's become like a mother to me that I never knew I craved, not having my own mother be there for me when I needed her.

"She's laughing more," Donna continues. "She has had visitors, and she talks about the world as if it's not something she's watching through a window. She's participating in life, now."

My chest tightens at her words. "Cal has..."

Donna shakes her head. "Cal isn't behind this one. This one is all you, my dear."

I don't know what to say, so I don't say anything.

"You have changed the temperature around here."

I blink back tears.

Donna shifts, tucking a leg under her. "You have changed him, too."

I laugh nervously. "I didn't do anything."

She gives me a look. "Sweetheart."

Her words rattle around in my head. I think of Cal in the kitchen this morning, barefoot, making coffee for me like it's already a ritual. Like he's been doing it for years and most of all, I've come to appreciate and anticipate our routines.

Donna leans forward slightly. "You know this man loves you more than anything, right?"

Her question is casual, but it lands heavy with me. I still have no idea what to say. I'm still coming down from the high of realizing she's actually in the room with me, much less praising me.

I scoff because it's easier than being honest with her...and myself.

Donna tilts her head. "You're adorable. You love him just as much. I can tell."

I cross my arms and grin at her, not denying it.

"This summer, you've helped my family greatly. I hope you realize that, Silvie. You've made more progress with my sister than I've made in six years. I've offered the best therapists, support, and I've tried everything. But you? You bring them both back to life."

That gives me pause.

"Cal has a hard time showing love and letting people in," she continues. "He will rearrange his whole life to protect the people he loves."

My throat tightens. I look toward the hallway again, suddenly aware of just how much Cal has given me without me knowing how big of a deal it is.

"And my sister," she says softly. "She hasn't let anyone in for a long time. And now she has a book club, gets makeovers, and speaks of you as if you are her new best friend."

That makes me smile. "She is my new best friend. I adore her."

The shower turns off down the hall, and Donna smiles, but there's something else there, too. Something watchful.

"I don't mean to intrude on anything..."

"You don't," Donna says. "That's the point. Has Cal ever talked to you about his father?"

I still. "Not much."

"Hmm," she murmurs.

Carly steps into the room then, smiling, a towel still wrapped around her hair, wearing shorts and a T-shirt. The tense moment breaks. But something has definitely shifted between us.

And now I'm wondering deep down, what else does Cal have buried? And why do I feel like it's starting to surface?

And I'm in too deep to step away.

cal

. . .

THE BAR'S packed in the way that makes Cocktails & Chaos feel alive. We have a live band tonight that is one of my favorites, and this is the night to be at the bar. The weather is perfect, the music is great, and Silvie's here. *My wife.*

I don't get tired of thinking that.

The Bees have taken over a few tables and somehow made this even more fun with a dartboard set up. No idea where that came from, but we'll go with it. Sometimes it's best not to ask the Bees any questions.

Silvie is at a table with Mia, Summer, and Wendy. They're all swapping stories, doing shots, laughing, and catching up like normal friends who do this. And that's what is fun to see. Silvie has become a local. Not an easy thing to do, but she's done it. She fits in here.

I'm working behind the bar, making drinks, and grinning like an idiot every time I catch Silvie's eye. I want to drag her home and fuck her senseless, but she's having a good time, and I need to work.

A hand reaches over the bar and rests on my forearm. I look over to see a blonde woman who looks to be in her early twenties. "You single?" she asks, shouting over the music.

289

I don't hesitate and lift up my hand, proudly showing off my ring. "I'm married."

And it feels good to say that. Who would have thought that I'd love being married? If you'd have asked me several months ago, I'd swear I'd never get married.

She laughs. "Figures. All the good ones always are. Who is the lucky lady?"

I nod toward Silvie, who is watching this, looking less than impressed by what is happening.

Silvie says something to the women, and they all turn and watch. Great, now we have an audience.

The woman follows my gaze and lifts her drink in a salute to Silvie. "Damn. Lucky."

"Yeah," I say quietly and mostly to myself. "We are."

She wanders off, and I'm still grinning when I feel the air shift in the bar. A woman steps in that I don't recognize, but she seems somehow familiar. Then it dawns on me that that has to be Silvie's sister. I don't know how I know, but something in me just knows. They look a lot alike, only Silvie has blonde hair, and this woman has dark, almost black hair.

She steps inside and scans the bar like she's entering a space she plans to conquer. She looks out of place. Perfect hair, high spiked expensive looking heels on the beach, her expression unpleasant and tight.

My jaw goes tight, and my body goes rigid. Because I was just thinking about how happy my wife looked sitting there with her friends. And then this terrible person comes and is about to fuck it all up.

She finds Silvie, and her gaze narrows and fixates on Silvie like a missile. My attention snaps to Silvie, my body going straight, shoulders squaring up.

Belladonna strides toward the table and Silvie's mid-sip when her sister stops in front of her, making Silvie practically choke on her drink when she sees her.

I want to throw Belladonna out of here. But I also kind of want to watch Silvie dress her down and put her in her place.

"What the hell are you doing here?" Silvie asks, coughing and wiping her mouth.

Belladonna smiles as if she's happy she caught Silvie off guard. "Hello, sister. Did you miss me?"

"Actually, no," Silvie mutters.

Belladonna smiles as if she's ready to attack in some way. "I figured out where you were. I knew you'd go where Birdie was. You two were always so freakishly close."

She says this like it's meant to sting like an insult, but there's something bitter underneath her words.

Silvie squints at her. "You came all this way to insult me? You could have just sent a text like you usually do."

"Well, that would mean you'd have to unblock me," she says with a pointed look.

Silvie stares at her and says nothing.

"I came to talk some sense into you," Belladonna says in a condescending tone, one I know isn't going to go well for her. I've watched Silvie take on board members. She won't put up with this.

"About what?" Silvie asks, already buzzed, already fearless. Silvie looks at Mia, Wendy, and Summer, who are all glaring at Belladonna. "Oh, this is going to be good, ladies."

Belladonna lifts her chin. "My husband. Tyler. I know you're mad that we're married now, but we're in love."

Wendy glances at the others as if she can't believe what she is hearing. "Is she for real?"

Silvie throws her head back and laughs. "Belladonna, I don't want your husband. Hell, I'm not even sure why *you* even want your husband."

Summer and Mia giggle. Wendy does not.

Wendy leans forward, eyes sharp. "Why are you really here? What's your problem with Silvie? She's not the one in the wrong here. You are. And she's finally happy now, and what, you're just going to ruin it for her?"

Belladonna glares at her. "This isn't your business. Back off."

"Silvie is our business. Why don't you go away?" Summer sits up straighter. "What's her name again?"

"Belladonna," Mia whispers. "I think. Can't remember. She's not very memorable."

"Isn't that poison?" Summer whispers.

Silvie sets her glass down carefully and straightens. Oh shit. She's turned into CEO Silvie. This is where it goes down.

"You know what?" Silvie says calmly with a smile. "I am happy. I have a hot six-foot-four tattooed husband who loves me. So, yeah, I'm happy. You can have...whatever Tyler is. And if that's what you want, I'm happy for you guys. But you need to leave and let me live my life."

Belladonna's composure cracks. "You don't understand what you've done. You've gotten Tyler fired and me cut off. How are we supposed to live?"

That's when Silvie finally notices me standing here, a few feet behind them, arms crossed, expression flat. Her eyes flick to mine and widen just a touch, and then she smiles.

Belladonna follows her gaze and turns. Belladonna's eyes widen in recognition when she sees me and waves. "Is that your husband? Aren't you going to introduce us?"

"Time to go, Belladonna," Silvie says calmly. "We're done here."

"No, we're not done," Belladonna snaps. "If you don't fix this, I'll ruin your life, just like you've ruined ours. Really, Silvie. You don't care about anyone but yourself."

Silvie looks at her with disgust. "Like what? What would you do, Belladonna?"

Belladonna's mouth twists. "I'll tell the tabloids. Everything. And I'll tell them where you are."

Summer glances at me and mouths, "Can I beat her ass?"

I shake my head.

Summer scowls and takes another sip of her drink.

"And all you'd be selling them are lies," Silvie says coolly. " I'll sue you for that. You have no assets, but I'll sue you for anything you have left. I'm an open book. I've made peace with what happened with you and Tyler. I have nothing you can throw in my face."

Belladonna's face gets red and hard. "You'll be ruined. No one will take you seriously."

"Maybe you just move on and get a life? Maybe a job?" Silvie offers.

"You're going to pay," she bites out. "I'm going to ruin you. I can promise you that."

Then she turns and stomps out, her heels catching in the sand and making her trip.

Music continues, drinks are being poured, the Bees are now forming a conga line out in the sand. And someone cheers on a drinking contest in the corner.

But nothing in this bar matters right now except my wife. She looks over at me, eyes bright, smile easy, like she didn't just stand her ground and win. I'm proud of her. God help me. I'm in love with a woman who loves me loudly and I'd have her back about anything. And I'd let the whole world try her just to watch them prove her wrong.

Wilby shows up and slides into a chair next to Silvie and grins. "Ladies. What did I miss?"

Mia snorts and summer raises her glass just as Wendy shakes her head like she's still processing everything. Silvie smiles into her drink, flushed, eyes bright.

"Her sister was just here," Summer says.

Wilby looks around and cringes. "I knew I smelled a rat when I came in."

Silvie says, "Oh, you missed it. Apparently, she's going to ruin me."

"Not sorry to miss that," Wilby says with a shudder.

"She's a real treat and was asked to leave. What can I get you to drink?" I ask.

"Surprise me. You always make me something good," she says. "I leave for a couple of hours and come back to craziness."

I bring them all another round, and Silvie catches my hand when I leave to walk away. "Thank you."

I lean down and kiss her softly. "You're welcome."

I turn to head back to the bar and hear Wilby say to Silvie, "When are we going back to New York?"

It dawns on me that she'll be going back again. And I can't go with her every time. My life is here in Coconut Beach. Hers is in New York. The thought hits me harder than I expect.

The night winds down and the music fades. The Bees drift out in pairs and laughter trails behind them.

Silvie kisses me before heading out. Her fingers squeeze mine and she says, "I'll see you at home?"

"Text me when you get there, okay?" I tell her.

She nods and waves and I watch her go.

Donna comes in and slides onto the bar stool when the bar has grown quieter and the lights are lower. She grins at me and says, "How's my favorite nephew?"

"Hi, Aunt Donna," I say as I walk around the bar to give her a hug.

She pats me on the back and says, "I was at your mom's."

"Is she okay?" I ask.

She puts up a hand. "She's doing well. In fact, I'm surprised, actually."

Relief floods my chest. "Yeah, she's made friends with Silvie."

"I met her, too," she says. "Nice woman."

I nod. "Yeah, she is."

She studies me for a moment, then sighs. "I am worried about you and your mom."

I give her a confused look. "What do you mean?"

"I am worried that if this doesn't work out, your mom will be so upset. She's so happy and it's been years since I've seen her like this."

I smile faintly. "I agree. It's kind of a wild story."

"It is," she agrees. "And I'm worried about you getting hurt."

That makes me pause.

"I worry about Carly the most," she continues. "If Silvie leaves, your mom will be devastated."

And I will be, too.

Her words land like a punch to the gut. I know she's right. She's looking out for us, but it still isn't something I haven't been thinking about myself. My biggest fears.

Donna's voice softens. "I want you to be happy more than anything. You have a way of self-sabotaging things when it comes to the people around you before they can leave. You always have."

After she leaves, I lock up alone. The bar feels too quiet.

Silvie's laughter echoes in my head. The way she looked tonight, like this town was hers, too. Like she could stay.

But she told me in the beginning, when this was fake, that she'd leave. This was a pause for her. A vacation from real life. And I knew it would hurt. I just didn't think it would feel like this.

I picture my mom waiting for her to have book club and her not being here anymore. And I think maybe Donna's right. It's not just me here that's going to be hurt. It's my mom. That makes my chest tighten. My mom has been so happy, and I can't have her lose that.

Silvie belongs in boardrooms, on planes, and has a future that doesn't need me. I belong here in Coconut Beach, behind this bar. We are fundamentally different. And for the first time she walked into my life and turned everything upside down in the best way possible, I wonder if loving her means I let my guard down and left me vulnerable and my mom as well. I have to make sure she doesn't get hurt if Silvie leaves.

silvie

. . .

"EYES UP HERE, MRS. BENNETT," Cal says as he catches me staring and practically drooling at the sight of his arms.

I can't help it. He's got his sleeves rolled up, forearms flexing as he slices limes, those beautiful tattoos on display. And who knew slicing limes could be that sexy?

"I'm working," I lie as I glance down at my phone and pretend to be doing something, not even able to hide my smile.

Cocktails & Chaos is in that beautiful golden hour, which is my favorite time of day, when the sun reflects off of the water at just the right angle, making it look like glitter, and everyone is tired from a long day of playing out on the boats and at the beach. The open tiki bar hums with tourists, salt air, and blender noise. I'm sitting at the bar with a basket of nachos, pretending to focus on my phone while absolutely unable to focus on my phone.

Cal smirks. "Sure you are."

Marina is also behind the bar, leaning over the counter and laughing at something a tall, good-looking tourist says. He's charming and definitely enjoying the attention.

Cal leans toward me. "That guy's not ordering drinks. He's flirting."

I smile at Cal, who's protective of Marina, as he is of all the staff. He's always looking out for them. Marina is like a sister to him, and I've never seen her seem this interested in a tourist. But he's laying on the southern charm thick with an accent.

Something about him seems off, though. I can't put my finger on it, but my Spidey senses are going off.

Marina flips her hair, rests her chin on her hand, bats her eyelashes at him, and says something that makes the guy throw his head back and laugh. He keeps glancing our way, and Marina doesn't seem to notice.

Cal shakes his head and goes back to slicing limes. "He better not break her heart or I'll break his legs."

I laugh. "That got dark."

He shrugs. "I've seen it happen a lot. Tourists come, and we're just temporary toys to them."

"Hey," I say as I reach across the bar and lay my hand on that deliciously muscular forearm. "Those days are over for you, husband."

He shakes his head and grins. "That they are. I've got what I need right here."

I raise a brow. "You're married now, and Marina gets to flirt. Are you jealous?"

"Of flirting?"

I raise a brow. "Yes."

He smirks. "I can still flirt."

I frown. "No, you cannot."

He laughs and leans across the bar. "I can flirt with my wife."

Ohhhhh. I squeeze my thighs together at him, calling me his wife in such a hot way.

Marina leans closer to the tourist. "So, you're here alone?" she asks sweetly.

The guy smiles, and he says, "Yes, I am."

I can't help but recognize that his southern accent has dropped slightly. Red flags are being raised.

"What are you here for?" she asks.

"For work," he says smoothly.

"What kind of work?" she asks as she wipes down the bar.

"Media."

Something in my stomach tightens. Before I can say anything, he casually reaches into his pocket, pulls out his phone, holds it up, and takes pictures of Cal and me.

Shit. Shit. Shit. Paparazzi. Damn it.

"Hey!" Marina yells and jumps back, hurt on her face.

The man's expression changes instantly, and his charm has evaporated.

"Silverlyn Montclair and her bartender husband at the local tiki bar," he says as he holds his phone up recording us.

My blood runs cold. I freeze and stare at Cal.

"You've got to be fucking kidding me," Cal says angrily. In one motion, he doesn't even hesitate as he drops his knife and vaults over the bar. The man shoves his phone in his pocket and bolts toward the beach.

"Cal!" I shout.

The man sprints across the sand, nearly wiping out. Cal closes the distance, furious, but then falls.

There's a waiting SUV parked beside the access path. The man dives into it and tires spray sand as it takes off.

Cal stands there for a second, breathing hard, chest heaving, looking very angry. Marina and I remain at the bar and watch as he turns back toward us. And as if they're multiplying like rats, there are more of them. Two more outside the tiki bar, taking photos and videos of everything that just transpired. They'd been waiting. They lift professional cameras, and flashes go off.

They're aiming at Marina and me. Cal storms toward us.

"Get out!" he roars at them.

They ignore him and keep taking photos, baiting him to keep yelling by hurling stupid accusations.

I gather my purse and go behind the bar, unsure where to hide from them. Fear flashes through me and Cal stands in front of me, protectively.

Erin Branscom

"Silvie! Did you pay this bartender to marry you to save your company?"

"Is this marriage under investigation by your trust?"

"I heard the board is reviewing the legality of the marriage?"

Tourists eating at the bar are staring, and a few are filming as well, equally into the drama.

I close my eyes, blinded by the flashes. It feels like being naked under floodlights. People are staring, talking, and pointing. I'm used to this back in New York, but not in Coconut Beach. My safe space.

Cal reaches under the bar, grabs his keys, and says to Marina, "I'll be right back."

Someone yells, "Temporary husband!"

Cal pulls me, his arm protectively around me, as we push out the back and race to his truck, him getting me in and racing to the driver's side.

More flashes.

He climbs in and peels out of the lot.

A black SUV pulls out behind us.

"You've got to be kidding me," he mutters.

They follow all the way down the coast road.

When we pull into the cottage driveway, two other cars are already parked along the street. We get out and run into the house, ignoring them as they call out more questions.

Once inside, we both exhale in relief as we shut and lock the door behind us.

"I'm sorry," I whisper.

They're here because of me. This is my fault. I'm shaking as I sink onto the couch and pull out my phone, which is buzzing with texts and calls.

"Why are you sorry?" he demands, a thread of anger still in his voice.

"I'm going home," I say quietly.

He freezes and looks at me. "Home?"

300

"This is my fault. If I go, maybe they'll follow. I can't do this to you, Cal. You didn't sign up for this."

He grabs my hand and doesn't let go. "Look at me, Silvie."

I peer up at him, my chest feeling heavy, and I see flashes through the window.

Cal stalks over and snaps all of the blinds closed. He sighs.

"Unbelievable," he mutters.

Panic rises in me. "This is what I was afraid of."

"Don't go outside," he says. "I have to go back to the bar and check on my mom."

I reach for my phone. "I have to call Birdie and Wilby."

"They're already coming," he says, glancing through the blinds.

I look out the peephole and open the door when I see Birdie and Wilby on the porch. Wilby's on the phone, and they rush inside.

Birdie shuts the door and peeks through the blinds. "Lord, have mercy. I haven't seen paparazzi like this since we lived in Manhattan and your family was on every front page."

I sigh. "It's not fun."

She softens. "No, sugar. It's not."

My phone buzzes and it's Carly. "Carly? Are you okay?"

She's frantic. "There are people outside my house knocking on the door and taking pictures. I can't reach Cal. Is he with you?"

My stomach sinks. "They're what? And, uh, yes, he's here."

"They're outside asking about you, filming and taking pictures."

"Tell her I'm calling her now," Cal says, "and I'll be back."

I hang up with Carly so she can take his call. He takes off and runs to his truck, taking a while to back up as they try to block him in.

I stand up and pace. "They're ruining everything. I hate this."

Wilby looks up from his phone slowly. "It was Belladonna."

I close my eyes. Because, of course, it was her doing.

"She leaked a full story claiming your marriage is strategic to steal the family company. It's everywhere," he says.

He sends me the link, and I quickly scan it. **Heiress Marries Local Bartender in Corporate Power Play.**

My stomach turns. I pull up my dad's contact and hit call.

He answers on the second ring, and he sounds furious. "What did you do, Silvie?"

"Wrong daughter, Dad. You should be asking Belladonna that," I clip, not having time for his accusations.

"I've been on the phone all day with the board."

"I saved the company, Dad. That's what I did. Your other daughter gave this story to the press."

"You brought chaos into this. The board is launching a full investigation. We look ridiculous."

"I did what I had to do! They were going to take it from us."

"And now they might anyway."

I press my hand to my forehead. "What do you want me to do?"

He exhales sharply. "You should've handled this differently."

The line goes dead, and he's hung up on me. Great.

Silence fills the cottage. Birdie is watching out the window and Wilby is on his phone firing off texts.

"Wilby, get the jet ready for tomorrow, please."

"We're leaving?" he blinks.

"Maybe if I go back to New York, they'll follow me."

Birdie steps forward. "And what about Cal?"

My throat tightens. "We have to go."

I feel so bad for Carly. She didn't ask for this. Cal didn't ask for this. I shouldn't have done this. And now I'm in a place where I can't walk away, or I will lose everything. And if I stay, I'll ruin their lives.

"I don't think you should run," Wilby says quietly.

"I'm not running."

But I might have to. I can't do this to them.

———

It's late. Wilby went back to Birdie's to pack and get ready. He got the jet to come pick us up tonight so we could hopefully leave in secret and not alert the paparazzi. Cal's cottage is quiet. The paparazzi seems to have gone for now.

I've packed a small suitcase, and I'm waiting for Cal to finish up at the bar and get home.

I hear his truck pull up and park, and I wait, on the couch, my feet tucked under me.

He opens the door and kicks off his shoes, eyeing my suitcase and looking over at me.

"I'm going to New York," I say.

He doesn't respond right away. He swallows and looks away, pissed.

Silence passes between us and the tension is thick.

"I don't understand why you're leaving," he finally says.

I swallow. "If I go back, they'll follow me."

"We handle this together," he says in a steady voice as he sets his keys on the table by the door.

And that makes this worse because even though I denied it, I am running.

"You shouldn't have to handle this," I say. "This is my mess."

He turns then, and his eyes are dark, hurt, and confused. "We're married."

"Fake married," I add softly.

"Married," he says firmly.

"And you didn't sign up for this."

He crosses the room and stares into my eyes. "Actually, I did. I signed up for marriage, which means I signed up for you. We are married, which means we handle things together. All of this."

I shake my head. "No, I messed things up. I brought this into your life, your bar, and into your mother's life. You both shouldn't have to fight my board members and psycho sister."

"I don't care," he says as he shakes his head.

"I do."

My voice cracks, and I hate it.

"I feel like I'm destroying us," I whisper.

He walks toward me slowly. "You think I married you for the easy version?"

I shake my head. "I think you didn't know what you were signing up for."

He cups my chin. "I know exactly what I signed up for."

My heart is in my throat.

"Did you?" My chest feels tight. "Because this is who I am. Private jets, board votes, and family warfare. I don't get to turn that off because I want to sit at a tiki bar and pretend I'm just some woman you met at the bar."

"You'll never be some woman I met at the bar," he says, softly. "When are you going to realize that?"

"I never want to hurt you."

His thumb brushes my cheek. "You'll hurt me if you leave me."

That almost undoes me. I shake my head. "I don't want to leave. But I feel like it's for the best."

"I want you."

I close my eyes. "If I stay, they'll keep circling. They'll keep pushing. And if I go, it will protect us."

"You don't know that," he argues.

"I know. But I do know that I can't sit here and watch them tear you apart."

"They won't," he argues. "They'll move on when they see there's no story."

Silence stretches between us.

"I don't want you to leave," he says finally.

"You could come with me," I say softly.

"I want to, but I can't leave my mom right now," he says, shaking his head. "And the bar...and Jonah..."

I nod. "Of course. I understand."

His honesty is raw. I can tell he looks torn by staying, torn by me leaving.

"I don't want to go," I whisper back.

He studies my face like he's memorizing it. "When are you coming back?"

"I don't know." I shake my head, sadly.

I step closer, pressing my hands to his chest. His heart is beating fast under my palm.

"I just need to get ahead of this," I say softly. "If I don't get control of the board, I will lose everything."

His jaw tightens, and something shifts in his eyes. "Okay."

That surprises me. I thought he would fight me on this. "Okay?"

"I don't like it. But I understand why you feel you need to go. I just hate that you'll be in New York and I'll be here and not able to protect you from...them," he says as he glances at the direction of the front door where the paparazzi was camping out.

He kisses me softly, pulling me to him, and murmurs, "I have an idea."

A small smile tugs at my mouth. "What are you suggesting?"

He leans in close, voice low. "We take the back path through the dunes. They won't know."

I glance out the blinds and notice that the paparazzi SUV is still idling at the end of the street. I can see a silhouette inside.

We slip out the back door quietly, Cal carrying my suitcase as if it weighs nothing. We carry our shoes and run barefoot through the cool sand under our feet. The ocean is loud, and the waves are the only sound.

We move through the dunes, my hand in Cal's. "Cal."

He turns, and I step toward him, pulling him down to me and kissing him. I glance at him in the moonlight and want to remember this moment. His face and how he looks at me.

"I hate that you're leaving," he murmurs against my mouth.

"Me, too."

"I don't want to lose you, Silvie."

"You won't," I promise, but I hesitate for a fraction of a second.

He tips his forehead to mine.

"I'm coming back," I say.

He searches my face as if he's looking for honesty, and he nods once.

"Then go win your war," he says. "I'll be here waiting."

We reach the airport, and Wilby pulls up, Birdie at the wheel. He nods, grabs his bag, and heads to the plane.

I hug Birdie, and she pulls me to her. "Travel safe, sugar. I'll be here when you want to come back."

I glance around and realize the paparazzi hadn't seen us leave, and we outsmarted them, something I love to do. Once they realize I'm gone, they'll flock after me, eager to chase the story. Coconut Beach will be safe from the vultures.

Cal waits, his hands in his pockets. I go to him kiss him softly. His hands come around me, and he pulls me close. He looks like he wants to say something, but he doesn't. He just looks sad.

I get on the plane and prepare for New York. And I have to decide whether I'm fighting for a company or fighting for us.

cal
. . .

THE FIRST THING I see when I unlock Cocktails & Chaos late the next morning is a tripod in the sand directed right at the front of the bar. It's out of place. Not a beach umbrella, abandoned beach chair, or a tent for a family to set up, reserving their spot. No, a freaking camera on a tripod with a long black lens pointed directly at the bar.

I stand there for a second with my keys still in the door. A guy in sunglasses hovers near the tripod and nods at me like we're acquaintances, as if he's not here to ruin our lives.

"Morning, Cal." He waves.

I shake my head and don't answer. I step inside and begin the inventory and paperwork.

I tried to sleep after Silvie left, but I couldn't. I wish I'd gone with her. I wish she'd just stayed. I wish for a lot of things, but that doesn't mean any of them will happen.

Five minutes later, I hear it. "Hey, kid."

I look up, and the paparazzi with the tripod is talking to Noah, my seventeen-year-old busboy, who is walking up to the back of the bar.

Noah stops and looks at the guy, confused about who he is.

"I'll give you two hundred bucks if you tell me some information that I need."

Noah glances at me and back at the guy.

The guy smiles and asks him a few questions. "What time does Silvie get here and leave?"

Noah shakes his head and backs away.

The guy continues as if this is a normal conversation. "Five if you tell me good information."

That's when I move and walk straight across the sand and step between them. "You're done."

The guy doesn't back up. "Relax. Just asking questions. Not a crime."

"You're harassing a minor," I add. "And trespassing."

He shrugs. "Information's information."

"You're trying to buy pieces of my life."

He laughs under his breath. "You married into headlines, buddy. Comes with the territory."

I step closer. "Step over that rope and I'll call the police. Talk to my staff again, and I'll make sure you're ruined."

He studies me for a second, as if gauging whether I'm serious, then backs up. He doesn't pack up and leave. He just stays within the boundary he knows he can't cross.

I shake my head and pull Noah inside and get to work.

"Sorry," he mutters.

"You didn't do anything wrong, buddy. It's okay."

By noon, there are three more SUVs parked along the beach access road, and locals are staring and talking. Tourists are searching for the person they're stalking. And every time I look over, there's a lens pointed at me.

One of the regulars claps me on the shoulder. "Must be nice, huh? Marrying into millions. Don't understand why you're still working at the bar."

I shake my head because I know he's joking. But it still lands wrong.

———

My shift is almost over when an older guy, maybe fifty, takes a seat at the bar. I note the expensive watch on his wrist and his clothes that look perfect. He's going bald and I note the thick gold wedding band on his finger. He glances around the bar and his eyes land on me.

Fucking great.

I don't look up and Marina helps him. He nods in my direction and she braces herself. I ignore him and continue my closing tasks.

He waits, still refusing when Marina offers him a menu. He's not here to eat and drink. He wants to talk to me.

He scoots down a few stools and says, "Are you Cal?"

I sigh and grit my teeth. Here we go.

He holds up his hands in surrender. "I'm not a reporter. I see you have a lot of those around here."

I glance over at him. "What do you want?"

He leans in and lowers his voice. "I'm your father."

I stare at him.

Then I go back to wiping down the bar. "Right."

I've had so many lies spewed at me. This, by far, is the one taken the farthest. The audacity.

"Marina," I call without acknowledging this asshole. "I'm out. Travis here?"

"Just got here," she calls. "Have a good night."

Travis steps up, and I nod at him and turn to leave. Footsteps follow me. Of course they do. These people are relentless.

"How is Carly?" the man asks behind me.

I spin so fast, I almost see red and step into his space. "I don't know who you think you are," I grit out. "But leave me alone."

"I'm your father," he says calmly. "It's true."

The words hit me in the gut like a punch.

"Prove it," I grit out, glaring at him. But he is my height and has dark hair like mine. But that means nothing to me because

309

my cousin Remy and I look alike, so I always thought I took after my mother's side.

"I met your mother while my family vacationed here for the summer. We were young and dumb. I went off to college. That's it."

He says it like he didn't just abandon my mother. Cast her aside like she was garbage. Like he left his sweater behind at his vacation villa.

Like she had a choice in the matter and wasn't just left pregnant and alone at eighteen.

The fucking audacity of this man. But I let him continue because if he is who he says he is, I want to know why. I have always wanted to know why.

"I always wondered what happened to her," he continues.

"What happened to her?" I echo. "Are you fucking kidding me right now?"

He shrugs. "When she said she was pregnant, it was too much for me. I was headed off to college. I told her to get rid of it but I see that she didn't."

Get rid of it. Get rid of *me*. Wow.

"What's your name?"

"Neil Harrington."

Harrington. "Like the Harringtons of Harrington Holdings?"

He looks taken aback. "Yeah. How did you know that? I mean...I guess you're married to a Montclair, but I didn't realize you knew about my family."

My family. That's laughable. As if we don't share the same DNA.

"Sometimes I wish things had worked out differently," he says, almost thoughtfully. "You could have had more opportunities as a Harrington than being a bartender in Coconut Beach."

My vision narrows. And he continues. I'm seething.

"Although I do think it's funny you ended up married to one of my family friends. I do business with the Montclairs. We're competitors, I suppose. But I've known them a very long time."

"You are such a piece of shit," I bite out.

He sighs. "I did what I thought was best. I was a kid too, you know."

"Joke's on you, asshole," I say. "I went to NYU and studied finance."

His eyebrows lift slightly in surprise.

"And I got a master's in business. Top of my class."

He stands up straighter, studying me now. He judged me, and he doesn't even know me.

"I worked in finance in New York," I continue.

"Why are you working here as a bartender then?" he asks, looking confused.

I don't miss the way he says it as if I'm a felon or doing something wrong. There's nothing wrong with working as a bartender. And the fact that he's judging me on this tells me everything I need to know about this man. He doesn't need to know anything about me, and definitely doesn't get to know anything about my mother.

"You have no right to come here and judge me. You don't even know me," I practically spit out.

He frowns.

"You are absolute trash," I say evenly. "And I'm grateful I didn't have to know you."

He doesn't react the way I expect. He ignores my insults. "How's your mother? What was it, six years ago, I last saw her? We talked, and she was upset, but is she still here on Coconut Beach?"

His casual words pierce me like a knife. Six years ago. My stomach drops and the pieces that I've been missing are now clicking into place.

Six years ago, I was in New York, starting my new job.

Six years ago, my mother stopped leaving the house.

She'd been bartending with Jonah at Chaos. Then suddenly she wasn't. She stopped leaving the house. Canceled all plans.

She had panic attacks. Severe anxiety. She started shrinking. Becoming a shell of who she was.

I stare at him, and the anger I feel toward him makes me see red. I feel dizzy as I stare at him.

"What did you say to her that day?" I ask.

He shrugs as if it isn't important. "I don't remember. I was here with my wife and kids."

Kids. He has kids. I have siblings.

The words hit me even harder than I thought they would. I always figured that my biological father probably married and had a family. Sometimes I wondered if I had siblings.

I shake my head back to reality and stay focused.

He was here with his wife and kids on vacation. While my mother was here alone. Raising a kid while she was practically a kid herself.

"Look." He spreads his hands like this is unfortunate, but inevitable. "We were young," he says. "Things happen."

Things happen.

I step closer again and shake my head in disgust at him. "You are really something."

My hands are shaking so badly.

He looks annoyed now and defensive. "It wasn't personal. I had a path. I couldn't just derail my whole life."

"So, you derailed hers instead."

He scoffs and sighs.

"You have no idea what you did," I continue.

He stiffens slightly. "I didn't force her to have it."

It. Meaning me.

He looks past me, over at the beach as if he's remembering something. "I did wonder about her. About you."

Bullshit.

"If you wondered," I say, "You would've checked in. Made right by her. Instead, you just pretended we didn't exist and went on about your life."

He's silent.

"I wasn't sure I should," he says finally.

"You didn't want to know. You didn't care," I correct him.

That hits where I wanted it to.

"I'm here now," he finally says.

I laugh and shake my head. "And why are you here? What could you possibly want?"

His jaw tightens.

"You're here because my wife and I are on every headline right now, and you saw an opportunity. What is this? A power play for your company since you're competitors?"

"That's not fair."

"Oh, you want to talk about fair?" I ask.

My chest feels like it's cracking open. I remember my mom being a shell of a person when I came back to take care of her. She never would say what happened. Nobody really knew. I remember her saying how much anxiety and panic she felt when she would leave the house.

I remember one time she was crying and said she wasn't enough. And now this man is standing in front of me and can't even recall what he said to destroy her that day. Because I can't think of anything else that could have done that destruction.

"Don't come near me again," I tell him. "And you don't come near my mother or my wife."

He opens his mouth to argue, and I step into him again.

"You are useless trash," I say clearly. "And if you set foot on Coconut Beach again, I will make sure it's the last time."

He studies me and nods. And for a quick second, I see a flash of something cross his face that looks like regret. It's not there long.

"As I said," he mutters. "Things could have been different."

"Yeah," I clip. "You could have been a decent person."

He walks away toward the parking lot and doesn't look back.

My hands curl into fists, and I wish this meeting had never happened. Mostly, I want to go to my mom's and find out what he said to her that day. What he could have said to her to make her feel discarded all over again and close in on herself.

And I think about how I built myself into the man I am without him. My mother was always a hard worker and encouraged me to become the man I am today. I chose her, this town, this bar, and Silvie. He doesn't get to choose when he becomes a part of my life. He doesn't get to act like I could have been more. I am enough. And I didn't need him to become it.

silvie

• • •

I **STAND BAREFOOT** at the window of my penthouse, looking out over the city, with glass and endless lights stretching into the city as the sun sets. My pink suit is still perfect, my lipstick is still on point, and my hair is still smooth. Although, my heels got kicked off by the door.

From the outside, I look like I have everything together. The CEO of Montclair Holdings. But on the inside, I'm a lovesick mess. I'm homesick for a place and a person who has stolen my heart. I cross my arms and realize that I don't even want to be here anymore. And that thought surprises me. I thought this was everything I wanted. To work and keep my family's company going. And now that I've got it close, I wonder if this is truly what I want. Because right now it doesn't feel like it.

Cal's working at Cocktails & Chaos tonight. He and I texted earlier, and he said that he's been busy. The bar has been slammed. He's been short on texts and calls. Not cold, just distant. He says he's working, but I feel like there's more to it. And I hate it. I'm homesick for a man at a beach in a tiki bar. I want to fall asleep next to him and wake up in his arms. I wrap my arms around my waist, feeling sad and full of longing for him. New York has been so lonely. And I'm questioning everything.

I haven't eaten all day. I had non-stop meetings, calls, strategy sessions, damage control, and was in full CEO mode. I open the fridge in my kitchen, and it's sparse. I have no appetite, yet I know I need something. I scroll through my phone and order Chinese food from the place two blocks over that I love. I need some ultimate comfort food. Something warm and spicy that I can eat and then take a long hot bath and soak the day away.

The apartment is too quiet. I wander around while I wait for my food and stare at the fancy decor that I realize isn't me at all. This place doesn't feel like home. It feels like a prison. I should sell it. Find something more...like me. Like home. Then I close my eyes and think of Cal. He's my home. Wherever he is. I don't think I'd find anything here in New York that would feel like that.

The buzzer sounds, and I walk toward the door, assuming it's the doorman with my food delivery. I open it, and it's not him. It's my mother. She steps inside before I can speak, her perfume sharp and familiar.

"What do you want?" I ask, feeling too tired for her crap tonight.

She looks around the penthouse, inspecting it, and says, "You've made quite a mess of things, Silvie."

I close the door slowly, sighing in frustration at her intrusion. But I also know that if I throw her out, it will make a scene and that is likely what she wants.

"What were you thinking?" she continues. "You've humiliated this family."

I walk calmly to the panel beside the door and press the security button. She's still ranting and hasn't even noticed.

She continues, "As if your wedding wasn't a big enough embarrassment, you had to go and marry a bartender from some beach town?"

"I find it interesting that I'm the problem in all of this," I say. "Did you forget that Belladonna slept with my fiancé?"

And this is exactly what she wanted. An argument and a scene. Here we go...

"Why can't you just be happy for your sister and move on?" my mother snaps. "She's happy, and Tyler could have helped out at the company. But no, you had to ruin him, too. I swear, Silvie, I don't know what your problem is."

I don't respond. Because what does one say to a mother who accepts treatment of her daughter this way and believes this nonsense? That I'm actually the problem. This is crazy. She's literally crazy.

"We could have found you a suitable match," she continues. "A man who understands our world. Someone appropriate."

Appropriate.

I stand there and let her continue because adding anything to the conversation right now would be like pouring gasoline on a fire. And what my mother wants is an explosion.

"You chose to make this an issue," she says angrily. "By marrying some random bartender."

There's a faint ding behind me, and the elevator opens.

Thank God. Security is here.

"Silvie, you've..."

Security steps into the foyer, and my mother turns, offended by the interruption. She realizes that they're here to escort her, and her face contorts with rage and embarrassment. "You can't be serious."

I hold her gaze. "Don't come to my home again. You're not welcome here or at my company."

Her face goes red with rage. "Silvie! I am your mother!"

"Then you should have acted like it," I hiss back as security gently but firmly guides her toward the door and escorts her out. The door closes, and the apartment is silent again.

I sigh, exhausted from her. I make a note to let my building staff know that she's not to enter the property. My food arrives a few minutes later, and the timing makes me almost laugh. I take the bag and thank them as the door closes behind them.

I set the container on the table and sit down. It smells warm and comforting. I take a bite and close my eyes. Lonely and needing to talk to someone, I call Birdie, and she picks up.

"Well, hello, sugar."

I put her on speaker and keep eating. "My mother just showed up at my apartment."

There's a pause. "And?"

"Oh, her same old stuff. How I embarrassed the family. And that I should have just let her find me a suitable match. As if I'm a piece of livestock she can auction off."

Birdie exhales softly. "I know, sugar. But are you surprised?"

I stare at my food in front of me. "No."

"She's always valued optics over happiness."

I push my food around with my fork. "I know."

Birdie hums. "You sound worn out. I don't like it."

"I am," I admit. "I've had nonstop meetings since I've been back. Trying to cram everything in."

"Are you eating? You know you forget to eat," she reminds me.

I glance down at the food I've been picking at. "I'm working on it."

She's quiet for a moment, then says gently, "Your mother was your very first bully."

I swallow, and tears prick my eyes at the memories that have haunted me for thirty years. She's right.

"I had you," I say gratefully.

"And you'll always have me, sugar. You know that," she says in her soft voice that has always comforted me.

My throat tightens, and I lean back in my chair, looking around the penthouse. "I hate it here, Birdie." She listens, and I continue. "I miss Cal, and I miss Coconut Beach."

"When are you coming back?" she asks.

"In two days."

"Two days," she repeats. "That's not too long, sugar. And you bring that Wilby with you. He's a hoot, and the Bees all love him."

"He's coming." I smile at the mention of him. "I have to finish up with the board review. I can't leave in the middle of this."

"I understand."

I stare at the skyline again. "It feels like I'm living two lives," I say. "In one, I'm powerful and necessary. In the other, I'm loved."

"You're allowed to have both, you know."

"Am I?" I choke out.

"Yes," she says firmly. "Just because you didn't have that growing up doesn't mean you can't have that now for yourself."

"I don't want to lose either," I admit. "I want to have my job, and I want to be happy."

"Then don't," Birdie says simply.

I think about the polished image I'm expected to have. Then I realize for the first time in my life, maybe this isn't my dream life after all. Maybe this was just a chapter in my life. And maybe it's time for a new chapter. Maybe I'm allowed to want more.

"I'll be back soon," I say again.

"We'll be here," she replies.

After we hang up, I sit at the table a little longer. The food is cold now. The apartment is still quiet and feels so lonely. My phone lights up with an email from legal.

I ignore it. Instead, I pick up my phone and open my texts. I type a text out to Cal.

Me: Miss you.

I stare at it for a second before hitting send. For the first time in years, I'm not chasing the future.

I'm hoping it includes him.

———————

I wake up reaching for him, but my hand slides across the cool and empty sheets. Then I remember that I'm in New York. But in my dream, I was back at Cocktails & Chaos. Cal was behind the bar, smiling at me like the world was simple again, and paparazzi wasn't waiting for me everywhere I turned.

Then I wake up to reality. I still feel nauseated, probably from not eating enough, and remember that we're leaving today. Wilby and I are going back to Coconut Beach for a while. My suitcase is packed and ready. I'm ready. I miss Cal.

I swing my legs over the side of the bed and stand. The hard floor is cool beneath my feet. It feels sterile and immaculate here. Not comfortable like Cal's cottage with rugs and mismatched cozy lamps. I walk out and stare out at the skyline from the massive windows and don't feel anchored here anymore. I feel done.

My phone buzzes on the nightstand.

Wilby: Car will be there in twenty.

Me: I'm ready.

That's not true, but twenty minutes is enough to get myself Coconut Beach ready. Because in Coconut Beach, I feel myself when I'm going there. I get to wear simple and comfortable clothes. I get to be me.

The ride to the airport is quiet. The city blurs past the window. I don't check the headlines or my email. For once, I let everything sit.

At the private terminal, Wilby is waiting for me next to his suitcase. I haven't missed how Wilby wants to go back as well. He loves it there. We both do.

"Hey, have you seen the weather they're calling for tonight at Coconut Beach? There's a bad storm coming."

I discuss this with the pilot, and he's convinced we're safe, so we prepare to take off.

"You sure about this?" Wilby asks.

"Yes," I confirm. "He says it's okay."

He studies me for a second. "Okay. If you're sure."

The cabin smells faintly of leather and recycled air. I buckle in and stare out the window as the plane taxis. As we lift off, the skyline tilts beneath us. For a moment, Manhattan looks small. Then it disappears into the clouds. I lean back against my seat and relax the further we get away from it.

The turbulence starts sooner than I expected. Not violent. Just enough to make the cabin sway. I grip the armrest.

"You good?" Wilby asks.

"I'm fine," I grit out.

The plane dips slightly, and my stomach lurches. That's strange. I've flown since I was a child. Private jets. Commercial flights. International travel. I've never gotten motion sickness. In fact, I usually read and do stuff on my computer regardless of turbulence. Something Wilby has always made fun of me for.

The cabin tilts again, and nausea rushes up fast and sharp. I've felt terrible the past few days. I chalked it up to exhaustion. But this was my father's life. Constantly working, moving, traveling. And I don't want this life. I want a balanced life. I want a life.

I close my eyes and wonder if I'd ever be able to have both. I press my palm to my stomach. It doesn't settle. I excuse myself and make it to the tiny bathroom just in time.

When I return, Wilby is watching me closely. "You're pale."

"It's just turbulence," I say as I close my eyes and try to focus on something boring like a spreadsheet, or anything to not think about the plane moving like this.

"You never get turbulence sick." He eyes me suspiciously.

I finally fall asleep, exhausted, and he gently taps my arm when we descend toward Coconut Beach. The storm is visible over the water. Sheets of rain move across the ocean like curtains, and the runway glistens when we land.

I thank the pilots, grateful to hear they're staying overnight at the Palm and returning tomorrow after the storm.

The second the cabin door opens, the salty, humid air hits me, and storm winds whip around us. It fills my lungs like oxygen I didn't know I was missing. I step down onto the tarmac, and the wind tugs at my hair.

Thunder rumbles somewhere out over the water. I don't care. I just feel sick and lightheaded. But I feel like I'm home. I didn't know I could be homesick for this place. For him.

———

The storm is already rolling in when Cal's truck pulls up. Wind whips sand across the driveway. The sky is dark and swollen with rain. Thunder rumbles low and steady.

He jumps out before the engine even fully cuts off. I barely have time to shut the car door before he's in front of me.

He pulls me into him so hard my breath leaves my lungs. "I'm so glad you're here," he says into my hair.

"Me, too," I whisper, sinking into him.

Wilby goes to Birdie's and gets settled and we wave to him.

Cal's arms wrap protectively around me. "This storm's supposed to be a bad one."

"I know," I whisper.

He pulls back just enough to look at me. Rain starts to fall in thick drops. "You shouldn't have flown in this. I was so worried."

"I missed you," I murmur.

Something shifts in his expression at that. He cups my face and kisses me. The wind pushes against us. The rain starts harder.

"Come on," he says, grabbing my hand. "Let's get inside."

The storm hits full force within the night. Rain pounds the

roof. Lightning flashes white across the windows. The power flickers twice before stabilizing.

———————

The next morning, I stand on Cal's porch with a cup of coffee in both hands and look out at the cottages. A few shingles are missing. One of the patio chairs is upside down in the sand. It could have been so much worse.

Cal is already down checking on the Bees and Carly with Jonah. His T-shirt is damp and clinging to his back, hair still messy from the wind, and there is something tight in his shoulders that was not there yesterday. He has always worn responsibility like a second skin for his mother and Jonah, but today he is on high alert, looking stressed.

I head to Carly's house before I talk myself out of it. I've missed her, and we need to catch up. And I could use a friend. She answers the door after a long minute. Her eyes look tired but clearer than they usually are. The house smells like lemon cleaner and coffee.

"Hi, sweetie," she says softly. "You made it through the storm."

"We did," I tell her, stepping inside. "How are you?"

She shrugs and wraps her cardigan tighter around herself. "A little shaken. But I'm alright. I don't love that the reporters have been camped out all over."

"I know," I say with a sigh. "I'm really sorry about that."

"It's scary feeling trapped like that."

"Actually," I say as I take her hands in mine. "I was thinking about that. How you can take back some control. When I go back to New York, I could help set you up with telehealth for therapy. We can find someone who can help. I know a few firms that work with executive mental health, and they're discreet. You wouldn't have to leave the house to do it, but maybe one day you'd be able to leave again with the right therapy."

"That sounds like a dream, but I don't know." Her eyes flicker with something hopeful and fear all at once. "You'd do that to help me?"

"Of course I would," I say. "And if you ever want to visit New York, even just for a week, you could stay with us. With me and Cal. We'd make it work."

"That feels so scary." She squeezes my fingers. "But thank you for thinking of me."

I notice she feels more anxious, and I hate that. Maybe I was too forward. But I had to try.

When I leave, Cal is waiting at the end of the walkway. He must have seen me go in.

"What were you talking to my mom about?" he asks, his voice steady but edged.

"I offered to help her find a telehealth therapist," I say carefully. "And I told her she could come to New York sometime if she wanted."

His jaw tightens. "Silvie, you don't need to do that."

"Cal," I say. "I'm trying to help."

"She's my mom," he says, looking irritated, running a hand through his hair. "I've got it handled."

I feel something in me bristle. "Do you?"

He looks at me like that question cuts. "Yeah. I do."

We walk back toward the bar, sand sticking to our shoes. I can feel the argument building between us. He's mad at me. Whatever was growing while I was gone feels even bigger now. And I want to fix this, whatever it is between us.

"You know you built this safe life for your mom," I say finally. "And then you show up for Jonah. You do so much for them. You stay here because you think they need you."

"They do need me."

"I'm not saying they don't," I reply, stopping in front of him. "But what about you, Cal? What do you want?"

He stares at me as if I had asked him something in a foreign language.

"I just want them to be safe," he says. "I want my mom to be okay."

"That's not what I asked." My voice softens. "What do you want for your life?"

He exhales hard. "Why does it have to be bigger than this?"

"It doesn't have to be bigger," I say. "But it has to be yours. Not just you cleaning up everyone else's mess."

His eyes flash. "And what about you? You're going back to your skyscraper and your board meetings and your billion-dollar company. Why do you care about us Coconut Beach peasants?"

"Cal," I say, my spine straightening. "That's not true."

We stand there, a new level of emotion between us and not emotions I like. I'm mad. I've never treated anyone here poorly. I am kind to everyone.

"You really think that?" I ask, tearfully.

He shakes his head and looks away. "We want different things, Silvie."

"I want to be a CEO," I say, and my voice does not shake. "I want to run Montclair Holdings. I want to build something that's mine. I also want to have a life, Cal. I want both love and ambition. But right now, I have to focus on my job. The board is circling. My birthday is coming. I can't pretend this is just a vacation anymore."

His face changes at that. Something shatters between us.

"So just go," he says quietly. "I'll keep playing along back here. That's what we agreed on, right?"

"Don't do that," I whisper. "Don't do this."

"And don't string my mom around," he adds, his voice rough. "She doesn't deserve to have her heart broken again."

Anger flares hot in my chest. "I would never," I say sharply. "Don't you dare imply that. I love her. I would never do that."

"Then what are you doing?" he asks. "Trying to get her to go to New York? Not everything is about you, Silvie."

"I never said that," I say tearfully, "but I'm not a villain in your small-town tragedy. Whatever happened to you and your mom is not my fault."

He rubs his face with both hands. "I just need space."

The words hang between us. I see the boy he must have been, the one who never knew his father and decided he would never be the one who left. I see the man he is now, terrified of wanting something that might not stay. And the one who builds a life for everyone but himself. As if he's not allowed.

"I'm sorry," I say, my voice softer now. "I'm asking you to think about what you want instead of what everyone else needs."

He shakes his head. "You think you know me, Silvie. But you don't."

Then he turns and walks toward the beach, shoulders rigid, hands shoved in his pockets.

I watch him go until he is just a dark shape against the pale sand.

My heart aches painfully in my chest. I don't know what to do. Everything feels wrong and confusing. It's like I'm being torn in half. With tears in my eyes, I head back to Cal's place. Giving him space feels like the last thing I want to do, but what choice do I have? I don't have the time right now to smooth this out between us and that hurts.

Back at Cal's cottage, I pull my suitcase out from under the bed. My phone buzzes with emails from the board, subject lines sharp and urgent. Cal is right. I should give him space and go back to New York.

I cry as I pack up my things because I don't want to leave him.

But I know I have to.

cal

. . .

THE STORM DID a number on Cocktails & Chaos, but it could have been worse. We lost part of our thatched roof and half of the string lights. But nothing we can't fix. The deck has been warped for a while and today is the day I decided to take my anger out on it. I drag a soaked patio table across the warped deck and set it upright with more force than necessary.

"You're going to tear up more than you fix," Jonah grumbles.

"It's rotten," I clip.

"So are you," Jonah says as he watches me out of the corner of his eye.

"It needs to be sanded and repaired." I glare at him.

He just lifts a shoulder and grunts in return as he stands a few feet away, stacking chairs and moving more slowly than usual.

It's been two days since Silvie left, and I'll admit I've been a bear. I've been waking up before sunrise and burying myself in work. My goal has been to stay as busy as I can so that I don't have to think of her. Or the way I told her to go. When what I really wanted was for her to stay.

I pry up another board and toss it into the pile. I look over and wipe the sweat from my brow as I glare at the paparazzi van parked across the street. Same black SUV with tinted windows. They've been circling like sharks. They don't care that she's gone. They're here for any dirt they can scrounge up.

The Coconut Beach locals are over it. One of the Bees tried to nonchalantly run them off the sidewalk the other day on a motor scooter. I can't say I didn't laugh. Because that was funny as hell.

And Lucille and Bitsy have been posting fake sightings on the Coconut Beach social media to watch them scramble. They're catching on now, though.

Jonah follows my gaze. "They're persistent little rats. I'll give them that."

"They're more like weasels," I grumble.

"Same thing," he says, running a hand over his beard.

Birdie walks up, her oversized sun hat and sunglasses perched on her nose. She surveys the deck and says cheerfully, "You both look grumpy."

"I'm not grumpy," I mutter.

She pats my cheek. "Of course you are, sugar. Jonah is always grumpy. But you? This is a new look for you. I don't like it."

Jonah snorts.

Birdie lowers her voice like she's about to share a secret. "You'll both be delighted to learn that the Bees have escalated operations."

I close my eyes. "I'm afraid to ask." Because when it comes to the Bees, this could mean one of many things.

"We've made it our personal mission to exhaust every single reporter," she says proudly.

Jonah clears his throat.

Birdie continues, "Wouldn't you know that they were under the impression that you and Silvie were out on the water yesterday? And they appear to have gotten stranded out there in the water. For hours."

Well, that kept them busy. Explains why I had peace at the bar yesterday afternoon.

If only it were true. Not having her here has left a gaping hole in my chest.

"Jonah happened to be out there fishing," she says with a grin.

Jonah holds up both hands. "I was not involved."

He doesn't meet my eyes.

Birdie beams. "It was a shame he couldn't tow them in right away. He told them it had something to do with tide patterns."

Jonah shrugs. "Can't control the ocean."

I shake my head . The smirk tugging at the corner of his mouth makes me laugh.

"You left them out there floating for hours?" I ask with a lifted eyebrow.

He huffs. "They were fine."

Birdie laughs like this is the best thing she's heard all week. "We've made it our mission to send them on wild goose chases. Summer convinced one of them that Silvie was in Aspen. We heard a few actually flew to Colorado to check."

I scrub a hand down my face. "This is all insane."

I wish it could go back to the way it was. Peaceful and quiet.

"Effective," Birdie counters.

Across the street, the SUV door opens and one of the photographers steps out, camera in his hand as he scans the area hoping he can get a good shot of something.

"Unbelievable," I groan.

Birdie checks her phone. "Oh, good. Bitsy just posted that we are planning a party for you and Silvie tonight."

I turn to her. "What?"

Jonah's shoulders shake with laughter. For once, it's funny to see him conspiring with the Bees and having fun with the paparazzi.

Birdie smirks. "They'll all be at the wrong beach at sunset."

The photographer pulls out his phone and glances at it, frowns, then jogs back to the SUV. Within seconds, the engine starts up, and he speeds off.

Birdie squeezes my arm before heading back toward the cottages. "We've got your back, sugar. Always."

I lean against the railing, staring out at the water. It looks calm now. Like the storm and fight between Silvie and me never happened.

Jonah steps up beside me. "You going to keep brooding like an angry bear?"

"I'm not."

"You're brooding," he says. "It's obnoxious."

I let out a breath. "I'm working."

"You've been working nonstop since she left."

"Yeah."

He studies me for a second. "You mad at her?"

I don't answer right away. The truth is messy.

"I'm mad at the situation," I say finally. "At the timing. At the fact that I didn't say what I should've said."

"And what was that?"

That I wanted her to stay. That I wanted her more than this bar and this beach and this safe little world I've built around everyone else.

I shrug instead. "Doesn't matter."

Jonah leans his elbows on the railing. "The whole town's tired of those vultures. We'll keep them busy."

"I don't need protecting."

"That's not what I mean."

I glance back at the empty street. "They're here because of her."

"They're here because she matters to you," he says quietly.

I let out a humorless laugh. "That's not why."

Jonah doesn't argue. He just looks at me like he knows better as he pats my shoulder and saunters off.

When he's gone, I pick up the crowbar again and get to work. I tell myself I'm just fixing what the storm tore apart.

But really, I'm just trying to stay busy enough that I don't check my phone every five minutes.

Trying not to wonder if she's sitting in some glass tower right now, choosing her future.

Trying not to admit that I'm still standing here, waiting to see if I'm part of it.

———

Her pillow on my bed still smells like her shampoo. Coconut and something flowery. It's torture because when I smell it, I remember her tangled in the sheets and her laugh muffled against my chest.

My throat tightens, and I mutter, "Get it together."

I hear my phone buzz and pull it out to see Wilby's name on the screen. I stare at it for a second before answering. What if something's wrong with Silvie?

"Yeah."

"You sound awful," he says. "Are you still being dramatic?"

"What do you want, Wilby?" I say dryly.

He sighs. I can hear city noise in the background. Traffic, sirens, the typical hum of the city that never stops moving.

"Listen, I'm just going to give it to you straight," he says.

That makes me pause.

"She's not doing good," he says. "She's not eating or sleeping. She looks awful."

My fingers tighten around the phone. "Why? She's where she wants to be. She got her company. This is what she wanted, Wilby."

"She's not happy," he says.

"She tell you to call me?"

"No, and she'd probably be pissed if she knew I did. She misses you like hell, and it's making her physically sick. I've never seen her like this."

Silence.

"She needs you, man."

I sit on the edge of the bed. "She's fine."

Erin Branscom

"She's not fine, not even close to fine. She's heartbroken," he says firmly.

"She's Silvie. She's built for this life. She'll bounce back and be okay," I reason.

"She needs you," he shoots back. "Look, I can't explain it. But you two? You are it, man. IT."

Silence again stretches between us and I close my eyes.

Then he says, "I can send the jet."

I let out a breath. "Wilby."

"I'm serious. You can be here by tonight. And fix her! She needs you."

"I can't."

"You can."

"I have a life here. I have to take care of my mom."

There's a pause, then he says calmly, "Cal."

"I'm not leaving my mom."

"You're not abandoning her. Listen, she has the Bees all lined up. Silvie got her to sign up for her first therapy appointment. She's been out on the porch twice. She's made progress."

I swallow, heart pattering wildly in my chest. I didn't know any of this. I guess you miss a lot while wallowing in self-pity.

"I can't," I say again, but it comes out weaker now.

"Are you staying for Carly," Wilby asks carefully, "or are you hiding?"

That lands harder than it should. Because I think he's right. Damn it. I know he's right.

"I've gotta go," I mutter.

He sighs. "If you change your mind, the jet's ready."

I hang up.

———

That afternoon, when I get to the bar, Jonah is there, his arms folded as he watches me walk toward him.

Jonah is never behind the bar. He hasn't worked at the bar in over five years. He gave it to me to manage, and he's taken a hands-off approach. I run it all, make all the decisions, and he lets me have free will.

"You look like crap," he says as his eyes scan my face.

"Hello to you, too," I say as I grab a few dirty dishes off a table and set them in the bin.

"We need to talk."

I pause and straighten. "This sounds serious."

He looks at me. "It is serious. You are messing up."

I move behind the bar automatically and grab a rag because it's habit and muscle memory. He puts his hand on it.

"You gonna keep doing this?" Jonah asks.

"Doing what?" I clip.

"You know what," he says calmly.

"I'm trying to work."

"You're hiding," Jonah says.

I slam a stack of coasters down. "Drop it. Why does everyone say that?"

"Because it's true," he says.

I glare at him. "No, it's not."

"You're fired."

I blink. "What?"

"You're fired."

"You can't fire me."

"I just did."

I stare at him. "For what?"

"For acting like a ghost in your own life."

I let out a humorless laugh. "You're dramatic."

"Marina's the manager now."

"Fine."

"Fine?" he snaps. "That's it? That's all you've got?"

"I don't care."

And I don't. That's the worst part. Everything feels like static. Like I'm watching my own life through fogged glass.

Jonah walks and stops in front of me. "You're letting it fall apart."

"I'm holding everything together."

"For who?" he demands.

"My mom."

"Your mom doesn't need you to martyr yourself."

I stiffen. "Watch it."

"No, I won't watch it. She means something to me, son. She needs you to be happy and not to punish yourself because of her. Stop being scared."

"I'm not scared."

"You are terrified."

Silence fills the air between us.

"You think if you stay here and hide behind taking care of your mom," Jonah continues, softer now, "it hurts less when Silvie leaves for good."

That hits somewhere deep and ugly.

"She told me in the beginning she'd leave," I say quietly.

"She told you she'd leave because she didn't think you'd be real. Everyone knows this is real."

My jaw tightens and I glance away.

Jonah reaches into the drawer behind the bar and tosses a folder onto the counter between us.

"What's this?"

"Open it."

I flip it open. It's the deed to Cocktails & Chaos with my name on it.

I look up. "What is this?"

"You're the owner now," he says.

"What do you mean? Why are you doing this?" I ask, confused. "Did something happen?"

"No, nothing has happened. I've been meaning to transfer it. Paperwork's done. It's yours. If we're being honest, it's been yours for a while now. We just needed to make it official."

"Jonah, I can't take this," I say, closing the folder.

"You can."

"I don't want..."

"You don't want what?" he interrupts. "Responsibility? Freedom? You can go anywhere when you own this bar. Marina is going to run it, and you know that she's more than capable."

My heart pounds in my chest.

"You're not tied here," he says. "You never were. I don't need you, and your momma doesn't need you. We all look after her."

"You don't get it..."

"I do get it," he says. "I've got it. Marina's got it. The damn Bees got it. Your mom will be fine."

I swallow hard. I think about what Wilby said.

"Carly doesn't need you hovering," he continues. "She needs you to live your life."

The bar suddenly feels smaller.

"I love you, son. You mean the world to me. It's my pleasure to give you this. But if you make me get all sappy, I swear I'll push you off the dock. Just take it."

I nod and give him a big hug. He tenses up first, then leans into it and pats my back.

"Thank you," I tell him.

"Silvie's not just another summer escape," Jonah says firmly. "She's your wife."

My chest aches. Wife.

God, I miss her. So damn much.

"She chose you," he says gently. "Now go choose her."

The truth is, I already have. I know, deep in my heart, I want her, but everything is so messy and stressful.

When you're with her it's not...

"I don't know if she still wants me," I admit, hating how true those words are.

I want to go to her.

Jonah steps closer and drops his voice. "Then go fight for her."

I really want to go to her.

I exhale slowly, and silence stretches between us.

I really, really want to go to her.

Jonah claps a hand on my shoulder. "Go get your wife."

I'm going to go to her.

For the first time in days, something sparks in my chest. Hope. I'm gonna go get her back.

silvie

. . .

I BARELY MAKE it to the trash can when I grip the sides of the metal can and throw up like my body is staging a hostile takeover. Again. I moan and grab a tissue, glancing around to see if anyone saw. It's not something I imagine baddie CEOs are supposed to do. I sink back into my chair and close my eyes.

"It's okay," I whisper to myself. "You're fine. You're absolutely fine."

There's a soft knock on my office door, and it opens because only Wilby doesn't wait for permission. He slips in like he owns the place, and honestly, he pretty much does.

He says nothing, just searches my face and sets a plate of toast down in front of me and a can of Sprite beside it.

"Thanks," I say, my voice hoarse.

"You look like hell," he says gently. "I rescheduled all of your afternoon appointments. Until further notice. You need rest."

"Okay," I say.

"Now, I know you're a mess. You never agree to rest," he says as he studies me. His eyes are worried, and that makes me nervous. He's not just my right-hand man. He's my best friend, which means I can't lie to him and pretend that everything is okay when he obviously knows it's not.

He plops a small brown paper bag onto my desk, and I glance at it and back up at him. I'm too tired to ask what it is.

"I have four sisters," he says softly. "Open it."

My fingers feel shaky as I pull the top apart and peer inside. A pregnancy test.

I freeze. "No."

"Silvie…"

"No, no, no," I plead as I look up at him.

He's so calm and annoyingly prepared as usual.

"Can't be," I whisper.

"Could be," he gently corrects.

My brain starts racing. I open my calendar app and think back to the last time I had my period. I scroll back, and back. And back again. Oh, shit. I can't even remember. I took my pills like clockwork, didn't I? Then I tilt my head. Maybe I missed a day or so. I didn't think I did.

My hand slowly drifts to my flat stomach. "Oh, God."

Wilby doesn't move. "Go take it."

I shake my head. "I can't."

"Yes, you can," he says.

I don't have time to be pregnant. I can't be a mom…

He crosses his arms. "Bathroom. Now."

I stand on unsteady legs, grab the bag as if it's radioactive, and head to my small, private bathroom.

Wilby closes the door and says, "I'll be right here. I'm not leaving you alone."

"I'm fine," I protest.

"You're so weak you can barely walk," he says. "You throw everything up."

"It could have been food poisoning or the flu," I call through the door.

"Okay," he says calmly. "Then take the test and prove it."

I move on autopilot, and my hands are shaking. I start breathing fast, I'm so nervous. I set it on the counter like it's a ticking time bomb.

"I can't look," I say.

Wilby opens the door and steps closer to the sink. "What do you want it to be?" he asks quietly.

I swallow. "This wasn't part of the plan."

He looks at me pointedly. "I don't think anything in your life for the past few months has gone to plan and thank God it hasn't, otherwise you'd be married to Tyler the Turd right now."

I sigh. "That's not comforting. That's a nightmare."

He leans his hip against the counter. "You'll never find a better man than Cal. He's the whole package."

My chest tightens at the mention of Cal. Because I miss him so much.

"That man loves you, Silverlyn."

"Not enough to fight for me," I say softly.

Wilby huffs. "He fake-married you. He helped you save your entire legacy."

"That's true."

"Also, you gotta make space for him. You told him you had to focus on your company. You didn't even include him."

Oh my God. I did that.

Wilby smirks. "You're not a pansy, Silvie. You can fight for him."

I glare at him weakly. "Did you just call me a pansy?"

"Yes. You can wear the pants. You can be the boss. You can fight for him."

I slide down the wall until I'm sitting on the tile floor.

"For your family," he says.

Family.

The word feels foreign and warm at the same time. Then I realize what he's telling me.

"Family?" I echo.

He looks down at the test and then back at me. His expression softens, and he smiles. "You're a mom. A mommy. Mamacita. Congratulations, friend."

The air leaves my lungs. Cal and I are having a baby. A family.

"Wait. Really?" I breathe.

He points at it and meets my eyes. "I'm not touching that thing. You peed on it. You're pregnant."

I smile and wipe tears from the corners of my eyes. My hand moves instinctively to my stomach. Pregnant with Cal's baby.

"I can't," I whisper. "I have a company to run."

"You can." Wilby rolls his eyes. "There's this thing called daycare and nannies. And duh…Birdie."

"No. It's not that. I don't know how. What if I turn out like my mom?" I say, suddenly feeling scared.

"You've been running a billion-dollar company. You've survived your mother. You've survived a lot. You can handle this. And you have Cal."

Cal. Oh, God. What will he say?

I laugh wetly. "This wasn't on my five-year plan."

"Maybe it's on the forever plan."

"What do I do?" I whisper.

Wilby smiles, and his voice softens. "You call your husband."

Husband. My throat tightens. "What if he doesn't want this?"

"He will."

"You don't know that."

"I do."

I close my eyes and picture Cal's laugh and his hands holding me. Kissing me. Taking care of me. And I picture him as a dad, and I can totally see it. I may not know how to do to this, but I think he'd be great at it. Maybe we could figure it out together. I'm going to need him. Because I can't even bake brownies.

"Come on," he says as he opens the bathroom door. "I made you a doctor's appointment. Let's go hear the little heartbeat."

"But how did you know I'd be pregnant?" I call after him.

"Sisters," he calls back.

"That's it?" I whisper as the elevator closes behind us.

I clutch the glossy printout of the ultrasound that resembles a blob. I tuck it in my purse in case a reporter is lingering around.

"That's your baby." Wilby shudders as he leans against the other side of the elevator. "It's real."

"I can't believe this is really happening. Not how I thought my day was going to go." I let out a shaky laugh.

The elevator hums as we head downward. I look at my reflection in the mirrored wall and I look pale. My hair is still perfectly blown out, my pink suit still sharp and tailored. I look like I should be walking into a board meeting, not carrying around a secret little heartbeat in my body.

Wilby guides me out to the waiting car, and I slide in and lean my head back. Cal should have been here. He might have wanted to be here. I think about the heartbeat we heard, fast and wild. He could've been holding my hand, making inappropriate jokes to calm me down, kissing my temple, and telling me he's happy.

"Thank you for coming with me," I say as I look over at Wilby, combing through work emails on his phone.

"Of course," he murmurs.

My penthouse still feels cold and lonely when we walk in. Wilby kicks off his shoes and pours us both waters. He throws a blanket over the couch and queues up the show he knows I've been watching.

"I'm going to get changed," I tell him.

"I'll order food!" he calls after me.

A shower sounds damn good.

After I've thrown on cozy and comfy light pink sweats, I join him on the couch.

He's already changed into comfy clothes and is under a blanket, his laptop open in front of him. "I ordered us pasta," he says. "You need carbs."

"I'm growing a human. My body deserves carbs."

"And garlic bread," he adds.

When our delivery arrives, he gets it and hands me a fork. We sit cross-legged on the big couch. The takeout containers steam between us. I pick the alfredo pasta, and Wilby chooses the penne vodka.

The ultrasound photo still sits on the coffee table, reminding me of the elephant in the room. I can't stop looking at it.

Wilby glances at the ultrasound and back at me as he reaches for napkins. "How are you going to tell him?"

I trace the edge of the takeout container. "I think I should do it in person."

He studies me for a second, then nods. "That's probably a good idea."

We eat in silence after that. When we're done and everything's put away, we watch a few episodes of my show.

When he finally stands to leave, he squeezes my shoulder. "Call me if you need me."

"I will. Thanks, Wilby."

He nods and leaves. "See you tomorrow."

When the elevator doors close, the loneliness rushes in. I carry the ultrasound to my bedroom with me, like it's sacred.

I change into one of Cal's old T-shirts that I stole from him when I left Coconut Beach. It still smells like him, and I miss him. I crawl under the covers and stare at the ceiling.

I last about five minutes before I sit up again and decide to go take a bath. I wait for the bathtub to fill slowly and steam curls into the air. I slide into the water and let the water comfort me like a warm blanket over my shoulders. I close my eyes and I can almost feel Cal here. That time, he brought me breakfast in the tub before my big day taking over. The way he'd sat with me while I soaked and told me I had this. That I'd be great. The way he kisses me like I'm his. The way he never rushed me, never yelled, never got mad at me. Until the day I pushed him too far.

Wilby was right. I'll never find a man like him. I know this in my soul. Cal is special. He's...mine. And I need him. I want him. And the thought of losing him makes me feel sick. I open my eyes and stare at the tile. There won't be another Cal. And this is just a job. Sure, it's a powerful one. But it's just a job. I wanted to show everyone I could do it. It could be mine. And I could be feminine and powerful, and I could do it. I don't need it. I need him. I don't need to fight for some stupid male-dominated board's approval. I don't need this cold and sterile penthouse. I could sell everything. Liquidate it all. Walk away and go live the good life in Coconut Beach. Chase sunsets with Cal in the sand while holding our baby. Dance in the kitchen while Cal cooks dinner, because let's be honest, I'd probably burn it down.

I press my hand to my stomach. We could have a good life. That idea doesn't feel reckless. It feels...peaceful. I make my way to bed not long after, feeling finally at peace.

———————

The next morning, I head to the office, even though Wilby told me to stay home and take the day off. He's sitting at his desk, drinking coffee and doing online clothes shopping when I walk up to his desk.

He closes his eyes. "Silverlyn. Why aren't you at home resting?"

"I'm selling it all," I tell him as I flop down in the chair next to him.

His eyes widen. "Selling what?"

"The penthouse, the building, anything I can. I don't want it anymore."

He blinks. "Where are you going to live?"

"Not here."

I slide into the chair next to him.

"Let's not be rash," he says. "Talk to me, Goose."

I snort at the *Top Gun* reference. Wilby and his movie quotes.

"I don't know where I belong," I admit quietly. "I just want him."

Wilby sets his cup down. "That's the most romantic thing I've ever heard."

I blink at him. "I have no idea what I'm doing."

He leans in and whispers, "You don't want this anymore?"

I shrug. "I don't know."

"You can have it all," he says. "You don't have to choose. Men don't choose."

I sigh. "I don't want what my father had. I don't want to work eighteen-hour days and live here. I want to live."

"You don't have to run things like Charles," he whispers, looking around to make sure no one is listening to us. "You can run this with a family and with healthy boundaries. Just because he didn't have any, doesn't mean you don't have to."

I stare at him and smile slowly. Because he's right.

"You're not him," he continues. "You can do this your way."

"You think so?" I whisper.

Wilby smiles. "I know so. And I think you're already doing it."

cal

· · ·

"HEY, MOM." I smile as she opens the door and holds it open for me.

I set a few bags of groceries on the table, along with three new paperback books.

"Honey, what a surprise. It's not Tuesday, is it?" she asks, looking confused.

I shake my head. "I'm going to New York. I wanted to make sure you were good before I head out for a few days."

She softens, shame filling her face. "Oh, honey. Thank you. I'm sorry you had to take the time to do this."

"Mom, don't say sorry," I tell her. "I love you, and I want to take care of you."

"Does this mean you're going to get Silvie?" she asks, looking hopeful.

I chuckle and nod. "Yeah. I've been an idiot too long. I shouldn't have let her leave."

I tell her about how Jonah gave me the bar, and she wipes her eyes. "That Jonah has always been a good man."

"Mom, I have to tell you something," I say, frowning, unsure how to talk to her about this.

"Okay," she says hesitantly, as if she knows this isn't going to be an easy conversation.

"What happened six years ago when my biological father came to Coconut Beach? What happened to make you not want to leave the house anymore?"

She swallows and looks down at her hands in her lap. "How do you know he came here?"

"He found me this week and told me," I tell her.

"He's here?" she asks, looking at the door and back at me.

Holy shit, she's scared. I want to pound that asshole in the face. But I need her to tell me what he did, so I need to stay calm. I need to figure out what broke her in order to fix her. I need her to let me in.

"Not anymore." I shake my head. "In fact, I told him he's never allowed on this island ever again."

She breathes a deep sigh of relief. "That seems a little extreme. It's not my island."

"He won't be bothering either of us. But I need to know. What happened?"

"He showed up one day after all these years." She exhales and looks over at her bookcase. "He was with his family. They came into Cocktails & Chaos, and he was joking with his wife and kids. He looked over at me and said to his family, 'That could have been your mother if I'd stayed here and not made a life for myself.'"

My jaw goes tight, and my fist clenches.

"I had a lot of shame at seeing him and his family laugh. They looked at me like I was just some server at the bar and not the woman who had you. It made me feel so ashamed. It brought back memories of when I was a single mom, pregnant, and just...alone. People judged me, and then I raised you alone, and that wasn't easy. Him coming here and doing that just made me feel...bad. Staying home is my safe space."

I'm going to kick that motherfucker's ass.

"I've been going to therapy," she admits. "Silvie's helping

me. I have had two sessions now, and I am talking about a lot of things I've kept buried. I think it's helping."

My heart squeezes. "I'm proud of you, Mom."

I had no idea that Silvie was still helping my mom. Even though she went back to New York and she hasn't reached out to me, she's still helping my mom. That gives me hope that there's still a chance for us.

Mom smiles. "Thanks. I'm proud of you, too. Which is why I want you to go live your life. Let me live mine. I'm figuring it out and getting better. I don't want you to think you have to stay here for me."

Damn it. Jonah and Wilby were right. I was hiding out here behind my mom. And she doesn't want that, either. I might have lost the best woman because I was too afraid to live my life. How sad is that?

No more delaying. I need to go get my wife.

———

Me: Still okay if I come?

Wilby: Jet's been in Coconut Beach waiting.
Can be wheels up in two hours.

Me: I'm coming. Thank you.

Wilby: I think you're making the right choice.
She needs you. You need her.

Me: I know. Don't tell her I'm coming, okay? I
need to do a few things when I get there.

Wilby: You've got it.

———

Erin Branscom

The elevator ride up to Montclair Holdings feels longer than it should. I am so nervous right now but not letting anything get in the way of what I need to do. I know what I want, and I know what I need to do. The numbers feel like they're climbing one by one. I adjust the cuffs on my sleeve and straighten my jacket. I'm wearing my dark navy suit that's tailored with clean lines. Light-blue button-down shirt, no tie. I'm drawing the line at a tie. I don't need one to impress the person I'm coming here for. I'm here to see one man. And one woman. And really, she's the only one who matters to me.

When the doors open, everything is familiar but still feels foreign. People glance up, and a few heads turn curiously. I recognize the look. They know who I am and what I'm here for.

I walk straight toward the front desk. "Good morning. I have a meeting with Charles Montclair."

Her eyes flick down to her screen, then back at me. Something shifts in her expression. It's respect. Interesting. "He's expecting you."

Good. This is a good sign.

The dark-wood double doors to his office are heavy, their polished handles shiny. I knock once and enter when I hear him call out. He stands before his floor-to-ceiling windows over-looking Manhattan. To some, he may seem intimidating, but to me, he's not. No matter how much he tries to be. He's staring out at the city as if he owns it, which I suppose he kind of does.

He turns slowly and takes me in from head to toe. He nods his head approvingly. "You clean up well."

I don't respond to that, because I feel like it's a test. Of whether he can get a rise out of me or not. I've had practice with people. While he was making deals, I was behind a bar for the past five years studying people like him. Seeing how they inter-act, how they tick, and I've got Charles Montclair's number. There's just one problem. He doesn't have mine. He has no idea about me. None.

"I've had practice."

He gives me a confused look and gestures to the chair across from his desk. "Sit."

I don't. Because I'm not a fucking dog. Or a cat.

"I won't take up too much of your time," I say. "I'm here to get my wife."

The words hit, and he's silent. His eyes narrow and his jaw tightens.

"I thought we were past this. You were staying in Coconut Beach and playing your part. Silently."

"With all due respect, Charles," I say evenly. "Enough. Drop the bullshit."

Silence stretches between us.

"I'm here because I want things to go differently this time," I continue. "I want a real wedding with family. I want Silvie to be surrounded by people who love her. Not whatever bullshit circus you had that first time."

He studies me, his eyes still narrowed.

"She's my wife. And I love her. And I'm not going anywhere."

He blinks and looks like he's not sure what to say. "You weren't supposed to be real. You're a bartender in Coconut Beach. She has a real opportunity here to change her legacy."

I step closer to him, not aggressive, but firm. "I am a part of that legacy. She is my family."

"What do you want? Is it money?" he asks in an even tone.

"I don't think you are understanding. See, where you come from, it's all about money. For me...it's about family. Big, loud, happy family. People who show up, even when it's hard to show up. They love each other and would do anything for each other. That's my currency."

A look of surprise crosses his face. He's thinking.

"You don't know me. You think I don't fit in your world. And that's fine. Maybe I don't. Maybe I do. But I'm here anyway."

His gaze flickers at that, and he continues to listen.

"Family is everything to me, Charles. I grew up with a

mother who loved me and encouraged me to have anything I
wanted in life. She told me I could be and do whatever I wanted.
She only just wanted me to be healthy and happy. So, I had a
good role model. Silvie didn't have that for a mother. And she
should have."

He sighs and looks away.

"Things are going to be different from here on out," I say.
"My wife will have her village that supports and encourages
her."

His eyebrows furl together.

"And she needs you to be a part of her village," I continue.
"She's been working for this her whole life and she loves it. And
she should have it. With all of us having her back and encouraging her."

His shoulders lower a fraction. "You think I don't know that
she needs that?" he asks quietly.

I swallow.

"I think you've been an empire," I say. "And somewhere
along the way, she got left behind to be abused and neglected by
her own mother. Now she thinks work is all she has and
somehow can't have both."

He walks back over to the window and looks out at it. Then
looks back at me. "You and I aren't so different."

I don't break eye contact.

He walks over to his bar and pulls down two crystal glasses
from the shelf. "I started as nothing. Did you know that? I was
the bartender at my wife's family's country club. I mixed
drinks for all of the men who thought I'd never become one of
them."

Holy shit.

His mouth twitches at my surprise. "And look at me now,"
he continues. " But I didn't come from a family like yours. I
didn't marry into a family like yours. I tried to create that...and
failed. But Silvie? Silvie is different."

"Silvie is everything," I say softly.

"She loves you," he says as he pours bourbon into two glasses. I don't tell him that it's eleven in the morning.

"I love her," I answer.

"I know."

He studies my face like he's looking for doubt or something to conflict with this. He won't find it.

"I was wrong about you," he says finally. "And I wasn't fair. I thought you were a rebellion for my daughter."

"I'm not."

"No," he agrees quietly. "You're not."

He steps closer and hands me a glass. I take it and hold it.

"What does this marriage and life look like for you, Cal?" he asks over his glass.

"I know you think I don't fit into your world. But I fit into Silvie's world. I can promise you that. I love her and I will take care of her and support her until the day that I die," I say with conviction.

He unbuttons his cuffs and rolls up his sleeves to reveal completely tatted-up arms. Wow. Unexpected.

"You mark everything important on your skin?" he asks.

I shrug. "Sometimes."

He nods once. "I did too, once upon a time. See? Not much different." He lets loose a sharp breath. "I'll support this," he says. "The board is still gunning for her. But having you by her side helps."

Relief pulses through me, but I don't let it show.

"I'm here for whatever she needs," I tell him. "I'll attend meetings and dinners. I'll be by her side if that's what she wants."

He nods.

"But I'm not playing golf. I draw the line there."

He blinks, and then he laughs. "That's where you draw the line?"

"That's where I draw the line. Golf is boring, Charles."

He shakes his head, still smiling. "Thank fuck."

"Do you want a family?" he suddenly asks.

The question surprises me because Silvie and I have briefly talked about it, but she seems pretty driven in her career, and it didn't seem like something she wanted. But then I think about what she said about what I wanted. And that I need to want for myself, not just for what everyone else wants and needs.

"I want Silvie," I say honestly and meet his eyes. "Whatever she wants. If that's kids, I'm in. If it's just the two of us, running back and forth between Coconut Beach and New York, I'm in. If she wants to run this company and have me support her, I'm in. I just want her. She's it for me."

Something shifts in him then. He's not a businessman standing in front of me. A titan of his industry. He's a father.

"You'd follow her anywhere, it sounds like," he says.

"I already did. I'm here, aren't I?" I grin.

He looks down at his desk for a moment.

"You don't have to like me, but you need to know I'm not going anywhere."

He lifts his chin and looks at me. "I do like you."

Then he straightens and buttons his sleeves again. He turns and walks toward the door. "Come on. Let's go get my daughter back for you."

silvie

• • •

I'M SITTING at my desk, trying to work while Wilby attends a few meetings for me, taking notes when my father's assistant knocks on my door and steps into my office.

"Your father would like to see you in the boardroom."

The boardroom. The room where decisions are made, votes happen, and where futures shift. It's where I've learned how to put up with men twice my age questioning me because I'm female. It's the place I've practiced never letting them see me sweat. It's where I've perfected my poker face. My pulse spikes immediately, and my stomach turns. This is it. This is when the board calls me a fraud and strips me of my company, no matter how hard I've fought to keep it.

"Now?" I ask, already knowing the answer. I glance around, wishing Wilby was here. He insisted on taking the meetings so I could get some work done. I'm regretting that now.

"Yes."

I close my laptop carefully, buying myself extra seconds to compose myself. I feel like I haven't slept well in weeks, and I'm so tired. If today is the day when I'm canned, so be it. I just miss Cal. I haven't talked to him since I left Coconut Beach. I want to talk to him and to tell him about the baby. I don't know how he'll react. I just miss him. I keep replaying the last moment we had together, where he was so distant and angry. He pushed me away. He told me to go and that he'd play his part. As if we were in a play, acting out our lives. Maybe that's what we were. But it's not what I want. Maybe it doesn't matter what I want, anymore. Maybe I just get whatever fate hands me at this point.

I stand and smooth my shirt, slipping into my hot pink blazer. Because pink is all I wear now. All the shades. I refuse to conform to the man's world any longer. Maybe I'm channeling my inner Elle Woods. I don't care. I'm going to be me from now on. And if they don't like it, I don't really care. If this meeting is about the optics of my marriage and choosing love, I will fight. I'll fight for myself and my family. Because while I'm tired of fighting, I won't stop. I am going to turn this company around and make room for any woman who wants to work and have a family.

I walk down the long hallway, heels clicking on the tile, portraits of the board lining the walls. Ribbon cuttings, deals closing, empires built. A lot of black suits and all men. Yeah, that's going to be changing.

The boardroom doors swing open as I step inside and everything stops. My dad is sitting at the head of the table. And Cal is sitting next to him.

Cal. *My* Cal. I start to feel my poker face fade away. Because when I look at him, there's no faking what I feel for him. God, I love him so much. I've missed him so much. And wait...he's here? And he looks so good in his navy suit and light blue shirt. He looks powerful and confident, as if he were made for this boardroom.

I look at my father, and he's sitting with his hands folded in front of him, smiling at me. Smiling. What the hell is happening right now? My gaze lands on the table and there are flowers laid on it. Pale blush roses. My favorite. Next to them is a light pink velvet ring box.

My lungs forget how to breathe. I tremble, and Cal rises and comes to me. He stands before me, smiling, his hands by his sides. He looks nervous.

I glance over at my father. Neither seems angry. In fact, they seem friendly around each other which is new.

"What's this?" I ask, my voice feeling small.

Cal looks like he wants to scoop me up. I want to run to him. I want to hold him so tightly and tell him that I've missed him so much. But I don't. He told me to go. And while he may be here right now, he hurt me. I don't know what this is. I'm not the one running this time.

My father clears his throat. "I believe this is your meeting. We can talk later."

My eyes follow him as he steps past me. "Whatever you decide," he says quietly. "You have my support."

Support. That word has never come easy to him. He doesn't give it easily. He's driven, and the one thing that matters to him is what's best for his company. It was never about support.

The doors close behind him, and it's just Cal and me in this massive space.

"What are you doing here, Cal?" I ask softly, lifting my chin up.

He doesn't try to touch me. "I needed to talk to you."

I look down at his stubble already visible on his jaw, even though he probably shaved this morning. "You told me to go."

He nods. "I did."

Something disarms me in his tone and the way he's so frank about this. "So, why are you here now?"

"Because I was wrong."

My chest tightens, and I cross my arms over my chest, feeling protective. Because he has no idea how much power he has here. The power to break me and shatter me if he wants. And I'm vulnerable at his mercy.

"Oh, yeah?" I ask.

"You were right. I was using her as an excuse."

"You were protecting your mom," I counter. "And I get that."

"I was hiding behind that," he says. "I was afraid." The honesty in his voice slices through me. "I thought if I braced for you leaving, it wouldn't hurt me as much," he continues. "I thought if I pushed you away first, you'd do what you needed to do, and I could control the hurt. It was dumb."

Control. I understand control. I live it. A carefully curated and controlled world that I now realize I hate.

"And did it work for you?" I ask softly.

"No," he says. "I just hurt you, and I'm so sorry, baby."

My throat burns as he steps closer to me. He's still giving me space. He's waiting.

He moves closer to the table and away from me. "I came to do this right."

I swallow at the word. Right. My whole life, I've been doing things right. I've been groomed to take over the family company since I was a teenager.

"Right how?" I whisper.

"Right for us," he says. "What fits us. I'm here for you."

He moves closer. "I don't need you to give anything up. I need you to thrive, baby. I need you to fly and soar as high as you want to. I want you to know that I've got your back every step of the way. I'm right behind you. I'll give you whatever you want."

He finally closes the distance between us. "I just need you to be happy," he says. "I need you to be you."

He turns and gestures to the boardroom and the skyline beyond the glass. "You want to run this company forever? I've got you. You want to be the most powerful CEO this city has ever seen? I'll stand behind you and clap the loudest. I'll kick anyone's ass who tries to get in your way."

My eyes sting because I didn't realize how badly I needed to hear this.

"You don't want a family? Fine. I'll be your family. You want to split your life between Coconut Beach and the city? I'll pack up."

He looks at me like I'm the only thing that matters to him. I've never been looked at like this. Chosen.

"And what do *you* want?"

He smiles. "I just want you, Silvie. All of you. CEO you. Beach you. Every version of you that you'll give me. I want the whole damn thing."

No one's ever said anything like this to me before.

"You're my wife," he says softly. "And I came to get you back."

He steps closer and brushes his thumbs across my cheeks, catching tears I didn't realize were falling. "You only run from things that don't matter. You run to the ones that do."

My heart aches because he's right. I ran from my wedding, and I almost ran from him. And it felt so wrong because he feels so right.

"Do you want this?" he asks, searching my eyes.

And there's the real question. It's not power, responsibilities or business. It's love. It's family.

"I love you so much. I've wanted you since the first moment I saw you, Callahan Bennett."

He opens the ring box, and it's a new ring. It's an oval set on a gold band, with an eternity wedding band encrusted with diamonds around it. It's me, and it's perfect.

He takes my hand and gently removes our old rings, the ones he bought online right before our fake ceremony. He slides the new ones on, and I love the way they look on my hand.

I step into him and kiss him like I've been starving for him. Because I have. Everything around us disappears, and it's just him and me. His hands are on my waist, his mouth covering mine as he's equally as hungry. He holds me like he's never letting go, and when we both come up for air, we just stare at each other. He rests his forehead to mine.

"I missed you so much," I confess.

"I missed you more," he says.

"I hated you a little for not fighting for us."

"I deserved it," he says softly.

"There's something I have to tell you. It might change everything."

His expression shifts, and he braces himself. I recognize the protective and focused look. "What is it?"

My stomach dips. "I found something out after I left."

His brow furrows. "Found out what?"

My hands shake because I'm terrified of what he's going to say right now. "I'm pregnant."

Silence.

"You're going to be a dad."

His eyes lock on mine, and he's still. For a second, I begin to panic.

"I know this is a lot," I rush out. "I didn't plan it. I don't know how I'm supposed to be a wife and a mom and run this company and be this person and..."

He cups my face gently. "Hey."

I pause and realize his eyes are glassy.

"I don't know either. I never had a dad. I had Jonah, but not a dad who lived with us," he whispers.

The vulnerability in his voice nearly breaks me, and he continues. "But we can figure it out together."

I close my eyes. Together. Yeah, we can.

"I'm going to be a dad," he says as he lets out a shaky breath, as if he can't believe it either. "You're going to be a mom."

His hand slides to my stomach, and he whispers in my ear, "I love you so much."

"I love you, too."

"We're building a family. And we'll do it together," he says quietly.

My heart swells, and all that fear that I had in me that he wouldn't want this is gone. Instead, he looks happy.

"I was scared to tell you," I admit. "I didn't know if you'd want this."

He looks at me like I'm insane. "I want everything with you. You never have to be scared to tell me anything."

I didn't know how badly I needed to hear those words from him.

Cal kisses me softly. "I think you're going to be a great mom."

"You'll be a great dad," I whisper back. "This baby is lucky to have you."

The diamonds on my finger shine in the sunlight, and I lift my hand to his chest, the steady beat of his heart beneath my palm makes my throat tighten.

He kisses me gently at first, and then he deepens it with his mouth, not urgent, or rushed, just confident. Like he's promising me something and I'm giving it to him.

He threads his fingers through my hair and picks me up and sets me on the boardroom table. I kiss him, wrapping my arms around his neck and pulling him to me, his hard body to mine, and moan a little.

"Silvie," he murmurs my name, low and reverent like he's choosing me again.

And for the first time in this building, I'm being chosen by the one who matters. He's holding me instead of me being the one to hold everything together. And somehow, I know that everything is going to be just fine.

———————

Cal and I walk hand in hand back to my office, and I close and lock the door. I turn to him and take my jacket off, and he grins.

"I've never had sex at work," I admit. "But I can't go another minute without you."

He slides off his jacket and lays it over a chair. He unbuttons his shirt, slowly. "You have to be quiet."

"I am quiet," I bite out.

He tips his head as he takes off his shirt and I sigh at the sight of his tanned and tattooed chest.

I slide off my shirt and unbutton my pants, kicking those down. I'm standing before him in a soft pink lace bralette and lace panties.

"Oh, shit. That is what you were wearing under that suit?" he grits out.

"Yep."

He grins and steps out of his boxers, letting them drop, coming toward me wearing nothing. He cups my face, kissing me urgently and hungrily. His hand dips to my panties and he groans into my mouth. "Fucking soaked baby."

"I need you," I plead.

"I need you more," he says as he slides them down and pulls my bra off quickly. He cups my bottom to him and slowly enters me while my body trembles.

"Cal."

"You have to be quiet, baby," he whispers. "You can be loud as you want at home, but at the office, I'm in charge of fucking you good at your desk."

I roll my head back and moan as he takes me hard and tension builds and builds until I moan, "Cal."

His hand cups my chin. "Come for me, baby."

I pant and moan as he goes harder, gripping me to him. "Come on..."

I let loose and let go, and he grips me harder, coming hard as he pants. "Good girl."

"That's so hot. I need you to do this more often."

He chuckles. "I plan to."

"At the office," I add, still breathless.

"Might be weird, but sure." He grins and then leans forward to drag his lips over my neck. In a sweet whisper, he says, "I love you, Mrs. Bennett."

"I love you, Mr. Bennett."

epilogue

. . .

Cal

SILVIE LIES ON A TOWEL, her legs stretched out, one hand resting on the small curve of her belly. She's not showing much yet. Just enough that I notice when she shifts her weight. And I can't stop noticing. I love everything about that woman.

I didn't know it, but Silvie and her dad have been working to establish an office here in Coconut Beach as well as back in Manhattan. It appears that most of the board doesn't mind the travel, and several have decided to move down here as well. This works out for Silvie, because she loves it here and says the beach air seems to soothe the nausea in a way Manhattan never could. So, we're here for now. I'm surfing and she's barefoot in the sand, the sun spilling over Coconut Beach, waking up the island.

I stare out at her and think of how we built this. I watch her close her eyes and tip her face toward the sun. Her hair lifts in the breeze, gold against the morning light, and I swear I've never seen anything more beautiful and powerful than the woman carrying our baby. The woman who could choose anyone and chose me.

I lay down my board and sit behind her, wrapping my arms around her waist, pressing my chin into her shoulder.

She sighs and leans into me, not caring that I'm getting her wet.

"How's the nausea today?"

"Manageable," she says. "The ocean helps. I have no idea how, but it does."

"It's yours," I tell her. "I bought it for you."

She laughs softly. "You can't buy the ocean, dork."

"Watch me."

She shakes her head and leans back into me, that simple trust that still feels unreal sometimes. For a long time, I braced myself for this to end. Because I never wanted to. But she isn't.

We found a new place together in Manhattan. It's more family-friendly, and she's got a designer making it into a home for us. I'm expanding my cottage here as much as I can. *Our* cottage. I told her we could find something bigger, but she assured me this was all we needed. She likes being close to my mom and Birdie, and I love that, too.

"You know," she says casually. "We're going to need to make the cottage a little bigger."

I kiss her temple. "It'll be fine. I've already talked to the contractor."

"No," she says, and there's something mischievous in her voice. "Bigger."

"We have plenty of room for the nursery."

She turns toward me, eyes bright, and says, "The babies need more room."

My brain catches on. "Babies?" I repeat.

She grins and reaches into the bag beside her, pulling out an ultrasound photo. She holds it up. "Babies."

For a second, I just stare at the image of two blobs in the picture. It dawns on me that there are, in fact, two.

"Two?" I say again, because apparently, I'm speechless and only capable of a few words. "But I thought there was only one."

"Me too," she says with a chuckle. "But there was another little one hiding in there."

"Holy shit."

"We're going to practically be outnumbered," she teases.

I let out a breath that turns into a laugh. "There are two of us, Silvie. They don't outnumber us."

My hands shake a little as I take the photo from her, stare at it, and smile. I wonder what they'll look like. I always grew up wondering whose eyes I had and who I took after. My kids will never wonder. They will always know both their parents. I pull her even closer, hand protectively over her stomach.

"As long as they're healthy," I murmur.

She softens immediately. "Yeah."

I kiss her slowly, tasting her mint toothpaste, my hands sliding down her arms, and she laughs against my mouth. "You're going to need a bigger truck."

"I'm going to need a bigger everything," I reply.

I kneel in the sand in front of her and press my lips to her belly. "Hey," I say. "You've got two parents who love the hell out of you. You hear me?"

She threads her fingers through my hair. "You're already a great dad."

I look up at her and grin. "My mom is going to lose her mind when she finds out it's twins."

That thought makes my chest tighten in the best way. My mom has been working so hard on herself. She was beside herself when we told her Silvie was pregnant. She even flew to New York with us last month. It was rough on the way, but once she got there, she felt good at Silvie's penthouse. She relaxed, and we had a great time. Progress.

She walked through Central Park with Silvie and even chatted with the doorman. She's working hard in therapy, and she told me last week that she wants to be the best grandma to this baby. Now there are two of them.

Donna is working on getting her up to visit Wisteria Cove at the end of the year. She's trying.

Silvie leans into me, watching me. "What are you thinking about?"

"Just thinking about how our kids are going to get to have skylines and sunrises at the beach."

She smiles slowly. "Yeah, they will."

I kiss her again, slower this time. Deeper. My hands slide along her back and settle at her hips, holding her steady against me. She sighs softly into my mouth, and for a second, it's just us. The ocean rolling in and out. The sun is climbing higher.

That night we have dinner at Cocktails & Chaos. My mom even shows up. She tells us she doesn't think she'll stay long, but I'm just happy she's here.

Wilby is here with Summer, Wendy, Mia, and Juniper. The Bees aren't coming. They said they had something to do, which could be alarming or exciting.

Jonah quietly pulls out a chair and sits next to my mom. I see her visibly relax when she realizes it's him. They have always been friends, and I love that we have him as part of our unofficial family.

Wilby is on one side of me, and Silvie is on my right. He's watching us curiously and grins. "You know...at the end of the day, it's the random girl that you became friends with on a completely random evening at your bar. And now you can't imagine your life without her."

I snort. "Isn't that the truth?"

"What are you two yapping about?" Silvie asks with a grin.

"You," Wilby says as he holds up his beer in cheers to us. Silvie holds up her water, and I tip my beer in as well. "Cheers."

I look around at this table and these people and I'm grateful for the beautiful life that we have.

Silvie

I'm sitting outside the window of the nursery with my feet propped up in a chair, a glass of lemonade sweating in my hand. The nursery windows are open behind me, white curtains lifting softly in the breeze. The room smells faintly of fresh paint and cedar from the new built-ins. Because apparently, we don't do anything halfway.

Cal is putting together one of the cribs on the floor of the nursery. He insisted on assembling them himself. He said something about knowing every screw and bolt that holds our babies together. And I'm not surprised. Cal has been thinking of everything. Wilby's got things covered at work and Cal covers things at home. Which is good, because pregnancy brain is a real thing.

Cal is shirtless and focused. It's also deeply unfair how hot fatherhood looks on him already.

"You missed a screw," I say sweetly.

He glances up, squinting at me and smirks. "No, I didn't."

"I can sense it."

He snorts. "CEO intuition?"

"Mother's intuition."

He glances through the window, as if he's admiring me. "You're glowing," he murmurs.

"I'm sweaty."

"Glowing," he corrects. "You're beautiful."

We both look up as Summer comes barreling through like a

gust of wind. Blonde hair piled on top of her head. Oversized sunglasses. Dramatic as ever. And that's why we love her.

"I bring snacks and gossip," she announces as she holds up a drink tray and a paper bag which I hope are treats.

"Come on over, hurricane," Cal teases.

She flops down next to me and kicks her sandals off.

"You two look disgustingly happy," she tells me.

"We are."

"I can't believe you're having twins," she says. "I can't even decide what I want at a restaurant."

Cal chuckles and disappears to probably give us girl time.

Summer leans closer to me conspiratorially.

"So," she says slowly, "Dayton's back."

My eyebrow lifts.

"Really?"

"Unfortunately," she says. "Apparently, he's able to work from here."

He and Summer have history. Complicated history.

"Why are you so bothered?" I ask gently.

"I am not bothered," she says quickly.

She's absolutely bothered.

I smirk.

"Good," I say. "Because last time he was in town and he walked by us at Chaos, he couldn't stop staring at you."

She blinks. "He did not."

"He did."

She exhales slowly and looks out toward the water. "That man thinks he can just buzzkill all of my ideas for my mom's house," she mutters.

Ah. There it is.

Cal comes outside and joins us. "Who are we hating?" he asks casually.

"Dayton," Summer says immediately.

Cal nods once and grins. "He probably deserves it. What did he do this time?"

Cal and Dayton went to school together, so they are friends but give each other crap.

She tosses the paper bag at him. "Exist."

I lean back in my chair, watching the way the breeze moves through the palm trees. The way the ocean glints. The way this place feels steady.

I never thought I'd split my life between Manhattan and Coconut Beach. Now I can't imagine not having both. I love my husband and the family we're making, but I hate seeing my friend go through a bad time.

Summer stares at the horizon like she's trying to solve something as well. "What if he ruins everything for me?" she asks quietly.

"What if he makes it better?" I say lightly.

She looks at me. "And, what if I want him?"

Cal makes a noise in his throat. "I didn't hear that," he says.

Summer laughs, but it's softer now.

The sun dips lower, painting everything in warm gold. My hand slides into Cal's automatically. His thumb brushes over my knuckles, grounding me.

"You don't have to decide anything today," I tell her. "Let's see what he does."

She watches a figure walking along the distant shoreline. Tall. Broad shoulders. Familiar stride. Dayton.

Cal leans closer to me and murmurs, "This should be interesting."

I smile slowly. Summer's story is about to get very interesting.

Six Months Later

"Who is Carl the cab driver?" Wilby asks and why are we sending him a Christmas card?"

I laugh. "It's a long story. But he's the cab driver when I left the wedding with Tyler. And if it hadn't been for him, I wouldn't have ended up in Coconut Beach."

Wilby nods as if this makes perfect sense. Because it does.

Sometimes life has a way of working out how you least expect it.

want more silvie and cal?

Check out this bonus scene for Just Another Summer Escape when you sign up for Erin's newsletter!

Scan the QR code to get your bonus scene:

Freedom Valley Series
Falling Inn Love
Baked Inn Love
All Inn Thyme
Love Inn Books
Forever Inn Love
Snowed Inn

Bridger Falls
Forever To Me
Wild As Her
Always You
High Road

Wisteria Cove
The Pumpkin Spice Spell
Mistletoe & Magic
Hexes & Honeysuckle

Cozy Creek Collection
Fall Too Well
Bagpipes & Buns

You can find all of Erin's books on her website:
Erinbranscom.com

about the author

Erin Branscom is a creator of happily-ever-after's, crafting spicy, Hallmark-like romances that make readers fall head over heels for charming small towns. When she's not writing heartwarming stories, Erin can be found anywhere there are dogs, with a cup of coffee in hand, or lost in a good book. As a passionate Scorpio, she brings intensity and heart to everything she does. Dive into her world and discover love, warmth, and a touch of spice in every story.

acknowledgments

To my family. I love you all and you are my reason for working hard every day. I'm so thankful for all of you and your support. To all my readers, thank you for always showing up for me and being excited!

a note from erin

Hey, friends! This book was so special to me to write. I loved writing it for all of you. It felt like I went on vacation to Coconut Beach and didn't want to leave. If you need an escape right now or a vacation, I hope Coconut Beach can be that place for you.

A big thank you to Lyra Parish for inviting me to write in this series. I loved writing with you, J.S. Cooper, and Ariel Hendrix. What an incredible group of authors I am thankful to have created such a beautiful world with.

Coconut Beach connects with Wisteria Cove in this book. If you loved Cal's Aunt Donna Bennett, you'll love the Wisteria Cove series that takes place in Wisteria Cove, Massachusetts. It has all the Practical Magic and small-town-romance vibes. I love keeping the worlds alive and making the characters pop up in other series.

Happy reading!

www.ingramcontent.com/pod-product-compliance
Lightning Source LLC
Jackson TN
JSHW031331270326
99672JS00009B/21